Praise for Peter Seth's What It Was Like*:*

"My obsession with *What It Was Like* is identical to the one the story's wry, intelligent, and completely unremorseful narrator has for the beautiful, sexually intoxicating and mesmerizing Rachel Prince, with whom he begins a romance that we know from the opening pages is ill-fated. Once I started reading, I had to finish the book as fast as I could. Reading *What It Was Like* made me experience all the joys – and dangers – of teenage lust with an immediacy that I haven't felt since *Splendor in the Grass*."
– Stan Chervin, Screenwriter, Academy Award nominee for *Moneyball*

"*What It Was Like* is a story about all kinds of love – the obsessive first love of two unforgettable teenagers as well as the layers of love that can lie in tortuous wait between parents and children, a love as deep and hidden as an ominous quarry. If indeed you've ever wondered what kind of parents J.D. Salinger and Patricia Highsmith would have made if they had gotten together, then look no further than Peter Seth, their literary progeny."
– Kevin Sessums, author of *Mississippi Sissy* and *I Left It On the Mountain*

"Just when you think you know where the story is headed it changes directions. It's a roller coaster ride to the very last page."
– Book Bug

"Passionate, stark, haunted fiction that nails it on the head about young adult romance gone awry."
– Crystal Book Reviews

"A great beginning of a career for Peter Seth."
– Literarily Illumined

When I Got Out

A novel by

Peter Seth

The Story Plant
Studio Digital CT, LLC
P.O. Box 4331
Stamford, CT 06907

Copyright © 2019 by Peter Seth Robinson

Story Plant hardcover ISBN-13: 978-1-61188-265-0
Fiction Studio Books E-book ISBN: 978-1-945839-28-3

Visit our website at www.TheStoryPlant.com

First Story Plant Printing: September 2019

Printed in the United States of America

0 9 8 7 6 5 4 3 2 1

To my parents ...
and for my grandchildren

March 30, 2015

PUBLIC NOTICE
Four sealed, notarized copies of this document
have been sent by certified mail—one each—to:

Ms. Janet DiFiore
District Attorney of Westchester County, New York
111 Dr. Martin Luther King Jr. Blvd.
White Plains, New York 10601

Mr. Daniel Stein
Chief, Criminal Division
United States Attorney's Office, Southern District
of New York
1 Saint Andrews Plaza
New York, NY 10007

Mr. Wilfredo A. Ferrer
U.S. Attorney
U.S. Attorney's Office, Southern District of Florida
99 N.E. 4th Street
Miami, FL 33132
Mr. David Bowdich
Assistant Director in Charge, Los Angeles Field
Office
Federal Bureau of Investigation
11000 Wilshire Blvd. #1700
Los Angeles, CA 90024

Should anything of a criminal or violent nature
happen to the writer of these pages or should he
unexpectedly disappear, these officials have directions to open their packages, read the contents,
and act accordingly.

PART I
GETTING OUT

ONE

My given name is Larry Ingber—Laurence Allan Ingber—but
some people may remember me as the Ivy League Killer from
this supposedly sensational trial on Long Island back in the late
Sixties, early Seventies.[1] It caused quite a splash in the media
for a while because it had all kinds of juicy elements: young love,
young love gone wrong, a double murder, class conflict, two dead
bodies in the trunk of a Cadillac, a car chase, Mafia connections,
other people's *multiple* tragedies. In other words, a little something for everyone. But that was a long time ago, and now most
people don't remember me at all. To tell you the truth, I sincerely
hope no one recalls that sorry episode. Unfortunately, some people have extraordinary powers of memory, and the dead never
forget a thing. I'm somewhere between the two. I don't want my
life to be defined by one very stupid thing that I did when I was
nineteen, but I guess, to some extent, that's what I'm stuck with.

I truly don't know why my name stayed in the public consciousness for so long. There are lots of murderers, more famous
and much worse than me: Manson, Speck, Chapman, Berkowitz,
Gacy, O.J., etc. *And* as I keep saying to everyone: I didn't kill
anyone. OK, I did witness two murders, did not do anything to
stop them, and helped dispose of the bodies in a way that demon-
strated a "reckless and depraved disregard for human dignity."
But forget about that (not that I can). The point is I didn't actually kill anyone. That fact always seems to get lost in my story.

I think, finally, what touched people is that, despite all the
violence and sensationalism, at the bottom of it all, they felt that
The Girl and I were *truly* in love. We were just a couple of teen-

1 On March 17, 1970, the Supreme Court of Nassau County, in Mineola, New
York, convicted Laurence Allan Ingber of two counts of second-degree homicide.

11

agers trying to make it in a hostile world when things got screwed up. Nothing all that special. It was like everyone's love story... except for the double murder.

The reason I'm writing this down after all these years—with the full and absolute intention of sending it to "the authorities"—is that my life is now in danger. Funny, after almost forty years in some of the worst prisons in "the land of the free, the home of the brave," after surviving with caged human animals, guarded by other animals, I've come out into the real world, into freedom, and now I fear for my life as much as I ever did in prison.

No, it's not funny.

That's why I'm getting this on the record, so that if I'm killed, the cops will know who did it, or, perhaps more precisely, who caused it. For several years in prison, I kept a diary—an extremely detailed, carefully documented journal of deliberate, systematic abuse—that I had smuggled out, but I got in big trouble for it. And before that, right after my trial, I wrote my version of what happened with The Girl and me and the whole Incident for my lawyer. He then tried to use it to influence the judge during the sentencing phase since I didn't take the stand and testify in my own defense, to my eternal regret. But nothing ever came of that. Just a lot of writer's cramp.

After my initial stretch at Sing Sing, when I had been sent upstate to Elmira, I tried to write a novel based on my case, but that got burned up in a cell fire started by some guys who wanted to kill me. Don't worry: later, they got theirs. One thing you learn is how and when to protect yourself. The drive for survival is primal and inexorable, which is what I'm worried about right now.

I stopped that kind of writing—two years up in smoke—and started writing for other inmates: letters to their lawyers or parole boards, doing research, and preparing briefs, things like that. I even wrote quite a few love letters to their wives, fiancées, and what are now called their baby mamas. Legally, you're not allowed to run a business while you're in prison, so I took payment in goods and services: better food, easier work assignments, new clothes, extra commissary, books and magazines, and, most importantly, protection.

Protection. That's a strange word. It means different things to different people. In prison, protection is a very physical thing:

"Stay out of my space, stay out of my face, or I will hurt you." When you are out, there's not quite the same risk to your physical well-being at every moment. But I've discovered that you need other kinds of protection.

When I first got to Sing Sing in 1970, I had an unusual form of protection. One of the people killed in the Incident that put me in prison was also the girlfriend of a certain Mr. Herb Perlov, a man I despise, even today. While he was alive, he did nothing but harm The Girl and me. I think he also might have abused her, but I'm not sure about that since I'm not sure about a lot of the things she said. But it turned out that Herb was no normal Harvard Law grad. He wasn't a corporate lawyer or an investment banker; he was, in fact, "Herb the Hebe," mouthpiece for a certain New York crime family. (I believe that is the technical term for a Mafia lawyer, and if you want to know which family, you can look it look it up yourself. "Google it," as I have learned to say.)

When I got to Sing Sing, being the Ivy League Killer, I was already a famous criminal and, as such, a big target for any of the assorted bored and violent maniacs who would love to knock off a "celebrity convict" like me. Just for the fun of it. But since I was also the Guy Who Killed Herb the Hebe's Girlfriend (which was actually not true), I got good protection for as long as I was in that place from members of a New Jersey crime family that was the *nemico mortale* of Herb's family. Although I was probably one of the most peaceful, rational people there, it was my reputation as the killer that made my imprisonment safe and semi-bearable.

At least in the beginning. I think I recall almost everything that's happened to me, but I have a "trick memory." Some years ago, I took a beating from two redneck hacks in an Oklahoma joint that left some holes in my past. Most things I remember with crystal clarity, as if they were happening right at this moment. But some things I don't remember at all. That's probably for the best.

Anyway, prison is now in my past—forever, I hope. I am much better prepared than most convicts getting out. I earned three degrees in prison from correspondence courses—all of them associate degrees (in Psychology, Applied Business, and Sociology) because I couldn't go for bachelor's degrees at the institution

I was in at the time. I also wanted to take some criminal justice courses, but the goon warden who ran that facility prevented me—even though I had worked my way up to his "honor block"—saying he didn't want me "getting ideas" and becoming a "pain-in-the-ass jailhouse lawyer." Of course, they don't equal the B.A. from Columbia that was once in my future, the Golden Passport to a Golden Career, but my future became a very different thing once I was convicted of double murder in the second degree.

Thankfully, I was left a legacy by my father. I remember my very last phone conversation with him. I was in a noisy prison hallway and his voice was very weak, but I recall every word he said.

"I saved for you," he said, "so when you get out, you'll have something."

(Notice how he said *when* I got out. He always believed in me.)

"You'll be able to have a life and do something," he said. "I gave everything to Mantell, so you'll get it from him. It's my legacy to you."

Those words have echoed in my mind many times.

The problem I had was Lester Mantell. Since my parole, I'd talked to Mantell exactly one time on the phone—very briefly—and that was after calling his office dozens of times. You'd think he'd be interested that his long-imprisoned client was getting out of jail after forty fucking years. Evidently he had moved on to other things. He mumbled something about my Dad's legacy money still being in a trust account that he was in the process of moving because it had been "stuck in probate." He said he'd be in touch with me when it cleared—and that was the last I heard from him.

My parents got very close to Mantell during my trial and came to depend on him for legal and financial advice, and almost everything after that. Most convicts come out with five hundred dollars of gate money, a parole officer to hassle them, and nothing else. With my Dad's legacy, I might have really had a chance to make his last wishes for me come true.

Did I mention that both my parents are dead? My Mom died before my Dad, which, from what I understand, is unusual. Men usually go before their women—ground down by life and stress and general male idiocy (cigarette smoking, violence, anger, alcohol). To tell you the plain truth, it was my incarceration that killed my mother. She couldn't take all the trips to see me, and when they moved me out of Elmira, after seven years, to a facility in Louisiana (a different hell), it was even more difficult for them. They could make only a couple of trips there. We all wrote a million letters trying to get me transferred someplace back East because of family hardship. No dice.

Mom wrote to me every day for *six* years. Every day, in this little, neat script, on this pretty paper (sometimes pink, sometimes blue). She had the best penmanship of anyone I ever knew. Her father—my grandpa Abe—was a CPA and made his kids practice their penmanship till their hands ached. At least that was the family legend.

My mother was always a somewhat nervous person, so when I got into trouble, she was not prepared. (Is any mother ever prepared to see her son charged with murder? Maybe Ma Barker, but that's about it.) After all the tension of the trial—the pressure from the police and the DA's office, the abuse she got from the press, the stares from our neighbors and "friends"—and then when I was found guilty, well, she was never really the same.

But finally, it was her decision to stop living. I can semi-understand it; I was her only child and the light of her life. But still, she shouldn't have stopped living. There should have been more to her life than just being the mother of a prisoner and trying to get him out. You see, she didn't only write *me* letters; she also wrote letters to the governor and the Bureau of Prisons and the Department of Corrections and anyone else she could think of, trying to get me transferred or released, or get my sentence reduced. She even wrote to a couple of the wardens of the institutions I was in, which caused me lots of embarrassment until I told her to stop.

Probably the toughest thing about being in prison was not being let out to go to my parents' funerals. Either of them. My Dad died about four years after my Mom. In a way, that wasn't surprising either: he needed her, and when she was gone, it was as if he were suddenly missing some essential part of his being. He couldn't live without his heart. They had been together since high school (Erasmus, in Brooklyn) and, except for the time my Dad spent in the Army in World War II, were never apart. They always said how lucky they were to have found each other so young.

"I didn't waste any time," my Dad used to say. "First time I saw her in her gym bloomers cutting through the courtyard, that was it. From that moment on, she was mine."

I guess it was probably for the best that I wasn't allowed to go to those funerals. I just would have embarrassed my few remaining relatives, and maybe some reporters would have shown up. You never know.

I thought I was old news when I made the mistake of talking to some snot-nosed young reporter from *The New York Times* who dug up my story on the twenty-fifth anniversary of the Incident. I thought at the time it would help my upcoming parole hearing if I showed the world how "rehabilitated" and "remorseful" I was. Only the article didn't quite come out that way, and a whole bunch of people got pissed off at me all over again. I guess it was my ego, wanting to be mentioned favorably in the holy *Times*, "The Paper of Record." Or maybe it was the way the reporter egged me on, and I wanted to prove that I was just as smart as that pissant.

Anyway, I shot my mouth off during that interview and got myself in trouble. Still, that warden—whose name I won't even write—should have let me out for the funerals. It wouldn't have hurt anyone. *I* wouldn't have hurt anyone.

But I have to forget all about that now. I'm alive, and they're dead.

When I was released in 2010 due to the hard work of some good people for many years, I was in surprisingly decent health, considering the hellish series of institutions (seven separate facilities in four decades, not counting innumerable short stays at various transit points), which have been my homes for most of my life. I use the word *homes* in the most ironic sense possible.

One thing about prison life: it gets you in shape. Either you get in shape, or you don't last very long. You have to get strong because you are tested every day. The cruel seek out the weak for the pleasure of inflicting pain. But I refused to be weak. I'm not the biggest guy in the world, but I might be the most obsessed. I have the strongest will of anybody I've ever known. Never forget that. I don't.

For many years, I did push-ups and sit-ups by the hundreds every day until I ached. I did jumping jacks and shadowboxed, even in the dark. It all made me strong enough to protect myself. Even today I'm pretty lean, especially taking into account all the fatsos out here in the real world. I may have a little potbelly, but the muscles themselves are rock-solid, and there's only a little layer of fat on me. Not much hair, not much height. But considering the kind of medical care I got in prison, I'm in remarkable shape.

"Medical care." I had this one cellmate in Oklahoma for three years, a guy with BO so rank that I was convinced it had to be microbial. I mean this guy stunk straight out of the shower! Later, it turned out he had advanced cancer of the intestines. He was rotting from the inside out. Of course, the prison doctor kept diagnosing his problem as "acute gas," right up until the tumor was practically bulging out of his belly. He looked positively pregnant with cancer.

The fact that I survived this kind of medical care and came out as well as I did is almost a miracle. Finally, I think I survived just to spite my tormentors and the System. To walk out of prison was to get the last laugh. And I think that, most remarkably, I am still fairly sane. Maybe that's not for me to say. We'll see what happens. But my willpower and personal drive to survive and not be destroyed by my circumstances remain intact and inviolable. As I said, I might be the most obsessed person who ever lived, but that's only because I had to be. I don't want to be obsessed anymore. More than anything, I want to be a normal person who lives a normal life...if I can figure out what that means. I'll get the money from Mantell and I'll have a chance to "have something" and "do something," just like my Dad wanted.

⌒

The real crazy thing now is, even though I survived so many years of hell on Earth in prison and I'm out in the world now, I'm in danger of being murdered. It could come at any time, so I have to hurry. How I got myself into this situation, after the good fortune of my release and my Dad's legacy, is a fairly twisted story. It's twisting me right here, right now.

I had been waiting for—and planning for—my release for many, many years. Yet when my dream came true, I confess that I was a little scared. It's funny: most people would fear prison and want freedom. But the thing is, I *knew* prison. I didn't know yet how I was going to do in the outside world.

For the first three months, I lived at the Four Winds, a halfway house in Westchester County, in the suburbs just north of New York City. Inevitably and unforgettably, I was assigned a parole officer—Kenneth Fusco—to report to for five years, but basically, I was *out*, albeit with lots of restrictions. The Four Winds, a big, rundown split-level in New Rochelle, just south of 95 that cuts the city in half, is owned by some huge company and run by a retired cop, Nate Edwards. A very large, very black, very serious dude.

"You know why this place is called the Four Winds?" he asked every guy who came through the house, including me. He would wait for you to say, "Why?"

"Because from here, you can go any which way the four winds blow. You can go up. You can go down. You can succeed, or you can go right back to the joint. It's entirely up to you."

And it was.

Now that I was getting out from the clutches of the correctional system, what exactly did I want to do for the rest of my life? I was no longer a young man; I was sixty, if you can believe it. I still can't. I didn't have that much time left, so what did I really want to do? It was a question of *focus*. I had to live a whole life—my true life, whatever that was—in a very short time. I had to ask myself: what was really important?

Survival. The first thing I had to learn was how to survive outside of prison.

Fortunately, from the day I was paroled until I got my legacy money from Lester Mantell, I worked in the city of White Plains, right in the middle of Westchester, at the offices of Clemency USA, the group that worked for many years for my release.

Clemency helped me adjust to life outside and deal with Lester Mantell. (More on him later. Much more.)

I commuted to and from Four Winds, in New Rochelle, by bus, until I got my own place. Clemency USA is a great organization. I say that not just because they helped me; they're part of a renowned international charity—World Clemency, based in Geneva—advocating for prisoners around the world to get justice. Their work and faith kept me going for many years. They arranged my release with as little publicity as possible (keeping in mind my sincere desire to resume a normal life). It was the perfect place for me to be once I got out.

I was lucky enough to be hired to work in their Northwest Regional Office as a clerk and general office helper, which is a whole lot better than most ex-cons, who become burger flippers at McDonald's *if that*. I'm also lucky in that Clemency has this young girl named Kelly Mott, who runs the Gateway Program, which helps the people they get released adjust to life outside prison. By young girl, I mean that she's probably in her midthirties or something. I'm old now, so everyone younger than me is young.

On Nate Edwards's short leash at Four Winds, I was the perfect halfway-house resident. I went to work at Clemency in the morning and came back right after work—nothing else. I rode the buses and tried not to talk to anyone. I never broke curfew. I didn't get into fights with the morons and jerks who were the house's other residents. I kicked back the required 25 percent of my salary to Four Winds to pay for my upkeep, saved as much of the rest as I could, and kept strictly to myself. I tried hard to do nothing wrong.

One resident at Four Winds, a young, skinny, nervous mixed-race guy named Sammy Zambrano, made it clear he wanted to hang out and invited me to go out to this local bar.

Once, when we were both in the kitchen getting something out of the refrigerator, I made myself clear: "I don't want to be your friend."

He laughed at that. "I love you old guys!" he said. "You got the wisdom."

"Do me a favor," I said, taking out an apple from my labeled bag. (Everything had to be labeled in the refrigerator or it got stolen. And even then...) "Leave me alone."

Zambrano loved that even more.

"Listen," he whispered, leaning toward me, "I know someone who needs smart, old guys. White guys. Guys who know the ropes."

"I don't know anything about ropes," I said and walked out of the kitchen, biting down hard on my apple.

"There is money to be made," he sang softly as I left him behind.

Zambrano really pissed me off. Here we were, just gotten out of the joint, and he was already scheming. I'm not really a criminal, but I've spent most of my life among them, and I know their ways. There are negative people in this world, and Zambrano was one of them. He definitely wanted something from me and kept after me.

That's why the time for me to leave Four Winds couldn't have come soon enough.

Kelly found this small, nice studio apartment in the city of Yonkers, on the other side of Westchester, a short walk from the Hudson River and right near the No. 6 bus line, which could take me right to Clemency's office in White Plains. I told Kelly that I had to live alone—I really had no friends, no one to live *with*—so a tiny studio apartment was all I could afford, and barely that. She found a place through Javier Flores, a nice young guy who worked at Clemency. There was a vacancy in his building, and the landlord was going to let me live there month to month, without a lease: perfect for me. And I could take the bus to work with Javier, so I'd have someone to commute with. I think she also wanted someone to keep an eye on me, but that was OK. Kelly thought of everything.

To help me furnish it, she offered to take me to a place called Ikea. I'd never heard of it, but she said it was good and cheap. "Good" and "cheap" are things I can live with. I thought that maybe a thrift shop or a Salvation Army store would be a good place to start, but she said that Ikea was even cheaper.

One thing I've noticed since I've been out: things are so expensive now. When I went into the system in the late Sixties, a hundred thousand dollars could buy you, if not a mansion, certainly a big, big house. Now a hundred thousand dollars can't even buy an apartment! The whole New York area is super expensive, but I really didn't have anywhere else to go. Manhattan is way too expensive, and since Clemency's offices were in White Plains—and I was essentially paroled into their shared custody with Four Winds since they assured the parole board that they'd give me a job—it made sense to try it up here in Westchester. After all, I did live here for about seven years: Sing Sing is in Westchester.

Of course, I couldn't go back to Long Island: that place was poisoned for me long ago by the whole Incident and everything. It's bad enough that we have the same damn initials—Larry Ingber and Long Island—following me around my whole life. In any case, I am much more likely to be anonymous here in Westchester. Anonymous and normal: my twin goals.

I can't tell you how much help Kelly has been to me. She helped me get my driver's license. She helped me buy a cheap "smart" phone and showed me how to use it, sort of. I'm still getting used to it. She showed me how to use an ATM for the first time. I called it an "AMT" a couple of times, but she didn't laugh at me once. She just, very sweetly, corrected me.

She got Ed Nyquist, Clemency's head of legal affairs in the White Plains office, involved with helping me find Lester Mantell. Nyquist was supposedly this very high-powered lawyer and a big deal around the office, so this was good for me. He hadn't gotten any results yet, but I was hopeful.

Kelly also helped me deal with both Edwards and Fusco. Edwards wasn't so bad, but Fusco was a real hard case, and the one I'm saddled with my whole parole, which was sitll more than four and a half years. I started my parole hoping Fusco wasn't going to give me an extra hard time. I understand that part of his job as parole officer *is* to give me a hard time so that I obey all the rules and don't kill anyone else, etc. But one thing I've learned in life is that some people really like to make things harder for guys who are already in tough circumstances, as if to pass on their pain, their inner unhappiness. I think Fusco is one of those guys.

Kelly was coming over to take me to Ikea. She has long dark hair like The Girl. I'm just saying that out of an obligation to notice these things. Kelly's young enough to be my daughter, if I had ever had a daughter.

All my life I've always said—with fingers crossed—that Luck evens out. Well, now that I was finally-finally-*finally* out of prison, maybe the good luck that I was owed would have a chance to kick in. It felt good to be out. Then why was I so nervous? Believe me, nothing could be worse than life in prison. This *had* to be better. But in prison, life was simple: *survive—today.* Out here, it was more complicated than that.

But I had no more excuses. For so long I wanted to be free. And since I was on the threshold of real freedom (no Four Winds, no Nate Edwards to sign in and out with), what was next? I had this fire within me, this drive to live. Why was I so scared? All my life, I faced down stone killers in dark passageways: why was I now so scared of life, and other people, and the strange, unfriendly country I returned to?

I remember my last night at Four Winds, the night before I was going to move into my own apartment in Yonkers and *real, unsupervised* freedom at last. I was so excited yet so anxious that I couldn't fall sleep. I lay there in my bed in the dark, practically vibrating with awareness and nerves. It reminded me of all the nights in prison when I couldn't get to sleep, especially when I was younger. That's when The Girl and everything that happened returned to me. During the day, I could stay busy enough to forget about her, but at night, everything came back. Visions from a past I couldn't escape.

In some ways, the purest thing I ever did was love The Girl, even if it wound up ruining my life. She was the best thing that ever happened to me, and then she wasn't.

During the day, I could keep our tragedy out of my mind, but at night sometimes, like that night, I couldn't help it. Thoughts of her—or were they dreams?—came over me like a fever.

We met in summer. That's when it had to be. We were so ripe for love, teenagers in 1968. Love and revolution were in the air, in the music, everywhere—even at that summer camp for rich kids. I was a poor working counselor, but it didn't matter to her. For some reason, she—this clever, wild, beautiful girl—loved me. I was warned about her, but I didn't listen. Maybe people weren't meant to love as deeply as we loved. Maybe love that deep is somehow unhealthy, but we couldn't help ourselves. It was so right, be-

fore it went wrong. All that passion got twisted. What started out as pure love became something else. One moment, she was in my arms. In the tall grass. In the shadows. In the sand. In the dark. And then there was all this blood.

I woke up in a sweat. Was I ever asleep?

I threw off my covers, staggered to the window, and opened it. It took me a moment to reclaim my senses. I cursed myself: if I'm going to deal with the future, I couldn't stay stuck in the past.

I took a few deep breaths and recovered my sense of reality. Despite everything that was still spinning in my head, I was lucky, and I knew it. I was out of prison, something I thought might never happen. And whenever I need to, I could open the window—a window without bars!—and look up at the open sky and breathe fresh air, with nothing between the world and me. For years, that was something that was denied to me. Now, anytime I want, night or day, I can look up at the open sky—*my sky!*— and have a Moment of Grace and Thanks. All I have to do is look up at the sky, and I'm a new man—at least, for the moment—free from my past and ready for the demands of "normal" life in this complicated, stressful, relentless new world.

How could I have known then that, a short time later, from a most unexpected source, my life would again be in jeopardy, just as it had been all those years behind bars?

TWO

I went to an Ikea, and it was fantastic! Kelly picked me up from Four Winds at nine o'clock sharp on a Saturday morning in a big, new-looking silver pickup truck that she borrowed from her brother and took me to, if you can believe it, New Jersey. Evidently, it was the closest Ikea store, *and* they have a lower sales tax there or something. At least it gives people a reason to go to Jersey. She had to get permission from Ken Fusco for me to leave New York State. Isn't that ridiculous? OK, it's part of the terms of parole, to notify your Field Officer whenever you leave the state, but still: can you believe it? And Fusco gave her a hard time.

"He said, '*Whut? He's too good to buy furniture in New Yawk?*'" Kelly said, in a perfect imitation of Fusco's humorless grumble.

"But you convinced him," I said, watching the scenery go by, listening to the piercing hum of the truck's engine. I had been taking the bus to my job in White Plains, and I hadn't been in many cars since my release, especially a nice new truck like this one. It still had that "new car" smell; some things *hadn't* changed.

"It wasn't easy," she said, checking traffic both ways as she turned onto Boston Post Road. "He does like his rules."

"Yes, he does," I said, thinking of how Fusco enjoyed making people squirm and beg. "But who could resist you?" I concluded, watching Kelly change lanes and speed up.

"Plenty of people!" She scoffed with a short laugh, tucking her hair behind her ear with a quick gesture. "You should have heard what it took me to convince my brother to lend me his truck today."

I was still getting used to being around females. Girls. Women. For so many years, the only women I ever had contact with were prison workers: nurses and clerks, the occasional psychologist, even guards sometimes, especially toward the end of my time. But they were workers, usually in uniform, and they were protected from (and usually scared of) people like me. But now women were just women, in regular clothes. In all these colors and soft-looking fabrics. Right there, in front of me, or next to me. Smelling like distant flowers. It's not easy for a convict like me, who spent a good part of the last forty years fantasizing about women, to get used to being around the real thing. But I'm learning, slowly.

"You must be pretty excited, Larry," she said. "Moving day, finally. Your first *real* place since you've been out."

"Excited?" I said. "Nah!"

That got a laugh out of her, as I hoped it would.

"I was up at five thirty," I said. "I've been jumping out of my skin since Tuesday. I did all my paperwork with Edwards and checked in with Fusco yesterday. I really can't wait to get out of there."

"Have you heard anything from Ed Nyquist?" she asked.

"Nothing," I shot back. "Zilch. So far."

Kelly didn't say anything. This was a sore spot, for sure. I greatly appreciated Clemency for helping to get me out. I just wish I hadn't entrusted Nyquist and his legal department with getting my Mantell money back. But I didn't want to change things and risk offending Clemency; they were being so good to me.

Once I even asked Fusco to try to get in touch with Mantell for me so that I could fire his ass after I got the money. "You're my parole officer—you're supposed to help me adjust to the outside world, right?" I think he tried, once. In any case, the next time I saw him, Fusco said, "Get yourself another lawyer."

Why I stayed with Mantell for so many years is a tough question. I think it was because my parents were so involved with him and depended on him so much, for legal and financial advice. They always said how he was working on different "appeals" for me. But nothing ever happened, not until Clemency got involved. But even without my money, I couldn't wait any longer to move out of Four Winds. My time was up, and I was being kicked out.

Besides, the situation was getting more uncomfortable for me by the day.

Sammy Zambrano made a couple of other advances on me. "There's money to be made," he said with the sleazy confidence that I dismissed at first as typical bullshit convict talk. But I really didn't like when he hissed in my ear, "I know who you are, Larry." After that, I stayed out of the crappy television room in Four Winds for good and kept my head down until I could get the hell out of there.

I changed the subject with Kelly. "Nice truck!" I said, feeling the smooth, fake leather on the dashboard.

"Jimmy's in total love with it," said Kelly as she shifted in her seat and pulled at her tight jeans. "It's a hybrid."

"Oh," I said noncommittally.

"That's a kind of engine that uses less gas," she explained. "And electricity, somehow."

"I know what a hybrid is," I lied. Now that I'm out, I keep running into Things I Missed While I Was Inside, and this was one of them. But I covered up pretty well, I think. I have to do quite a bit of that.

"And you know you have to wear your seat belt now," she said, "or they'll practically throw you in jail. There are laws against all kinds of things now. Legally, you can't sell a big soda in New York City, but you *can* smoke pot in the state of Colorado."

"Well then, let's move to Colorado," I cracked.

"Don't talk like that!" she said, giggling. "You're on parole."

"I know," I said. "I was only kidding. And don't tell Fusco. His favorite thing in the world is testing people's pee."

"Nice job," she said as she stepped down on the gas or the electricity, or whatever it was that made her hybrid go.

"This is so cool," I said as we made good time on the Cross-Bronx Expressway, on our way to the George Washington Bridge.

"What's cool?" she said.

"Everything," I answered. "There's a map on your dashboard that moves. We're going to buy furniture for my new apartment. I can't even believe those words—'my new apartment'—and I never had a girl pick me up in a truck...or in any car at all, for that matter."

But that last part was a lie: The Girl picked me up a bunch of times in that bad-luck red Mustang of hers.

"I'll pay the toll," I said, starting to reach for my wallet, which was only fair since we were going to buy stuff for me.

"Don't worry," she said, putting out her hand. "The toll is on the other side, coming back."

"Oh," I said, sitting back. "I'll get it then. How much is it?"

"Twelve dollars."

"*Twelve dollars*!"

My head almost hit the roof of the truck. OK, not really; I'm not that tall.

"Twelve bucks?" I repeated. "Shit...sorry...I don't remember what it was when I went away, but it wasn't any twelve bucks!"

"I bet," she said. "And I bet there wasn't any E-ZPass either."

"What's that?"

She explained how it worked as we started to cross the bridge. It was another Thing I Had Missed. Then she complained about the new email system the office was breaking in, and the IT consultant that Clemency used. As she talked, I looked through the passenger window, up the Hudson, to see if I could spot Sing Sing. It was hard to see through the traffic and the metal girders of the bridge that flashed by. There was still a mist clinging to the shoreline that hid the land. And I don't think you can see that far north anyway. But I could imagine Sing Sing there, imagine my "home" for those first years, imagine the two thousand guys wishing they were where I was. Wishing they were anywhere else.

"Jersey!" she said as we crossed the bridge. "*Sopranos* country!"

"I hate to keep saying this," I said, "but what's that?"

Kelly tsked and said, "Sorry. It's was a TV show. About the Mafia in north Jersey."

"Oh," I said neutrally. "Yeah, I've heard of that one." Another Thing I Had Missed. For many years, I didn't have access to a TV or any outside media, only books. It was how I was penalized by one particular warden whose name I refuse to write. So I missed a lot of TV shows and movies. Some I know, but most I don't. The show with the sopranos was just one of them. I could have kept a list.

"Oh, it was the best show ever," she went on. "I'm originally from Paterson. Eastside High. So, I grew up with those guys. Or, at least, their sons. Some very scary people. Of course, now it's all African American and immigrants from all over. But, hey, everything's different nowadays."

I snorted in agreement and said, "It sure is," and didn't say anything else when she kept talking about the Mafia. Nothing about Herb the Hebe, etc. One thing about prison: you learn to keep your mouth shut.

⁀

The Ikea parking lot was packed, and so we had to park a long way from the enormous box of a store. I guess Saturday is still a big shopping day, and everyone wants cheap furniture: families with strollers, couples holding hands.

"Very blue and yellow," I said, looking up at the huge store-front, which seemed to get bigger as we approached. I almost felt as if Kelly wanted to take my arm, but she had her purse on the side closer to me.

"It's from Sweden," she said.

"Of course!" I said. "What a dummy." I don't know why I didn't make the obvious connection. I guess I assumed that Ikea was, from the name—I don't know—Japanese.

We were barely into the lobby before we got caught in a jam of parents and kids. I admit that I was still a little uneasy in crowds. I didn't like being bumped. All my life, being bumped could be someone's hostile, provocative act. My negative reaction to contact from other people is a very hard reflex to break.

"C'mon," she said, leading me toward the escalator. "Do you have the list?"

"Yes, I do," I said, patting the pocket on my shirt. "Absolutely!"

I gave it to her as we rode up the escalator. We had printed it out in the office on Friday on "Clemency USA" paper with its red, white, and blue wings, and had the headings *Bedroom*, *Kitchen*, *Living Room*, *Bathroom*, and *Miscellaneous*. Even though it was a small studio, it still had "areas."

"The first thing you need is the bed," she said as I followed her off the escalator onto the main floor.

Everything looked bright, clean, and colorful. There were lots of sample rooms, some with their actual square footage listed so you could compare your room: very smart. I saw walls full of chairs, three rows high; entire closet *systems*; very big, super thin TVs; and a whole area for media storage. There were all different kinds of kitchens, with counters of granite and wood, and huge steel appliances. You could pick out your own cabinets and choose different styles of doors and handles and finishes. They even had free pencils and tape measures made of paper by the cash registers.

"Wow," I said. "This is unbelievable. My father was a salesman in a furniture store but nothing remotely like this." I thought of the dingy store on Old Country Road, where my Dad used to work and where I worked for a couple of vacations. A store like that, with a few dark, cluttered rooms, couldn't compare to something like this.

"Their prices are really good," Kelly said, "because they sell a bajillion of them, all over the world. But you have to put everything together yourself."

"*Everything*? Wow," I said. "And people do it?"

"If you want to save money," she said. "I mean, look at everybody!"

Did I mention the place was extremely crowded?

"What kind of a bed do you like?" she asked as we entered a whole giant room of them. Bed after bed after bed, with different kinds of mattresses and covers and headboards.

"A new one," I said.

I spent almost a half hour testing beds, but for a long while I just gazed at the mattresses—so clean, so white, so pure. I thought of all the foul places where I'd had to sleep over the years: the hard surfaces, the disgustingly used and abused mattresses that smelled like other men's fluids. I've slept chained up. I've slept standing up. I've slept while insects crawled all over me— that was almost impossible. But struggling *not* to sleep because you think someone is going to kill you if you do fall asleep—that's the toughest.

"Get what you like," said Kelly.

"That's very good advice," I said. "In life too."

We spent the good next hour buying and crossing things off the list. I got a big shopping cart, and we gradually filled it with dishes and glasses and silverware and utensils —four of each, Kelly advised. All nice and plain and clean and Swedish.

There was a huge section of knives of all sizes. I picked up one chef's knife, with a wide gleaming blade, and turned to Kelly.

"You have no idea how much trouble I would have gotten into for having one of these," I said, looking at the shining steel and the sharp point. "Prison knives are actually smaller," I continued. "Easier to conceal."

"I bet," she said.

I could tell by the uncertain flicker in her eyes that I had mentioned prison once too often. Kelly was very understanding, but I had to remind myself that people didn't want to constantly hear about my prison experiences. Of course, that's almost everything I know, except what I've read in books. Still, I can't keep advertising it so much if I want to be "normal." Which I very much do.

We got into a huge line at the checkout. They must have had ten lines open, but all of them were long and slow. We waited there long enough for me to also get a lamp for twelve dollars and a complete tool kit for eight. I couldn't help but notice that the enclosed hammer, wrench, and pliers made excellent weapons, but I remembered to keep my mouth shut.

I paid with a debit card, which Kelly help me set up at the Bank of America near the Clemency office, but was a little surprised to have to pay for a bunch of big blue bags *and* have to pack the stuff myself.

"That's how they save money," said Kelly to me as she showed me how to wrap glasses in paper, one at a time. "You do the work. They save on everything." It was a lot of packing into a lot of big blue bags, but we did it.

"We gotta get going," she said, rolling up all the silverware in tissue paper, one piece at a time. "I promised Jimmy that I'd have his truck back by four, and we still have to drop all this off at your apartment."

"Whenever you say," I responded, wrapping right along with her. "I am ready."

⌒

I waited with the two carts in the outside loading area while she got the truck from the parking lot. As I guarded my purchases,

I watched other groups loading their Ikea booty: excited families and groups of students and young couples fitting their packages into their cars and vans. Everyone seemed so happy and busy, putting down rear seats and tying down car trunks. No one seemed interested in stealing my stuff, but I was so used to watching my things like a hawk, from decades of living among predators and thieves, that I stayed on guard against these cheerful, innocent people involved with their giant plants and framed posters. They didn't even notice me.

I started to think about how I was going to arrange the furniture in my new apartment. *My new apartment!* I just can't get enough of those words. There was a big window in the longest wall, and I could put my new chair right next to it so that I could see the sky anytime I wanted to. I wouldn't let Kelly talk me into curtains because I told her that I would never *not* want to see the sky. I think she understood.

We started loading the stuff in, putting the heaviest things in first. Good ol' brother Jimmy had some thick packing straps in the big compartment behind the front seats in the cab, and Kelly got busy tying everything down. As I emptied the two carts, I watched Kelly out of the corner of my eye, tying knots and cranking on the clamps to tighten the straps. She knew what she was doing.

She caught me watching her.

"Jersey girl!" she said proudly, explaining her expertise.

We got everything in, and after one final check of the carts and surrounding area and an extra retightening of everything in the flatbed, we climbed into the truck.

"Do you know that song?" she asked me as she put the keys in the ignition.

"What song?" I asked.

"'Jersey Girl,'" she said, buckling her seat belt.

"No," I said, buckling my belt too.

"Bruce does it," she said. "The Boss...Bruce Springsteen. But I think it's a Tom Waits song."

I wish that I knew the song, but I didn't.

"Sorry," I said, "I missed a lot of music. I went from teenager to golden oldie, with very little in-between. I do know what rap

31

is. I heard a lot of rap inside. And hip-hop, whatever they call it. I still like the Beatles."

"*Everyone* likes the Beatles. Even my kids like the Beatles," she said. "I'd disown them if they didn't."

"Good parenting!"

We laughed, and I felt good being with her. Being with any woman. It felt so good and natural that it made me feel a little nervous. It wasn't easy, this being normal. I was getting better, but it was still hard for me to completely...*unclench*.

By now, we were back on Route 17, heading back to the George Washington Bridge. Traffic was heavier now.

"Oh, would you look at this!" Kelly fretted as we came to a near halt behind a long line of cars.

We were sitting for a few minutes in the stopped traffic when Kelly broke the silence.

"Larry," she said, "can I ask you something?"

"Sure," I said. I wondered what she was going to ask me, especially when I saw her hesitate to begin.

"Why did you take all those pencils and tape measures from the store?"

"What?"

"Why did you take so many of those little yellow pencils and tape measures from the Ikea?"

OK, she caught me. I didn't think anyone saw.

"They were free, weren't they?" I defended myself. "What if want to measure a lot of things?"

"I'm just asking," she said.

"I know, I know," I said, blanking with embarrassment. "What can I say? I'm crazy. It was a crazy thing to do. I saw something that was free, and I just took it. Because I could. It was...it was, y'know, my Prison Mind working, not me. ...I really had no good reason, Kelly. None at all."

I felt so stupid. Inside me was my Prison Mind, still working as if I were in the joint. I fight it every day, but it's long-established and very strong. After all those years, prison became part of the DNA in every cell in my body.

"What can I say?" I sighed. I have to tell myself, over and over: only do things when there's a good, logical reason to do them.

Why did I take those pencils and tape measures? Sure, I spent a lot of money at that store, more than half of my whole bank account, but why did I feel the need to take so many stupid little yellow pencils, and so many worthless paper tape measures, just because they were free? Once I got my money from Mantell, I could buy a million little pencils. Maybe I still am crazy from prison. *Permanently* damaged goods. The best thing I could do was just sit there, have the money ready to pay the toll back across the Hudson to New York, and work on not being so crazy.

"We'll drop this stuff off fast," I offered, "so you can get this beautiful truck back to brother Jimmy. And you gotta thank him for me. You saved my life—again."

Which made Kelly flinch a little and take her foot off the gas.

"You and Clemency, I mean," I continued. "And Jimmy too. The whole...enterprise."

"I know what you mean, Larry," she said, in an understanding voice. It was as if she were talking to a child. I felt like such a jerk. One thing I found: in the outside world, people treat old people as if they were children, talking down to you as if you are stupid or deaf. At least in prison, a convict is just a convict. Age doesn't matter; we're all equal dogshit.

In any case, I was saying too many wrong things. I should just shut up for a while and not screw up a good day any further.

"Thank God for MapQuest," she said as she turned the truck skillfully off the Saw Mill at the Yonkers Avenue exit. "We're real close now."

"Javier showed me MapQuest at the office," I said. "And Yelp. They're very cool."

"There are lots of cool things these days," she said. "Except they all tend to cost a lot of money."

"Not *all*," I corrected her. I didn't mean anything by my comment, but instantly I realized it could be seen as a *romantic* comment. Which it was. Only I didn't mean it that way. At least at that time. And I didn't want to say anything else to make Kelly feel uncomfortable; I had done enough of that already today.

"Here we go!" she said, sparing me any further embarrassment. "Home sweet Yonkers."

I was lucky to get this apartment right near the No. 6 bus that will drop me almost directly in front of the office. When I got my legacy money from Mantell, I'd get a car, but this arrangement would do for now.

The funny thing is that I had mentioned just once to Kelly that I'd like to live someplace with a view of the Hudson. I always had this thing about the Hudson River. When I was at Columbia (very briefly), I used to like to walk down to where I could see the river. There's something about the sight of water when you're trying to walk off your troubles. It doesn't actually work. It doesn't solve anything. But it makes you feel vaguely better, and walking is good for your overall health. When I was at Sing Sing (for a much longer time), the rare sight of the Hudson lifted my heart, even if any thoughts of floating away from that particular hell were completely futile. So, the idea of living near the Hudson now, as a *free* man, was extremely appealing. I couldn't afford an actual river view—yet—but this apartment was very close to Trevor Park, which was right on the water, so I could go down to the Hudson anytime I wanted. "Anytime I want." Can you believe that? Talk about Grace and Thanks.

"What's the building number again?" she asked.

"Seventeen thirty," I said, leaning forward in my seat eagerly. "It's on the second floor, and there's an elevator, so it shouldn't be too hard to carry the stuff up."

Famous last words. I almost gave myself a hernia carrying those giant Ikea boxes. Kelly helped, but she's—if you'll pardon the expression—"a girl" and has no real muscle mass. She tried and tried, pushing as best she could, but a twelve-year-old Boy Scout would have been better.

But I shouldn't complain about anything. It was a great moment when we stood the first big box up against the wall outside the front door of my apartment, and I took out my new set of keys.

"You have your keys on a *paper clip*?" she asked jokingly.

"As long as it works," I replied coolly.

I didn't tell her all the things I could do with a paper clip, how I could weaponize it in a matter of seconds. More thoughts to drive out of my head.

By the time we were finished unpacking the truck and getting everything into the apartment, I was pretty sweaty, and so was Kelly. Except that I looked grungy, I'm sure, and she looked wonderful. Her hair was a little messy, her cheeks flushed with vitality.

"That's everything from the truck," I said.

"Yeah," she said, taking a deep breath. "Look at all this stuff."

"Wow," I said, looking at the piles of boxes on the floor and the big blue bags in the corner. "I guess I bought out Sweden."

On an impulse, I said, "Hey! Let's order a pizza!"

I understood immediately from the frozen look on her face that I had said the wrong thing.

Then I tried to save myself, instantly remembering: "Sorry, I forgot: you've gotta get the truck back. Only kidding about the pizza. It's enough that you gave up your Saturday to help an old guy. I should listen to myself and learn to keep my mouth shut."

"Thank you, Larry" was her response. Finally, I had said the right thing.

"You're the best, Kelly."

"I gotta go," she said walking over to a chair to pick up her purse. "Jimmy's already texted me twice."

After a moment of hesitation, she came across to me and gave me a peck on the cheek. "See you Monday."

She turned and practically ran out of the apartment. She looked good, even going away. I had said so many stupid things, and still she gave me a little kiss.

She slammed the door, and I was alone.

Alone.

By myself. With no one to supervise me.

I took a deep breath and stood there, in my own apartment, surrounded by boxes of stuff I bought with my own money, money that I earned.

No sign-in sheet at the front desk. No curfew. No one to watch me. No one to lock me in. For the first time in a very long time, I was my own jailer. It was a strange and wonderful feeling. From now on and forever more, I would lock *myself* in.

⌒

I spent most of the next forty-one hours putting Ikea furniture together. Sleeping, cursing, occasionally eating something, and putting more Ikea furniture together. I wish I knew how to curse in Swedish; maybe the furniture would have put itself together. I quickly learned to hate those stupid little L-shaped wrenches. I hated the little wooden pegs that held the cheap composite boards together. I hated the little cleats that tightened everything. I hated the little diagrams that supposedly told me—without words, of course—how to do everything easily. Sure. I wonder if Ingmar Bergman ever made a movie about putting together Ikea furniture. Nah, way too bleak.

The best moment of all? Maybe it was the easiest, when I took the plastic off my new mattress on the first night. I hadn't had a new mattress of my own since, I think, 1959. I'm not kidding.

And I did order in a pizza that night. All for myself. Half mushroom, half pepperoni, just like we used to order from Jerry's, where I grew up on the Island. I should have asked if they had any cheese sticks. Next time. I even had to buzz the delivery guy through the front door of the building. Javier said that it had good security, and he was right. And I tipped the guy, just like a normal person.

I also had a six-pack delivered with the pizza, which might have impaired my Ikea-assembling ability. OK, which *definitely* impaired my Ikea-assembling ability. I apologize to the entire Swedish nation.

After my third piece of pizza and third can of beer, I realized that I wasn't going to be able to put everything together that first night. Not even close. The last thing I did was make up the bed. I opened the package of nice, clean white sheets and spread them out on the nice, clean white mattress. As I pulled the fitted sheet over the four corners of the mattress, one at a time, I felt a twinge from my trick memory, recalling something about some kids at that summer camp, hiding candy in the corners of their bed sheets. That was such a long time ago, to come back to me now. Funny, those kids are all adults now, probably with kids of their own. I wonder whatever happened to them.

I took a shower, a long hot-cold shower like James Bond. There was excellent water pressure, which I had tested before when Kelly and I looked the place over. Here there was no one banging on the wall, telling me to hurry up. There was no one threatening to attack me or beat me up around the corner when the bulls weren't watching. I figured if I showered long enough and if the water was hot enough, someday I could wash the prison off me.

I used one of my nice, soft, new white towels to dry myself. I couldn't believe that I had more than one towel. For many years, I had just one towel: one gray, practically see-through towel. And now I have Q-tips. Unlimited Q-tips. I've rediscovered that you don't really feel dry until you Q-tip your ears. Twice.

Before I went to sleep, I got out of bed and double-checked to make sure my front door was double locked, and the windows too. Javier said that this was a pretty safe neighborhood, but different people have different ideas of safety.

I left a light on in the bathroom. If I got up at night to pee, I didn't want to trip and break my neck in the unfamiliar dark. That would be perfect on the first night in my new apartment.

Then I just lay there in the semi-dark, on my clean, smooth white sheets, thinking how far I'd come to get here. The nightmare I had lived for so many years was becoming a dream come true. It's late in the game, to say the least, but now I could maybe live some of the life I was always meant to live, whatever that was.

I spoke bravely to no one: "Hello?"

"*Hello*?" I shouted.

As I fell asleep, I felt cautiously optimistic about the future. Was there any other way to be? I realized that this was one of the best days I'd had in a long, long time...maybe since those golden days with The Girl, walking together on Jones Beach or lying on the grass in some quiet, hidden place or in an actual bed before all hell broke loose.

When I turned over and stretched out on my super clean, super new sheets, my body's bone-tiredness finally hit me. I'm not as young as I used to be, or maybe I'm losing a little of my prison toughness. Either way, what I needed was sleep. A long time ago,

I slept on sheets this sweet smelling...at The Girl's house, the weekend when her mother was away. As I fell asleep, drifting on Ikea whiteness, dreams from long ago came back to me.

People said, "Summer things never last." But they were wrong. We fought for our love—a losing battle, as it turned out. Her parents hated me. I suppose that was to be expected. They hated that I made her happy, that I gave her the love that they were incapable of giving. No matter what they say in books and movies, the world hates lovers. The world is jealous of love and tries to destroy it. Lovers must be strong, and we were just not strong enough. It was going to be so beautiful, so good, when I started my freshman year at Columbia. It seems like a million years ago. My parents were so proud of me. Letting them down was perhaps my deepest shame, but then again, I have so many. Maybe if I had spent less time on frustrating phone calls with The Girl and more time in Butler Library, I might not have flunked geology. But she was so beautiful, with those blue-blue eyes and long dark hair. And she was smart—wicked smart. We had this Zone of love that was supposed to protect us.... So why did things turn so ugly? There were so many pure, perfect moments—at the beach, in the grass, in cramped backseats, in each other's arms—until everything ended suddenly.

I woke up, drenched in sweat, not knowing where I was, twisted in my perfect new sheets. Someday I had to learn to let go of what I couldn't change.

THREE

⌒

On that next Monday morning, I got up bright and early in my own apartment and went to work, just like a normal person, like any regular American. (You have no idea what it means for me to say that.) I had jobs before I went to prison, but they were summer jobs when I was a teenager, like at that camp where I met The Girl or in the store where my father worked. I had jobs in prison—library, laundry, grounds keeping, food service, etc.— but that's a different thing. It's not the same when there's some-one with a gun watching you do your job. Sure, I went from Four Winds to Clemency for three months, but that was under strict, sign-in-and-out supervision, with big Ned Edwards breathing down my neck. Now I was going from my own place, on my own time. With zero supervision, except for checking in with Fusco every three weeks and the possibility of his dropping in on me unannounced, I'm flying completely solo. For the first time in just about forever.

No question I'm extremely lucky that Clemency USA gave me this job. Lots of guys who get out of the joint are lucky to get some job scrubbing floors someplace. Once an employer finds out that you're a convicted felon, well, would *you* want to hire a guy who has been in jail for a long time, even if it's only to flip burg-ers? And that's if you can get that job.

Honestly, I would have been happy for any job at all, but I was working for an important organization that actually tried to do good in this world. (It helped get *me* out of prison, didn't it? That's only half a joke.) The office in White Plains is just one branch, the Northeast branch, of Clemency USA, which is head-quartered in Washington, D.C. And Clemency USA is just one branch of World Clemency, an international organization head-quartered in Geneva, Switzerland. At various times, our branch gets pressure from Washington to do things. And if something is really important, we get pressure from Geneva. Everyone gets really agitated when Geneva wants something. It was exciting to be part of something that big, doing good all around the world. Even if I was only delivering packages, answering phones, making coffee, or entering contributors' phone numbers and addresses—regular mail and email—into the database. I was OK with that. I used to have big dreams. But I was happy with this little dream: my own little place, a little job, and a little life.

Almost every morning since I moved in, I met Javier at the bus stop a couple of blocks from the apartment a little after eight, and we'd take the 8:15 bus together. I bought a Metrocard at the bodega on the corner to pay for my bus rides. I could even use it on the subway. Kelly showed me how when I first started commuting to Clemency. Another Thing I Had Missed. But I was lucky that I had people who were willing to help me.

I took pleasure in the simplest things. I liked standing in line for the bus because I knew that people in line with me almost certainly didn't have knives or shanks they might stick me with. I still didn't like being bumped or run into. But I was getting used to the accidental nudge, the inadvertent touch.

I used to hate taking buses. The city buses, the bus out of Jamaica down Merrick Boulevard, those camp buses, all the prison transfer buses I was shackled and chained into, over the years—all of them. Their diesel fumes and their rough rides.

But this one, the No. 6, wasn't so bad. I even became friendly with the driver, Jaynelle, a large black woman. I developed a nodding relationship with some of the other commuters. There were two older women: nurses, who always nodded back and returned my smile. Also, there were a few teenage boys with full backpacks who went to Archbishop Stepinac High School in White Plains, looking good in their chinos and blue vests with a red *S*. They all had little earphones in, listening to music, and were constantly looking down at their phones, which seem to have taken over everybody's lives.

"How was your weekend, man?" asked Javier after we settled into one of the rear seats of the big Bee-Line bus.

"Great," I said. "I spent the whole weekend putting Ikea furniture together. How about you?"

"Busy too," he said. "I had a big exam on data management, and then I had to work all day Sunday in my cousin's liquor store."

Javier was going for his B.S. in Information Systems and carried an old-fashioned black leather briefcase. He was in his midtwenties, kind of heavy-set, and still living at home with his family. I'd been thinking about going back to school, but I decided to put it off for a while, to make sure I did well at my job and got accustomed to living alone, etc., before I took on too much. As I said, I was trying to be careful with everything I did. It only made sense: I didn't want to make any mistakes that would put me back in prison. That much was clear.

"At least Rosemary gives me time off to study, when I need it," he said.

"She *would*," I said with a chuckle. Rosemary Dandridge was the office manager at Clemency and my direct supervisor. She was a substantial, middle-aged black woman and one of the down-deep nicest people I've ever met. I'm not saying this because she gave me an old laptop and some other equipment that her department was throwing away. She was strictly no-nonsense, and I had to stay in her good graces to grease things with Kelly and the Gateway Program and not get in any trouble that could be reported to Fusco. Even though I was wary of her, I liked that she was calm, had a good sense of humor, and was the same way to everybody. I tried to listen carefully to everything she said.

"*You* should go back to school," said Javier, moving closer to me as the bus was filling up with passengers, constricting my personal space. "You could do it," he encouraged me. "I've seen you, man. You can *work*. You have a ton of energy."

"You mean 'for an old man.'" I laughed nervously.

"No!" he protested. "For anyone."

"No, you're right. I am pretty obsessed," I admitted, patting his arm lightly, telling him to relax. "But in a *good* way. I'm not just some crazy old con—"

I stopped myself before I said anything else, but he flinched a little and resettled in his seat, as I realized what I had let slip out. Javier, like everyone at Clemency, knew about my background, but I had to be careful with what I said and how I behaved. When you're an ex-convict, especially a "famous killer," you have to be *extra* careful. People think you're prone to violence, and that is not true. I am not prone to violence, but I have been exposed to a lot of it. I know what it is and how to deal with it. But people are sensitive, so I had to be watchful—over myself. I wanted these people—the people at Clemency—to like me. No, I *needed* them to like me.

"A crazy old guy from Long Island who likes living in Westchester now," I concluded. "In fact, who likes it quite a lot!"

I also liked getting to the office early. So did Javier. What I didn't like was that a cup of coffee cost *four dollars*. At first, I resisted it. I mean, isn't that ridiculous? Four dollars for some hot water and ground-up beans. OK, there's the money for the rent of the store and paying the kids who make the coffee. But still: *four dollars? For a cup of coffee?* I sound like my old man.

There are lots of office buildings in White Plains. It's not Manhattan or anything, but it's quite a collection of tall steel-and-glass buildings. We're in one of the tallest towers on Martine Street, right in their downtown. I must say that, although I miss the city, I don't mind the shorter commute to White Plains. Manhattan wasn't so good to me the last time I lived there, my freshman year at Columbia. I was a bridge-and-tunnel kid who never really fit in. Besides, Manhattan is now ridiculously expensive, or so I hear, even more expensive than Westchester. As it is, White Plains is busy enough for me; everybody seems to be in that Manhattan I'm-a-very-important-person-and-I'm-five-minutes-late rush anyway.

I know that email and texting is the big thing now, but we still get regular mail at Clemency USA, and I'm responsible for distributing it to people's desks. This is after all our mail has been screened by an outside security company. You might ask, "Why?" and "Screened for what?" The answer is that everybody seems to require extra security these days because of terrorism, but especially Clemency because we're a do-gooder organization. We sometimes criticize governments, corporations, and other groups. (That includes the United States government. Is that surprising? It shouldn't be.) We stand up for human rights. So sometimes we are harassed and threatened by bad people. Crazy people send crazy stuff in the mail. A few years ago, someone sent some white powder to the head of the Washington office after someone called for a reinstitution of the assault weapons ban. The powder turned out to be nothing very harmful (not anthrax or any other poison), but there were also lots of phone threats. Clemency has a lot of enemies—tyrannical governments, out-of-control state and local prison systems, the private corporations that run prisons, the prison guard unions, hate groups both in and out of the system, multinational corporations that corrupt small countries, union busters, gun nuts, neo-Nazis, white supremacists, religious extremists of all kinds, and on and on. No one was ever charged in the white powder incident, but they decided to have all the mail screened before it comes to us in White Plains. I guess I'm happy about that; I don't want to sort the mail someday and have it blow up in my face or give me the plague. There are a lot of crazy, angry people out here, I'm finding out. I understood it in prison, but all this anger out here in the outside world is a whole other thing I can't quite comprehend yet. But I'm working on it.

Thanks largely to Rosemary, I'm getting much better on the computer. I think that's the biggest "thing" I missed in all my years of incarceration: computers. And phones! They've really taken over the world. Everyone, or almost everyone, is either carrying one or working on one. By the time I left prison, the phones had fully infiltrated the system. To put it bluntly, once guys could "keester" a small phone, the guards couldn't keep them out. Now guys keep running their drug rings and their women from prison on their phones. Hell, you can transfer funds, make movies, whatever the hell you want with these phones. Boundaries are nonexistent. I didn't have one when I was inside; I had no need and didn't want to get in trouble and jeopardize my release at the end, if and when it came. But now I can see that they are pretty much a necessity, a fact of life.

Another of my regular jobs is updating the computer list of contributors. Clemency depends mostly on contributions from regular people. They get some matching funds from some foundations and, now and then, a big donation from a left-leaning billionaire, but a lot of it is fund-raisers and mailings to individuals. Doing good isn't cheap. So, I enter the new names in the database. I have a security code and everything. They trust me.

I had very restricted access to some old computers in a couple of the prison libraries, but nothing like these sleek machines out here. I wish I'd had one of these, with a fast search engine and internet access, in my cell while I was in prison. Who knows what I could have accomplished.

⌢

It was Monday, and I was burning to talk to Ed Nyquist. Now that I was out of Four Winds and in my apartment, I could really concentrate on getting on this Mantell thing. But I knew enough not to bother Nyquist on a Monday morning. People at Clemency were super busy on Monday morning, so maybe it was like that in other places. I knew it would be better if I waited until the afternoon. Truthfully, from the beginning, Nyquist seemed to treat my Mantell issue as a lesser problem compared to the capital punishment and big-time international humanitarian issues they deal with. And because they were handling my case pro bono—I had no funds to pay a lawyer—I kept my mouth shut...most of the time.

Nyquist was one of those guys who radiated self-importance: you could see it in his perfect suit and perfect hair. Rosemary defended Nyquist, saying that he was "a very well-respected man," hinting that he came from old money, though she didn't use that term. But later I overheard her complain to someone about Nyquist: "He think his shit don't stink."

So I waited to approach him and reported to Rosemary instead, as I did every day, for my assignment.

"I want you to go out and get this," she said, handing me a piece of paper that had just been disgorged from her printer on the floor next to her desk. "I already emailed Sheila in business affairs. She'll give you the party card."

I glanced down the list of things. It was Naomi's, a secretary in business affairs, last day before her maternity leave, and there was going to be a party for her that afternoon. The list wasn't complicated: red wine, white wine, some food, paper plates, plastic forks and spoons, and a cake that Rosemary had ordered, with a copy of the receipt attached: nothing unusual.

"Cool," I said, folding up the papers and putting them in my shirt pocket. One of the first things I did when I got this job was buy a whole bunch of nice, new white dress shirts (on sale). That way, even if I'm wearing jeans or chinos, I still look kind of sharp and neat. And when I put a sports jacket over it, I'm good any-place.

I thought of one slight problem.

"One thing, Rosemary," I said. "I don't have a car to—"

"That's OK," she said. "Derek will take you wherever you need to go."

"Great!"

Derek Ellison was a student intern who was working at Clemency for the semester. When I was young, an intern was a doctor in his first year after medical school. Now apparently there are all kinds of interns working in various businesses. But instead of money, they get college credit and practical experience in whatever field they're interested in.

After I had gotten the credit card from Sheila, I approached Derek, waiting outside his cubicle. "You ready?" I asked.

"Yeah," he said, rummaging around on his messy desktop, "let me get all my stuff first."

"Take your time," I said, amused at his semi-frantic searching.

Derek was a good-looking kid, no doubt about it. He was like me when I was young, except he was taller, had more hair, handsomer features, big brown puppy-dog eyes, and a straighter nose. He dressed well but casually, in chinos, sports jacket, and blue Oxford shirt. He had that eternal messy-but-cool, privileged prep-school manner. But he seemed nice enough and eager to please.

"Let me just get my keys and my phone," he said, "and we're outta here."

I had to step quickly to keep up with the kid's long stride as we walked to the parking structure a block down from the office.

"Parking this far away's a pain," he said. "They should have their own lot."

He dashed across the street to beat a yellow light, and I stayed with him.

"So, Derek," I said, "what college you go to?"

"Dartmouth," he said.

"Good school!" I said. "You must be a good student."

"Well, that's one way to look at it," he non-answered me. "It's this way."

He turned into the parking structure's first stairwell, and I followed.

"So if you're an intern," I said. "Does that mean you're going to be a doctor someday?"

"Not even close," he said with a snort. "But it's their way of dignifying a lot of unpaid labor with a nice title."

"But you get college credit for it, right?" I asked, walking with him while I dodged another pedestrian coming the other way.

"Yeah," he said, starting up the metal staircase.

"So let me get this straight," I said as we trudged upwards. "Your parents are paying tuition at Dartmouth, so that you can come here and work for free, doing basically the same stuff I do for money."

"That's one way to look at it," he said.

"Wow," I said. "This job with Clemency must be a real plum. You must be a really good student."

He let out a gassy laugh. "Well," he said, "if you really want to know, I got a couple of incompletes last term."

"Too much partying?"

"It depends on your definition of 'too much.'"

"Partying happens," I sympathized with him. "Especially at Dartmouth, right?"

"And unfortunately I'm living back home, but just for this semester. I grew up right near here in Scarsdale."

"So how is that?" I asked.

"Need you ask?" he croaked.

"Don't worry, kid. Everybody smart fucks up some time or another."

He liked that and laughed as we walked off on level three. He took his keys out of his pocket. I followed him down the aisle.

"Nice wheels," I said when I saw the lights blink on the sleek, silver sedan he had opened with a beep of his key.

"Eh," he sniffed. "It used to be my mother's."

"I used to drive my mother's car too," I said. "Only it wasn't a—a—what is this?"

"It's a BMW," he mumbled, getting into the driver's side.

"Oh," I said, getting in on the passenger side, "a Beemer!"

"Please don't call it that," said Derek with a pained expression as he turned on the engine.

"Hey, it beats my mother's Ford Falcon that I used to drive. By a long shot."

"Ford Falcon?" he mused, putting the car into gear and turning around to back out of the space. "That sounds like the name of an old movie star."

Which got a laugh out of me. The kid was sharp.

"You know where we're going?" I asked him, as I buckled my seat belt, like Kelly taught me.

"Oh, yeah," he said, expertly whipping the car backward out of the parking space. "Party store, liquor store, supermarket."

We were down two ramps and out on the road in a flash. Derek liked to drive fast.

"So," I said, "how do you like Dartmouth?"

"It's OK. My father and his father went there, so...."

"Dartmouth," I mused. "A minor Ivy."

That made him snicker.

"What?" I said. "I figure if it's not Harvard, Yale, or Princeton, it's not worth bragging about, right?"

"You went to Columbia, right?"

Briefly, I froze. Of course, he knew that. Everyone at Clemency knew my background and who I was; they were the ones who got me out. But I was surprised that this kid, this intern, knew my history.

"Right," I answered. "Another *very* minor Ivy. Turn here."

We got all the stuff from Rosemary's party store list. I pushed the cart, and Derek threw everything in. Paper tablecloth, napkins, paper plates, plastic forks, little candles, streamers—all in blue baby colors; Naomi was having a boy.

I paid with the credit card, no problem. They asked to see my ID, and I had my employee badge and these business cards from

Clemency with my name on them that Kelly had made up for me. (I was really touched.) Derek and I walked out of there with three giant shopping bags of goodies.

Next was the liquor store on Mamaroneck Avenue. I grabbed an empty shopping cart and pulled it from the rack.

"Do you know anything about wine?" I asked Derek.

"A little," he said as he led the way down the aisle toward the wine.

"Yeah, I figured. Dartmouth always was a big drinking school."

"Besides that!" He laughed. "My father collects wine. Many, many bottles of wine."

"That's nice," I said, noting his ambivalence. "Rosemary said four bottles of white, four bottles of red."

I pushed the cart down the aisle while Derek slowly scanned the rows of bottles. Bottle after bottle after bottle.

"I have a friend, a serious wine fanatic," he said, putting two kinds of white into the cart. "Wants to get his Ph.D. in—what's the word—*viticulture* at UC Davis. His father runs some big investment firm, but he just wants to make his own wine. They say it's very satisfying to make your own wine."

"Pruno." I couldn't stop myself from saying it.

"What?" asked Derek, pivoting to face me. "What's pruno?"

I hesitated, but I had to tell him.

"It's the hooch you make in prison," I said. "Homemade wine. You put stuff in a plastic bag like apples or bread—whatever you have—with some sugar, and you let it ferment in the tank of your toilet for a week, and presto! You've got wine. Or something like it."

"Pruno," Derek repeated with a slow-growing smile. "Sounds like a great name for a winery: Chateau de Pruno. What do you think of this red?"

At the bakery counter at the supermarket, it was the same easy thing.

The skinny clerk read from a computer screen while he pushed his glasses higher on the bridge of his nose with his index finger. "You ordered gluten-free?"

"Did we?" I asked Derek.

Derek took the receipt out of my hand and scanned it. "Yes," he said crisply so that the clerk could hear, "we did."

I paid for everything. Again, no problem with my ID and the plastic from Clemency.

"It's a business card," said Derek as we went out to the parking lot. "They shouldn't give you any trouble."

I didn't want to tell him that I was accustomed to being suspected for everything I did, every move I made. But I could tell that Derek was a child of wealth and privilege and was extremely comfortable with life and all the advantages and prerogatives of freedom, mobility, and money. I mean, c'mon: *Scarsdale*! I was raised lower-middle class, but I went to Columbia (briefly) and know something about rich boys.

"What's wrong with gluten?" I asked Derek as I pushed the shopping cart full of snack food, cheese, cute little raw vegetables, and a big platter of cut-up fruit through the parking lot. He very carefully carried the cake himself.

"Don't ask. Gluten is evil," he said. "And forget about peanuts."

"What's wrong with peanuts?" I exclaimed.

"Hey," he said, getting the car unlocked, "a peanut can kill a kid these days."

⌐

"Good work, Larry," said Rosemary, taking the cake from me and giving it directly to Svetlana, her small, roundish secretary with a Russian accent.

"Take this to the kitchen," she told Svetlana, "and put it on the side."

"We got everything on your list, Rosemary," I said. "Derek is parking the car, and I'm gonna give the card right back to Sheila."

"Good," she said. "Then take anything cold and put it in the refrigerator, and after lunch, you can help me set up the conference room."

"Derek's a good kid," I said.

"I'm glad you like him," she said. "His father's on the board of Clemency."

"Oh!" I said. "That explains everything."

I hadn't been to a party in a very long time. There had been a couple of going-away get-togethers with punch and Twinkies at the Four Winds if a guy was getting his FR, his final release—I told Edwards to forget about mine, and he gladly complied—but this was an actual party with real people, not convicts. It meant circulating and talking to people, even to some people I didn't really know. Clemency was a pretty big place. I wasn't nervous, but I wanted to make a good impression. So I guess it kind of did make me nervous.

At first, I concentrated on helping Svetlana set up the refreshments and keeping them neat, making sure the ice bucket was full, the drinks were cold (all the cans of soda fully submerged in ice water), and the plastic glasses lined up exactly. It wasn't long before the conference room was filled with happy, chatty Clemency workers, drinking wine and eating snacks. I watched with pride as people came by and took cheese and crackers or little plates of the fruit salad that Derek and I had bought.

"Lots of people," I muttered to myself, looking out at the room full of secretaries and researchers and department heads and IT guys and media people.

"Everybody like Naomi," pronounced Svetlana.

"Who doesn't like a nice young, pregnant girl?" I said, looking across the room at Naomi in the corner, surrounded by well-wishers. Naomi was usually a quiet girl, always very nice to me when I went into her cubicle to put her mail on top of her in-box. But now, big-bellied and bubbly, she was talking a mile a minute to the women, mostly, who were her audience. She was dressed up on her last day before her maternity leave, in some kind of small, lacey, yellow circus tent.

Rosemary came up next to me, checking to see how the refreshments were going.

"Doesn't she look pretty?" I said.

Rosemary tsked me. "The word I'd use is *fat*. She'd better watch herself or she's gonna have trouble when the time comes to push."

She put her hand on my back. "Now *you* get out from behind this table and go circulate. Talk to some people. They won't bite you." And she gave me a gentle shove.

I took a plastic cup of Coke off the table and walked out among the partygoers. I saw that Nyquist was by the window, talking to Sylvia Lemaire, executive assistant to Geoffrey Blackburn, who was the head of the whole White Plains office. Nyquist had a glass of wine, *my* wine, in his hand. He didn't seem to be as prissy and irritable as usual, but I wasn't sure if I should approach him now. Was it better to do it in a social setting like this, or during regular business hours? I just wasn't sure.

I looked around for Kelly, but she wasn't there. Not seeing anyone to talk to, I walked over to the longest wall of the room and started to look at the many framed newspaper and magazine clippings about various prisoners around the world who were freed with the help of World Clemency, Clemency USA, and the other international branches. Some were labor leaders or anti-government or human rights crusaders. Some were just regular people like me who got caught up in some horrible prison system somewhere. There was one tiny, framed clipping from *Newsday*, the only newspaper left on Long Island, about my release. I was glad that during Clemency's push to have me freed that I didn't have to open myself to any interviews or publicity. I was finished with that, especially after that kid from the *Times* humiliated me.

Fortunately, Derek came along to save me. "Nice wall," he said, standing next to me.

"Yes," I said, "it is, isn't it?"

"I guess it's OK that they have these parties," he said, sipping his red wine. (I had never heard of Malbec before.) "Even though this is a *charity* and all, and the money could go directly to the prisoners. And their *families*."

"These people work hard," I countered, turning with him to look out on the room.

"They have a right to have parties when something like this happens."

"Something like *this*?" Derek repeated archly.

"You know what I mean," I protested.

He laughed and bumped against my shoulder, just as a friend would. I didn't have any real friends when I was in prison. It's not a good idea to get too close to anyone in prison. In fact, it's dangerous. But I do, in fact, *remember* friendship.

"Hey!" said Derek, bolting away from me. "I gotta see Linda!"

And he walked straight across the room, directly toward Linda Pirroux, the very attractive young blonde who was the main public relations and social media person in our branch, and immediately engaged her in bright conversation. As I said, Derek wasn't stupid. But I was left alone.

I saw Kelly at the snack table and made a beeline for her. She was taking a bite just as I approached her.

"You like the cheese?" I asked her. "I picked it out."

"It's very good," she said, dabbing her mouth with a little napkin.

"Actually," I said, "it was on Rosemary's list."

I made sure that I got into her line of vision and, lowering my voice, asked her, "You think this is a good time to ask Nyquist about, you know, Mantell and everything?"

"Your guess is as good as mine," she said as we looked over at Nyquist by the window. "Why not? He has a glass of wine in his hand. Maybe it *is* a good time."

"All I want to do is ask him a simple question," I said, reasoning with myself.

"That is very good cheese," said Kelly, turning back to the snack table. "Maybe you should go talk to him."

I started to walk across the room toward Nyquist. But just then, he was hijacked by Blackburn, the Big Man himself, who I hadn't seen come into the room. Geoffrey Blackburn was tall, frail, silvery, and scholarly—not the kind of guy you'd think of as the head of anything, at least at first glance. But his résumé was solid: from Yale to Oxford to Yale Law School to Supreme Court Clerkship and finally the State Department, along with a bloodline that went back to the Mayflower voyage of 1629, the second Mayflower. When he was a baby, his diapers probably came from Brooks Brothers. But from what everybody said, he knew where the big charity donors were and how to get them to open their wallets for unpopular causes, such as helping jailbirds like me.

Just then, Rosemary started the cake-cutting ceremony. Naomi made a little speech, thanking us all, saying how much this meant to her, and ending with "And don't you dare give my job away! I'm not kidding!" which got a big laugh from everybody.

I got in line along the edge of the conference table and shuffled forward, inch by inch, until I got a piece of the cake from Rosemary, who was wielding a mean cake slicer.

I stood in the middle of the floor, taking the first bite when I saw that Nyquist was free. At least Blackburn was gone. Now was my chance to catch him. I walked over to him with a confident stride and a smile.

"Excuse me, Mr. Nyquist!" I called. "Can I talk to you for a minute?"

Nyquist turned to look at me, pulling back at the same time.

"Yes?" he said, with a measured tone. His suit and tie and shirt and haircut were absolutely perfect.

"Hi," I said, trying to sound casual and friendly. "I was wondering if you've heard anything about Lester Mantell—"

"You asked me about this last week, Mr. Ingber," he said, cutting me off. "Didn't I tell you that I was working on it? We're doing the best we can. We're in touch with the FBI and the SEC. I was in Washington over the weekend. The board of directors meeting is coming up, and I'm afraid that, for now, you're going to have to find a wee bit more patience."

My first instinct was to smash the piece of cake into his face and shout, "Patience? Do you have any idea what patience means to a person who's been in prison for thirty-nine years, ten months, seventeen days, fifteen hours, and sixteen minutes? Do you have any concept of the meaning of the word, you self-righteous, silk-tied, supercilious asshole!"

But I didn't say any of that. I kept it all in, even as I flushed inside with white rage—my Prison Mind—that almost blinded me with its force. Instead, I controlled myself, just as I was instructed to do in a million group therapy sessions.

"...OK," I said, exhaling, keeping my balance. "OK. But when you hear something —"

"You'll be the first to know," he curtly finished my sentence for me.

I turned and walked away, still dizzy with anger. It happened so fast. I had planned the conversation for so long, and it was over so quickly. And I didn't learn anything other than that Nyquist was a nasty, rude, condescending person, which I sort of already knew. But the way he dismissed me, barely treating me like a person... On the one hand, I was used to it from prison. But on the other hand, I didn't expect to find that attitude out here, in the real world, especially in this organization of do-gooders. Some things are different out here, but some things are the same: certain human beings, wherever they are, are simply assholes.

After the party, I stayed for a while to help Rosemary and Naomi's friends clean up until Rosemary sent me home.

"What's wrong?" she asked me.

"Nothing," I lied, replaying my encounter with Nyquist over and over again, each time finding something unsatisfying about it. The FBI? The SEC?

Going home on the bus alone, I was better. The toughest part was balancing the little plastic bag with a piece of the party cake in a little box that Rosemary made up for me and trying to keep it level all the way home so the cake didn't get smashed. It was a relief after a difficult day not to have to make small talk with Javier. I spent the whole bus ride that morning convincing him not to drop out of the computer program at Pace. He said it was too much work, and his girlfriend wanted him to be with her more. I told him to tell his girlfriend that he was going to school *for* her: to improve their future *together*. I threw a good scare into him, about the need to work hard while he was young, to safeguard the future for both of them. Then I was all out of small talk and advice. (Who was I, anyway, to give anyone advice about anything?)

But, in a way, it was a good day, except, of course, for Nyquist. Why were they having such trouble getting to Mantell? I tried to concentrate on the good things that happened. I did a lot of work that morning, updating the database, and Rosemary said that soon she was going to let me start answering more routine emails. The more work, I told her, the better, because I was going to ask her for a raise. And Derek, the kid, he was nice and smart and respectful, and I was happy that we helped with Naomi's party. It made me feel, more and more, a part of Clemency. I have to say it: Derek reminded me of myself when I was young. Smart but a bit rebellious, not that I'm comparing his incompletes at Dartmouth to my involvement in two murders. He was still a rich kid with a golden future, even better than mine. After all, I didn't grow up in Scarsdale—far from it. I wondered how rich and how ambitious he really was.

What I would give if I could go back in time and start all over. I guess that's "unprofitable thinking," but sometimes I can't help but dream *backward* and think what my life would have been minus The Girl...and what I did.

The lobby of my building was warm; someone was cooking something comforting, something cheesy. I got my little key out and checked my silver mailbox, the second to last one in the row. I love getting mail; always have. Even so-called junk mail I find interesting. Everything, even the most worthless stuff is mailed for a purpose. It means something to somebody or they wouldn't have mailed it, right?

Of course, there were a couple of bills. My Dad used to say, "Bills don't stop," and I guess he was right...about a lot of things, as it turned out.

I had leftovers that night. I am becoming a Master of Leftovers. I made a lasagna the other night, which should last me at least four meals. I followed the recipe on the box and felt like a chemist. It was actually fun. I had to buy a big pan, but I figured it was worth it. I'll be cooking other big meals for myself for a good long while.

I cleaned up right after I finished eating. I was tired and didn't want to let things hang. There was a Mets game on the radio, and I wanted to fall asleep listening to that. I needed something to keep my mind off Mantell. I couldn't let thoughts of him constantly eat me up from inside.

I washed the dishes, thinking instead about the piece of blue cake and milk waiting for me. That would hit the spot. Despite the missing money, my Dad's legacy unfulfilled, and so many desperate, lost years, I never thought I'd ever have *this*: my own place and leftovers and time alone with no one to threaten me, no one to fear. When you think about it, *I'm* a leftover too. A leftover from another time, a leftover from a family that is gone, a leftover from distant memories.

As I fell asleep, I got lost in the life I might have had with The Girl: the big career, the big house, the big life. I couldn't help it. What I could have had, if only, if only, things hadn't changed.

She tortured me with her love. A week of unhappy phone calls, followed by a passionate weekend of apology and reconciliation. And then the same thing would happen all over again. Some of our problems she couldn't help—hateful mother, hateful home— but some of it she could. I didn't choose a troubled girl on purpose. Love chose her for me. And Love eventually doomed me. I should have known when I saw the bruises on her arms. But her apologies were so sweet and well-intentioned. Love is forgiveness, and I forgave. So many ups, so many downs. Isn't love supposed to be like that? Passionate, tempestuous, and rapturous? When you're "in" love, sometimes you can't see out. She blinded me with her love, and I got lost and couldn't find my way out. But when it was good, it was so good. That's what I kept telling myself. I didn't know where we were going until it was too late to stop.

FOUR

I hated going to see my parole officer Kenneth Fusco every third week—Thursdays at four o'clock sharp—but I had no choice. Fusco was fanatical about missing appointments. Once, I missed one—entirely my fault—and he read me the riot act. Later I found out that he actually got one guy's parole revoked because he missed too many appointments. Technical violations led to a revocation hearing, and bam, the guy was back in the joint. I think that Fusco considered that some kind of victory, making the guy an example.

And since four o'clock was right at the beginning of rush hour, I was nervous about making every single appointment. I didn't want my freedom to be subject to the whims of the Westchester Bee-Line Bus system, but to some extent it was. Once, I ran so late that I had to take a cab in the rain to get to Fusco on time, and I couldn't afford cabs.

But I made it for this one with ten minutes to spare; ten minutes in the drab waiting room listening to Fusco in the inner office make life miserable for another poor schmuck parolee like me, another "case." I didn't have to hear Fusco's exact words. Through the door, I could tell by his tone that he was reading the riot act to someone. When the door finally opened, who came out was practically a *kid*: a skinny Latino guy in his early twenties with his eyes all red. Fusco made the poor kid cry.

"Next!" Fusco barked as the kid dashed past me, head down, out of the waiting room. He couldn't even make eye contact with me.

I walked into Fusco's small, stale office and sat in the chair next to his desk as he stared at his computer screen with his dark, vindictive eyes. He made me sit there for a good two minutes in silence. I waited for him to speak, and he waited for me.

Finally, I said, "Well, I'm glad we had this talk, Officer Fusco," and got up from my chair as if I was leaving.

"Sit the fuck down!" Fusco ordered.

"And I'm happy to see you too," I said, sitting back down with a satisfied smile. For some reason, he hated me, and I hated him right back.

Reading directly off the computer screen, he asked me a series of questions about my work, about where I was living, and who I was seeing.

"What about your pal Sammy Zambrano?" he asked.

"Zambrano?" I almost rose out of my chair again. "I have nothing to do with him."

Fusco chuckled. "That's not what *he* said."

"Fuck what he said!" I shot back.

That got a nasty little laugh out of Fusco. I didn't want to let him upset me, but I couldn't help it. He still had some control over my life, and he just loved it.

"You don't fool anybody, Ingber," he said with a smirk. "I know you. I'm just waiting for you to fuck up—and you will. Fuck up. Guaranteed."

I didn't say anything. Sometimes I knew when to keep my big mouth shut.

"Just once, smart guy, you fuck up, and you're mine. I cannot wait to send you back where you belong" was his goodbye to me. This was after I left my monthly supervision fee with him. Can you believe that I have to help *pay* for the cost of my parole, which includes Fusco's salary? I pay for him to make my life miserable. Well, fuck him: I refuse to be miserable. The lard-ass never even got out of his chair the whole time I was there.

But I'll admit the encounter rocked me, more than a little. I was going to have to be very careful about my dealings with Fusco. No question, he had it in for me.

⌒

The next day when I got into work, I went straight to Nyquist's office, but he wasn't even in that day. I asked his assistant, Jan Cavilli, if she knew whether Nyquist had heard anything about

Mantell or had made any calls. She thought that he had made some calls but didn't have anything new to tell me. She was sympathetic, but that did me no good.

I went back to the job I was doing for Rosemary, sorting old journals in the small library on the fourth floor, trying to keep a positive attitude, but my mind kept coming back to the same things: Fusco, Mantell, money I needed and didn't have. Money, time, and loneliness.

Kelly came up from behind and surprised me.

"Oh," she said, "I didn't mean to scare you."

"You didn't scare me," I lied.

Kelly had a sweet, concerned smile, her arms wrapped around a stack of files. I hadn't seen her in a couple of days.

"You know I was thinking about you the other day," she began.

I liked that.

"I think I mentioned this once before to you. You haven't been back to Long Island since you've been out, right?" She paused. "Don't you think it's about time?"

That stopped me. Just the thought of going back to Long Island sent a sudden chill right through me, but it was a strange, *warm* kind of chill. It was true that I hadn't gone back to Long Island since I had been out. Part of it was that I didn't have a car to drive there, nor anyone to drive me. And part of it, I suppose, was that I didn't want to deal with my past and any unresolved Long Island memories. I had enough Long Island still within me; did I really need any more?

"You once told me that you were thinking of someday going to visit your parents', uh..." she trailed off. I understood what she was getting at: she didn't want to say *gravesite* or something explicitly morbid.

"Oh, yeah." I saved her. "Maybe I did say that once...since I wasn't allowed to go to their funerals. Either one."

"Then maybe you should go now," she said in a tender voice. "I bet there are lots of places on Long Island you'd like to see again."

"What?" I said. "To raise some ghosts?"

"Or bury them," she said right back.

She let that sit in the air for a moment. Of course, she had a point. Maybe I was stuck in the present *because* I was avoiding dealing with my past. Maybe there was something I could do about it. "Proactively," as people say these days. And maybe I could unstick myself so that I can move on with what's left of my life.

"But I don't have a car and—"

"I think I can get Derek to drive you," she cut me off with a note of confidence in her voice, making me think that she had already asked him.

"What?" I quizzed. "On a weekend? On a Saturday? 'Cause it would take a whole day to—"

"That's OK," she interrupted. "He loves you." Quickly she changed her tone: "I don't mean *loves* you. I mean he looks up to you. You know he likes to hang out with you."

Which was true. Coffee breaks and bag lunches in the lunchroom.

"He's like a big puppy dog," she said as my mind was filling with visions of places I'd like to go on the Island, in addition to my parents' graves. "Why don't you ask him?"

So I did. That afternoon. And he instantly said yes.

"With one condition," he said.

"What condition?"

"You never call my car a Beemer again," he said. "Ever."

"Deal."

⌒

Derek picked me up the next Saturday morning, right on time. In fact, he was a little early. I hardly slept the night before, thinking about the places I wanted to see...and the places I didn't. I had a great childhood on Long Island until it ended.

"I told you it didn't have to be this early," I said as I got into his unnamed German car. "It's *Saturday*."

"No!" he said with a real smile on his face as we took off from the curb. "I wanted to get going. This will be fun. I really don't know Long Island. I've been to the Hamptons once, a long time ago."

"Well, I know the Island," I said. "At least, I once did."

"Summers, we go to the Cape. My grandfather has a place there," he said.

"I hear that's nice too," I said, silently amused at how easily he dropped "the Cape." Child of money. I remember guys like him from Columbia.

"So, Larry," he demanded happily, drumming the steering wheel, "where are we going?"

"Make a right," I said. "I spent all last night on MapQuest."

Out from my back pocket I pulled a wad of folded up papers: maps I printed out last night.

"Rosemary gave me an old printer," I said, flattening out the papers. "But the cartridges are so damn expensive."

"No kidding, but you don't have to print stuff out like that," said Derek. "There are maps on your phone."

"I know," I said, "but I still like paper. Paper gives me...confidence. What about if the whole internet goes down? Then how would you find your way around?"

"If the whole internet goes down, the whole society goes down, and we'll all have to walk," he jeered. "So I wouldn't worry too much about it."

"Good enough!" I admired his carefree attitude. "Take the next right."

It was a warm, beautiful, sunny day, even though it was well into the fall. There were still some leaves left on the trees: some big yellows and reds and oranges. The sky was blue and practically cloudless. Let me tell you something about weather. When you're in prison, normal weather hardly exists. Whatever it is "outside," hot or cold, it's always basically late winter in your heart. Now that I see the sky every day, I love it more than I ever thought I would when I was inside.

"You got any music in this thing?" I asked him, looking at the elaborate dashboard and fancy console between us.

"What do you like?" he asked me, reaching for the radio knob.

"Play me what you listen to," I said, just as some blaring rock started, right in my ear.

Some chunking, ringing guitars started churning, filling the car with clear sound.

"Nice," I said, continuing to listen. "Vaguely Byrds-y. Who are these guys?"

"The Decemberists," he said, pronouncing it distinctly for me.

"You mean The Decembrists?" I repeated. "As in early Russian revolutionary Decembrists?"

"Yeah," he said uncertainly. "I think so."

"They sound good," I said, trying to sound sincere. Guys like to be complimented on their taste in music. "But don't go by me. I never got beyond Jimi Hendrix."

"*Nobody* did," he countered as he turned up the volume.

We were making good time now. Very little traffic, even for a Saturday. I hope we'd have such good luck all day.

"You just can't beat good loud music in a fast-moving car, can you?" I said, as the Bronx sailed by my window.

"Cannot be done," he agreed, turning up the volume even more and playing with the sound balance.

I shouted, "You're really nice to do this, to drive me. To give up your whole Saturday—"

"I'm not giving up my *whole* Saturday," he cut me off, raising his palm in a gesture of peace and self-defense. "Besides, Kelly said you needed a ride. Everybody needs a favor sometime."

"Right! Maybe someday I can do a favor for *you*."

"I'll tell you one thing you can do for me right now," he said.

"Yeah?" I said, a bit surprised that he had something so soon.

"You can get some toll money ready," he cracked and laughed out loud.

"Smart-ass," I muttered, digging into my wallet.

The Whitestone Bridge stood tall and silver in the sun as I gave Derek the cash for the toll. "*Seven-fifty! Are they kidding?*" I didn't say that, but it's what I thought. I didn't want to constantly be the crabby old guy complaining about everything new. That's not who I wanted to be...even if it was partially true. Ridiculously high bridge tolls were another Thing I Had Missed, thankfully.

The last time I crossed the Whitestone Bridge I think I was being taken from the Nassau County jail up to Sing Sing, but maybe that was the Throgs Neck Bridge. Regardless, this was definitely the bridge that The Girl and I drove on the night of the Incident. And on this clear, almost traffic-free Saturday morning, it looked pretty damn beautiful as we cruised straight toward its gleaming towers and graceful cables. Was it this beautiful on that night when I was driving that humungous Cadillac with two bodies in the trunk? Probably not.

Derek and I talked a little about Clemency and the people there. Nothing nasty, just the normal, good-natured making-fun-of-people talk, but as we touched down on the other side, onto actual Long Island soil—and I intend it to sound like a moon landing—I felt a tightness inside and an honest shiver to my bones. Yes, I was going "home"...back on L.I. But what did I really want to see?

If it wasn't a Saturday, I would have made Derek drive to Mineola, to the Nassau County Courthouse and the building where Mantell's office used to be, and ask around, but everything would be closed there on Saturday. I should never have let Nyquist and Clemency handle the Mantell thing for me. I thought about asking Derek if his father knew Nyquist and could put some pressure on him, but I figured I would wait for that, when the time was right.

"So," barked Derek, "which way?"

"Oh. Turn right here," I shouted, jarred back to the present and my duties as navigator. I pointed, indicating a sign for the Cross Island Parkway. "The Cross Island! Quick!"

He swerved the car smartly, getting in the right lane, squeezing between cars.

"Good move," I murmured. "Sorry."

"That's OK," said Derek magnanimously. "No problem. German engineering."

"So," Derek said in that little bark of his, "where are we going first?"

"OK, you ready?" I sighed, having thought this all out last night. "We're going to my parents' gravesite. Now, aren't you happy you offered to do this?"

"Hey!" Derek shot back. "I *love* cemeteries. Cemeteries are very cool. Have you ever been to Père Lachaise in Paris? That's a fantastic place! I went to Jim Morrison's grave there. And, God, who else? Lots of famous dead people."

"Well," I responded, "don't expect this to be Père Lachaise." Pronouncing it, even though I took French in school, seemed foreign on my tongue. And what kind of a question was that to me? Derek knew what kind of life I've lived: *had I ever been to "Pair La-shez?"*

"I spent last summer in Paris," Derek recalled, a wolfish smile crossing his face. "This girl took me there—a girl from Calais— and we brought a picnic with us. To Père Lachaise. It was...*très jolie.*"

Paris. I remember my roommate when I was at Columbia, a schmuck by the name of Darryl Gingrich. This jerk I used to call "Roommate A" testified against me at my trial. He used to brag about his summer at the Sorbonne and smoke those stupid, stinky French cigarettes. I googled him: he's a corporate lawyer now, in Silicon Valley... and, apparently, a major antique car collector and Republican Party contributor. And still an asshole, I'm sure. Hence, the name I gave him: the *A* was for Asshole.

We zipped along the waters of Long Island Sound as I tried to put the past behind me, for just a moment.

"You know what's over there?" I said, pointing to the land on the other side of the inlet. "F. Scott Fitzgerald's West Egg. From *Gatsby.*"

"Wow," he said.

"Or it might be East Egg," I allowed, "and he reversed them in the book. But it's one of the Eggs, that's for sure. Long Island has a whole crazy history."

Then I stopped myself, realizing, unfortunately, that I was part of that crazy history. A small part, but a part. So I shut my mouth for a while and let the radio play and the miles pass by.

We got off the parkway easily and followed my perfect-so-far directions past Belmont racetrack, where there seemed to be some activity, a few blocks down Hempstead Turnpike. Drab stores, fast-food joints, and gas stations. We were getting to the south shore of Long Island, where it flattens out. This is where I grew up. I had to ignore a strong, almost pulling feeling within me and cleared my head to concentrate on the directions.

MapQuest took us right to the entrance to the cemetery. It was at the edge of a residential area, off a well-traveled, truck-pound-ed road full of potholes, badly repaired. It all looked familiar, like something from an old photograph or a childhood dream.

"Wow," said Derek, as he waited to make the left turn through the open gate, "this looks nice."

I looked over the low walls of the cemetery across the acres of gravestones stretching, block after block, over the dead and said, "It's OK, Derek. You don't have to lie. This isn't for a grade."

We parked in one of the narrow spaces by the front and got directions in the Condolence Office to my parents' plot. The clerk, a little old lady (I should stop saying that: she was probably about my age), found my parents' names in the computer registry. I was happy that she didn't seem to recognize their names—she might have figured out who I was.

She quickly printed out a little map of the grounds, showing me the way to the actual site.

"Wow," I said as we walked out. "Everything is computerized these days. Even death."

We found our place on the map and set off crunching along the narrow gravel pathway. Fortunately, there were no burials that day, or it really would have been a drag for Derek.

The map proved to be less than ideal because although there were row letters and plot numbers on the map, there were almost none on the ground itself. Most of them had been overgrown or washed away by Nature long ago and never replaced. Still, the map gave Derek and me the general location, and after a few minutes of "let's spread out" searching, I found my parents' headstones.

Their names had been carved on two low, rectangular slabs of gray granite, set right next to each other, into the flat, dead grass. I stood there for a moment, my mind flooding with irreconcilable thoughts and buried memories until it went blank.

"I think I was here before," I said, "for my grandmother's funeral." I wasn't really sure: my trick memory again.

Derek stood behind me and didn't say anything. Which was the right thing to do.

I stood there feeling the light breeze blowing over all of us: Derek, me, my parents, and all these dead people under the ground. All the gravesites were kind of squashed together. Many generations of dead people. Here was my grandmother's grave. And my grandfather, although I really don't remember him. And all these strangers. I stood there not saying anything, thinking about their lost lives, and mine.

65

After a while, I said, "I had forgotten how flat Long Island was."

Derek came a little closer to me. "I bet they have a Bible or a prayer book, if you want to read something over them."

"No," I said, "no thanks. That's not my thing. But I should have brought something to say or read. Maybe—what is it—that Dylan Thomas poem about 'Do not go gentle into that good night'? I wish I remembered that."

Then, like we were in a movie, Derek said—in this calm, assured voice—the first lines of the poem.

> *Do not go gentle into that good night,*
> *Old age should burn and rave at close of day;*
> *Rage, rage against the dying of the light.*

And then, to my absolute, jaw-dropped amazement, he went on and recited the whole poem. *The whole damn poem*! By the time he ended with—

> *And you, my father, there on the sad height,*
> *Curse, bless, me now with your fierce tears, I pray.*
> *Do not go gentle into that good night.*
> *Rage, rage against the dying of the light.*

—I had all these tears streaming down my cheeks. Really. I'm sorry, but I couldn't stop them. I thought they had tortured all the tears out of me in prison long ago, but I was wrong. I loved my parents, and I, their only child, had ruined their lives. And now they were dead, under this ground and these stupid pieces of stone. And, really, they were not even there. They were...somewhere else. All that was left were memories, tears, and the money Mantell had, my legacy.

"Mrs. Stearne," Derek declared. "A.P. English. Scarsdale High. Fuck the Eagles."

It was sweet of him, making his little joke to break the tension—for the both of us.

"She was completely nuts about Dylan Thomas. She made the whole class do Under Milk Wood," he said. "For Christmas."

"You're kidding," I said, turning away from him, drying my eyes.

"No, really!" he insisted. "I was Organ Morgan."

That cracked both of us up, and my tears kept flowing.

"Sorry, kid," I said laughing, wiping my cheeks with the back of my hand. Make that both hands.

"Hey," Derek said, "it's OK. I don't even want to think about my parents dying."

"How old are your parents?" I asked him, turning away from the gravesites.

"I don't know. In their forties or fifties, I guess," he said.

"Good! You still have plenty of time for them to drive you crazy. Now," I said, holding back the last of my tears and composing myself. "Let's go do something fun! Let's get some lunch."

"What did you have in mind?" said Derek, joining me as I walked away without looking back.

"Have you ever had steamers and beer at the beach?"

"No," he said. "Not really."

"You spend time with your family at *the Cape* and never have had steamers and beer?" I replied, picking up the pace of my gravel-crunching walk. "Oh, man! Let's get the hell out of here."

We drove away from the cemetery as if making an escape from Death Itself. I think we both audibly breathed sighs of relief when we crossed back out of the gate. I felt embarrassed having cried like that, in front of a kid. All those many years in prison, I taught myself to never show any weakness or emotion.

"I do not fear because I do not feel." That was my motto.

But maybe crying at your parents' gravesite is the right thing to do. Isn't that a Moment of Grace and Thanks? Maybe I was on my way to becoming a normal person.

⌒

It wasn't that far, so I had Derek drive us to one of my old haunts, the strip of clam shacks down by the ocean at Freeport. It was just a few minutes on the Southern State and the Meadowbrook. It was scarily astonishing how well I remembered these roads. Some things looked different but not completely, as if I were recalling a vision from long ago.

When we eased onto Merrick Road, Derek adjusted to non-highway speed. Slowed down, everything still looked sort of the same—the strip malls and gas stations and fast-food places—but starker, more run-down. But after a few turns, we were suddenly in a vaguely familiar area of Freeport—just what I was looking for. Everything suddenly had that gray, sea-bleached, clapboard look. There were boatyards, seafood restaurants, and dry docks; smaller boats on trailers and large boats on lifts behind high chain-link fences. You could see flashes of seawater—the Atlantic Ocean!—between the buildings we drove past.

"What street is this?" Derek asked, whipping the car into the turn. "Who is this Guy Lombardo?"

"Never mind, kid." I laughed. "Not everything from the past is worth remembering." Before he could ask me anything else, I saw a parked car's brake lights turn on. "Hey! That guy's moving. We got a space."

"Brilliant!" said Derek, scooting the car over to the side to protect the parking space from poachers.

"Street parking," I said. "This is our lucky day."

Derek and I spent the next hour pigging out on steamers and talking about a million and one things. Whether Derek was looking forward to going back to Dartmouth—an honest "not really." Whether to order the garlic bread or the mozzarella bread— "Both." What hip brand of beer to order since I knew nothing about such things—Derek's choice: "Stella Artois." The Knicks' recent draft choices. Where the real money in his family came from—"my mother's grandfather was a lawyer for the Rockefellers."

I "allowed" Derek to have one beer since he was driving, but I had two. Big mistake. By the end of the meal, I was completely stuffed and pretty beer-buzzed.

"Guy Lombardo..." I recalled for him, "was a bandleader... and the absolute personification of New Year's Eve." I had trouble getting personification out.

"The whole holiday?" he said leaning back in our comfortable red-leather booth. "Like Times Square and Ryan Seacrest and everything?"

"Who's Ryan Seacrest?"

He snorted and laughed. "No one you need to know. Not everything from the present is worth remembering."

"OK," I said, realizing that I'd stumbled into another Thing That I Had Missed. There were so many of them: I was a Stranger in My Own Land, with these huge gaps of knowledge. I had lost so much damned time I could never get back. But I went on.

"Yeah," I recalled. "Guy Lombardo. And his—I forget who it was, his band. The Royal somethings. At the ballroom of the Waldorf Astoria. Which I assume is still on Park Avenue. And every single New Year's Eve, they played Auld Lang Syne as if he wrote the damn song, with all these old, dressed-up corpse-looking people dancing on black-and-white TV."

"Sounds vaguely depressing," said Derek.

"It was! It was horrible," I said, maybe a bit too loudly. "It was old-fashioned and square even when it was new. It was never good! I should keep my voice down. His kids probably run this joint."

As the second beer and the heavy food started to take effect, I thought about my parents' graves, and what I had just dragged Derek through.

"So," I said, "you gonna be a lawyer like your father?"

He snorted. "That's what everyone asks me."

"It would make him proud, I bet. You want to make your father proud. It's a natural thing to do."

That's when it hit me: I remembered.

"Hey!" I said, almost losing some beer from my mouth. "I bet your father knows Ed Nyquist!"

"I don't know. I suppose he does." Derek put down his glass with a sullen look. "My father knows lots of people."

"I bet he could light a fire under Nyquist's ass," I grunted.

"What do you mean?"

I told Derek about Mantell and my missing legacy.

"That sucks," he said.

"Damn right it does! It sucks big-time."

Looking back, I probably shouldn't have asked the kid to intervene; his father was a sensitive topic for him. But I had this incurable Mantell fever in my brain, and it could flare up at any time, in any situation. It was something I couldn't control. In any case, he promised to ask his father to call Ed Nyquist about my situation.

69

I paid the whole check even though Derek wanted to split it.

"No," I insisted. "This I have. And it's great, what you've done, driving me and everything. Whether you mention anything to your father or not."

We walked out into the afternoon sunshine, and feeling the beer in me, I stretched my arms out and half yelled, "Stella!"

I wonder if he knew what I was shouting about, whether his generation knew Marlon Brando. Here I was, stuck in the past, trying to find my way in the present, making jokes to a kid who didn't even know half of what I was talking about.

"So, Larry," said Derek. "Is there anyplace else you want to go? As long as we're here. On the Island."

I stood there for a moment, thinking through the buzz and the bright sunshine. Then I answered honestly.

"Yeah," I said. "As long as we're this close...I guess I should go see my house. I mean my parents' house. The house I grew up in. As long as we're here, we might as well do the whole thing. The whole nine yards."

"Great!" said Derek, beeping his car open with his key as we approached. "Let's do ten."

⌒

I hadn't MapQuested the way to my house from the restaurant, but hell: that way I knew in my sleep. No trick memory here. Some things are implanted in my brain and cannot be erased. For good and for bad, I guess, is the unavoidable conclusion to that thought.

We breezed by a lot of stores, standing alone or in strip malls. Some seemed to be doing business, but there were quite a few empty storefronts, too, with "For Lease" signs. We passed vacant lots, parking lots, and used car lots as well as Freeport High— "Home of the Falcons"—and the good ol'/bad ol' Long Island Railroad on our right. How much time, how much life did I waste on that train going in and out of the city in those depressing, clattering cars?

We drove by a water tower, some ball fields, and more stores and vacant lots, with the railroad always there on our right.

"Lots of places out of business," I said, almost to myself as we drove past a whole row of empty storefronts.

"Hey," Derek said with a shrug. "The economy sucks," as if it were a natural fact of life.

"I suppose so," I muttered. I never remember so many empty lots and cheap discount places. Coming into winter with the trees almost completely bare, it all looked so run-down and depressing. I just don't remember it looking this grim, this downtrodden. Maybe it was because I was a kid seeing things with a naïve eye, but I don't think so. I think that, in many ways, things were better then. How the hell did this happen?

It didn't take more than fifteen minutes, and a few automatic "take this right" and "left here" directions from me before we turned onto my street. As we got closer, I felt very excited yet somewhat tense. There could still be some old-timers from when I grew up. Not that anyone would necessarily recognize me. Forty years in prison will do things to a man's appearance, even if I felt almost exactly the same inside.

I had forgotten how small the houses were, and how close together. But that was OK. What I couldn't believe was how depressed the whole street looked. There were potholes in the road, and don't people paint their houses anymore? There were lots of cheap-looking aluminum siding and some big new dormers that expanded the second floors of some of the houses. Some people had enclosed their yards with bare chain-link fencing and put metal gates on their windows. There were a couple of broken-down trailers parked in-between the houses. Many of the big trees that used to shade each front yard were gone. And there were no kids playing in the street on a Saturday afternoon like there used to be. At least a few kids should be out, throwing a football around on a late autumn afternoon like this. But now: nobody. Zilch.

"Which house was yours?" Derek asked, jarring me out of my memory trance.

"There," I said, "on the left," pointing at the small, not-quite-the-same house with, thank goodness, the same big maple tree still in the front. The leaves were gone—I remember raking a ton of those and then leaf-diving with my friends—but the tree was still there.

The front of the house had been remodeled. Someone enclosed the front porch with aluminum siding, which gave the place a weightier and cheaper look. The evergreen bushes under the windows looked sparse and undergrown. My Dad used to spend a lot of time, trimming all those shrubs with these big clippers. This new owner obviously needed a lesson...and some fertilizer.

Slowing way down, Derek asked, "Want me to park?"

Fighting the conflicting instincts within me—go, stay, go—I finally stammered, "Yeah. Why the hell not? We're already here."

Drawn as if by a magnet, I got out of the car and started to cross the street for a closer look, first letting a car pass in front of me. Derek was lost in his phone, like so many people are these days.

"Checking your mail?" I asked him. "Or is it a text? From a girl, I hope."

"Both," he said. "Sort of." And he followed me across the street.

As I got closer, I looked down the driveway along the side of the house to the detached garage at the back of the property. The basketball hoop on the front of the garage was gone. What a disappointment. I must've taken a million shots at that hoop. I remember when my Dad put it up. We must have replaced the net a dozen times. Nothing is sadder than a gray, shredded basketball net. I remember the exact place in the garage where my Dad kept the inflation needles and hand pump for when the balls needed air. I remember his miracle hook shot from the back porch one Fourth of July barbeque. I was becoming almost dizzy with memory when Derek spoke, bringing me back to the present.

"Nice-looking house," he said, trying to sound sincere, but he couldn't keep the condescending tone out of his tone.

"It's no Scarsdale," I said as we walked closer.

"Scarsdale isn't Scarsdale," he said with a snort.

I had to smile. All kids, no matter where or when, no matter how rich or how poor, can't stand their hometown.

The house itself looked dark and empty, and there were no people around.

"Where are all the kids?" I asked.

"Inside, playing Xbox and PlayStation Four," answered Derek. "Or surfing the web for porn. Kids don't play the same way anymore."

"I guess so," I muttered. "Still...on such a beautiful day."

He stepped up next to me. "You want to knock on the door and say—"

"No!" I shot back. I don't know why I reacted so negatively to his suggestion. I started to explain myself. "I just don't want to bother the guy who lives here. And I can see everything from here."

My father sold the house a few years after my mother died. He said it was too big for him after she was gone. "Too big to keep clean" is how he phrased it. He moved into an apartment somewhere near the water in Far Rockaway, and then a nursing home. I wrote him letters but eventually he stopped answering, and I lost touch. Now all that's left of him is the money that Mantell has.

I could see some frilly curtains in the window of my old upstairs bedroom in front of a pulled-down shade. That room always did get a lot of sun. It was my Fortress of Solitude, where The Girl and I would go to hide from the world in our Zone of love. So much happened in that room: my mind overloaded with memories of my childhood—so many that I couldn't think.

"So, tell me about this girl," I said to Derek, who was on his phone again.

"She's no one, really," he said, putting it into his pocket.

"That's OK," I said. "You're right not to talk about girls. It gets you nowhere."

The front door opened suddenly, and a man swung the storm door wide.

"Can I help you?" said a man with a clipped accent, possibly Indian or Pakistani. He was wearing a white shirt and dress pants, and he sounded angry.

Both Derek and I were surprised; there were no lights on in the house, and no car in the driveway.

"No!" I replied, taking a step back on the sidewalk. "Not a bit." Derek moved with me. "It's just that I used to live here," I said in a loud but friendly voice. "A million years ago."

The man didn't smile or seem to acknowledge what I was saying. He just stood there, looking at us. He didn't invite us in or ask me if I wanted to see my old bedroom. He also didn't ask me if I minded that he took down the basketball hoop on the garage. He just kept looking at us in the most unfriendly way.

There was nothing for me to do but say "OK...thanks, anyway."

And I turned away from the house and went back toward the car.

"Let's get out of here," I said to Derek.

As fast as I could, I got in the car on the passenger side while Derek got in on his side.

"The dick could've at least offered to let us come in and take a look...and a leak," I said, gazing across the street one last time at what was definitely not the Ingber house anymore: it was the House of the Angry New Guy.

"You know," said Derek, "I could use a bathroom too."

"Wait," I said. "I know just the place. Let's get out of here. I've seen enough."

⌒

I couldn't wait to get to the Lexington, my favorite old diner, right by the Long Island Railroad station. First of all, I did have to pee pretty badly (two cold beers, one old bladder), but most of all, I loved the Lex. *That* couldn't have changed very much. Diners were a constant around New York. There were even a couple in Westchester—one near Four Winds and another not far from my Yonkers apartment. But I hadn't come across one as good as the Lex. Or at least as good as I remember it.

But of course, I should have expected it. I'm sure social scientists or economists would have predicted it, but when Derek and I turned at the corner beyond the railroad station into view of the Lex, it wasn't there anymore.

"Wouldn't you just know it!"

Where my favorite diner once stood was now a small strip mall: a tax-preparation place, a discount beauty supply/vitamin store, a nail salon, a Mail Boxes Etc., and a Subway to eat at. And that was it.

What the hell happened to my hometown?

"At least the Subway'll have a bathroom," said Derek as he zoomed toward a parking spot at the far end of the lot.

We got lousy Subway coffee, took turns using their bathroom, and stood outside, drinking the lousy coffee, leaning against the fender of the BMW.

"So where do kids hang out now?" I asked, sipping through the hole in the white plastic top.

"Starbucks, probably," answered Derek. "There must be one around here. I'll check."

He whipped out his phone from his shirt pocket, but I put my hand over his and said, "Don't bother."

We stood there, sipping the coffee, listening to the hum of the continuous traffic on Sunrise Highway.

"You know," said Derek thoughtfully, "it's still pretty early, Larry. Isn't there someplace else you'd like to go?"

His question stood in the air like a ghost. I tried to ignore what was in my mind.

"What about the girl in your phone?" I asked him, pointing at his pocket.

"Forget about that," he said. "I know there's one more place you want to go."

"What the hell," I surrendered. "I might as well get it all out, over and done with. Run the whole damn table."

They say that a criminal always revisits the scene of his crime. I guess that could be true. It just took me forty years to do it. Not that I hadn't been to that house a million times in my daydreams and nightmares. I knew the way there like I knew my face in a mirror. Sure, some things had changed in her town, but it was still basically the same; the rich change slowly. Oh, there were a couple of new, fancier stores that I don't recall, and the obligatory Starbucks that didn't exist then, but the feeling of driving into a privileged preserve of the truly wealthy remained the same. There were a couple of new, supersized mansions, enormous even by local standards, but the overall impression was still Old Money. Serious money. Permanent money. No changes here. Funny how the rich stayed rich while my neighborhood got poorer. Or not so funny.

"Which way now?"

"Go left," I said automatically. "Left two blocks, and then a right."

I started to quiver inside: what did the House of Horrors look like today? Was it still the same massive block of brick with forbidding black shutters and that big, unwelcoming black door? Still that pretty prison where my beautiful blue-blue-eyed girl was tormented, the place where so many lives, including mine, ended?

As we drove nearer, I felt myself tense up—I told myself not to, but I couldn't help it—as I recognized the name of every street and every pretentious, fake-European-sounding court, terrace, or way. What a bunch of nonsense. Still I felt shivers all through me.

No matter how long I had been gone, I was still entering Enemy Territory. Even before what happened happened, I never felt comfortable here. I always felt watched...and unwelcome. Maybe this car—Derek's sleek gray sedan with its German engineering and fancy, lit-up dashboard—was acceptable in this neighborhood, but my parents' cars were never good enough. I was never good enough. I was always an intruder, a poor kid trying to steal one of their princesses.

"Tell me when to stop," said Derek.

"Stop!"

This was the way in, the opening to the famous cul-de-sac—Buckingham Court—where stood the House Where It Happened. In prison, I did a lot of remedial reading of stuff I missed at Columbia, and something Montaigne said hit me pretty hard: "Nothing fixes a thing so intensely in the memory as the wish to forget it."

But when I looked past Derek through the driver's window—to my immense shock, disbelief, then relief—the house wasn't there anymore. The enormous brick prison that kept so many secrets was gone. In its place was a huge glass-and-steel modern thing, even bigger than her mega-mansion.

"Thank goodness." I sighed. "They tore the fucker down."

Derek eased the car to the curb, and I immediately got out. I walked, was pulled really, down the sidewalk toward where the old house was. I couldn't stop seeing it in my mind, even though what was now there was an ultra-modern monstrosity; all odd, aggressive angles. It was like a dissolve in a movie that wouldn't stop dissolving. The original kept coming back.

Derek came up and stood next to me, putting his phone back in his shirt pocket.

"Is she still on for tonight?" I asked him.

"Maybe. This is pretty ugly," he said, nodding toward the house.

"It's very ugly," I agreed. "I just hope they remembered to salt the earth."

We stood shoulder to shoulder on the sidewalk, taking in its glistening, show-offy awfulness.

"So, this is where it happened?" asked Derek.

"The house is different. This is all new, but in this space," I said. "This same block of air...almost half a century ago."

"So how do you feel about all that?" he asked.

"What are you," I scoffed, "a psych major?" I didn't mean to jump on him. I just wasn't exactly sure what I was thinking. I groped for an answer. "Looking back on the whole thing, minus the murders, it was like a good bad dream. We were so in love. At least I was in love. That was all that mattered, what I could escape into. But hell, I was a kid, even younger than you: I wasn't thinking straight."

"Was she that hot?" asked Derek.

"Does it really matter now?" I replied. "But the answer is yes."

I stood there for a while—I don't know how long precisely, remembering things from years ago yet feeling feelings as present as today. I could see the house as it was the night it all happened, right there in front of me—the palace that I conquered, which then conquered me. I didn't even have to imagine it. My dreams came to life.

"I didn't think that coming back here would hit me this hard," I muttered to myself, not really knowing if Derek was near me or not. But I didn't care. I do not fear because I do not feel.

"You OK, Larry?" he asked.

"Me?" I said. "I'm great. I mean I am great." I tried to shake off the spell the place had cast over me. "I'm not in prison anymore. I can breathe this fresh air and walk the streets freely. You know what that means after years and years of close supervision? Now no one's watching me. Absolutely no one, except for my asshole of a parole officer. But I can raise my voice! Or I can whisper. I can dance around if I want to."

For the hell of it, I did a crazy, loose-limbed jig, like Dick Van Dyke in Mary Poppins, trying to dance away all the memories, all the nerves, all the guilt.

Derek stood back and laughed, even as he was checking his phone again.

"I can sing toooooo!" I sang out. "But I'll spare you that. That's the last thing you need."

"I am so glad I brought you here," he said, a very broad smile across his face.

Realizing what a spectacle I was making of myself, I quickly tried to self-sober, slapping myself across the face.

"Hey, we gotta get out of here," I said. "There really is nothing to see here, after all."

"Isn't there any last thing you want to say?"

"You mean like, 'I'm sorry?'"

I felt a sudden snap inside: it felt good to say those words out loud, right there on Buckingham Fuckingham Court.

"I'm sorry," I repeated. "I'm sorry! I'm sorry!" I spread my arms to embrace the whole scene. "I'm sorry, I'm sorry, I'm sorry, I'm sorry! I apologize to the entire human race and the entire Island of Long!"

"Uh, Larry!" Derek grabbed my arm. "You wanna maybe keep it down a little?"

I resurfaced from my trance of whatever-it-was—remorse? despair? bad clams? What the hell was I doing yelling in the middle of street in this nice neighborhood? If I were in one of these giant houses, I would be calling the cops right now about these two unknown guys hanging out shouting strange oaths and probably drunk. Fusco would love to hear about that. I'm surprised someone didn't send some dogs out after us, to scare us away. I've had dogs used against me, and believe me, you get scared. No, I wasn't good enough for this neighborhood when I was a bright young Ivy League freshman, and I certainly wasn't good enough for it now.

"You're right, kid," I said. "Let's get the hell out of here. This neighborhood was never any good for me anyway."

I don't know why I always come here in my dreams.

We started to walk back to the car. When we got close, Derek beeped his key and unlocked the doors.

He pulled open his door. "One more thing, Larry."

"What?" I asked, opening the passenger door.

"Do you want to go to her gravesite?"

"No, I do not!" I answered without any hesitation. "Let the dead bury the dead. I need to get off this fucking island—now."

⌐

I was glad that Derek was a fast driver. I couldn't get back home fast enough. Westchester was my home now.

"So, you got big plans for Saturday night, Organ Morgan?" I asked Derek, who seemed very intent on his driving in these last miles. I'm sure he wanted to get home too. It had been a long day for him with this crazy old con.

"Big enough," he said with a sly smile.

"So when do you go back to Dartmouth?" I asked.

"Not till after New Year's," he said. "I've got a while until then."

"The Royal Canadians."

"What?"

"Guy Lombardo's band!" My memory finally "untricked" me, hours later. "It was called the Royal Canadians. He was from Canada. I don't know what the hell I was thinking."

Derek laughed and shook his head. "You are too much, Larry."

"Don't mention it," I said. "I'm the next block."

We finally pulled up in front of my apartment building. It was dark and cold, and it seemed like I had left here a long, long time ago. It wasn't just the hours.

Derek slammed the car into park. "There. Safe at home."

I undid my seat belt and clapped him on his upper arm. "You did a nice thing for an old man."

"Bullshit," he laughed as I got out of the car. "I had a blast. Just what I needed."

I thought about reminding him to ask his old man on my behalf, to put some pressure on Nyquist, but I let it go.

"See you Monday, kid." Just before I slammed the door shut, I added, "And thanks again."

I stepped back from the car as he pulled away fast. I stood there, zipping up my jacket, watching his car speed back to Scarsdale. It was definitely getting colder. I felt that first real bite of winter wind, and it chilled me straight to my core. I was going to need a heavier coat for the long winter ahead.

I wasn't in my apartment for more than a minute before my cell phone rang in my pocket, startling the hell out of me. Almost no one had my number: Kelly, Fusco, Nate Edwards, Javier. Maybe it was Derek. Did I leave something in his car? I couldn't think of anyone else as I opened the phone. The screen read "Caller Unknown" with a number I didn't know.

I hit the answer button, held it up to my ear, and said a cautious, "Hello?"

"Larry?"

"Who is this?" I didn't recognize the man's voice.

"This is your friend," he said. "You don't know me?"

It was Sammy Zambrano—that skeeve from Four Winds.

"How did you get this number?" I demanded.

He just laughed nastily. "You underestimate me, my friend."

"I'm not your friend, Zambrano," I shot back.

That made him laugh even harder. "I know you don't like me, Larry, but I like you. I can't believe you don't want to make some money. Easy green."

I was about to cut off the call—and I should have—but I kept listening.

"I need a couple of smart, old white guys for this doctor who has a real good thing going. The money all comes from Medicare, from the government, so nobody gets robbed, nobody gets hurt. It's easy green, man. Two G's! Can't you use two G's?"

I ignored his question because the real answer was Of course I could. Clemency doesn't pay me much at all. Forget about the money Mantell had.

"Do me a favor, creep," I told him. "Lose my number."

I cut off the call like I should have when I first answered it and shut down the phone completely. I didn't want any callbacks from him. Zambrano was just the kind of person I needed to avoid. What a crazy day. It was bad enough that I was haunted by my past, but I was being haunted in my present too.

Right before I fell asleep, it occurred to me that I should have had Derek drive me to fucking Lester Mantell's office in Mineola. Even though it was a Saturday and it was probably empty, somebody might have been there, or in a nearby office, somebody I could get some information from.

Damn, I berated myself, I had to stop making mistakes. No question about it: prison was simple—survive. Being free in this real world was a lot more difficult than I thought it was going to be.

If I hadn't been so tired, I would have gone outside and looked up at the night sky. You can't see many stars at night in Yonkers. I don't know if it's too much streetlight or too much pollution. If I went down to the river, it would be darker and maybe I could see more stars.

Maybe that's what I needed: more stars. I knew I needed something.

I was almost asleep, and just when I thought I was too exhausted to have another thought, visions of what I refused to see that day—the inside of the house on the night of the murders—came back to me.

It happened so suddenly, and then in slow motion. She was an angry girl inside, schooled in cruelty, and it all came out at once. Years of rage built up this desperate force within her, and one night, it was ignited. Twice. And there was all this blood. An impossible amount. And we cleaned it all up—logically insane. The two bodies too. It was her idea where to take them, and where to dump them. But I helped. I drove her mother's Cadillac with the bodies in the trunk while she followed in her bad-luck red Mustang. I led the way all the way upstate to—I can't even say it. And two people were dead, along with my life. Who was that lost boy? I still don't understand how what started so innocently became so...un-innocent. How could a love so pure lead to so much death?

I woke up the next morning with a brutal hangover. I couldn't even look at myself in the mirror: too many memories, too much truth.

FIVE

⌒

I made the mistake of missing a Fusco appointment (no bus after an hour in the rain, and me with the flu), and he got pissed
even though I called and told him. I had dodged a couple of his
phone calls, letting them go to my voicemail, and postponed
once before, pleading overwork until I finally ran out of excuses. Whatever I did, I knew he had it in for me. It's not as if I
were actually "absconding," the official term for ducking your
parole officer, but I was definitely avoiding him and stretching
out the time between appointments. One problem, besides having this instinctive, reflexive dislike for him, was not wanting
to tell him about the phone calls from Zambrano—there was
more than one—which I was required to. I didn't want to tell
Fusco anything. And, I admit, I didn't exactly enjoy taking the
bus all the way to New Rochelle and then back home to Yonkers after work. The whole trip took more than two hours, not
counting my ten unpleasant minutes with Fusco, but I couldn't
afford to take cabs. And I certainly couldn't afford to buy a
car, even a crappy old used one. In fact, money was so tight
I was thinking of getting a part-time job on the weekends,
although I didn't know what it could be. Everything out here
was so expensive. I just had to get my money from Mantell.

⌒

When I finally sat down with Fusco, it was like this:

"You always think you're the smartest con in the room, don't
you, Ingber?" he said sneering, not looking away from the computer screen where my file was displayed.

"Did I ever say that, Officer Fusco?" I replied calmly, not taking his bait, looking around at the drab office I knew so well, decorated with printed flyers and statements of various kinds of rights.

"You don't say it out loud," Fusco grunted as he typed with two fingers, hunt-and-peck style, but continued quickly, "but you don't have to. I know you."

I said nothing.

"Any change of address?" he asked by rote. "Any disciplinary actions or notifications from your supervisor? Any traffic violations or encounters with any law enforcement officers?"

"No and no," I answered, "and none except you."

"Have you been doing any drugs?" he said, clicking the mouse next to his keyboard.

"No," I said. "But I'll pee anyplace you want me to."

He ignored my offer, turning from his computer screen to face me. He looked tired and older than when I last saw him. Part of it was the dismal lighting; part of it was his dismal job, persecuting convicts like me, and part of it was who he was: a vindictive prick. I'm not saying that most convicts don't need some kind of supervision on getting out of the joint, but what they don't need is more oppression.

"Have you been in contact with any known criminals or past associates from your time inside?" he asked.

"No," I lied. I did not consider hanging up on Zambrano as contact.

Fusco got suspicious.

"Listen, Ingber," he said, rubbing his nose roughly, "you maybe got those do-gooder libtards you work for buffaloed, but you don't fool me."

"Come on, Officer Fusco!" I laughed to tamp down my anger. "I know you've got guys a lot worse than me to deal with."

"Yeah," he said, "but I don't have anyone as wise-ass as you."

I could have come back at him with some zinger, but I kept my mouth shut. Fusco was one of those always-bring-you-down, have-to-win guys. Just because he hated his life, he had to make everyone suffer. A lot of people in the penal system were like that. Nonetheless I knew it was time to get out of there before I said something I would regret.

"I want to see you in three weeks," he barked. "And three weeks don't mean three months."

"It can't be soon enough," I said, getting up from my chair.

"Don't make me chase you, Ingber," he said as I walked to the door of his stifling office. "And don't forget your supervision fee."

I dug the thirty dollars out of my wallet and put it on Fusco's desk. He printed out a receipt and handed it to me.

"It's always a treat to see you, Officer Fusco," I said, taking the doorknob in my hand. "Because every time I see you brings me closer to the last time I'll see you."

"Like I said." He snickered, shaking his head. "A real wise-ass."

"I'm just trying to make my way out here without hurting anyone," I said. "And trying to salvage what's left of my life. Is that OK with you?"

And I closed the door hard and walked away from his office.

I cursed myself all the way out to the sidewalk to get the bus back to Yonkers. I shouldn't have said that last thing. It was a stupid, indefensible thing to do. He had no right to hear my inner thoughts. Nobody did.

⌒

Then one morning I got a welcome piece of good news.

Kelly leaned prettily into my cubicle as I was proofreading an email notice for Rosemary and said, "What are you doing for Thanksgiving?"

"Oh, nothing really," I said.

Thanksgiving was only a week away, and I had tried not to think about it. I try not to think about holidays in general. I learned from many years in prison that holidays only made you more depressed than usual.

"They're having something at Four Winds. I might go there," I lied. "Or maybe I was thinking about going to a movie—"

"Nonsense. You're coming to my house. I'm having a bunch of people. Nothing fancy, mostly family. So don't consider saying no." And she moved on before I could say anything.

That picked up my spirits. Kelly looked nice, with her dark hair spilling onto her shoulders as she leaned into my space. Of course, she was way too young for me. But on the other hand, who knows? Maybe she likes older, more experienced guys. What a ridiculous fantasy. But it was something to think about as her scent filled my cubicle and my imagination.

Then I got a call summoning me to Nyquist's office.

"Right now?"

"Right now," shot back his efficient assistant, Jan.

"Great," I said and hung up. Finally! This was the call I'd been waiting for.

⌒

"Completely disappeared."

The words repeated in my brain—and seemed to echo in Nyquist's book-lined, tomb-like office—as I stood there, hearing the news that I knew was coming.

"Really, Larry," said Nyquist, sitting in his high-backed leather desk chair, "I was hoping to give you better news. We've been talking to the FBI. People in Washington and White Plains, and the district attorney's office in Mineola."

He said "Mineola" as if he were talking about Mars.

"Quite a few people are looking for your Mr. Mantell," said Nyquist, his hands folded across his vested stomach. "And unfortunately it seems as if he's covered his tracks fairly well."

I felt the room starting to tilt, so I sat down.

Nyquist kept talking: "But I've gotten Rob Verdugo in the Washington office involved with this. He has *very* good contacts. I've talked to people at the Nassau County Bar Association. They're taking the lead on this. Mantell is primarily *their* problem."

"So when were you going to tell me this?" I finally managed to say.

"I was hoping to have *good* news for you, Larry. We didn't want to disappoint you," he said, leaning forward with a little smile. "After everything you've been through."

This expression of sympathy from cold-fish Nyquist stopped me for a moment.

"Unfortunately," he continued, "since your parents made him executor and trustee of virtually everything, that gave him access to everything, all the accounts. *Carte blanche.*"

I hated the way he said "carte blanche," in a real plummy, French-type accent, as if he cared more about his correct pronunciation than about my money.

"I *am* truly sorry, but we're doing everything we can for the present moment," he said.

There seemed to be nothing more Nyquist wanted to say. He wanted me to get up and leave his office. So I did.

But I stopped just at the door and turned back to say, "Thank you, Mr. Nyquist." I don't know why I thanked him; he had delayed, obfuscated, screwed up—*whatever*—getting my money. I guess I thanked him because it was a reflex: he was a boss, a well-dressed, rich white guy behind a big desk, the man in charge helping a poor ex-con.

When I walked out of his office closing the door behind me, I got a deeply sympathetic look from Jan and moved past her desk on shaky legs.

"Sorry, Larry," she said.

"Yeah," I said. "Me too."

I went straight to the men's room and threw up my lunch: my economical, healthy, brown-bag lunch. I know that people must have heard me, but I didn't care. I was just happy that I made it to the toilet and didn't have an accident all over the floor.

It took a while for me to recover. Finally, Javier came in and asked me if I was OK, but I said it was just some "bad fish tacos" for lunch.

"Yeah, man," said Javier. "That's the worst."

He left me sitting on the cool tile floor, my stomach and my mind slowly settling down. I should have known something was off with Mantell long ago. And I shouldn't have left things to Nyquist; I should have taken care of the situation myself, no matter what Fusco said. When I was in Elmira, I found out that my cellmate was stealing money from my secret stash. What did I do? I had him beaten up and the bones in both his hands broken. That got him transferred out of my cell to the infirmary, where he couldn't even wipe his own ass for a month; an orderly had to do it. I hope he used a wire brush. P.S.: Nobody ever stole from me again, at least while I was in Elmira. But now, this disaster.

⌒

I stayed after work on the computer in my office, searching again for Mantell on the internet. It had been a couple of days since I did a search, and now, sure enough, there was a new little article on *Newsday*'s website about the "missing local attorney." There wasn't even a byline on the article so I could call up or email the reporter to ask if they could give me any more information. Even if I did call, I couldn't tell them who I was; I wanted to stay anonymous. The last thing I wanted was to draw attention to myself.

"You're not going to find him tonight," said Rosemary, standing just outside my cubicle, winding a scarf around her neck, ready to go home.

"I know," I said, not taking my eyes off the screen, not wanting to believe her. "One more minute."

I felt her looking at me, but I didn't say anything. I just kept searching, hitting "enter," and hoping I'd get lucky. There had to be a strand, a clue, something somewhere in all this wonderful new world of infinite information.

When I looked over, Rosemary was gone. I was glad.

I didn't stay much longer at work. The clean-up ladies were starting their vacuums, so I knew I had to go. By the time my bus got to my stop in Yonkers, it was dark and too late to cook, so I got some salami at the bodega near my bus stop.

As soon as I got into my apartment, I took out the big, battered manila envelope that held all my correspondence with Mantell from over the years, when he was with Bishop, Hosker, etc., and when he went out alone. They were friendly letters on his law firm's letterhead and some Xeroxes of old accountants' worksheets with listings for my mother's and father's IRAs and other "investment accounts." The printing was faint in some of the photocopies—Mantell had all the originals—and many were over twenty years old. I was surprised when I first saw those numbers. I couldn't imagine how my parents saved that much money, especially with all they spent on my defense and the appeals. There were even two ancient birthday cards he sent to me, signed, "Your friend, Les." What a two-faced bastard.

The rest of the night I searched the internet until my eyes burned and were too tired to focus. Even cleaning my glasses didn't help. Then I took one of my James Bond hot-cold-hot-cold-hot showers for so long that I had to steady myself against the tile wall, nearly passing out.

I went to sleep, going over the keywords I had used so many times to search for Mantell: *lawyer...attorney...trust...Bishop...Hosker...Finch...trusts*...my name...my parents' names...even The Girl's name. After a while, the words didn't make any sense. It reminded me of the countless nights I tried to get myself to sleep in prison. Nights trying to remember those damn state capitals. Nights when you were afraid to go to sleep, and afraid to wake up in the morning because, after that first flickering moment of consciousness, you remembered that you were still in prison—and were going to be there for many, many, many years.

At least that was over. But I could see a whole new set of challenges in front of me leading to an uncertain future. Everything was defined for me in prison. All this freedom is confusing. Life had more angles out here in the world—more difficulties, more enemies. I couldn't let Mantell get away. But what was I going to do? What *could* I do? At that moment, I just wanted to go to sleep and forget about everything.

⌐

The next day, I got the call I'd been waiting for. Michael Rathbun, a guy from the Westchester D.A.'s office, wanted to know everything I knew about Lester Mantell.

"What took you so long?" I asked him, cutting him no slack.

I sensed he was on the verge of hanging up, so I loosened up and told him everything I knew about Mantell: the whole history, all the accounts, all the promises. I said that I hadn't seen him in a long time, though I talked to him on the phone a little over a year ago, when he assured me my parents' money was safe. Hah.

Rathbun said that his office was coordinating with the SEC and the Nassau County Bar Association.

"They don't like crooked lawyers either," said Rathbun.

I offered to make him copies of all my Mantell papers, and he said to send everything I had. He gave me his cell and office numbers and told me that I could call him or his partner Gil Cuellar anytime. And that was that.

I hung up the phone, satisfied that I had finally gotten my story out—personally—to the authorities. This Rathbun guy did sound sympathetic. But then I realized I was at a dead end. That didn't seem right. How could I make this only a *temporary* dead end? Inside, I knew I had to do something; I just wasn't sure exactly what. But the fire inside me was lit, and I damn sure wasn't going to let it go out.

⌒

The best thing that happened was that Kelly's Thanksgiving dinner rolled around. I'll admit that I had concerns. Kelly was nice, but how would I fit in with her family and friends? I'd been doing OK with the people at Clemency, but it was a humanitarian organization dedicated to fairness for prisoners, so they had to be nice to me, at least on the surface. But how would I do in a family situation? In someone's home? I hadn't been in someone's home with regular people since I was a kid. Would Kelly tell them about me? And would some of them object to having the Ivy League Killer at their Thanksgiving celebration? I could totally understand that.

The day before, we were standing in the Clemency kitchen. Kelly offered to have me picked up at my apartment, but I told her it was OK. The No. 7 bus went right to Pelham, where she lived, and it was a short walk from Lincoln Avenue to her place.

"One more thing, Kelly." I stopped her. "Will these people know about me?"

"'These people' are my family, Larry," she replied patiently, "and yes, some of them know about you. They know what I do, so they know who you are."

I wanted to say, "They might *think* they know who I am, but they don't." But by then she had turned away with her yogurt.

"Wait! Can I bring anything?"

"Just your appetite," she said, walking away before I could say anything else.

I wound up bringing flowers. Nice, fall-looking chrysanthemums: yellow and rust-colored. It was a safe choice and only a couple of bucks. I had to bring *something*, right? I think my mother would have approved.

The day before, I had checked with the bus service and, as I expected, they were running an abbreviated schedule for the holiday. I wanted to make sure that I would not be late. Kelly told me "around one o'clock," and that's when I was going to get there. Kelly's house was in Pelham, down by the Bronx border, on Long Island Sound. I really didn't know too much about Westchester, but I was learning. The years in Sing Sing don't count.

I decided to wear a blue blazer, some nice chinos, and a light blue Oxford shirt. Sort of what I wore for work, but I didn't want to look like a bum at Kelly's—make that I didn't want to look like a convict. Better to dress too nice than not nice enough. That's probably a good rule of thumb for life.

But despite all my plans and preparation, all my rationalizing and self-protecting in advance, I just couldn't fall asleep the night before. I kept thinking and trying not to think about being among people again, about being exposed to public eyes and private whispers. I know what it's like to be looked at as a monster, a deviant, an "other"—and it kills your soul. I remember when they started calling me the Ivy League Killer in the papers so long ago. I tried to sleep, but I kept falling into memories of my arrest and trial...

People hated me, but then again, I did a hateful thing. They put me in a cage, to protect society. And to punish me. I deserved punishment. People took my picture and stared at me. They yelled my name, and they yelled curses. I was manhandled by cops and transported places in chains. Chains. I sat mute during my trial—"on advice of counsel"—and I was judged guilty. I couldn't believe what was happening to me. I tried to somehow live "above" my life, observing it intellectually while having to defend it physically every day. What I wanted to do was disappear. I see why guys in jail commit suicide: to disappear. To relieve the pain. To get it over with.

I woke up in the middle of night, sweating and alive, my mind flashing with old visions of cracked walls and unmovable bars. I swung my feet over the side of the bed and sat up, catching my breath, remembering where I was. I was out, I was free, and yet...

Sometimes I honestly don't know why I'm still alive. There must a reason, I keep telling myself. I've been through so much hell to get here.

SIX

Thanksgiving arrived on a cold, clear perfect-for-football Thursday. The bus was almost empty, but the female bus driver said, "Happy Thanksgiving!" with such enthusiasm that it made me smile. Here was a woman having to work on a big national holiday, away from her family, and she was trying to be cheerful and upbeat, wearing a big turkey pin on the front pocket of her uniform. I was slowly but surely getting over my reflexive hatred for anyone in a uniform.

I got to Pelham super early, so I killed time walking around. It was only in the mid-40s, so it wasn't too bad. Kelly's house was just a few blocks off Lincoln, the bus route, so I was OK on time. Nice little houses in this neighborhood, very close together. I shouldn't say *little*; they were bigger than the house I grew up in. Someone had a fire going. I couldn't see which chimney was smoking, but it was a great pure autumn smell. I saw a family getting out of a minivan at one house where they were all greeted by their laughing, delighted, hello-shouting relatives. One young woman was carrying a baby who they made a fuss over. It was like a scene out of some TV commercial for soup or insurance, but the people really seemed to mean it. I stood there watching them until they all walked into the house, this sweet little brick house with dark green shutters and a slate roof. What a nice scene: just regular people enjoying one another and the holiday. Nothing threatening or complicated or unusual, just normal human life. How strange. I think I could live around here. Maybe not every place was poisoned to me, as Long Island was. For me, it was another Moment of Grace and Thanks under the open, blue sky, and I hadn't even gone to the party yet.

"What lovely flowers!" said Kelly as she opened her front door the moment after I rang the bell. I could tell she wanted to be the first one to welcome me. (I had killed enough time in her neighborhood so that I rang her bell at exactly 1:05. I figured five minutes late was just about right.)

"Happy Thanksgiving, Kel'," I said, handing her the flowers as I walked in. "You have a beautiful house."

And I meant it. She had one of those little brick cuties. It could've used some maintenance—some paint on the trim and a shutter on the second-floor dormer needed replacing—but it seemed like a pretty sweet place to live.

"Hey, everyone!" Kelly shouted as we walked into the living room filled with people, some on the couch, some in chairs, watching football. "This is Larry Ingber. From work."

The room was dark except for the big glowing TV. I smiled and gave a friendly wave to everyone, trying to take in the whole scene.

"Hi," I said cheerfully. "Happy Thanksgiving!"

I knew instantly from a few blank/hostile looks that Kelly had told them who I was.

I think a couple of people said, "Happy Thanksgiving" back to me, but I wasn't sure. The football game was on pretty loud.

"Everything smells so good," I said enthusiastically. "I love turkey."

It was warm in her house, and the air was filled with thick cooking smells. Good smells, but they were strong, almost overpowering.

Kelly quickly introduced the people in the room, but it was a blur for me, and I'm very bad with people's names anyway. "These are my neighbors Bob and Eileen Selwyn, my cousins Carl and Donnie, my brother Jimmy—"

"The man with the truck," I said, acknowledging the husky, goateed guy in the middle of the sofa, straight in front of the TV.

"His wife, Jean, is somewhere," Kelly continued, "and there are a whole bunch of kids out back."

"Great," I said.

"Come on," Kelly said to me, seeing that the TV watchers were basically ignoring us, "let's find a vase."

I followed Kelly and my flowers as she led me though the living room, past the TV. I mumbled "Bye" and hustled past the screen through the big, sun-filled dining room with the long table fully laid out with white tablecloth, silverware, glistening plates, and twinkly glassware, and into the kitchen, which was in a state of high activity.

Four women were busily at work: one at the sink, one chopping, one carrying a stack of dishes, and the other with her back to me doing something I couldn't see.

"Hey, everyone," said Kelly, holding the flowers high. "This is Larry. He brought these beautiful flowers."

"Hi, Larry," said voices in chorus.

I watched as Kelly went to a cupboard and took down a large, cut-glass vase.

"I was going to bring something to eat," I said, standing back from the action, "but I'm not a very good cook. The best thing I cook is leftovers."

One woman—stout, curly-haired, and serious—whizzed by me, saying sarcastically, "I *think* we have enough food."

Kelly cut in front of a little blond woman who was standing at the sink, saying, "Can I get in here?"

The little blond woman in yellow rubber gloves stepped back, wiping a wisp of hair off her forehead with the back of her wrist. "Kelly, I'm moving. Can't you wait a minute? Everyone's in such a rush!"

The little blond woman smiled at me.

"Those are lovely," she said. "Flowers are always correct."

"Larry, this is my aunt Betsy," said Kelly, as she turned from the sink with the vase filled with water. "My mother's little sister."

"Nice to meet you, Aunt Betsy," I said with a smile and a nod. "And where's your mother?"

"I'm afraid she passed away, what, six years ago." Kelly sighed and I saw Aunt Betsy's pert smile suddenly fade.

"Oh!" I said. "Sorry."

I winced inside. *Great*, I told myself. I hadn't been in the house five minutes before I said something wrong.

"That's OK," said Aunt Betsy. "It wasn't your fault. You didn't—" She stopped herself with a slight pause while her unsaid words—"*kill her*"—hung in the air and rang in my ears.

"Thanks," I mumbled. "I know."

"And just Betsy is fine," she said. "I'm not *your* aunt. At least, I don't think I am."

She looked at me with lively greenish eyes and a kind attitude. I could tell she definitely knew who I was.

"No," I said, standing back as Kelly cut between us carrying away the vase of flowers, "I think I would remember if you were."

I watched Aunt Betsy go back to washing the dishes in the sink, with a bounce in her step. She had on these long, colorful socks and chunky shoes below her short black skirt that made her look like a large elf.

"Just Betsy" is fine with me too, I told myself, cementing her name in my mind.

Kelly came back into the kitchen, introducing the other two women: "And this is my cousin Rita, and that was Dorothy with the serving dish."

"Cousin Rita, meter maid," I said, mumbling a Beatles reference to help me remember her name, "and Dorothy with the dish."

"Come on, Larry," said Kelly, "let me show you where to put your coat."

Before she led me out of the kitchen, I said to the ladies, "I'm on clean-up crew! I'm very good at pots and pans."

"We'll take you up on that," said Betsy at the sink as Rita kept on snapping beans at one counter. Dorothy disappeared behind the open refrigerator door.

I followed Kelly down a dark hallway. I could hear the football game from the living room and some pinging sound from somewhere else.

"You can throw your coat in here," she said, leading me into an unlit room—her bedroom, with a big bed piled with coats.

"Thanks, Kel," I said as I took off my coat and folded it. "Just one thing?"

She stopped and turned back to face me.

"If any of your family doesn't want me here," I said softly, "if they feel uncomfortable, I'll be happy to go."

She flipped on the overhead light. "Don't be ridiculous. This is my house, and I'll have whoever I want come for Thanksgiving."

She seemed pretty sure about that.

"And Larry?" she said, taking my coat from my hands and tossing it onto the pile. "Don't be so worried about what other people think all the time—especially *my* family. Just be yourself and relax. Come on, let me show you the playroom."

And a playroom it was. Five kids were spread out across the floor of the large, sun-drenched room, playing among a lot of toys, games, and open books. The room extended into the backyard and was surrounded on three sides by windows. Kelly had a nice backyard with dark green hedges, a basketball hoop over a black-topped area and a doghouse that looked like a log cabin. Two of the older kids were sitting against a wall, staring into the phones in their hands. Three littler kids—two girls and a boy—were playing on the floor with little plastic toys.

"Are any of these yours?" I asked Kelly.

"No," she said, "mine are upstairs. Staying out of trouble. I hope."

I looked down at the children on the floor. They were very cute. I suppose all children are cute in some ways, but these children were objectively cute.

One little girl with short brown hair in a party dress—she must have been about three or four—looked up at me with these big eyes and said, "Do you like Legos?"

Then I said the wrong thing. "What are Legos?"

All the kids—even the two who were buried in their phones—instantly turned and looked at me like I was some strange creature from some diseased planet.

"What?" I said dumbly.

Kelly had pivoted away, stifling a laugh.

I looked at the kids' horrified faces. I had never seen such looks of pity *and* disbelief.

"They're those little plastic toys," Kelly said, tugging my sleeve and pointing to the zillion little plastic things on the floor. "They're very popular."

"Oh," I said. "Cool."

The kids were still looking at me.

"So, you build things with them?" I asked.

⌢

Half an hour later, I was the King of Legos, and Emily, the little one with short brown hair, had already asked me to come back for Christmas.

Several times, some adult came in to watch me while I was playing with the kids. I can't blame them; they didn't know me from Adam. All they knew was that I was this famous "rehabilitated" killer who Kelly vouched for. If I were a parent, I probably wouldn't trust me either.

After a while, Kelly came into the playroom. "Larry, we're getting a count on who likes white meat and who likes dark."

I looked up at Kelly from the floor, holding up a couple of Lego pieces. "These are great! We never had toys like this when I was a kid. We had things to build with, but these have little *spears*. And what are these again, Emily?"

"Hobbits."

"Hobbits," I repeated to Kelly, who stood there with a grin on her face.

"When I was a kid," I explained to my new friends Emily, Georgia, Henry, and Evan, "we had Lincoln Logs. And Tinkertoys. Ever hear of them? How about Erector Sets?"

"That sounds *gross*," said Evan, the oldest boy.

I ignored him. "What about Mr. Machine? I won't even *ask* about electric trains. Lionel trains?"

"You're funny," said Emily. "Make another tower. A bigger one."

"OK," said Kelly. "Who wants white meat and who wants dark?"

⌢

The meal was spectacular. There was almost too much food on the long, long table that doglegged out of the dining room and into the living room, where the kiddies' end was. I couldn't help but think of all the prison Thanksgivings I'd spent—some better than others, depending on the sadistic whim of whoever the current warden was. I remember one dick who canceled Thanksgiving over some missing garden tools. And I do remember the distant Thanksgivings from when I was a kid, but nothing, *nothing* like this. I wish I could remember all the different foods that Kelly served and who cooked what. But more, I remember what people said, these crazy exchanges. (A couple of times, I had to bite the inside of my cheek to keep from laughing.) It was like this:

"That ambrosia is disgusting." "It is not!" "Ambrosia is a traditional Thanksgiving side dish. Everybody eats it." "Of course it is!" "It's well-known that the pilgrims served tiny little marshmallows at Plymouth Rock."

"I love stuffing." "Stuffing is the best part of the turkey." "It's not part of the turkey, dummy!" "Watch your mouth! You know what he means." "Can someone pass the cranberry sauce this way before I expire?" "Can I go to the children's table?" "You're already there."

"We went to some open houses. Everything is so expensive." "And if it's not expensive, you wouldn't want to live there." "You have to have so much money. Who has that much money?" "If you're not rich these days, you're poor." "It takes a lot of money to be poor these days." "The middle is completely gone." "I wish your middle was gone." "Oh, pass me the gravy and leave me alone."

"These little carrot sticks look like those little wrenches from Ikea." "I hate Ikea." "What's wrong with Ikea? You don't like a lamp for twelve dollars?" "And the Swedish meatballs are good." "They have horsemeat in them." "They do not!" "Yes, they do. From Swedish horses. I googled it." "Can I please sit at the children's table? It's more fun there." "No, you sit with the adults and make conversation." "I hate conversation." "Would you stop that?" "Stop what?" "Ma! He just cut a fart that woulda killed a midget!" "You mean 'short person,' dear."

"I wanted to take the girls to see *Wicked* because they love the album so much, for Georgia's birthday, you know? But the tickets were over a hundred dollars each—and those were for the worst seats in the place, a mile away from the stage." "When I was young, my parents used to take me to a Broadway show every so often. They weren't rich, but they could afford it, now and again as a treat." "I love a good musical." "Now it's just for tourists and rich people." "I saw *Annie* and *Phantom of the Opera* and—" "The sun'll come out tomorrow—" "Please! People are trying to eat."

"Did Mikey go to that girl's family's house?" "Don't ask." "You can get 'em off the couch, but you can't get 'em off the payroll." "Oh, hush!" "You should see his friends. They're even worse. It's all porn and pot, porn and pot, all the time." "Will you watch what you're saying?"

"All he does is listen to that angry radio all the time and watch that damn TV. Then he'll go on the computer and find that *World Net Daily*—" "*World Nut Daily*, if you ask me—" "And see the same things he'd heard on Rush and what's-his-name? The harp on Fox with the square head." "Which harp with the square head?" "Don't you laugh!" "That's not a very nice expression." "You should see how he types all angry-like. And then I make him turn that off and come to bed." "And then does he you-know-what?" "Of course not! He's too angry! So I read a book, and he goes to sleep." "Do we really have to talk about this at the table?"

"Why isn't Dennis here?" "He has to work." "Why?" "Because his boss wants him to work." "But it's Thanksgiving." "Dennis wants to keep his job." "But it's Thanksgiving." "Not to Walmart." "Nuts to Walmart."

I listened to the music of their ordinary conversations—their concerns and worries, big and little—lost in all that I had lost, all the ordinary things I had never done.

"Are you OK, Larry?" Kelly asked me, startling me back to the moment. "You're being very quiet."

I swallowed the food that was in my mouth. "Everything is so good, I just can't stop eating." I picked up the dainty little salad fork and held it in the air. "Even the silverware is beautiful."

Everyone seemed to like my comment, smiling or mumbling in agreement.

Then Jimmy said, "What, I bet you're used to plastic?"

My eyes met Jimmy's. He obviously knew that in prison they use only plastic cutlery.

"I used to be, Jimmy," I said, locking onto his gaze like a cold laser beam. "But now I'm completely into heavy metal."

I know how to stare down guys. I didn't spend my time in prison with the most violent, psychotic scum of the earth and learn nothing.

Jimmy kept his eyes on me for just a moment, then looked back down to his plate, probably feeling foolish. Good: he should've. I was a guest: why try to make me look bad in front of everyone?

From the head of the table, Kelly clinked her knife loudly against her wineglass.

"Attention, please! Attention!" she sang out, clinking her glass once again, almost knocking it over. She had been drinking. We all had been drinking, myself included, this very nice-tasting white wine.

"Whoa!" She righted the glass and continued. "OK, now, even though our mother is no longer here, at least physically, there was one thing she always liked to do at Thanksgiving—"

"Aw, Kel!" Jimmy cut in from the other end of the table. "Do we hafta?"

"Yes, we do," she shot back.

"Come on," Jimmy protested, but Kelly looked over to Betsy for support and asked, "Betsy?"

Sitting at the very end of the long table, Betsy carefully pronounced, "This was one of Sharon Marie's favorite things, and so—"

"So it's a way of bringing her here, so just be nice and do it, OK, James?" Kelly emphasized. "Thank you, Betsy. So we're going to play the Thankful Game now."

She turned to me and explained. "Larry, this is something we used to do when my mother was still alive. We go around the table and, one at a time, you say what you're grateful for this year. *Thankful*, I mean."

"Well, I think that's a lovely thing to do," I spoke up. "A real family tradition."

"That's exactly what it is," said Eileen, the mother of a couple of my Lego friends who was sitting next to me. "A family tradition."

"Sorta like alcoholism," someone from down the table said.

"And depression," another wit added.

"And divorce."

"Very funny, the three comedians down there." Kelly snorted. "I'm sure we'll hear more of their brilliance later. OK, I'll go first."

We all turned to look at Kelly.

"Who wants more bread?" someone said.

"Ssshhh," Betsy gently silenced them.

Kelly cleared her throat. "This year, I'm thankful for my two darling sons." She then raised her voice: "I hope you're being good around there. Someone look at them."

"Yeah! We're good," sounded two semi-annoyed boys' voices around the corner at the kids' end.

"OK, I'm also thankful," Kelly said, "for our continued good health, knock wood. And I'm thankful my brother, Jimmy, and his friend Al for putting in that new closet for me."

A couple of people laughed and looked at Jimmy.

Kelly continued, "I'm thankful for old friends, and new friends." She nodded at me. "And I'm thankful that we all can be together on a beautiful day like this. Next."

The man next to Kelly—one of her cousins—said, "I'd like to thank Kelly for having us all here again this year. And I'd like to thank God for bringing us all together today."

"Amen," several people said.

Next was Jimmy's wife, Jean, a rather heavy blonde wearing a tight, frilly blouse.

"Of course I'm thankful for my family," Jean trilled out. "And for my mother, even though she can't be here, but she's in a very nice assisted-living facility my sisters found for her in Minnesota, so I'm thankful for that."

A kid around the corner wailed "W!" and started to cry. A parent on the other side of the table instantly got up from her chair and went to see about the fuss.

Jean went on, "I'm thankful for Jimmy's new job going so well because the kids' new school is good. And expensive. And, and...I'd like to thank whoever made that delicious green bean salad."

Even before the Thankful Game got around to me, I started to get nervous. What should I say? How honest should I be with these strangers?

102

Next to me, Eileen was finishing up with "And I'd like to thank all the peacemakers in this world, for helping beat our swords into ploughshares."

"Unfortunately," Betsy across the table from me joked, "there is still more money to be made in *swords*." Which distracted me, just when it came to my turn.

"Larry?" asked Kelly as all eyes turned to me.

"OK," I panicked. "Uh, I'm thankful to all of you for having me here," I said before I could think of anything else. "And I want to thank Kelly for inviting me in the first place." That seemed obvious. And redundant. "And I'm thankful for all this good food," I continued. "And I'm thankful for this beautiful, sunny day. I'm thankful for every new day."

Then I got a little carried away, but I couldn't help myself.

"I'm thankful for my freedom...and I'm thankful for the future, now that I have one. I'm thankful for being alive, right at this moment, on this beautiful planet, as long as it lasts, with you extremely nice people. I'm thankful for more things than I can possibly express. This is my best Thanksgiving in many, many, *many* years."

It was very quiet around the table. I knew I had said too much, but I said what was in my heart. Blame the wine.

"That was lovely, Larry," said Betsy, with a sweet, encouraging smile.

"Next?" barked Jimmy, and the guy next to me—an older relative named Ned, who was hard of hearing on my side (I found out later)—started with "I'd like to thank whoever brought the peppermint schnapps."

Which gave the whole room a much-needed, tension-relieving laugh.

I didn't hear much of what people said after that. Had I said too much? And what did it matter now; I couldn't *unsay* what I had said. By the time we were finished with the turkey and everything, I was so full—of food and wine and regrets—that I was thankful when Kelly asked me if I wanted to wash some dishes.

"Do I?" I shot to my feet with enthusiasm. "I am a master dishwasher." I actually stood up so quickly I had to find my balance by holding onto the edge of the table. But I was all right; I had simply underestimated my wine intake. This real wine was as disorienting as my best pruno.

A minute later, I had my sleeves rolled up and was elbow-deep in suds, head down in the steam of the hot water. *This* I knew how to do; I was on kitchen duty at several lockups (and that was a good job). I had to scrub giant metal vats, ten times the size of Kelly's little pots and pans. This was child's play, and a lot easier than chatting with strangers.

There were all kinds of activity and talk behind me, people buzzing back and forth, clearing the table and putting out more dishes for coffee and dessert.

"Where's the aluminum foil?"

Someone dumped a whole lot of silverware into the sink.

"Thank you," I said, moving aside while I kept scrubbing. "Keep 'em coming."

"This is when you appreciate really good Tupperware," a woman declared."Somebody open a window. I'm sweatin' like a whore in church."

"Who's going to want to take some turkey home?" someone sang out. I almost said, "I do," but I stopped myself. Even though I'm the King of Leftovers, I figured they should keep the turkey in the family.

Someone came up behind me and whispered in my ear, "Do *you* appreciate really good Tupperware?"

I turned and looked to see Betsy giving me a nice sly smile as she put more dirty dishes next to me.

"I liked what you said at the dinner table," she said softly. She grabbed a few sheets of paper towel from the roll hanging over the counter. "Slight emergency in Legoland."

She turned and went away. Betsy was nice and friendly, just like Kelly, but even...I don't know, warmer.

Almost splitting my eardrums, a high voice demanded, "OK, who wants decaf and who wants regular?"

I washed until there weren't any more dishes or pots to wash. Twice, people tried to drag me away from the sink, saying that I had done enough, but I was resolved to wash them all. Every last one.

Before we all sat down for coffee and dessert, I stepped outside into the backyard to get a breath of good, cold autumn air as the kids played basketball and chased the dog under the bright floodlight mounted on the corner of the house. I watched as the boys scrambled after the ball, fought for rebounds, over-dribbled, and took bad shots, just like kids have always done.

Kelly came out the back door. "Mikey! Erin! Sean! Go back inside and put on your coats, please. Your mothers asked me to tell you."

Walking up next to me, she commanded the kids, "You can come back outside later. Just go get your coats. You too, Connor."

"'Connor? Erin? Sean?' Are you *all* Irish?" I asked her.

"No!" she said with a snicker. "But my ex's family, they all were, and weren't they proud of it? We're mutts on my side. A little English, a little Welsh, a little German, some Austrian. Nothing to brag about."

"But one hundred percent American," I said.

"That is the correct answer." She nodded.

"Anybody can be an American," I agreed. "We'll take anybody."

"As long as you don't sneak across the border," added Kelly. "Or wear a headscarf."

"Unless you want to cut my grass cheap," I returned.

Betsy called to us from the back door.

"Kelly! Larry! Everybody!" she trilled. "The dessert and coffee's ready. If you all don't hurry, you're going to miss out on my chocolate clouds."

"We'll be right in, Betsy!" Kelly called back. "Come on, kidlets. Time for dessert."

She didn't have to repeat herself because the kids reacted instantly to the word *dessert*, running right past us and back into the house before we had a chance to move.

"Your aunt is really nice," I said to Kelly as we followed the kids across the nubby brown autumn grass. "She's so...perky."

"Oh, there's no one like Betsy," said Kelly, as if stating an accepted fact. "And she's been through some very tough times."

"Tell me," I asked.

She whispered, "Her husband got cancer, and she had a very rough time with him before he passed. That went on for a long time."

"That's too bad," I muttered. "What was her husband like before?"

"Ma!" yelled Kelly's younger son, Brendan, as he came bursting out of the door. "Connor won't let me play *Black Ops*, and he told me I could for as long as I wanted if I helped him with the garage, and now he says he won't!"

Kelly turned to me and shrugged. "Sorry, but I gotta referee this. You get some coffee."

"Black Ops?" I inquired.

"Don't ask," she said with a rueful smile and went back in with Brendan.

I was the last person left in the backyard except for Kelly's dog, who was lying contentedly in the last of the afternoon sun against the wooden fence, happy to collapse after all the chaos of the kids at play.

I took a pause too. "You and me, Lassie. *People*! Sometimes they just wear you out."

And I walked inside to rejoin the party. Which was a good idea because the choice of desserts was quite unbelievable; there was practically an entire bakery spread out on the kitchen table. When I think of all the years I spent listening to guys talk about food. One cellie of mine used to talk for hours and hours about his grandmother's "knuckle bread."

"What would you like?" Dorothy asked me, holding a wedge-shaped cake cutter like a weapon.

"A little of everything," I replied honestly, looking over the pies (pumpkin, apple, and mince, I think), cakes (layer, Black Forest, and pound), and assorted cookies as well as little holiday pastries. Tiny chocolate cupcakes that looked like pilgrims' hats, and tiny apple tarts that looked like turkey faces, with candy corn for "feathers." They reminded me of stuff my mother used to make.

Dorothy gave me a heaping plate of almost everything, pulling me back from the far edge of my trick memory, and pointed me to the coffee that was set up on the counter. I followed the line, picking up a cup and saucer, and pouring myself a cup, using lots of half-and-half.

There were only a few people at the dining room table. I could hear the TV in the living room, playing loudly what sounded like another football game.

"Who's playing in the second game?" I asked as I stood there, careful not to spill my too-filled cup and too-crowded plate.

"Dallas and the Patriots," someone said.

"Good game," I replied.

"I hope they *both* lose," the old man from the coffee table wisecracked. He reminded me a little of my old man, who loved the New York Giants and, even way back then, thought that Dallas was a bunch of jerks. I met a lot of convicts from Texas. They seem to have a big problem down there with violent people. I think it might be a case of too much football on the brain.

"Have a seat, Larry," a woman's voice said. "You've been working much too hard for a new guest."

I turned around and it was Betsy, already sitting down in a chair behind me.

"This is an amazing party," I said. "Do you do this every year?"

"Something like this," she replied. "It depends. There are different people, but we always do something."

"That's really great," I said sincerely.

"Thanksgiving is my favorite holiday," she said firmly, "because it's not about buying presents or patriotism or somebody's religion or drinking large amounts of alcohol. It's just about *family*."

That made me sit down right next to her.

"You didn't have any of my chocolate clouds," she said, looking unhappily down at my plate. "Why not?"

I didn't know what to say, sputtering, "Uh, I don't know, somebody filled up my plate and—"

Betsy stood straight up. "Well, we'll have to rectify that," and she walked out into the kitchen.

I looked down at my half-eaten plate of desserts and didn't think I could stand another bite of anything.

"Here!" Betsy clanked a little plate bearing a large blob of dark chocolate in front of me on the table and placed a little fork down firmly next to it.

"Tell me if you've ever tasted anything as good," she practically ordered me.

Obediently I picked up the fork, cut off a chunk of the blob, making sure that I got some of the soft brown inside cake, and carefully put it in my mouth.

"I've never...tasted...anything...as good," I said. "Excellent," Betsy purred. "Dorothy's always been jealous of my chocolate clouds," she added matter-of-factly. "But I don't care. I'm above that."

"This is some serious chocolate," I said sincerely. It was a helluva dessert.

"Chocolate is very healthy," she said. "Especially dark chocolate. They say it's the flavonoids. Flavonoids act as B-vitamin antioxidants, and there are a ton of them in dark chocolate."

"Flavonoids?" I repeated. "Are you a chemist?"

"Noooo," she said, laughing. "I'm a school secretary. At the Thomas Paine School in Rye. You know it? It's a private school. Four through twelve. Anyway, I do know some science teachers, and *they* know a lot about chemistry." She had short blond hair in a choppy, flippy kind of style. And she had these brownish-greenish eyes that seemed interested in everything.

"Thomas Paine?" I asked. "You mean the Thomas Paine who attacked organized religion, was imprisoned in France, and died in disgrace with only six people at his funeral?"

Betsy countered, "No, we're more about Thomas Paine, hero of the American Revolution and writer of *Common Sense*. That Thomas Paine."

I asked, "Do your kids ever say, 'This school is a pain'?"

"No, never," she deadpanned. Which made me laugh.

"TOUCHDOWN!" several people screamed from the living room, making both of us flinch. There was lots of yelling and cheering and some groaning from the TV room.

"Should we go see what all the yelling is about?" I asked her.

"What do *you* want to do?" she asked me right back. She looked straight into my eyes and really seemed to want to know.

For so many years in prison, my choices were severely limited. The system was designed that way. You did what the guards told you to do, according to a schedule, and that was it. Inmates—presumably violent, dangerous people—needed control. But now, in the real world, everything was a choice; *my* choice. Did I want to go into the living room and check out some silly football game and watch some stupid touchdown that would be replayed a zillion times on the TV news or, if I really wanted to see it, I could catch on YouTube—or did I want to stay there and keep talking to this very nice woman, who was about my age or a little younger, and who seemed to like talking to me as if I were a regular human being and not the Ivy League Killer?

"Betsy," I said, "how would you like to get me another of those delicious clouds of yours?"

I spent the rest of the evening talking to Betsy—and a few other people—at the dining room table. About politics. About sports. About television shows and movies, some that I had heard of, most not. About books. (Betsy was in a book club she mentioned enthusiastically a couple of times.) About everything. Well, almost everything: I tried to avoid talking about my past because it's really nothing to talk about among nice people, especially people like Betsy. I deflected personal questions that came my way and hoped for the best.

Somebody started little glasses of the peppermint schnapps going around. And soon after that, the room started to go around, at least a little for me. The football game was over, and somebody turned on the stereo, or whatever they call it these days. Some of the songs I knew, some I didn't.

"Please keep it down, Connor!" said Betsy to Kelly's son. "People are trying to talk."

Connor had been running around for a lot of the party, making noise with some clacking toy, and getting into little fights with some of the other kids.

I watched as Betsy pulled him aside calmly and talked to him.

"Connor, honey?" she said. "You still want to go to Nicky's sleepover like your mother promised you if you behaved yourself today, right?"

"I guess so," the boy muttered, looking at the floor.

"We talked about this before," she said, gently holding his chin and directing his face so he had to look at her. "You're making things hard for yourself. I've told you before: the hard way is the easy way, and the easy way is the hard way. What you think is hard—behaving properly and doing what you're supposed to do—isn't really hard. It keeps you out of trouble and is actually the easy way to get what you want. What you *think* the easy way is—running around like a little nutcase and disobeying your mother—gets you into trouble and is actually the hard way. You understand?"

I watched as the boy stood there, resisting her message, just as I had watched a million young guys react to different therapists' advice in a group session.

"I think so," Connor replied with a sigh.

She kissed him on the forehead, turned him around, and pushed him gently away. I liked the way she handled him.

She came back to sit down next to me. "Sorry. That was a little of my detention room speech."

"Does it work?"

"Sometimes," she said. "Some kids listen. But adults can only do so much. After a certain point, it's up to the kid."

"Amen to that," I said, then immediately shut up. I didn't want to think about what I did when I was a kid—or have to explain it to Aunt Betsy.

⌒

It was getting late, and I saw Kelly getting coats from the bedroom. Soon everyone was crowded into the foyer, organizing packages of leftovers, yawning, yakking, taking a few last photos and some "selfies," which I stayed far-far-far away from. The last thing I wanted was having my picture taken.

I took my coat from Kelly, who looked pretty but exhausted. "I can't thank you enough, Kelly, for inviting me."

"Oh, you were great," she said. "You're the best dishwasher we ever had."

"Are you serious?" I said. "I just had the best Thanksgiving I've had in—in a very long time. So that's something."

For some reason, that completely silenced the room.

"Amen, brother!" said Jimmy, of all people, patting me on the back as he got his keys out of his pocket. "Great meal, sis," he added, pulling Kelly to him for a hug and a peck on the cheek.

"Take care of him," Kelly said to Jean as she turned her cheek. "He's been you-know-whating."

"Do not worry," said Jean. "I'm driving. Come on. Where are the kids?"

"I shouldn't've had that peppermint schnapps," someone groaned. "It's like brushing your teeth with a martini."

"How're you getting home, Larry?" asked Eileen, turning down the collar on her daughter's jacket.

"Oh," I said, surprised that someone asked me something. "Same way I got here: the number seven bus. It goes right by my place in Yonkers."

"But that's ridiculous," Rita commented.

"You can't take a bus at night," piped up Emily, my little Lego friend in a pink jacket from some Disney movie.

"I do it all the time, Miss Emily," I said, looking down at her.

"But not on *Thanksgiving* night," reasoned Evan, one of the bigger boys.

"Don't worry!" said a clear voice. "*I'll* take him home."

It was Betsy.

A moment of embarrassed silence suddenly seized the room as they all looked at each other worried about the same thing: was it right, this little middle-aged lady, their beloved aunt, driving somewhere with this guy they barely knew, this famous killer?

"I have plenty of room in the Jeep, and it's not that far," she said. "If it's only Yonkers."

"Oh, it's definitely only Yonkers," I responded, secretly happy to get a ride home and not have to take the bus—and very happy that it was Betsy who offered. Placing myself at their mercy, I asked, "Are you sure this is OK with you all?"

No one said anything.

"Of course it's OK," Betsy broke the silence. "I've been to *Yonkers* before."

Everyone laughed at that, releasing the tension in the room.

The next moment I was standing at the front door, holding it open as Kelly made sure everyone had their packages of leftovers, while Betsy made sure that she had her keys. Everybody said goodbye to me as if they knew me, and in a way, they did. I got a few kisses on my cheek and some handshakes and hugs. It felt good and strange at the same time. I'm still uneasy with contact from other people.

"Time to hit the road," announced Betsy, shaking her keys in the air. "You sure you're OK, Kel'?"

"I'm fine," Kelly said with a deep, satisfied sigh. "Absolutely. Another great Thanksgiving, Bets, thanks to you."

"Thanks to *you*, sugarpie," Betsy responded, hugging her closely. "You give those boys a kiss."

"I will," Kelly said. "And tell Roland that we were thinking of him. I'm sorry he couldn't make it."

"I will," replied Betsy. "I tried to get him to come, but you know how he is."

Kelly held open the door. "You take care of this Larry guy. Get him home. He looks exhausted."

"I am *partied out*," I said broadly, going along with her joke. Did I look that exhausted?

Betsy had opened the storm door, indicating that I should follow her.

I stepped forward and said, "Thanks, Kelly," giving her a quick kiss on the cheek. "For everything."

She tolerated my kiss and gave me a warm smile in return. "It was my pleasure. Honestly."

She grabbed me by both hands, gave them a little squeeze, and let them go. I could tell by the compassionate look in her eyes, once and for all, that she regarded me as a nice, old guy: nothing more.

I turned and stepped outside. That's when I realized how cold it was. And how inadequate my jacket was for the winter. It was late November. I needed something heavier, and longer too. I also realized I had lost sight of Betsy.

"This way, Larry!" she shouted.

I turned my head two ways before seeing her on the other side of the street—she was quick on her feet—walking toward a big, old black Jeep. Just as I reached for the passenger door handle, lock clicked open.

"Excuse the rust," she said, turning on the engine, "but I live on City Island."

"Where is City Island?"

"In the Bronx," she said, revving the engine twice to keep it from stalling. "So," she chirped, "where to in Yonkers?"

"Do you know Yonkers?" I asked her.

"Not very well," she said, pounding the heat control panel twice with her small fist, to try to get it to function.

"Can you get to the Cross County?"

"I think so," she replied.

"Then get on the Cross County West," I said, "and I'll tell you from there."

There wasn't much traffic on the roads, and we got to Yonkers pretty quickly, bumping along in the high-riding Jeep.

Betsy didn't say anything at first, and I was shy about breaking the silence. But then she said, "Can I ask you something, Larry?"

"Sure," I said, a bit nervously. "Ask me anything you want."

"How did you know how many people there were at Thomas Paine's funeral?"

"Well," I said with a laugh, stalling for time and a good answer. "Uhhh...well, at one point in my life, I had a lot of free time on my hands, so I used to do a lot of reading."

"Lucky you," she said tartly. Obviously, my answer didn't fool her one bit.

We drove for a while longer while I looked at her sideways, her hands high on the steering wheel. I wanted to keep the conversation going. I didn't want her to shut me out just because I was somewhat defensive about my past.

"Why does living on City Island make your car rust?" I asked.

"It's right on the ocean," she said. "On Long Island Sound. All that salt air makes everything rust. But it's like a little New England village, City Island. If you've never seen it, it's very charming."

"I bet it is," I said, watching her drive so attentively. So daintily.

"Where to now?" she said, jarring me out of my thoughts.

It was only two more blocks, and she drove me right to the front door of my building. When she slowed the Jeep to a careful, perfect stop at the curb, I said, "Thanks a lot, Betsy. This beats the bus by a bunch."

"Oh, it's nothing," she trilled. "Lots of things are better than a bus."

"You know what I mean," I said looking directly into her eyes. Which surprised her a little and ruffled her. Which was the last thing that I wanted to do.

Before I closed the door, I said, "Thanks for the lift. In more ways than one."

And she took off before I could say anything else, like asking her if she knew her way back to City Island. But I had a feeling she knew her way back. I had the feeling she knew a lot of things.

As I got out my keys and walked to my front door with a spring in my step, I realized I hadn't felt this "up" feeling—this strange light-heartedness—in a long, long, *long* time.

I went upstairs, showered, and fell almost immediately into dreamless sleep, happily exhausted, thinking of Betsy Hull, her chocolate clouds, and her sweet, sane smile.

SEVEN

After that, things got much better and much worse, both at the same time. First, the worse.

Mantell was completely gone. Vanished. I got sort of friendly with Rathbun and Cuellar, only too well over the next few months.

"Evidently Mantell had been preparing for this for a while," Rathbun told me during a phone call. "He sold his condo in Garden City a year and a half ago, and he'd been slowly liquidating his visible assets. He let his office lease run out. He even dropped his car lease."

"How *old* is he now?" I asked him, and myself too. My trial was in 1970, and here this guy was still messing with the law.

"In his midseventies," Rathbun said.

"Damn," I muttered, remembering, "my excellent new lawyer" when he was young, idealistic, and on my side.

"We're working with the FBI," said Rathbun, "and the SEC, following anything with his name on it."

"I checked out his old partners," I volunteered, "and I've been searching on the internet every night for anything that can lead to him."

"You and me and six other guys," he snorted.

I realized that the powers of the Justice Department and FBI were far beyond mine, but still I never liked that superior tone that the law took with people like me.

"Well," I said, "what about his home in the Virgin Islands, in St. Croix, I think?"

"We checked that out. Mantell is gone from there now."

"It's still on his website."

"That website is dead," he said. "It's not even an active mailbox. The domain has expired. We have our IT guys on it. He's moved his operation somewhere else. To China or the Cayman Islands. We're looking there."

"Isn't that where tax cheats go?" I asked.

"Mantell's expertise was in tax *avoidance*," said Rathbun. "That became his main legitimate enterprise for a while, once he stopped defending people like you. He wasn't very good at that."

"Tell me about it," I agreed.

"He wasn't stupid," the cop said, "and he *was* greedy. That's a bad combination. Over the years he apparently assigned the income from your parents' trust—and a lot of other people's money—to a Virgin Islands corporation and then gradually siphoned all the money out. Then he created what they call passive foreign investment companies to move money to the Caymans. He also set up fictitious partners to dodge the IRS."

"So, what do we do?" I asked. "The longer we wait, the colder his trail gets." Rathbun didn't have any immediate answer for that because it was the truth.

"Just be patient, Larry—" he began. But that word—that word, again!—made me cut him off instantly.

"*Patient*?" I snapped. "You're talking to me about being patient?"

It was the only time I really raised my voice at Rathbun, a guy I was beginning to like in spite of the fact that he was a cop. Technically, he might have been from the DA's office, but to me, they're all cops.

"I'll call when I have something, Larry."

"Please do that."

And we both hung up simultaneously.

It was probably not in my best interest to alienate Rathbun, but I felt I had no choice. I had to light a fire under him.

And why? It wasn't just because it was right, and it wasn't just for revenge: I was having trouble paying my bills with what I was making at Clemency. I know I was lucky to have the job at all, but numbers don't lie and bills don't stop. My apartment was so small I couldn't even bring in a roommate, like a lot of people including almost all the younger people at Clemency have

116

to. Either that, or they're living with their parents. Why should Mantell be living high someplace on my legacy money, the money my father sweated for and saved?

⌒

I was sitting in the kitchen at Clemency, eating my brown-bag lunch and figuring out my bills. Rosemary came in to get something to drink out of the soda machine, though in fairness to Clemency, the machine didn't have much soda: it was more green iced teas, protein shakes, "power waters," and something called kombucha. Whatever they were, they were too expensive for me.

Rosemary pushed one of the buttons and something heavy fell to the bottom of the bottle catcher. She bent down and retrieved it with a comical grunt.

"Why they put these things down so low, I'll never know," she said, walking over to me.

I closed my open checkbook and took a bite of my sandwich.

"You've been looking down lately, Larry," she said. "You been missing your little buddy?"

I really didn't know what she meant.

"Derek Ellison," she said. "He used to follow you around like a shadow."

It had been a while since Derek had gone back to Dartmouth. There were other interns now from different colleges.

"He was a good kid," I said, remembering Derek and that wild day driving around Long Island.

"Well connected," said Rosemary with a raised eyebrow.

"I assume all these kids are well-connected kids, right?" I responded.

That's when I decided to mention what I'd been meaning to for weeks. There was nobody else there, and after doing my bills, I just couldn't keep my mouth shut. My old story.

"Y'know, Rosemary," I started, turning around in my chair, "I was thinking. I've been here, I mean here at Clemency, for a while now, and I've done everything you've asked me. More than everything. And I want to do more. But I'm finding it hard to, frankly, pay my bills. I hardly spend any money; all I do is pay my rent, buy food and my bus pass, and come here to work, but there's almost nothing left after that. I was wondering if you could maybe talk to someone about a raise or something. Not a lot. Just enough to help me pay some of these bills."

She nodded, even as I saw in her eyes the negative message to come. "I know, I know, Larry—"

"It's not like I'm asking for a lot of money," I interrupted her. "And I'm not even paid for the overtime I put in. But I'm living paycheck-to-paycheck and—"

"Larry, I hear this from everybody," she said.

"Everybody?" I repeated.

"Everybody who reports to me," she confirmed. "Other people have asked me about more money, people who've been here a lot longer than you. And frankly, upstairs, they want me to take more interns."

"It's free labor," I conceded.

"As many as I want," she added. "I just don't have any place to put them."

I could tell, just from that comment, that my request was futile.

"Look, I can ask," she continued, "but I'm already being asked to cut my budget by ten percent, and I'm fighting *that*. It's hard to ask for more when they already want to give you less. But the good news is that, even though you're still technically a contractor, you're finished with your probationary period, so you'll be able to join our benefits program."

"That's good," I said. I was still a couple of years short of Medicare age. I was still pretty healthy. Prison toughened me like hammered steel, but health coverage is something everybody needs, right? In case of emergency. For when the inevitable happens.

I thanked Rosemary for listening to me. It wasn't her fault that Clemency USA didn't have a ton of dough to pay their employees. After all, it was a nonprofit corporation. Still, a working person has to be able to live. I was going to have to find a way to make more money. Or get some kind of second job on the weekends. And I had to find Lester Mantell.

I went down to Human Resources to find out about the medical benefits I was now entitled to. I walked into the office, with its wall-to-wall posters of government health, safety, and employment regulations, and explained to the HR person—her name was Maria: dark hair, dark eyes, lots of makeup—why I was there, and she had me fill out a form. Make that a bunch of forms of very small type that would have taken me an hour to read and even more to understand. Does anybody actually read those forms? You just have to sign and hope for the best. Face it: we're at the mercy of these systems, even out here in the world of the free.

I handed the forms back to Maria and started to leave, when she called me back.

"You haven't checked off your choice for your deductible and everything," she scolded me.

She then sat me back down and patiently explained the details of the medical plans that Clemency offered.

"Wait a minute," I realized. "To get a monthly rate I can handle, all I really get is catastrophic coverage in case I get hit by a car or something. I can't really afford anything else. And forget about the dental."

"I'm sorry, Larry," she said, "but these are the plans we offer. In order to meet the needs of all our employees."

"But if your people can't *afford* the plans," I asked tartly, "what does it matter, what you offer?"

She really didn't have an answer for me. I didn't want to put her on the spot; nothing was *her* fault.

"OK, let me think about it," I said, rising slowly. "I do have another option."

"And what's that?" asked Maria, rising with me.

"Not get sick ever," I said and turned to leave. I didn't mean to zing her. It was just something I had to say. And *not get sick ever* was always my health plan in prison.

"Thanks anyway, Maria," I added.

"Uh, *Larry*!" she called sharply.

I stopped.

"I'm sorry," Maria said extra-politely, with this little chuckle, "but it looks as if you've spelled your name incorrectly here. Your first name. It looks like there's a *U* here where there should be a *W*."

"What?" I said, not sure that I heard her.

"It looks like you spelled your name with a *U* instead of a *W*," she said with a snicker.

"I'm sorry, but that's the way it's spelled," I said.

She looked at me with blank eyes.

I continued my explanation: "Not *all* Lawrences spell their names with a *W*. Haven't you ever heard of Laurence Olivier? He's a Laurence with *U*."

"Lawrence whooo?" she said, drawing back from me condescendingly.

"Laurence Olivier," I shot back. "One of the greatest actors of the twentieth century!"

She had no idea what I was talking about.

"I'm sorry," she said acidly, "but this is the twenty-*first* century." And she gave me a smug little smile.

I couldn't help but respond, "You've never heard of *Rebecca*? Or *Wuthering Heights*? Or...*Spartacus*?"

She just looked back at me with blank eyes.

"How about *Hamlet*?" I cracked.

That made her falter a little. "Why don't I keep these papers until you decide how you want to proceed? Until you get back to me the next time, with what you want to do."

"OK, Maria," I said, going to the door and turning the knob. "But next time—*por favor*—I know how to spell my own name." Then I left.

OK, I maybe shouldn't have said that last crack in Spanish, but I couldn't help myself. The señorita pissed me off. It wasn't her fault that she was young, but it *was* her fault that she was ignorant and proud of it. Then again, who was I to talk? I didn't know half the movies and TV shows and music that people talked about. Of course, I had an excuse: I was in cold storage for forty years.

And my name! That stupid *U* that my mother put in my name because she loved Laurence Olivier. Really. Especially Olivier in *Wuthering Heights*. The stupid *U* I've come to tolerate after detesting it, even though it's caused so much confusion and misspellings over the years. How many times have I had to say, "That's Laurence with a *U*," and people respond with a "Huh?" I've sometimes thought it was maybe the *U* that gave me such a

Heathcliff complex so that I became obsessed with that beautiful, mixed-up girl when I was young, foolish, and crazy-lost in love.

And my middle name: they had to spell *Allan* like Edgar Allan Poe, not the normal way with one *L* or even *Allen*. How many times did I have to correct that spelling with people? Even after my name became famous...or rather, infamous.

I went back to my cubicle, simmering with multiple angers: Mantell, money, this HR girl, not to mention the vanished possibility of getting any health care before I turn sixty-five or die. All this, and my bus was late that morning. My regular driver, Jaynelle, had been out, and the new guy was hopeless. Maybe he was just temporary. But, as they say, everything is temporary.

Also my right knee had been bothering me lately. My right leg was the one that was smashed up in that ending-everything car accident outside Loomis, New York, so many centuries ago. It's usually pretty good, but every so often, the pain flares up. Maybe I'm just finally getting old, and with nothing to fight against, I'm finally breaking down.

I went home, had my dinner of leftovers, and listened to the Mets game, trying not to think about what I was going to do about Mantell. What *could* I do? I knew some old mobsters, but they were from a long time ago. And would I dare go outside the law? There had to be other angles I wasn't thinking of.

And as if to mock me, in the morning there was a text from the Probation Department—the automatic one I got before every appointment—but underneath was a personal message from Fusco: *do nt u dare miss it genus*.

All that was the worse. The better was all Betsy.

EIGHT

First thing Monday morning after the Thanksgiving party, I went to Kelly's office to get Betsy's phone number. I debated about whether to ask her for it. Sorry, but I debate everything. The thing is I really liked Betsy. And I think she liked me. So what if I was who I was?

"Why do you want her number?" Kelly asked.

"So I can call her," I said.

I thought that Kelly liked me; why the cool response?

"Betsy's very dear to me," she said, as if that was some argument against me. I felt somewhat dismayed—no, hurt.

"I just want to *call* her," I said. "For coffee, or something. That's what people do nowadays, right? It's OK, she'll probably say no."

"No, she won't," Kelly shot back. "She liked you. I can tell. But after what she's been through—she pretends to be all cheerful—but she's a very vulnerable person. And I'm just...well, protective of her."

"OK." I shrugged. "If you don't want to give it to me, I'll—"

"No," she snapped. "Here it is. I'll give it to you." And she blurted out a string of numbers from memory, beginning with a 718 area code. "You want to write it down?" she asked.

"No," I said. "I got it." And I pointed to the side of my head.

"OK," she challenged me, "what is it?"

I recited the numbers back to her perfectly: "Seven-one-eight-six-eight-three-three-five-oh-nine." Occasionally, I can still show off my considerable powers of memory; I'm not senile...yet.

"Thanks, Kelly," I said. "I appreciate it." I opened her door and was just about to leave. "Thanks again for Thanksgiving," I said. "And everything else."

I left, closing her door behind me, and entered Betsy's number in my phone contacts as fast as I could before I could forget it. Then I smiled: I had gotten what I came for...and more.

She *liked* me.

⌒

Why did I feel like a nervous teenager, calling Betsy for the first time? Kelly already told me she liked me, even though she knew about my past. I wasn't expecting anything more than having coffee someplace. Still, right before I punched her number into my phone, I thought, *What if she says no?*

It would be perfectly reasonable for her to say no to me: Mr. Damaged Goods. No matter how grateful I am to be out of prison, how cheerful I try to be for every day I spend outside prison walls, I know who I am. I know that I'm a closed-in, difficult person. I've had to become that out of necessity. For so many years, what was outside of me was so bad, so horrible, so anti-life that my only choice was to go inside. Deep inside. I've witnessed and experienced things in prison that no normal, rational person should have to endure. I have dark, dark places inside me. And maybe that makes me the wrong man for any woman, ever. But I'm selfish: I was lonely...and I genuinely liked her. So I called her.

"Hello? Is this Betsy?"

"Larry?"

"Uhhh," I mumbled, caught off guard. "How'd you know—?"

"Kelly warned me that you'd be calling."

"*Warned* you?"

"She *told* me," Betsy clarified, "that you were thinking of calling me."

"And now I am...calling you."

"Do I *need* a warning, Larry?"

There was a moment of dead air. She was sharp, so I didn't want to say anything obviously stupid. Or too smart-ass either.

"What do you want, Larry?" she said, after I didn't fill the silence fast enough.

"I want to see you," I said finally. "Again. Us. Together."

"That's generally the way people see each other," she said. "Together."

Remembering my goal, I blurted out, "Coffee. How about coffee first?...Isn't that what people do? That way, after fifteen minutes, you can bail on me if you don't like the way things are going."

"That sounds very enticing," she said, making fun of me but gently.

"You know what I—"

"Fair enough," she cut me off. "You convinced me. I accept."

I was happy; she said yes. But there was more dead air.

"Then coffee, it is," she said deliberately. "For fifteen minutes...or less."

⌢

The plan was to meet Saturday morning at eleven. There was no Starbucks near me. It's not "upscale" enough of a neighborhood to warrant a Starbucks. But there was a nice coffee shop within walking distance of my building called Chic's, which looked like a little old cabin and had good coffee and muffins and a decent view of the river, so that's where we decided to meet. Meeting near me was the obvious thing to do; Betsy had a car. It would have taken me three buses and two hours to get to City Island. Besides, this way she would have her own wheels, in case she wanted to make a quick escape.

I told her that I would meet her at Chic's at 11:00. I was there at ten to eleven. Old habits die hard. I was always a prompt, attentive boyfriend. (Wasn't that my fatal mistake?) I found a table in the corner and sat down, figuring I would order something and wait for her to get there.

Boyfriend? What was I thinking? Why do I always get ahead of myself? This was just a nice lady I met, someone vaguely my age, who might be fun to hang out with. Nothing more, nothing less. Of course, there was the possibility of physical contact, something from my long, lonely, distant past, something I was even more nervous about. But talk about getting ahead of myself! I resolved right then to try to keep things light, uncomplicated, and completely casual.

I was checking out the pastries in Chic's display case—everything was so expensive—when, she appeared at the front door, looking for me in a blue parka, pressed chinos, and little black boots. She looked good, with her perky blond hair and smiling face. She was having trouble seeing in the dark interior of Chic's.

"Betsy," I called her name softly.

"Larry?" she said, squinting and holding her hand over her brow to shade her eyes. "There you are!"

"Here I am!" I said, meeting her halfway across the room. "So nice to see you."

I almost leaned over to kiss her cheek, but I held back. Instead, I took both her hands and gave them a little shake.

"You were right about the river," she said with a wide smile.

"Come. I got us a nice table. With a view. You want something first?" I brought her over to the glass case filled with muffins, pastries, and bagels of all kinds.

"Oh my," she said, looking at the goodies. "Look at all that."

"Have whatever you want," I said, making sure she knew that I was paying. I didn't have a ton of cash on me, but I had enough. Ancient habits die hard.

"This is all very tempting," muttered Betsy still peering into the glass. "How about...a plain bagel, toasted, with cream cheese? Low-fat cream cheese if they have it."

"Bagel and low-fat cream cheese," I confirmed. "Classic."

"And a medium-sized...cinnamon-roast special blend latte," she concluded.

"Cool. Did you hear all that?" I said to the counter guy, and he repeated her order back perfectly.

"Excellent!" I complimented him and turned to Betsy. "Why don't you go back to our table? I'm sitting over there, in the corner. And I'll bring everything."

"OK," she said a bit cautiously. "Sure."

And she drifted back to our table.

"Just a regular coffee for me," I said to the counter guy. Chic's was cheaper than Starbucks, but it was still overpriced. But then again, everything is overpriced these days.

When I got back to our table with my plastic tray, Betsy had her parka off and was sitting there waiting for me. She was wearing a little black cardigan over a nice white blouse. Without the big jacket, she looked much smaller.

"You didn't get anything?" she asked me as I put down the tray.

"I had a late breakfast," I said, lying to her. I just didn't want to spend four bucks on a muffin.

"I'll give you some of mine," she volunteered. "I'll never eat this whole thing."

I sat down. "Have whatever you want."

I removed the plastic covers on the coffees and spread out the bagel and cream cheese for Betsy to prepare.

"This place is nice," said Betsy.

"Yeah," I said, "it's very un-Starbucks."

"Starbucks isn't so bad," she said, starting to spread the cream cheese on the bagel with a plastic knife, "but it's the same wherever you go. This place is unusual. I like unusual...usually."

"Me too."

I watched her quick little movements, her neat knife work, the cute way she licked a little cream cheese off her thumb. I stirred some sugar into my coffee and tried to think of something to say.

"I had a really good time at Kelly's."

"Me too," she said, smiling warmly.

"And you do that every year?"

"Yes, we do. Some form of it. Sometimes there are different people. Like you."

"Well, I'm different," I said. "I'll grant you that." I watched her eat a small bite, chewing it thoroughly.

"Betsy," I murmured. "That's a great name."

She took a little sip of hot coffee and held up her hand until she was finished chewing.

"My real name is...Elizabeth. Elizabeth Anne," she said. "But I've always been called Betsy. I tried to be Elizabeth once, in my twenties, but it never stuck. I guess I'm just a Betsy."

"Betsy's a *terrific* name," I insisted.

"I think it's kind of silly," she said. "Especially at my age."

"There's Betsy Ross," I offered. "Everybody loves the flag."

"Yeah, and who else?" she shot back.

"Well..." I stalled, "there's...Betsy Trotwood. From *David Copperfield*."

"Oh my!" she said with a gasp, putting her cup down with a little splash. "You know *Dickens*?"

"Well, not personally," I joked. "But I'm *almost* that old."

"No, I'm not kidding," she said, mopping up her spill. "I don't meet that many men who actually read novels, other than the teachers at my school."

"Well, I like to read, and I had a long time to read a lot of very long books."

"So you said," she countered gently.

Was this the time to tell her all about me? All about my past? I probably revealed some things to Betsy when we first talked on Thanksgiving. I didn't want to scare her away, but I felt that I owed her the truth. At least, *some* truth.

"So you know all about me?" I asked her, looking directly in her clever green eyes. "Did Kelly tell you everything?"

She looked straight back at me and said, "No one knows everything. But she told me some things. And I looked you up a little on the internet."

"Oh." I winced. "I wish you hadn't done that."

"You were just a kid," she said tenderly.

"*Still*," I said. I refused to accept her explanation.

"But you've paid your debt to society."

"Yeah, that's what they say," I said, trying not to laugh at the platitude.

I took a drink of my coffee and ripped a piece off her bagel, thinking, *Why did I bring this up? Didn't I want to make things light, uncomplicated, and casual?*

"You were only nineteen years old, for God's sake, right?" she insisted. "You were a baby! After all this time, you don't think you deserve a second chance?...I don't know about you, but I believe in second chances."

I heard her words, but more than that, I studied her face and hands and the kind, positive gleam in her eyes. She was technically old —about the same age as me, maybe a little younger—but there was something youthful and hopeful and affirmative about her, making *me* feel younger. She seemed to believe in me more than I believed in myself. Or maybe she was just being kind.

"You like your bagel?" I asked her.

"Are you listening to me, Larry?" She put her coffee down.

"Every word," I said. And I meant it. "You wanna get out of here? Let's get some fresh air."

"We don't have to talk about what you don't want to talk about," she said.

"No," I said. "You say anything you want. I *want* you to say what you're feeling and thinking. Why would I want you to hold back anything...or, worse, *lie*?"

"Why? Because most people don't want to hear the truth," she said. "Not that I know what 'the Truth' is."

"I bet you have a pretty good idea," I said.

"Well." She laughed and looked down. "*I* happen to think so. But that doesn't make a person especially popular in some circles."

"But who cares about circles?" I said.

She looked at me, her head slightly turned, with what I can only call her "female X-ray eye."

"OK then, Larry," she said, nodding slowly. "Let's get some fresh air."

⌒

Outside Chic's was brisk and breezy. The sky was light gray, and the river dark gray. I heard a train going by, the Metro North Hudson line that went right along the river.

"So, you want to do something else?" I asked Betsy. "Go someplace maybe?"

She turned the collar of her big, blue parka up and said thoughtfully, "Well, the coolest place around here is probably the Bronx Zoo. When I have visitors from out of town, especially if they have kids, I take them to the zoo. It would be beautiful, even on a day like this. Not so many people around."

"The zoo?" I said, letting the picture form in my mind. "You mean...animals in cages? Let me think about that a minute."

"Sorry," Betsy said, frowning. "I didn't think of it that way. It really is a beautiful place."

"I bet it is," I said. "I went to the Bronx Zoo once when I was a kid, I think, on a school trip."

"OK, then," she said, giving me another choice, "why don't you let me show you City Island? Where I live. It's a pretty interesting place."

"That sounds great," I said, happy that she came up with an alternative to animal jail and even happier that it was a trip to *her* neighborhood. "I'm all in favor of 'pretty interesting.'"

⌒

Betsy's Jeep was cold and rode hard, but she seemed to enjoy driving it so much that I didn't mind.

"I need new suspension," she said, "but some things have to wait their turn."

"It's nice to have any wheels at all," I said. "Thanks for the ride."

"Oh, pish," she said, laughing. "It's good for me to get out. Just on principle."

"Well." I laughed. "I'm glad to be your principle."

"No, thank you," she said and snickered. "I already have a principal and his name is Victor Croll. Headmaster Croll. Who is a pain in my—and everybody else at Thomas Paine's—*life*."

I liked how she avoided cursing.

"Then how did he get to be headmaster?"

"Two things, I think," she replied with clear-eyed certainty. "Ambition and inertia."

Betsy drove quickly, changing lanes and checking her mirrors regularly. I think she was humming to herself, but I wasn't sure.

"I hate driving in weekend traffic," she said.

"Well, life is filled with risk," I said, watching the plain Yonkers scenery go by—stores, people, and the cars in the on-coming traffic.

"You don't have to make fun of me, Larry," she chided.

"I wasn't!" I protested. "I was just making an observation. I didn't mean anything."

She laughed again. "It's OK. Say whatever you want. I have very thick skin."

"I bet that's not strictly true," I said, and it was out of my mouth before I realized the sexual implication, something I had resisted doing so far.

That left us both silent for a while.

Then Betsy had the good sense to turn on the radio.

"NPR," she said. "My *Bible*....At least, my *radio* Bible."

We drove for a while, saying nothing. I resolved not to say anything inappropriate again. This was a nice woman who had had a tough time with her late husband and his cancer, according to Kelly, right? I didn't want to be a jerk and scare her away. There was enough about me already that was scary. If she had any idea of the thoughts in my head sometimes, the horrible memories I can't erase, she'd run in the other direction as fast as she could. But here she was, driving me in her Jeep, relaxed, chatty, and able to take care of herself. Still, I didn't want to force anything. I had to be cool and let things happen normally. I just had to keep focusing what "normal" is.

"How long have you lived in...uh, City Island?" I asked her.

She turned down the radio.

"How long?" she asked. "A long time. Over thirty years."

"Wow," I said.

"My husband liked boats," she said.

"Do *you* like boats?" I asked her.

"I learned to, a little," she said with a dry laugh, as if remembering something that amused her.

"Boats," I mused. "I like to look at the ocean, but boats are a different thing."

"They certainly are," she said. "But now I love it here. It's like getting away from the real world, even if it's just an illusion."

"Do you like illusions?" I asked her.

She waited a moment and smiled. "Some illusions."

I watched Betsy as she drove. She seemed so honest and frank about things, so open. She didn't seem to be the "very vulnerable person" who had "been through so much" who Kelly described. Were there dark shadows in Betsy? There had to be some; everyone has some darkness inside. Maybe not as much as me, but some.

"Summers it can get pretty crowded here," she said. "But then again, that's good for local businesses, so it's a double-edged sword. To be perfectly honest, we need the tourists and can't stand 'em, both at the same time."

We swung off the Cross County and down the Hutchinson River Parkway—"the Hutch"—and we were soon in those flat, reedy grasslands that meant you were getting near the ocean.

"Orchard Beach," I read the exit sign as we slowed on the curve.

"Orchard Beach is famous," she said.

"Famous for what?" I asked, not really expecting an answer.

"Oh, lots of things. Race riots!" she wisecracked. "Being crowded...loud radios. You know: *da Bronx*."

Another big rainbow of laughter came out of her mouth. "I shouldn't insult the Bronx. Especially since I'm a lifelong resident."

"But isn't that what gives you the right?" I said.

"Exactly!" she concurred. "I can say anything I want about *my* family. But *you* say anything?" She made two quick slitting-the-throat gestures across her neck with a thumbnail, swish-swish. Very precisely and sharply. I was impressed. She was not entirely soft and "vulnerable."

Right then I saw the water between the reeds, what must be some little pocket of Long Island Sound. We were getting close to the ocean. Not only could you see it, you could feel it and, when I put down the window, smell it.

"It's nice here," I said, closing my eyes, feeling the sea with all my senses. It reminded me of growing up on Long Island, driving close to the ocean. Jones Beach and The Girl. I opened my eyes.

"People sometimes forget," said Betsy, driving easily, at home on these roads, "New York has one of the largest natural harbors in the world. There are all these hidden inlets and islands and other places that no one knows about. Or very few people do."

Zzrrrppp, we were suddenly going across a noisy, old metal bridge with a big "Welcome to City Island—Seaport of the Bronx" sign overhead.

"Back that way," she said, pointing to the left, "is Orchard Beach. But this is the way onto City Island. Which actually *is* an island."

As we drove down the street, gradually things began to look like a New England fishing village. There were marine supply stores and bait and tackle shops and lobster shacks and boat repair yards and clam houses and antique shops. In a way, it was like that Guy Lombardo area in Freeport, where I took Derek for steamers, but this was much bigger and nicer.

"Wow," I said. "I can't believe this is the Bronx."

"That's what everyone says," she commented, looking carefully for cross traffic.

"And you moved here because...?"

"My husband was born here," she said. "That made him a clamdigger. I, on the other hand, am a resident who was not born here, so I am what's known as a musselsucker."

"That sounds...ridiculous," I said.

"I know," she said. "But it's sort of cute. And they like it, the Chamber of Commerce types, to keep up the special identity of the place."

"Does that matter?"

"It's good for business," she said. "For the restaurants and everybody."

"But does that matter *to you*?" I pressed her.

"Absolutely" she answered strongly. "This is my community. These people are my friends. Some of them I can take or leave, but most of them are good people. And of course, there's Roland."

"Who's Roland?"

"This is Roland's," she said, swinging the big Jeep into a parking space next to a dumpster at the back of a two-story gray building.

"He's my landlord. I live over his store and help him out," she said. "He's getting a bit slower lately, but he's still quite a—well, you decide."

There was a big, rusted "Reserved Parking—Do Not Park Here—No Stopping" sign on the wall in front of us, and next to us, an old, white cargo van, dusty with grime and dirt, in front of a similar "Reserved Parking" sign.

"I have my own parking space, which is important," she said. "Parking around here in the summer can be just impossible. Let's go. Last stop."

She was out of the car and had closed her door before I could say anything. I got out as fast as I could, just in time to see her take a deep breath.

"Great air!" I said, thinking she wanted me to admire the quality of the ocean air, fresh and salty.

"Sometimes it really stinks," she said, wrinkling her nose a little. "You know: *fish*. But today it's good. Come on."

She locked the Jeep and walked up the alleyway next to the building. I followed.

The alleyway was narrow—these were old buildings—and I noticed an old-fashioned metal fire escape overhead, with the long ladder that slides to the ground. A much larger person might have trouble walking down this alley without scraping against the sides. I was glad get out of there into the open space.

"It's a little snug that way," she said with a big smile as I emerged, "but it's much faster because here we are."

I turned around and saw a wide gray building with painted-white Victorian trim and a big picture window with a large, fancy, weatherworn sign: "City Island Nautical Treasures and Antiques."

Betsy walked lightly up the front steps and in the front door, which swung inward to the sound of jingling sleigh bells. I tried to get in front of her to open the door for her, but she was too fast for me.

It was dark inside the store, and it took my eyes a moment to adjust. After a couple of blinks, I started to focus on the overwhelming profusion of "nautical treasures and antiques" all around. Old birdcages and lobster traps, fishing tackle and little lamps with fringes on the shades. The walls were covered with paintings of ships, old advertising signs, and ancient license plates, all the way to the high ceiling. There were several tables and a great many glass cases filled with nautical items: brass instruments and barometers, sextants and compasses, lots of ship models, some large ships' steering wheels, tons of scrimshaw, and racks of telescopes of different lengths in a long rack on the wall. And there were shelves and shelves of old books and magazines, aged kitchen utensils, stacks of wicker baskets, mason jars of seashells and marine specimens, and what could charitably be described as "interesting junk."

"Larry!" Betsy called me from far in the back. "Come meet Roland!"

I made my way down the aisle toward the rear of the store, past the counter with an old brass cash register, past dozens of printed notices and business cards pinned to a big bulletin board, and into a small office, where I heard voices—Betsy's high chatter and a low, rumbling growl.

As I walked in, I saw sitting behind a large, old wooden desk angled into the corner a big-boned man with combed-back white hair and a beard like an Old Testament prophet.

Betsy stood on the other side of the desk, just finishing a story. "And that was that for *him*. Period, the end. Don't ever do business with him again."

Then she turned to me with a big smile.

"Larry!" she sang out, happy to see me. She pointed to the man behind the desk. "Larry, this is Roland Elias, proprietor of this wonderful establishment. Roland, this is Larry Ingber."

"Hi," I said with a wave as I noticed his long, untrimmed eyebrows and the grimy suspenders with anchors strapped over his broad shoulders.

"Hello..." Roland said back to me as if it were a weighty decision. I decided to be nice.

"This is some store you have here," I complimented him.

"You wanna buy something?" he shot back.

"No," I calmly returned fire. "But you have some nice stuff."

"'Nice stuff?'" he grunted back to me.

"Roland," Betsy cut in, "was Debbie here?"

I looked around the crowded little office while Betsy peppered Roland with questions about Debbie, who was some kind of a medical person, and the results of some tests. Betsy and I had to stand because there was really just room for the old man behind the paper-littered desk and a couple of dusty bookcases. Lots of stuff hung on the wall: old, framed maps; ancient fishing tackle; yellowed photographs of men holding or standing next to very large fish; pictures of ships with sailors, ships with sails, and enormous Navy vessels. In the corner, there was a little computer station—a chair and a big old monitor— that didn't seem to belong to the rest of the room.

"What about Sonya?" Betsy asked. "Did she do all the accounts that Bob wanted?"

"Here and gone," he grunted.

"Good," Betsy said, satisfied. "Can I get you anything?"

"Not a thing," he said. "I'm going in. You should close at six sharp."

"How has it been today?" she asked.

He got up from his chair with some difficulty, almost in segments. When he reached full height, I could see that he was very tall—well over six feet—but he was bent a little so he was probably even taller than he looked. He straightened his back and almost growled, "Too many talkers."

Betsy calmly asked him as he moved away from behind the desk, "And you have your dinner?"

"I have several, thank you," he said dryly. "I just wish I had an appetite."

"You will later," she assured him.

"If you say so," said Roland as he picked up a cane resting against the wall. He started to walk out of the office, leaning heavily on the cane with each step. I could see that he had a bad limp and a stiff leg.

As he slowly advanced, Betsy said, "Call me if you need anything."

"I won't," he said amiably.

As he passed by me, I said, "Nice meeting you, Roland," being polite for Betsy's sake.

"Ah, yes," he said, stopping as if seeing me for the first time. "The Count....Nice to meet you too."

And he ambled out of the office.

I was about to ask Betsy, "What did he mean by that? The Count? What Count?" but the sleigh bells rang at the front door.

"A customer!" she said, bolting out of the office into the front of the store, greeting someone with a lovely, musical hello before I had a chance to move an inch.

I spent the rest of the afternoon watching Betsy run the store, trying to stay out of her way, and only talked to her in-between customers. I liked how she waited on people and chatted with them just the right amount: not pushy, just friendly and helpful. I liked how she carefully showed an antique brass sextant to one guy. I liked how delicately she locked the sextant back in its case with one of the keys from a big silver ring of cabinet keys when the guy didn't buy it.

I settled in a little chair in the corner by the books and magazines and read all about "The Greatest Sea Battles," while customers came in and out, the bells on the door ringing when anyone entered or left.

135

Betsy came to check on me, peeking around the corner of a tall bookcase that was not even half of the nautical history section. "Are you OK? We haven't been this busy in weeks!"

"Great! I'm fine here," I said, resurfacing from the book in my lap. "Did you know that after the Battle of Actium, Cleopatra tried to cut a deal with Octavian, even after Mark Antony was dead?"

"That tramp Cleo!" Betsy laughed. "Always out for herself. You want some tea? I made some."

"Uh, sure," I said.

The door bells rang, and more customers came in. She whispered, "Be right back," and darted away.

I hate tea. I shouldn't say that. I've had all kinds of "teas" over the years, but I generally prefer coffee, even the vile, watery kind I got in prison. But if she offered it, and it was already made, I felt it was the right thing to do, to say yes to things. That was the normal response, right?

She brought me the tea—with two plain cookies sticking out from the saucer—and put it down next to me on the wide arm of the reading chair.

"Here," she said. "I made the cookies."

"You are too much," I said, looking up from my book.

"No, I'm not." She leaned toward me and whispered, "I think these might be actual buyers," pointing with her thumb toward customers in another part of the store. And she was gone.

The tea was...hot. But the cookies were great. I dunked. It was pretty damn nice: a good book, a comfortable chair, and homemade cookies. Was this one of those Moments? I tried to refocus on my reading, but my mind kept wandering to reflect on my good fortune. I used to read to *escape* my surroundings, to fly outside walls of misery. Now I wanted to be exactly where I was, being waited on by this very nice woman, out here in the free world, in this very cool store, with no one guarding me. My eyes started to fill with tears as I realized this was actually happening to me. And her tea wasn't so bad, once you got used to it.

At six o'clock on the dot, I heard her close and lock the front door, with a peal of bells and a firm click.

"Come on," she said, appearing from around the corner and beckoning me. "We are *closed*. Let's go upstairs. I have to change my shoes."

I followed her down a hallway toward the back of the store and up a very long flight of stairs to the second floor.

"This is why Roland rents out the upstairs," she said, half turning to me as she trudged upward. "He can't handle stairs. But he has a couple of nice rooms on the first floor."

"Great," I said, as she unlocked a door at the top of the stairs.

"There's another entrance from the outside," she said, swinging the door wide open, "but sometimes I use these stairs from inside the store."

"Nice," I mumbled, impressed at her setup, following her into the apartment.

"Take a seat! I'll just be a minute."

She left me standing there, in the little hallway, and disappeared.

"Cozy!" I shouted out to her, admiring the rooms as I walked into Betsyland. There was a living room with a small couch and a chair for reading, and a little dining room and kitchen beyond that. Framed pictures and photographs of her family—lots of them—hung on every flat surface. The ceilings were low and all angled oddly so that the rooms weren't rectangular boxes. And there were books everywhere, crowded into shelves but in a neat, highly organized way.

"Small, you mean!" she shouted back.

"No!" I said. "It's terrific!" And it was. I didn't say, "Betsy, you don't know the meaning of small." I just let it go.

She came briskly back into the living room, carrying a pair of pink tennis shoes.

"Sorry," she said as she sat down on a chair and switched out of her shoes right in front of me, "but these things are killing me."

She quickly slipped off her boots to reveal a pair of colorfully striped socks.

"As you can see," she continued, "I'm a slave to fashion."

Two minutes later, we were walking down the sidewalk at a healthy pace.

"I used to run," Betsy said, "but now I walk. I walk all the time. It's good for you; it gets oxygen into your brain."

"Well," I said, "my brain can use all the oxygen it can get."

She hooked her arm into mine, and we walked in step down City Island Avenue.

"So who's this Roland?" I asked, the first of the many questions I had accumulated in my mind as I read about so many naval battles and dead admirals.

"I told you," she said. "He's my landlord. And an old friend. I watch the store for him sometimes. And I help keep an eye on him. He has no relatives. Roland's a real character and a legend around here. He's like an oak tree: tall...and weathered."

"So I saw." I chuckled.

"I also help a little with his accounts," she said. "Mainly getting all his paperwork to Bob Jensen, who handles all his affairs. All the receipts for his taxes and such. And I make trips to the bank for him sometimes."

"You do all that?" I asked.

"It's not that much," she said. "For a friend."

"Wow. Do you have other hidden talents?" I said, looking at her sideways to see if she was blushing.

She snickered, ignored me, and immediately switched the subject back. "I've known Roland for a long time, but to tell you the truth, the store isn't doing so well lately. I think he's just keeping it open for the two apartments. He used to get two containers a year from Europe, but nothing like that now.

"He was very nice to my husband while he was alive, and he's the smartest man I know—Roland, I mean. He worked as a merchant marine for forty years. He knows people from all over the world and gets letters from famous professors and writers. He showed me one from Nelson Mandela. You'll see: you'll like him a lot. He's read everything—much more than me. Scholarly books too. He went to Harvard."

"Good for him," I said as her H-bomb detonated. I never quite finished my Ivy League education, and Columbia ain't Harvard.

I changed subjects on her. "So, why did Roland call me the Count?"

"Oh, pish," she said, crestfallen. "I was hoping you'd forget about that."

"Sorry," I said. "I don't forget much, generally speaking."

"I'll try to remember that," she said.

For a moment, I wondered if she was making fun of me.

"It's really nothing." She shrugged. "I told Roland about you and your story, and he said that you were like the Count of Monte Cristo: returned from a long time in prison to avenge those who wronged you."

I stopped walking and, touching her arm, stopped her too.

"I *should* be more like the Count of Monte Cristo," I declared. "I *should* be obsessed."

"Is that what you want to be?" she asked.

"It's what I *have* to be," I said. "I really want to be a normal person and try to live a quiet life. But I also want to get my money back from the guy who stole it from me. It was the legacy from my father, the last thing he left me. But I'm not out for revenge."

Betsy's eyes never left mine as I told her what I was feeling.

"OK," she said, accepting my explanation even if I myself wasn't sure how far I'd go in pursuing Mantell.

"Now can I ask *you* something I probably shouldn't?" I said carefully.

"With that kind of a build-up," she said with a smile, "how can I say no?"

"Why aren't you married to someone?"

"I *was* married to someone."

"I mean, now," I insisted. "Why don't you have a fella?"

"Who says I don't?" After a pause, she said, "You're right. I don't. But it's not because I'm not interested. I'm just realistic. Most of the men I meet are either married or gay or too young or too old. Or they want a Kardashian."

"What's that?" I asked.

"A girl!" she answered with a laugh. "A young girl. A dumb, young girl. Anyway, younger and dumber than me."

"You're not so old."

"Thanks," she said with a half smirk.

"No!" I raised my voice, maybe a bit too much. "I mean it. You're *alive*. More alive than a lot of people I see younger than you."

"Well, thank you," she said carefully. "I try my very best to be alive."

Instantly I was sorry to be so direct, but I couldn't help it. I wanted her to like me, but I didn't want to scare her off. So I put my hands back in my pockets, and we kept walking, side by side.

She told me more about the history of City Island and Roland's adventures as a merchant marine and how he inherited the store from one of his old shipmates. As we strolled, two people said hello to her. I let the first remark pass, but when another person—a middle-aged man in overalls—said, "Hi, Betsy!" I just had to say, "Does *everyone* around here know you?"

She smiled and shrugged. "Only the people who know me, know me. They really know Roland." She stopped suddenly. "Am I talking too much?"

From the bright, honest look in her eyes, I could see that she really cared what I answered.

"Not a bit," I said.

She seemed to like that. And she took my arm again and we continued down the street. She told me more stories about the Bronx, about Kelly growing up, and Kelly's kids. I told her about Clemency and my first apartment and what I was learning about this new (for me) planet, just happy to feel her arm in mine and not tense up. She didn't say anything about her marriage or her "troubles," and I didn't ask her. I figured that would come in time.

We were near the tip of City Island, where it stuck out into Long Island Sound and you could see the Throgs Neck Bridge all lit up with Manhattan beyond it. We stood there for a moment, taking it in. The scene, the night, the clean air, and the uneasy feeling of being with a new person.

"You remind me of something we have painted on the wall in the lobby of our school," she said. "Something that Thomas Paine said: 'We have it in our power to begin the world over again.'"

She then took me to her friend Gassim's seafood restaurant on the water, with "the best lobster rolls in the world, or at least, the Bronx." It was getting late, and we had to eat something. It was a casual place, nothing fancy, and Gassim Khalidi—stout, gray, and almost suspiciously good-humored—welcomed us like family. Unfortunately, I was getting low on cash. I checked my wallet when I thought Betsy wasn't looking, but maybe she did catch a glimpse because she insisted on paying half the bill. I objected, saying that I was "old school," but she was pretty stubborn, taking pity on me. I'm actually glad she chipped in. I was down to singles.

It was cold when we left Gassim's with the lobster rolls we didn't finish, so we walked close together, arm in arm, for warmth and stability against the gusts coming off the Sound.

"It's good to walk off a nice meal like that," she said, dragging me along at her pace.

"Whatever you say," I agreed, keeping up with her.

"Only a few blocks," she said. "And then I should take you home."

She waited and when I didn't say anything, she laughed. "You don't think I'm going to invite you upstairs on our *first date*...do you?"

That comment stopped me cold. I mumbled, "Was this our first date?"

"What would you call it? Do you realize that we've been together for more than eight hours now?"

"Oh," I said. "It doesn't feel like that long."

"I know."

We walked along in silence for a while until we got back to her Jeep, parked behind the store.

Driving back to my apartment, I didn't have to remind her of the way; she remembered. I don't know if *I* would have remembered.

A few minutes later, we were in front of my apartment building. She put on the parking brake and sat back in her seat.

"Thank you, Betsy," I said. "You are a very nice person."

She turned to me. "You don't really know me, Larry. Not after just one day."

"Do you mind if I kiss you anyway?" I said. I couldn't resist asking: she looked so...kissable.

She smiled shyly. "No, I don't."

I unbuckled my seat belt and leaned over to kiss her. At the last moment, she turned her face and took it on her cheek. She was right: a cheek kiss was the correct thing on a first date. Best not to push things too hard, too fast. But even so, it was very nice.

Of course, I was dying to touch her, but I was also completely unsure of myself: drawn in yet borderline terrified.

I got out of the Jeep and before I closed the door I asked, "Can I call you?"

She smiled. "Sure."

I closed the door and watched her drive away in the cold, black December night. She beeped the horn twice as she sped down the block. I waved back, in case she could see me in her rearview mirror.

I had been out of prison for a while, but for the first time in a very-very-very long time, I felt the inside of me completely unclench. I walked toward my building feeling a faint spark of real life light within me. No matter what Mantell did, no matter what Fusco did, no one could take this feeling, this big Moment from me.

And just when there was this glimmer, this possibility of a sliver of a happy, normal life and maybe even love, the whole world fell in on me once again.

PART II
GETTING ON

NINE

In the following weeks, I was pulled in all different directions. I did some of that pulling myself. I put in extra hours at Clemency, doing whatever Rosemary needed whenever she needed it, unspoken pressure on her for a raise. I spent time on the phone with Rathbun and Cuellar. Did I make myself a pain in the ass to them? Maybe. But they gave me the name of someone at the Long Island Bar Association—Elaine Kingston—so I called and made myself a pain in the ass to her too.

I kept getting texts from Sammy Zambrano, asking if I was *ready yet*. I deleted them as soon as I got them. In-between, I couldn't stay away from the internet, looking for the ghost of Lester Mantell.

I spent all day, every day, trying not to spend money.

And, of course, I had Fusco.

What saved me was Betsy. It just started: at night, she would pick me up from work, take me back to her apartment for dinner, and then drive me home to Yonkers. We missed a couple of nights; once because of her monthly book club meeting, which was important to her, and once to babysit for Kelly, but otherwise we started seeing each other just about every night. I wanted to spend as much free time with her as she would permit. I mean, I had my job, and she had hers, but I know what a good thing is, and I was going to do my best not to let it slip away.

She even let me help decorate the Christmas tree in her apartment. Another Moment of Grace and Thanks. I hadn't decorated a Christmas tree since Miss Egan's sixth grade class in 1962. I felt—what is the right word?—*blessed* that this nice, intelligent, decent woman appeared to like me. Seemingly without any effort on her part, she gave me a whole host of Moments. They might look like nothing, but they were everything: reading a book in bed at night with her reading next to me...filling my tea cup without my even asking ...putting away my clean laundry and making my stuff neater than I ever could...holding me in a way that didn't make me flinch... letting me hold her, and more. Maybe I wasn't completely ruined as a human being by my years in prison. If I was "damaged goods," at least someone had found some use for me.

Of course, I also started hanging out at Roland's store on the weekends, to help Betsy help Roland. Weekends were their busiest time, but business wasn't all that good.

"It's a combination of things," she told me. "The economy, I think, has a lot to do with it. Two other antique stores closed farther up City Island Avenue in the last three years. There's competition from the internet and a hundred garage sales every weekend. And, when it gets down to it, with this great so-called recession—I call it a depression—people have necessities to pay for and really don't *need* nautical antiques."

Nonetheless Betsy stayed cheerful and waited on all the customers. Roland would wander in and out of the store from his apartment in the back, but you could never be sure when he would appear. So it was mostly on Betsy during the weekends, which made it perfect for me to help her. And it was interesting to watch her run the store. Over time, she showed me how to record the sales, how to run the cash register, where the cash box and deposit bag for the bank were, where all the keys were and what they unlocked, how to lock the whole store up and set the alarm—a little bit of everything. I had never watched the store alone, but I was sure I could handle it. Handling Roland was another matter.

Right from the get-go, I realized it was in my best interest to keep Roland happy. He was Betsy's landlord, and I couldn't screw up her good situation. As you can imagine, I've met some extreme characters in my years, but Roland Elias was one Supreme Odd Fellow. Quick to anger but quick to joke too, he talked in spurts, going on long, involved rants and then remained silent for hours. I knew a couple of guys like him in prison—faraway guys—with deep wisdom and deep wounds.

I'll say this for Roland: he knew a lot of stuff. I think I know a lot from my years of enforced reading, but Roland's breadth of off-center knowledge was a source of amazement to me, time and time again.

"You have a lot of time to read at sea," he explained to me once.

"In prison too," I said back. That got his attention.

I told him my story one long rainy afternoon, when there were almost no customers, over a couple of glasses of Jim Beam.

Nodding his head, he said, "Smart men can do stupid things."

And he told me about his life. A brutal childhood in the Midwest: booze-addicted father, church-addicted mother.

"I kept the booze but not the church," he cracked. "It's an old story from the American prairie. Too many kids, not enough money. Winters are long: what else are you gonna do for excitement except drink and beat your wife and kids?"

"How did you wind up at Harvard?"

"I had a teacher who believed in me," he said. "Mrs. Edna Harris."

"And what happened when you got to Cambridge?"

A sad smile crossed his face. "I just wasn't the Ivy League type," he said.

"Neither was I," I admitted.

"I just wasn't meant to be part of the ruling class." He chuckled. "It's an idea I never approved of."

He "made a narrow escape" into the merchant marines.

"I've seen the world," he said, chomping his cigar end, "and let me tell you: you're not missing anything." He waited a moment. "That was a joke. I suppose I'm grateful that I traveled some and saw a fair enough assortment of human beings in different native habitats. But it's all the same in the end. I'm still sitting here, with the same mug, stuck in my own thoughts, drinking the same booze, the same pile on the same piles."

"Some things don't change," I agreed, even though I've never been plagued by that last particular problem.

I remember the first time he deigned to show me around the store, tossing off information at random about the merchandise for sale.

"That's crap," he said, pointing a crooked finger. "That's good. That's a very good three-mirror presentation sextant: rare, and in excellent condition. Original box. Don't take less than five hundred for it. Same for this Mercer chronometer."

He machine-gunned more information at me, which I took in just as fast.

"You know what the difference is between an antique and a piece of junk?" he quizzed me. Before I could answer, he said, "Fifty bucks."

And then he turned the corner, walking down the aisle on his stiff, swinging leg.

"This you should know about," he said, going behind the front counter and reaching under the cash register. He pulled out a short but lethal iron pipe with some old electrical tape wrapped around one end to make a better grip.

"Just in case anyone gets argumentative," he said with a twinkle. "Or sticky-fingered."

I had to laugh. "Yes, Roland, I recognize that instrument. I've had to use something similar myself. Once." I said nothing more.

"There are video cameras all around." He pointed them out to me. "Did Betsy show you how to set the burglar alarm? Human beings have been known to steal."

Over time, I began to learn about the world of nautical lamps and instruments, whistles, scrimshaw, compasses and clocks, gauges and scopes, ships in bottles, and all the other miscellaneous junk/treasure he had crammed into the store. Roland knew everything in his inventory, but it wasn't in any particular order. Everything was kind of random and looked like nothing had been moved in years. I guess that was part of its charm, that it was like some old sea dog's attic, and it was quaint in an old New England kind of way, but it was hard to see what exactly was for sale. I could see that people got lost in the tangle of everything, a jumble on the shelves.

Roland told me he won the store in a poker game from an old shipmate of his, a "degenerate gambler and pack rat." But I believed it when Betsy told me that Roland had simply lost interest in the store and kept it open for the sake of the apartments.

"Things always pick up in the summer," she offered with a hopeful smile. "When the tourists come back in force."

I decided that I should do something, for her and the store.

The next Monday, the Clemency offices were closed (fumigation of the entire building all weekend), and they gave us the day off *with pay*. Mondays the store was closed, so Betsy was going to work at Thomas Paine, early as usual. It gave me the chance to do something I'd been thinking about for weeks.

"What would you think if I moved some things around in the store?" I asked her. "To make it a little easier for customers to see things."

Betsy turned to me with some concern. "You'd have to ask Roland."

"You think he'd mind?" I asked.

"You can ask him," she said, "but he's pretty set in his ways. See you after school."

I was sitting at the kitchen table, drinking the rest of my tea. She came over and gave me a peck on the cheek, natural as anything. Then she went out the door and down the outside staircase to where the Jeep was parked.

I immediately went into action, quickly straightening up the kitchen while rehearsing what I was going to say to Roland and what I was going to do when I got the go-ahead. I went down the inside stairs into the store and first turned off the burglar alarm at the panel at the back door. It felt good that Betsy and Roland trusted me with the code, but it also made it easier for them, the more things I could do in the store.

Fortunately, I heard some activity from inside Roland's apartment, which meant he was awake. Some days he might not appear until noon. I knocked on his door, waited, heard the shuffling of his steps, and braced myself as he opened the door.

He was a good head taller than me, and he looked like hell, having just woken up, his hair all wild and woolly.

"Yeah?" he said, focusing down on me, swaying a little.

"Good morning, Roland," I said, making my play. "Listen, I've got some extra time today. Do you mind if I move some things around in the store? Maybe straighten some things up, give it a little change, a new look? Just to make things easier for the customers to see."

His heavy-lidded eyes opened a little. He stared at me for one hard second, then said, "Knock yourself out. I'm going back to my bunk."

He closed the door and was gone. That was all I needed.

For the next few hours, I worked on the store like a mad-man—a *good* madman. First I swept up the place, going in deep corners that hadn't seen a broom in too long. Then I started moving some of the merchandise, always dusting where things had been, putting items in more attractive arrangements. I didn't break a thing.

I carefully shifted two tables so that customers could walk through the store easier. I straightened up the bookshelves and old magazines, moving the flashier covers to the front to make a better display.

I found an old bucket, sponge, and squeegee in a back stor-age closet and washed off the wide front window. While I was outside, I rearranged the window display, which looked tired and dirty. I took several of the shiniest brass things and a few of the telescopes and prisms and set them so that the sun would catch them and attract passersby, whether they were on foot or in their cars. I took a big ship's model with an American flag, put it right in the center, and angled a spotlight on it. Then I carried two very nice, very heavy ship's figureheads—a mermaid and a milkmaid—and set them up alongside.

I worked my ass off, but it was fun. I only went upstairs once to make myself a quick sandwich, but I basically worked straight through until Betsy came home.

One close call: I was lifting a large, expensive ship's wheel and it got away from me. I almost dropped it, but as I caught it, I almost dislocated my left shoulder. I was once suspended from a heating pipe for four days, and it permanently damaged that shoulder. I can slip it in and out of its socket when I want to. When I put the ship's wheel down, I had to ram my shoulder against the wall to pop it back into its socket. That hurt like hell, but I was sort of used to it. It had happened before.

All the time I was working, I couldn't help occasionally think-ing to myself: *I should be spending this time looking for Mantell— that should be my mission every day.* Or *I should be doing this work at a store where they would pay me.* Then I would remind myself that what I was doing for the store was for Betsy, and that made it the right thing to do, at least for the time being.

I didn't even have time to shower when I heard her Jeep pull up in the back. I hoped she would like what I did. I wanted to surprise her, to make her proud of my good idea and my industriousness, to show her that I wanted to make things better.

Betsy burst in from the back entrance already talking: "You wouldn't believe what Croll did, right in front of the faculty! In the middle of the front office—"

Then silence.

I watched Betsy's reaction unfold—from shock to horror to amazement to joy—as she looked around the store.

"Oh. My. God," she intoned, stepping carefully into the store as if the floor were wet.

She picked up a small pewter vase in the shape of a lighthouse that I had found on one of the back shelves.

"What is this?" she asked, turning the vase over in her hands.

"It was over there," I said. "Behind the diving bell."

With a worried look she turned to me and said, "Has Roland seen this?"

"No," I said. "He's been inside all day. But he gave me the complete go-ahead," slightly exaggerating perhaps Roland's license to change things.

"This is...amazing," she said, slowly making her way around the "new" store. "Everything looks different. And newer. You know what I mean. I love how you redid the lures!"

"Thank you," I said modestly. In fact, I stuck myself a bunch of times, rehanging the delicate antique fishing lures with their nasty hooks, but the display did look better.

She stood in the middle of store, shaking her head as she turned around in slow wonder, to see everything.

"Now I feel guilty," she said sadly, "about not doing all this, years ago. "

"You couldn't have done it," I quickly absolved her. "It was a lot of heavy lifting and moving things, and there are a couple more things I think we should do."

"You are the best!" she said, reaching out her arms.

She walked to me with a grateful smile, and I took her in my arms and kissed her. It was a good kiss: long and warm, but not too long.

I pulled away for a moment, looked right in her twinkly green eyes, and said, "You know I did this for you."

The next kiss was even better.

Betsy and I began moving more things around. I was at the top of a ladder, carefully transferring a stack of old wicker traps to Betsy's outstretched hands, when the old man emerged from his apartment and came into the room.

"*What in the holy hell happened here?*"

He stood there, his white hair standing straight up, a tower of disbelief and incipient indignation.

"Roland!" Betsy instantly went to pacify him. "Wait till you see what Larry's done."

She left me standing on the ladder, but it was perfectly all right; she immediately went to work reassuring Roland.

"Look over here at the clocks!" she enthused, taking him to the cabinet where I rearranged the clocks, setting them among seashells I found in a box behind an old sea chest. There was actually a lot of nice stuff in the store; Roland had just neglected it. I understood: he was an old guy and things got stale to him. I had fresh eyes.

"See how all the gauges and instruments look better over here," she said, steering Roland to a corner shelf I had completely re-done.

"'Better'?" he grumbled dubiously. "But how am I going to find things when I want to?"

"Not everything is changed," Betsy reasoned.

From the ladder, I said, "Y'know, I think you probably coulda sold some of these dust balls as antiques."

"Very funny," Roland said without a trace of amusement. He glanced up at me. "Smart guy."

When people call you "smart guy," it's not a compliment, but I let it pass because I could see that Roland, begrudgingly, liked what I had done.

"*Hmmff,*" he grunted several times as he circled around the place. "Did you think about moving the diving bell out here?"

"Too heavy," I said. "But you and I can do it, easy."

"Easy-peazy!" echoed Betsy, happy to see that my remodeling—and everything else—just might work out with Roland.

The three of us worked for another hour, moving the things that were too heavy for me alone. Betsy had even better ideas than I did, and Roland went along with almost everything. We even discussed plans for a new paint job, both inside and out.

"Place looks better," Roland declared when we finished.

After we washed up—we were all pretty dusty—we celebrated with dinner and a pitcher of beer down the street at Gassim's, at the very tip of City Island. For a guy with a stiff leg and a cane, Roland got around fairly well, except for certain challenges like flights of stairs. But on a straight path, he kept up with Betsy and me.

"Three, in the corner pocket, Gassim," he called to the owner as we walked in and went toward the booth in the corner. "And something nice and tall." He indicated the pitcher of beer he wanted.

"Good evening, Captain!" Gassim said when he saw Roland ambling across the floor. "Long time, long time!"

Gassim rushed over to escort us to the well-used, red-leathered booth.

"And Miss Betsy too!" he added with obvious happiness.

"Hello, Gassim," said Betsy sweetly. "Nice to see you."

"I have some lovely minestrone. Been cooking all day," he said. "You'll have a bowl?"

"I'd love some," replied Betsy as she sat down and slid across the seat.

"Make it two," I said, moving in next to her.

Roland groused. "Aww, what the hell. Make it three."

By the end of the night, we had also finished two plates of lobster rolls, a whole bunch of side dishes, and a second pitcher of beer. Roland got very mellow—for him.

"I have to admit it," he said reflectively between sips. "I've let the store go somewhat...adrift."

Betsy kicked me lightly under the table. She told me that when Roland used any nautical terminology, that meant he was "happy-drunk."

"It's good to change things every so often," Betsy added earnestly. "Shake things up. Everyone needs a shaking up every so often. It just makes sense."

"You believe her?" Roland shook his head. "How can someone be so nice and positive all the time?"

"I know," I agreed with him. "Sometimes it just boggles my mind."

"To heck with both of you," Betsy shot back. "I'm not that nice! Just try and cross me."

That made both Roland and me laugh even louder.

At the end of the meal, Roland paid the whole tab. We walked back to the store, Betsy between Roland and me, happy and full from the food and the beer.

"It's only fair," he said. "For all the work you did."

"And the work I'm *going* to do," I added sincerely. "We're gonna sell a lot more stuff. You just watch."

Betsy squeezed my arm closer to her side when I said that, and I didn't even mention my plans to get the store's neglected website running more profitably.

"You keep working this hard," Roland said, "and I'm just gonna have to pay you something."

"Offer accepted!" I replied, and we all laughed. But I was going to hold him to that when the time came.

"Smell that air," said Betsy luxuriously, and she was right: the wind was just right to blow the tangy sea air inland to us. The lights on City Island Avenue were lit all the way down to Belden's Point, the farthest point south. There were people on the sidewalks, walking back to their cars or back home. Nobody seemed rushed or unhappy. It all had a fairyland, small-town feel about it, with the sky covering everything with soft black velvet and the hush of the ocean breeze in the background.

As Betsy took my arm and pulled closer to me as we walked, I thought to myself, *This just might work out.*

We kept working on the appearance of the store. We rehung the antique signal flags across the store, making it look cheerier. I bartered with some nice gay guys who owned a nursery on Ditmars Street: a few old lobster traps for some tubs of geraniums for the front of the store.

And we did get a lot more compliments about the fresh look from shoppers and other store owners on the street who were glad to see someone taking better care of Roland's quirky, old dump.

I studied up on all the merchandise—there's an amazing amount of stuff on the internet. Nautical antiques are actually quite fascinating: windows into a whole, largely vanished way of life.

Through Javier, I found a computer whiz named Maurice, who modernized the store's website and set us up on eBay for a very reasonable rate. (Betsy had to convince Roland to spend the money, but it was obviously the right thing to do.) Maurice showed me how to take photos of our merchandise and "upload" them to our "store." It was laborious work and it took some time, but Betsy and I put a whole bunch of things in, at a whole range of prices—from the most expensive, rarest instruments to back issues of *Proceedings*, a naval magazine. (Frankly, we copied some classy London antique stores' sites.) I checked Roland's prices against those on eBay and other competitive sites. Of course, not all the sellers had the overhead of a store to support, so their prices were rock-bottom, almost always lower than what Roland was charging. But one thing I learned from poking around on different websites was how tough and competitive business is.

Another thing that surprised me: I actually liked selling things. Besides making the money, I enjoyed seeing people find some little treasure in the store, falling in love with it, and buying it. My father was a furniture salesman, and I always felt slightly ashamed whenever he'd talk enthusiastically about some sale he made, either making a good deal for a young couple he liked or sticking someone he didn't like with some white elephant. It all seemed so trivial: who cares who bought what? But now I began to see that maybe life is nothing but little things: small purchases, everyday encounters, and odd occurrences that add up to...what? A life.

At first, business did pick up at the store somewhat. Walk-in traffic definitely increased; more people, mainly tourists, came in. Unfortunately, the shoppers were mostly browsers, not buyers. I guess that's always the ratio in an antiques store, but it still was disheartening for me, every time someone came in and then walked out, without buying something. And there was almost no action on the eBay site. I checked it several times a day. Nothing was moving.

"I'm so proud of you," Betsy said, peeking over my shoulder. I was looking at our site and the eBay page after closing one Saturday. "I think you've really helped Roland and the store."

She gave me a hug from behind and a kiss on my cheek. And I only flinched a little. She spun me around on the office chair.

With a big smile on her face, she added, "Roland's gonna start paying you, for all the work you've been doing. He says he'll pay you two hundred dollars a week. Which is a lot for him."

"Well, that's something," I replied, trying to sound grateful. Which I was. More would have been nicer, but two hundred was better than nothing. It would pay a couple of bills. "I really appreciate it."

The thing is, I would hang out in the store anyway, just to be with Betsy.

I stood up and gave her a long kiss, but I was thinking about the appointment I had with Fusco on Thursday, the bills I had to pay, and Mantell: things that were never far from the surface of my mind.

In fact, the next night, late on a Sunday after Betsy dropped me off, I got another text from Sammy Zambrano. All it said was: *Hi honey. Need money?* Of course, I didn't answer it and immediately erased it, but it stayed with me. I could just picture that skeeve nastily texting me. I knew what he was talking about: that Medicare scam.

Zambrano was right about one thing: money was tight, even with the extra two bills a week from Roland. Keeping my little apartment, even though I was spending most of my nights at Betsy's, cost me too much. It takes a lot of money to be poor these days. If I could only get my money from Mantell, everything would be better. Sure, Fusco was on my case, but I had Betsy in my life, and I was surviving. As long as anything else didn't go wrong, I figured I would be OK.

I figured wrong.

TEN

It was an innocent Monday morning right when you could feel spring about to break. I went into the office early, feeling good, because Rosemary had some sorting for me to do before a big mailing with an important deadline. I wanted to please her because I was going to ask her again for a raise that day after work. Mantell was still on the lam, and I was thinking about setting up some kind of a website for "victims of Lester Mantell" to try to find him, but it cost money to set that kind of thing up, and it would mean coming out into public view. But I couldn't spend all my time thinking about the money that was stolen from me: I had to also worry about the money that was—or wasn't—in my paycheck.

At one time, I would have brought in an extra coffee for Rosemary—there was a shop right near the bus stop—but I had stopped buying outside coffee altogether. It was just too damn expensive. Instead I had started bringing teabags to work and using the hot water in the kitchen. Betsy showed me that there are all kinds of interesting teas out there, especially if you give them a shot of honey—and one box of twenty-four tea bags is not even one Starbucks coffee.

Even with my long hours at Clemency and helping out in the store on weekends for Roland's two hundred clams, I was thinking of looking for some other kind of extra job. I started checking Craigslist for part-time jobs, wondering what exactly I could do and who would want to hire an old ex-con anyway. I loved being with Betsy, and that was important, helping her and Roland. But thoughts of money—or rather my lack of it—were always in my mind, breeding anxiety. Clemency was going to have to give me a raise. And I—or someone—was going to have to find Lester Mantell.

On the Monday that changed everything, I remember dropping my coat and knapsack in my cubicle, planning on putting my lunch in the kitchen refrigerator like always. As I walked down the hallway to the kitchen, I caught the eye of Jane McElroy from Fund-raising at the other end. I was about to say, "Happy Monday!" when she suddenly ducked into an open doorway, purposefully avoiding my gaze.

That was weird, I thought. Jane likes me, or so I thought. Maybe it was just my imagination.

I continued down the hallway and turned the corner into the kitchen. Sitting at one of the tables eating an Egg McMuffin was Dae-Ho Park, one of the accountants in Business Affairs. Everybody called him Dae.

"Hey, Dae," I said as I opened the refrigerator. "How was your weekend?"

"OK. Have you been online today?" he asked, his mouth a mush of yellow and brown.

"No," I said, surprised he hardly answered my question. "Why?"

"What about your email?" he asked.

"No," I said. "I just got in." I wasn't like all these kids, checking their phones and email every two seconds. On the bus, I was reading a Swedish mystery Betsy recommended.

"Forget about email," another voice spoke up behind me. "Check out Drudge or Huffington. Vulture. Radar online. It's all over the place."

I turned around to see that it was Lee Pearson, a pasty-faced guy I barely knew with a smirk on his face.

"What do you mean?" I asked as he got up, wiping his lips with a paper napkin.

"You'll see," he said and turned away, picking up his coffee cup on the way out.

I turned to Dae and commented, "Nice guy," but he was tossing his McDonald's into the wastebasket on his way out of the kitchen.

What is up with these guys? I asked myself.

I made my tea, hustled back to my cubicle, and turned on the computer. I put in my security code, waited a moment, and then

I was online. I opened my email: nothing strange there. Just the usual Clemency stuff: emails from Rosemary, Blackburn's office, and HR.

Then I checked Drudge; it loaded the fastest. And there it was, right on the home page: "MY BFF, THE IVY LEAGUE KILLER."

And two big photographs of *me*. One was from my trial—the one I really hate, with my hands being held behind my back by that shithead anti-Semite guard who hated me, and it looks like I'm going to cry.

The other one was from just a few months ago, when Derek and I visited the murder house, the selfie he took with both of us smiling.

"Returns to the Scene of the Crime" read the type in the upper corner above the headline. "Relives the Bloody Night in 1969... Works for Liberal Do-Gooders...Lives in Secret After 40 Years... Still Loves His Killer, 'Juliet.'"

It took me a moment to comprehend what was on the screen: how did Drudge get all this stuff? So I clicked on the big headline, and it brought up an article in *The Dartmouth*, the college news-paper, or rather the *website* of the newspaper—but there it was on the front page in the corner, with the headline "Old Murders Never Fade Away" and that picture of Derek and me.

And the byline was by Derek Ellison. *My* Derek. And the ar-ticle was super-long, all about how he befriended this "legendary criminal" during his internship, dredging up the whole case in all its shameful details: the whole Ivy League Killer thing. The Romeo and Juliet–Leopold and Loeb–Bonnie and Clyde circus of it all. I could barely read it as my brain started to burn with rage. How could Derek betray me?

I scrolled down to see that picture of The Girl, the one they always used, the one that made her look especially perfect, like Natalie Wood but with longer hair.

I went back to the top and started to read again. It was horri-ble. Everything about me: all the terrible things about my past— the murders, the escape with the bodies, the car crash when the cops were pursuing us. (Why I let her drive, I'll never know.) And *all* about me now, with pictures! And where I lived—and saying that I worked for Clemency. All my efforts to live an anonymous, private life, all my hopes to be "normal" again were suddenly blown to hell, in one shot.

And blown to hell by a kid I thought was my friend!

It hit me: what a sucker I was. How vain and silly an old man am I, to think that Derek would have anything but an ulterior motive for hanging out with me—and driving me all around Long Island that day. Why would a kid like that waste his Saturday on some old jailbird if not for some devious, selfish purpose? And what a sneaky bastard he was! How he let me talk, encouraging me with his smile and that fancy beer. I kept scanning the article—it was so damn long—and there were whole chunks of things I said. About my prison life. About Clemency. About The Girl and me.

I tried to keep reading, but the words kept smearing in my mind. I flashed back to all the time driving around the Island. Of course I had to open my big mouth, showing off for the kid. Showing him that I was just as smart as he was, just as quick, no matter what my life had been, what my background was. And *twice* the man. How stupid and arrogant of me.

And the little prick didn't mention anything about Mantell disappearing with my father's legacy until almost the very end of the article—the one thing he could have written about that might have actually *helped* me if he'd put it at the top of the story; instead, it was buried. There was almost nothing to make me sympathetic.

Just then, Kelly came into my cubicle, looking concerned. She hadn't even taken off her coat.

"I saw it at home and came straight in," she said. "I'm so sorry, Larry. I tried to call you, but your phone went straight to voicemail."

"Did you know about this?" I said.

"About what?"

"About Derek," I said. "That he was writing this about me."

"No!" she said. "Of course not."

"Just look at this...*disaster*." I sighed, scrolling down page after page of Derek's article. It was all there, even pictures of the two dead people. I hadn't seen them in such a long time. I knew every inch of their faces from memory, but to see them again *visually*, not just in my mind—and online, where millions of people could also see them—was too awful to comprehend.

Kelly kept talking as I continued through to the rest of Derek's article. I couldn't believe the research he must have done to dig all this up. He must have been working on it the whole time he was here at Clemency, worming his way into my confidence, learning things about me. I admit it: I was totally dumbfounded. Bewildered. Numb.

"What in hell am I going to do?" I said out loud.

"We'll talk to Linda," said Kelly.

It took me a moment to focus and realize that she was referring to Linda Pirroux, Clemency's head of social media. Maybe she *would* know what to do.

"I'm going to call her," she continued. "But I don't think she's in yet. We'll take care of this, I promise," she said, trying to sound confident on my behalf. "Look, I've gotta go, but I'll see you later. OK? Larry? This will all be all right."

With a worried look on her face she couldn't conceal, she left my cubicle, shaking her head slightly. All I could think of was that I wanted to talk to Betsy. I picked up my phone and redialed her cell phone out of my recent history. I knew that she kept it off during school, but I still wanted to leave her a message.

"Hi, Bets'?" I said, keeping my voice low. "You wanna call me when you get a chance? Something's happened, and I need to talk to you about it. OK?" I realized I was sounding like there was something wrong—*and there was*. But I didn't want to upset her, not while she was at work. "Just call me, OK?...Bye."

I hung up the phone. Instantly I regretted leaving the message. Maybe I should have just texted her—that wouldn't have been as alarming as the message I left. But the thing is, I *was* alarmed.

I looked at the article again on my screen. All those pictures, all those terrible memories—now brought back from the past for millions of people *today*. I had thought that all those years in prison had knocked all the feeling, all the shame out of me, but I was wrong.

"Hmmm," murmured Linda as she sat sideways, reading from her huge, slim computer screen behind her big, wide desk, "he writes fairly well."

"Oh, please don't say that," I groaned. Kelly put her hand on my shoulder to restrain me.

"It's not about his writing," said Kelly. "It's what he wrote. The way he violated Larry's right to privacy."

"Well..." muttered Linda as she continued reading for a few more moments, "it looks like he certainly did *that*."

Linda turned to face me. She was very pretty, very blond, and had a pleasant smile that almost distracted me from her words.

"Don't you think that Derek wrote this to embarrass not just me but Clemency too?" I asked. "Isn't his father on the board or something?"

Linda said, "I don't know why he wrote it, Larry, but that isn't the point now. The point is how can I help you?"

"Help me?" I echoed.

"I'm not sure what you want me to do," she said. "Do you want to talk to the media?"

"Of course not!" I said, almost rising from the chair.

"Well, the problem is," she said leaning forward, "this"—she tilted her head toward the article on the computer screen—"is already out there. It looks like it's been picked up rather widely. People are still very interested in the Sixties. Looks like he's already gotten-" Again she turned to the computer and hit some keys. "One hundred and sixty-thousand hits, and it's still early in the day."

"Oh, shit," I mumbled. I instantly regretted swearing, but it just came out.

"Once these things go viral," she said, "they're impossible to control."

"*Viral*," I repeated the horrible word.

"Well," said Linda, "we have some options. We can put out a statement."

"Saying what?" asked Kelly.

Linda offered, "Saying that Larry has paid his debt to society and that he's a valuable, trusted worker here at Clemency. And that events in his past have no relevance to how he is today."

Kelly countered, "But what about everything Derek says about Larry?"

"Let's all read it over," said Linda calmly, "and see if there are any defamatory comments."

"It's *all* defamatory!" I said, gripping the chair arms so tightly that I practically rose out of my chair. Again, Kelly put her hand on my shoulder.

"That's a very good idea, Linda," Kelly cut me off. "We'll reread it and see whether there is anything actionable in it."

"Actionable?" Linda repeated doubtfully. "That's going to be a stretch."

"Why?" I asked.

"Because," said Linda sitting back in her high, deep leather chair, "we here at Clemency believe in the First Amendment."

Right then, I saw that I was in deep, deep trouble.

"You said we had options," I appealed to her. "What else can we do?"

Her face brightened. "Would *you* like to make a statement? Do a press conference where you could deny everything?"

"A press conference?" I panicked. "You mean get in front of a bunch of people who could ask me about anything and everything?"

"You could answer Derek's article and—"

"Are you kidding?" I almost shouted. "All I want to do is disappear and live a normal life. The last thing I want to do is—!"

Kelly put a strong hand on my shoulder, cutting me off.

"Larry," she said. "I think what Linda means is we can respond to this in various ways."

"But *this*, I'm afraid"—Linda pointed at Derek's article—"has made your disappearing kind of impossible."

⌒

It was decided that I would reread the article and compile a full list of any discrepancies or problems I had with it, and we would see about releasing a statement.

But in the back of my mind, I suspected that sweet Linda Pirroux had already made up hers: she wasn't going to go out on any limb for me.

On the way back to my cubicle, I passed two people in the hallway going the other way, and I swear one of them—a young girl I knew who was carrying some folders—looked at me darkly and held her folders extra tight as she passed me extra far away.

I forced myself to re-read Derek's article, to make a list of all the errors and misinterpretations he made. I got out a yellow legal pad, put it next to my keyboard, and got started. But as I dug into it, I realized it wasn't a question of errors of fact; it was his attitude. It was *the way* he described me, not the facts he stated.

My mind blurred as I remembered that whole day on the Island versus what was in the article. Did I really say those things? Is that how I talked about the murders, how I talked about jail, how I talked about getting out? Couldn't he tell that I was just being jokey and funny, showing off for a kid *who urged me to show off*?

What a sucker I was. (There was that word again. Herb the Hebe once called me that, and maybe he was right.) When I ran my mouth for that smart-ass *Times* reporter, showing I was just as smart—no, twice as smart—as his "paper of record" ass, it got me in trouble with that idiot warden. It brought more attention to my family, just when things were dying down, just when my Mom was really getting sick. And now the same thing was happening all over again.

I kept reading. He made me seem so callous, so flippant, so bloodless. Was that *me*? Unrepentant, twisted and, yes, still possibly dangerous? There was really no response to the article except to say, "He's totally wrong; I'm not like that at all."

And even worse, there was nothing about Mantell until the very end! I thought he hated lawyers. Maybe if he had mentioned my Mantell problem more prominently, someone who read the damn article could help find him! Instead, I got nothing.

There was only one positive thing in the whole article. Derek found out the quarry where we dumped the bodies had been closed. Apparently it had been poisoned by chemical runoff from local farms and had to be sealed and filled. In 1994, it was converted into the Shehawken Clean Water and Sewage Treatment Facility. That was one fact Derek got wrong. Chemical runoff didn't poison the Quarry: The Girl and I did.

I sent Betsy a text to call me as soon as she could. I wanted to make sure that I talked to her before she saw the article or someone told her about it. I wanted to explain things before she read it and formed an opinion. That was the most important thing: to make her understand that I was not the guy in the article.

The whole day was hell. It was obvious that everybody I saw had read the article or heard about it from someone. When I entered a room, groups of people would suddenly stop talking. Wherever I went, I was watched. I know it sounds paranoid, but when your face is all over the internet, when you are *hit* half a million times in the first day, you get the feeling that people in general are looking at you a little bit extra.

By late morning, Clemency was deluged with calls from the media about the famous killer who worked for them, right there in their White Plains office. Linda had to get involved with people from Washington—and from Geneva, which was the worst thing that could possibly happen.

Finally, by late afternoon, I had to stop myself from looking at how many places were picking up Derek's story, how the threads were multiplying, and the disgusting "Comments" that people were making on the Clemency website and everywhere else I looked. When do people have time to write such horrible things? Why do they even care? Don't they have anything else to do with their lives? And why are they so mean and deep-down hateful? I thought that only prison was cruel—but now I see it's happening all over America. People feel and say ugly things, and they're not one bit afraid to let them out into the open. When my trial was going on, there were only three TV networks, some local TV stations, some local newspapers, some radio stations—that was it. Now everything is free and instantaneous all over the world, all at once, in a zillion places.

I couldn't *believe* what was being dug up. Not just what Derek found—all kinds of other things were being posted about the trial, me and The Girl, her parents and my parents, and everything. After a while, I had to turn away, or I would have been sick all over again.

Clemency wound up releasing a completely innocuous statement late that afternoon, saying that, yes, I was employed by them as part of their Gateway Program, and yes, I had paid my debt to society, and that was it. Nothing like "We repudiate this scurrilous article written by a traitorous worm of an intern." It was a classic damning with faint praise. I felt like a complete schmuck. Double-crossed first by Derek and now by Clemency itself.

"That's it?" I asked Kelly. "I paid my debt to society? That's the best they could do? I'd be better off with a 'No comment!'"

"I'm very sorry, Larry," said Linda. "I didn't write this. This came straight from Washington. Which means it must have been cleared by Geneva."

The word "Geneva" hung like a black cloud in the room.

"Think about if you'd like to do some interviews," Linda suggested. "I'm sure we can find someone to tell your side of the story."

"Interviews?" I repeated, my heart sinking. "Oh, Jesus."

⌒

Before I went home, I found a Clemency baseball hat in the back storage room that must have been from some company picnic. It had the Clemency logo—a *C* with wings—with crossed baseball bats on either side of the brim. Before I went out into the street, I put on the cap and pulled it down over my brow. I kept my eyes low all the way to the bus stop and made it home without anyone noticing that I was anyone but some weird, old guy lost in his paperback—and *not* the monster who was all over the internet that day.

Betsy had texted me—*call u soon*—but I guess she hadn't yet. It was a Monday, her busiest day, when she supervised the after-school activities for a group of underprivileged, "at risk" girls, so there was no reason she should have responded to my texts. This was the good/bad side of this instantaneous world: instant communication with someone you want to/need to reach, and constant anxiety when you can't.

As soon as I got in my front door, I dropped everything and phoned Betsy. The call went straight to her sweet, perky message.

I just said, "I'm home. Call me. Please," and ended the call.

Then I texted her—*I'm home*—under the two other ones I had sent her.

I should have stopped and gotten some Tums or Rolaids or Pepto Bismol. Instead, I went to my little desk and turned on my laptop. Just to see what, if anything, was new there.

What a mistake! Derek's article was *everywhere*. I started clicking from site to site, reading everything, and I wound up re-living the whole damn thing—the Incident—all over again. God, I loved that beautiful, stupid girl. No, *I* was the stupid one—she was just...troubled.

The doorbell buzzed, jarring me back into this century.

When I opened the door, Betsy was standing there.

"Oh, you poor baby!" she said.

She reached out and took me in her arms. She just held me, and I held her.

"I'm so sorry," she said, close in my embrace. "My phone broke. It just quit! So I had to go to the computer store right after school and deal with it, and it was so hard to find, and the line was forever and it was so expensive. I'm so sorry. I wanted to call you so badly!"

"So you saw everything?" I asked.

She pulled back from me and said ruefully, "I saw a lot."

I held her by her shoulders, looked her right in the eyes, and pleaded, "I'm not the person in that article."

"I know that!" she said.

"You have to believe it!"

"I do, Larry," she said ardently, taking an extra moment. "I do."

I held her to me again, thinking how those words were like a wedding vow. I wondered if she noticed too.

"It'll never go away, will it?" I asked her, but it was a statement, not a question.

She looked hopeful. I tried to be hopeful. Why am I suspicious of Hope?

"Oh!" She suddenly smiled a little and reached into the pocket of her jacket. She pulled out a bright pink box.

"I brought you some Pepto Bismol," she said, putting it into my hand. "I knew we were low and, after today, you might need some."

"What are you?" I asked, cracking a smile, "a mind reader?"

"No," she replied simply, "I'm a *stomach* reader."

⌒

She spent the rest of the night trying to calm me down in other ways—talking sense sometimes or trying to distract me with stories about school, news, or the latest plot turn of this month's book club selection. But my mind kept circling back to Derek's article.

"And it's only the first day," I railed, getting up from the couch and beyond Betsy's touch, to pace the floor. "All I want to do is put the past behind me and start fresh. Everybody says don't bring prison with you out into the real world. So how am I supposed to do that when, suddenly, in my face and everyone's face, is *me*, committing this crime in 1969—and laughing about it *now*? So I'm screwed both ways? In the past *and* the present?"

Betsy let me get it all out of my system, or at least try. I thought about calling Derek and confronting him. I had controlled my Prison Mind all day, but it was starting to emerge, and I realized I was starting to make Betsy uneasy, so I stopped talking.

"You'll see," she said. "I promise you. In a few days, this will all die down."

"Maybe." I sighed. "Everything is temporary."

"Exactly!" she agreed. "There'll be something else on the internet, another old scandal, or some new scandal, and people's attention will switch to something else."

"And that's my best hope?" I said. "Trusting in the stupidity of the American people?"

She came over and tried to kiss me, but I didn't feel much like responding.

"No," I said, shaking my head. "It'll never be over. Not until I'm dead and gone."

I took a step away from her. "You'll see: it'll get worse. It's funny, I had more respect in prison than I do out here."

"What are you talking about?" Betsy touched my arm. "You're not in prison anymore."

"That's OK," I mumbled, not wanting to explain things to her. "It's all right." I smiled. "I'll be fine. Really."

I could tell she didn't believe me, and, in truth, neither did I. Maybe I didn't deserve to be happy, for what I had done all those years ago.

It was as low as I felt since I got out.

And, I had no idea how much worse it was going to get.

ELEVEN

Of course, I was right: things got worse, and fast. The very next morning on the bus, I got a strange, delayed "Hello" from Jaynelle, and the Archbishop Stepinac kids I used to exchange smiles and nods with all the time were out of their headphones for a change, whispering among themselves and looking at me. I think one of them took a picture of me as I got off.

Even on the bland, impersonal streets of downtown White Plains, I felt that I stood out. I walked the few short blocks from my bus stop to the office with my head down, under my Clemency hat brim, not meeting anyone's gaze. Still I thought that one passing guy recognized me, and I don't think it was just my imagination.

I tried to be casual, even invisible, walking into Clemency—just another day, nothing special. But even though I showed my pass clearly before I swiped it on the reader and smiled my way through the metal detector, I could swear Big Jose, the security guy, another "friend" of mine, moved his hand a little closer to the gun on his hip as I passed through.

One of the first things I did every day was deliver any large packages that didn't fit in people's mail slots. Whereas people used to say hi as I pushed around my cart full of packages or we'd exchange a few words about the Yankees/Mets/Knicks/Giants/Rangers or their kids, today no one wanted to talk to me. And I understood why: there was nothing to say. But not even a single smile of sympathy? Not even *eye contact?*

I tried to stay all day in my cubicle. I asked Rosemary, "Do you have anything especially stupid and mind-numbing that you need doing?"

"How do you feel about straightening up some file cabinets?" she replied sympathetically.

"Nothing could please me more." I sighed.

That filled up most of the morning, but still, you know me: I couldn't leave bad enough alone. I had to check my email. I had resolved to stay away from any websites that would have more comments about the Derek article, but maybe there was a work-related email I had to be aware of. Besides, there could have been something from Betsy.

But when I started my computer and checked my email, I saw—in the midst of all the regular stuff—an email with the subject "hello?" all in lowercase. The address was dEllison@dartmouth.edu.

Instantly I knew who it was. My first thought was admittedly half impressed: "What nerve this kid has!" I debated a moment, deciding whether to open it or not. I even moved my mouse over to the delete button and was just about to click it—*this pissant doesn't deserve my attention!*—when I held back. Yes, he didn't deserve my attention, yet I couldn't control my curiosity. I still wanted to see what he wrote. How would he try to bullshit me, to justify his actions? What could he possibly say?

I opened the email. (Later I printed out a copy, so here is what it said, verbatim.)

> By now, I'm sure you've read our article. What do you think, Larry? I can't believe how many places picked it up! You're famous again, and now ME TOO!! Isn't the digital world fucking amazing?
>
> I was going to run it past you before I submitted it to my editor, but I thought you might want to cut some things, and I couldn't have that. As you can see, I left out a lot of things—things you said about people at Clemency, etc. You can't imagine how hard I worked on it. You're a great subject and an amazing person.

Thank you for your cooperation. I hope there are
no hard feelings.

I'd love for my father to meet you.

Your friend and disciple,
Derek

And that was it.

I got up from my chair and paced around my little cubicle. *Disciple, my ass!* I almost kicked the wastebasket, but I stopped myself. Then I sat down and read it again. The second time, I could see through his crap like he was *shitting glass*! What, a few compliments to the old man, and he thinks he can get away with this?

No hard feelings? An honor to know me? I'm surprised he didn't invite me up to Dartmouth for a kegger. And what was that bullshit about meeting his father? Did he ever press his father about getting on Ed Nyquist about Mantell? Smart-ass punk! Thinking he could flatter his way out of this.

My initial impulse was to forward the email to Kelly, Linda Pirroux, *and* Ed Nyquist *and* Blackburn, and Rosemary, and everybody else I could think of. Let everyone see what a sleazy, sneaky little bastard he was!

But I hesitated. The email didn't exactly make *me* look good either. What was that stuff about "things I said" about people at Clemency? It was just gossip and banter. Still, it didn't sound good. I had a couple of beers in me; who knows what I said exactly? Maybe I shouldn't show the email to anybody, at least not until I had to. I would ask Betsy.

The only comfort I got that morning was from two texts from her: "*Hang in there, honey*" and "*How about Chinese from Loy's tonight? Mu shu me?*" You see what a kind person she was.

But it only helped a little. For the rest of the day, wherever I went, I felt looked at, whispered about, and disapproved of. It wasn't that people were actively hostile to me, but I could tell that things had turned for me—turned as sure as the seasons turned. I was on my way to becoming a pariah at Clemency. Even among these polite, liberal do-gooders. It was probably destined to hap-

pen, wherever I went. I just didn't expect it here... and so soon...
and this way. And for it to hurt quite so much.

At a quarter to five, my phone rang. (I use the old-fashioned
phone ringer sound, like a lot of old people do.) It was Betsy.

"Hi," she said. "You ready to be picked up?"

"I'll give you zero guesses," I said gratefully.

"Meet you in the back," she said. "But I'll be a while if there's
traffic on the Hutch."

"There's *always* traffic on the Hutch," I concurred.

At least I had Betsy.

I slunk out of the office without saying goodbye to anybody.
Despite myself, I was behaving like a guilty person. But I didn't
know what else to do.

⌒

We got back to Betsy's by way of a good, inexpensive take-out
Chinese place we found off Pelham Parkway—the special treat
that Betsy insisted on. I had us eat dinner and clean up before I
showed her Derek's email.

"OK," she said, when I had her sit down on her little blue
living room couch, "what's the big surprise?"

I showed her the printout and asked, "What do you think I
should do with this?"

"Wait," she said, "let me get my glasses."

I didn't say anything.

When she came back and started reading, I watched her
closely as she read it; she stayed completely stone-faced.

"So what do you think I should I do?" I asked.

She looked up and countered, "What do *you* want to do?"

"That's what I'm asking you," I said, focusing on her bright,
wise eyes.

I watched her think. She looked down, then up, trying to give
me the right answer.

She spoke carefully: "I'd say ignore it."

"Ignore it?"

"Yes," she said, offering the letter back to me. "Don't make a
thing bigger than it already is. Ignore it; it'll go away. You're still
on parole and—"

"I know I'm on parole," I said, taking the paper from her and refolding it. "You don't have to tell me that."

"But if you don't like this boy, this Derek," she said, "why continue any involvement with him? Wouldn't that be just what he wants?"

"So what do you want me to do? Nothing?" I asked.

She paused for one patient moment. "I want you to think about what's good for *you*."

"What's good for me?" I said, folding the paper and putting it deep into my back pocket. "What's good for me is if people didn't think of me as this famous killer!"

She leaned forward, cocked her head, and said simply, "Then don't act that way."

That shut me up. I closed my eyes and tried to think clearly, tried to remember all those "techniques" from the one million therapy classes I attended in prison in order to earn easier time. How to "ride the wave" and "adjust expectations" and even "count slowly to ten." Of course, like it or not, I *am* a known person. I am branded by my past, and I have to accept the fact that some people will always see me that way. There is no way to un-murder two people.

Betsy stepped around the coffee table, put her arms around me, and held me close. She didn't have to say anything else.

Sometimes Betsy drove me back to Yonkers, but mostly I stayed over in City Island, even if the next day was a workday. The next morning, she would drive me super early to the No. 60 bus that ran to White Plains from Pelham Manor. It was a hassle but totally worth it. Sometimes I just had to stay the night. I can't—and won't—tell you how patient Betsy has been with me when it comes to physical matters. When you've been in prison for almost forty years with no normal human contact, some things aren't so easy.

But you can bet I stayed over that night after the kind of day I had. If I'd gone home, all I would have done is turn over and over in my mind Derek's treachery and his stupid letter. Which is what I was sort of doing at Betsy's, only she could bring me out of it every fifteen minutes or so and get me back on the ground, into a calmer state of mind.

We were in bed asleep—well, Betsy was asleep; I was trying—when my cell phone rang on the end table. *Who could be calling me at this time of night?* I looked at the screen and saw a phone number with a 603 area code I didn't recognize. I pressed answer and said a cautious, "Hello?"

"You didn't answer my email, Larry," a soft voice said. "I thought your generation believed in good manners."

It was Derek. And he sounded like he'd been drinking.

"You got a lotta nerve calling me," I whispered, "you sneaky little pissant."

"Pissant?" he chirped. "That's a good one! Hey, wait a second. Let me write that down."

I pulled on my robe and tiptoed out of the bedroom so I wouldn't wake Betsy.

"You didn't seem to have any trouble remembering stuff I said before," I shot back as I closed the bedroom door behind me.

"What," he said, "don't tell me you didn't like the article."

"No, I didn't like the article." I raised my voice just a little, walking into the living room. "Are you out of your fucking mind? Why the hell would I want all this shit about my life dredged up now and splashed all over the internet? You know I'm trying to live a quiet, anonymous life."

"Now I didn't write the headline," he said. "That was my editor."

"It wasn't the title!" I spat back, visualizing the "My BFF, the Ivy League Killer" blazed across every computer screen in creation. "It was the whole fucking thing."

"I don't know," he said. "I thought it kind of...*ennobled* you."

"*Ennobled* me?" I countered. "Are you kidding? It ennobled *you*!" I switched to a lispy, little kid's voice. "Oh, look who *I'm* friends with: the scary, terrible, dangerous criminal. How brave and benevolent and condescending I am!...You patronizing piece of shit."

"Wow," he muttered. "I'm really surprised at your reaction, Lar'—"

"Then you're younger, stupider, and more naïve than I thought you were. And as long as you were writing so fucking much, why the hell didn't you talk more about Lester Mantell and how he stole from me? Maybe someone would have read it and had some lead on finding him? You could have done some *good* for me, but you buried it at the end!"

"Wow," he mumbled. "I probably should have...I didn't think of that."

"'I didn't think of that!'" I mocked his stupid answer. "Thanks a whole fucking lot, Derek."

"You know," he said, "I think you're looking at this the wrong way, Larry. This, man, is an *opportunity*. You should run with this. This is, like, new music. You should think about looking for an agent and trying to get a reality show out of this. 'The Ivy League Killer Comes Back. Stranger in a strange land: famous killer tries to straighten out his life.' How's that for a log line? It's a natural."

"You're *drunk*," I shot him down. "A *reality show*? You are one sick fuck."

"People love stories about death," he slurred. "It makes them feel alive."

"You poor, pathetic child," I pronounced.

"Come on, Larry, don't hate me. It was a good article! A good read! I tried to make you like a real character. Let's be frien—"

I ended the call with a press of my thumb. Then I powered down the phone so I wouldn't hear it if he called me back—if he was that stupid. I put the phone down on the coffee table, and Betsy was standing there with her robe pulled around her.

"Would you believe—?" I said. "It was Derek Ellison."

"What did he want?"

I laughed bitterly. "He wants to be friends."

Betsy just shook her head.

"He'd been drinking," I continued. "I mean, *Dartmouth*!... Some things don't change. Still a bunch of bully boys freezing their asses in the woods with nothing to do."

"Come back to bed, Larry. It's late."

"He told me I should try to get a reality TV show. Can you believe that?"

She shook her head again. "Whatever happened to people's values?"

"I think they were sold on e-Bay," I said.

⌢

I was up most of the night, tossing and turning so much I finally moved into the living room so I wouldn't disturb Betsy. But I must have slept sometime because when she shook me gently at six fifteen, I awoke from a fog of Derek dreams and prison nightmares.

"Act like it never happened," Betsy advised just as she dropped me off at the bus stop in the early morning chill. "Pretend it's just another day."

Well, I could pretend all I wanted, but from the first moment I walked in the building and got that cold "cop" look again from Big Jose to the sudden silence whenever I walked into the kitchen, I could tell it would never be "just another day" for me at Clemency. I could see it in people's eyes.

Then I got a call from Fusco, who raked me over the coals.

"All this shit about you makes *me* look bad, Ingber," he said.

"How do you think *I* feel?" I shot back.

"I don't give a flying fuck how you feel!" he barked. "You still owe me time. And I have a call into this woman, your boss, this Miss...uh...uh"—the schmuck had lost his place—"Mott. And I'll see what *she* says about what the hell's going on over there."

As soon as Fusco and I hung up, I hightailed it over to Kelly's office, telling her to expect a call from Fusco and what she should say to him.

"Don't worry, Larry," said Kelly in a soothing voice. "I've talked to Ken Fusco before. I think I can handle him."

"This is just the last thing I need," I said, pacing back and forth in front of her desk. "Fusco up my back."

"And there's one more thing," Kelly said.

I stopped pacing. "What?"

"Blackburn's office got a couple of calls," she started slowly. "Parents of some of the interns."

"The *interns*. You mean like Derek?"

"These are powerful people, Larry," Kelly whispered, sitting forward in her chair. "Not just anybody gets an internship here. You have to have some pull. You met Derek. His father is an *enormous* fundraiser for Clemency. He's a very influential man."

"Is he the one who complained?" I asked. "Derek's father?"

"And," Kelly continued, shaking her head slightly, "a couple of people said something to Human Resources. Colquitt got involved."

"Then I'll go talk to Colquitt. He knows me. Everyone here knows me. Or am I suddenly a stranger?"

Kelly had no answer for me.

I hammered on. "I thought that Clemency believed in...clemency. Forgiveness. Paying your debt to society. All that pious liberal crap that everyone seems to spout around here continuously."

"Can you just try to take it easy, just for now, Larry, please?" she said. "And let's hope this blows over."

"Hope?" I repeated.

"People are funny," she said with an anxious look on her face. "With what they actually care about."

I liked Kelly, but I wondered how much she would back me up here at Clemency, if some people really wanted to push me out. I could see that she was genuinely worried, and I didn't want to press her too hard. At least, not yet.

"Thanks, Kelly," I said, "for listening."

I made a move to leave her office.

"Uh, Larry?"

I stopped at the doorway and turned around.

"So how is my aunt?"

Very deliberately I answered, "Your aunt is fine."

Her face registered no emotion—either way—at my statement.

So I just left her office and walked down the hallway back to my cubicle, double-stunned. Was *Kelly* now against me? How could that be? What had changed? What had I done? I hadn't done anything different since yesterday. I was the same person. Why was everyone in the world's attitude toward me now different?

That article! That fucking article. Everything was going so well, and Derek ruined it. He fucking ruined it.

But the writing was on the wall: I could see that I was becoming an embarrassment to them. I wasn't a freed "political prisoner" like Jennifer Latheef in the Maldives, the trade union leaders in Honduras, the poet monks from Nepal, or the female health counselors from Uganda—all of them major global heroes, all of them freed by Clemency. I was just me.

So I did something pretty desperate. I went to Linda Pirroux and said, "What if I agreed to give an interview?"

TWELVE

"I think you've made a good decision," said Linda, with a bright smile and new energy. "Let me think who I can call."

I stood in front of her desk and emphasized, "But you've got to tell whoever's going to interview me that they have to ask me about my missing lawyer, Lester Mantell."

Linda was already scrolling down a list of names on her computer.

"Sure, Larry," she said absently. "But I find that it's best not to make preconditions on these things. Let me make a few calls and see what I can get for you."

She was completely absorbed in what was on the screen.

"OK," I said, uncertain of what I had committed to.

I'd talked it over with Betsy the night before.

"Are you sure you want to do this?" she asked.

"No," I answered honestly. "But maybe I can undo some of the damage that stupid article did. And it's my chance to get out the word about Mantell. Maybe someone will see me on TV who knows where Mantell is. Everything else is at a complete dead end."

I waited nervously for a couple of days for Linda to tell me something about an interview. Meanwhile, I tried to keep my head down at the office. I just did my job and tried to look harmless and friendly, which is what I am. If people's perceptions of me were all off because of that article, maybe an interview could help me, once and for all, set the record straight about who I really am.

"Channel 11?"

"I think it's a good place," said Linda. "It's been a couple of weeks since that article broke and some of the heat has died down...and I know Miranda Jakes, the reporter, from the Women's Media Caucus."

"OK," I said cautiously, "I'll give it a shot."

Channel 11 was one of the smaller, local stations in New York. So maybe a lot of people wouldn't see me. Is that what I wanted? I didn't know what I wanted, other than to get out some message about Mantell. Maybe someone watching would know something about Mantell's whereabouts, so it was worth the risk.

Linda prepared me for the interview. I sat across from her in her office with Kelly in the corner, watching.

"Just relax," said Linda. "That's the main thing. And don't worry about making a mistake. Everything is edited anyway."

She asked me a few sample questions—about how it felt getting out, how I liked working at Clemency—easy ones that I didn't stumble over too badly.

"Don't make any jokes," she said. "People might not like to see someone with your"—she paused—"background, making jokes."

I wanted to say, "Linda, if I couldn't make jokes, I couldn't survive my life."

Instead, I looked over to Kelly, who said, "I think she's right."

"I don't think Miranda is trying to play gotcha," said Linda. "I think she just wants to do a nice human-interest story on you."

"Good," I said. "That's just what I need. Human interest."

Human interest in finding Lester Mantell.

⌢

The night before, Betsy tried to keep me calm using several methods: tea, jokes, a couple of hands of gin rummy.

"I know you're nervous," she said. "Who wouldn't be?"

She suggested that I take a bath.

"Hydrotherapy?" I replied. "Like in the looney bin."

"Yes," she said with a smirk. "Exactly like that."

I hadn't taken a bath—I mean, *lying down* in a tub—in I-don't-know how many years. My studio apartment had a little shower, which was more than enough for me. But this lying down in warm, tranquilizing water was a new thing for me.

"Take your time," said Betsy, closing the door as she left. "And use those bath salts if you want."

She left me there to soak and think. It was such a "girl's" bathroom, with pink soaps and flowers on the towels, but I didn't mind. I could stretch out my old muscles still hanging on these old bones and try to relax.

How could I relax? Going on TV and exposing myself to *more* public scrutiny? Was that the right thing to do? I didn't want to say the wrong thing and embarrass myself. What exactly was I opening myself up for? The uncertainty was as bad the thing itself. But with Mantell still out there, with *my* money, *my* legacy, it would all be worth it. I thought about what I'd say about him. I didn't want to sound like an ex-con just grubbing for money. I had to strike the right tone...in everything I said. I can't deny that I was nervous about the whole thing, but it was worth the try. And when I got my money, I'd buy Betsy all new towels. Or so I remember thinking in that bath tub, trying to relax away the tension that never *ever* seemed to go away.

⌒

The day before the interview, I tried on some ties, which I borrowed from Roland.

"Why do you want a tie?" he scowled.

"Don't ask," I said, looking through the rack of ancient ties in his musty bedroom closet.

"Take whatever you want," he said. "I haven't worn one in years."

"Well," I said, picking out a quiet, maroon-and-blue stripe, "I guess this one is as good as any."

"Perfect for a hanging," Roland said with a cackle, and I couldn't disagree with him.

⌒

The Channel 11 people set up their gear in the big conference room at Clemency while I got ready in Linda's office, with Kelly standing by for support.

"Do you have a comb?" Linda asked Kelly as she looked me over. I sat nervously in the chair across from her desk.

"I don't have that much hair," I said.

Nonetheless, she ran Kelly's comb through what's left of my hair and fluffed it up a bit. I felt like a little boy being readied for my class picture.

When Linda finished, Kelly said, "You look beautiful."

That made me laugh. I needed a laugh right then. I just kept telling myself, *Relax...be yourself...and be sure to mention Mantell.*

As they walked me down the hall, Linda said, "I think you'll like Miranda. She's here to get your story and get home."

"Fine with me," I said, thinking about what my "story" was, and how I wanted to undo the damage that Derek had done.

Just before we walked into the conference room, Kelly pulled me back and said, "Pretend you're at my house, and it's Thanksgiving and you're talking to Betsy. Be *that* Larry."

She gave me a big, encouraging smile and a little hug, but what she said troubled me. Wasn't I the same "Larry" all the time? Who was I supposed to be? Nonetheless I walked into the conference room, a tight smile pasted on my face. No matter what was ahead of me, I wanted to seem confident, even if I felt the exact opposite.

There were quite a few people at the far end of the room, beyond the long conference table: most of Linda's staff and their assistants, a tall woman with long blond hair, and a man with a camera and video equipment. When I entered the room, they all turned and looked at me.

I whispered to Linda, "Do they all have to watch?"

She whispered back, "Lots and lots of people are going to be watching on TV. What do a few more matter?"

Lots and lots? Was I about to make a big mistake?

"We have arrived," Linda announced, leading me into the room and straight to Miranda Jakes, who was waiting for me with a big smile, one hand holding a clipboard and the other extended toward me.

"Mr. Ingber," she said in a most welcoming manner. She was tall, pretty, fluffy, and blond and knew how to focus her considerable charm. I admit, her smile made me feel instantly better.

"Larry," said Linda, "this is Miranda Jakes. I've been so looking forward to getting you two together."

"Me too," I said, rather mindlessly, focusing on sparkly eyes and very long, must-be-fake eyelashes. "Nice to meet you, Ms. Jakes."

"Nice to meet, you, too," said Miranda, looking down at me. She towered over me in her high heels and long legs.

I had looked her up the night before: she had been a sideline reporter for ESPN before joining Channel 11 and went to Florida International University. After all these years, I was still a snob about where people went to college. OK, maybe not a first-class brain, but she seemed nice so far, and she was the one with the microphone.

"This is Mark." Miranda pointed to a bear of a man standing near us holding a camera and some other equipment. "He'll do our sound and picture and whatever else is necessary."

Mark laughed once, heaving his big belly, and grunted, "Don't you wish!" Evidently that was some private joke between them.

"So let's get set up," Miranda said brightly, "and we'll just talk and see what happens."

"Great," said Linda. "Where do you want him?" Him, being me.

"Over here," said Miranda, pointing to one of the two chairs by the window. "What do you think, Mark?"

"That should be good," said the big man, hoisting the camera onto his shoulder and looking through the viewer. "Yeah."

"How about it?" Linda asked me, waiting for me to obey.

"OK," I said enthusiastically and moved over. It felt like I was taking a chair at the dentist's.

Kelly came over to me, straightened my tie, and said a firm "There!" She gave me an encouraging smile and whispered, "Good luck."

The way she said it made me feel like I really did need some luck—serious luck—right at that moment.

Mark approached me, leaned over, and clipped something—a little microphone—onto my jacket lapel.

"Just talk normally," he said.

"I'll try" was my very truthful answer.

Miranda sat in the chair across from me as Mark adjusted the blinds until the light in the room was bright but soft.

"Don't be nervous," said Miranda to me with kind eyes. I think she could see how tense I was.

"I'm not," I lied, trying to concentrate on why I was there. "As long as I can talk about my lawyer."

Miranda smiled and joked, "No matter what, everyone hates their lawyer," with a little laugh. And they did. I saw that I was going to have to push that line of talk if I wanted her to take me seriously.

"Let's get a level here," Miranda said. "I'll do my introduction later, so let's just start talking now, and we can cut in the rest."

"Sounds good to me," I said.

She looked so prepared and fresh-faced. I could see her get ready for the camera, as if coming fully and brightly to life. I realized that I should try to do the same thing, only I didn't know exactly how.

"Well, Larry," she started suddenly, "it's nice to talk to you. You're quite a mystery man."

"No, I'm not," I said by reflex. "Everybody knows about me."

"How is that?" she asked straight back.

"Or they think they know about me, know what I *did*," I qualified my answer. "But I can't help what other people think. All I can do is take care of myself and try to be a good, solid, law-abiding citizen. People can remember back to the Sixties, when I was a teenager, but I'm different now."

"Different? How?"

"Well..." I said. "In almost every way."

Miranda leaned in. "There was that article about you that appeared widely in the media a few weeks ago—"

"Totally bogus!" I snapped.

"What do you mean, 'bogus?'" she asked, her eyes narrowing.

"I mean, *bogus*!" I almost stuttered. "Everything in that article was wrong about me."

"Such as?"

I almost laughed. "Where do I start?"

I looked over at Linda and Kelly, and from their serious expressions I could tell I wasn't doing well. I was being too—what—defensive? Maybe I was, but that's because she was attacking me.

"Tell me, Larry," said Miranda in a lower, more serious voice, "how often do you think about what happened back in 1969, what happened to those two people?"

It was such a direct question that I had to pause and take a breath.

"Every day," I said simply. Sometimes the truth is complicated, but not this time.

"And we know that you went back there a few weeks ago," she said. "Do you often *visualize* the scene, even today?"

I drew back. "Do we have to relive that whole thing all over again?"

"You call it a *thing*?" she emphasized.

"No!" I responded. "I don't call it a 'thing.' I call it the tragedy of my life. And their lives. Everybody's life!"

My leg started to shake.

"Can we stop for a minute?" I asked.

"What do you say to victims' rights groups who say that you should still be in jail?" Miranda pressed on.

"I say to them"—I stalled, trying to think precisely—"they have their right to think what they want. I can't blame anyone for feeling the way they feel. As I said, I can't help what other people think. All I can do is take care of myself and try to behave with genuine contrition and remorse. I accept responsibility for what I did."

"But Larry, those people are still dead," Miranda continued. "And you're alive and free."

I didn't know what to say to that.

"Yes," I confessed. "I am alive and free. I guess I should be sorry for that."

Miranda stiffened. "That's entirely up to you, Larry."

"I don't know what you want me to say," I admitted. "I'm as sorry as I can be. That's what I'm trying to say. And because my lawyer—"

"Have you made restitution to the surviving family members?" she interrupted. "Have you even tried to contact them?"

"No," I said. Her question threw me off. "But I'm pretty sure those people don't want to hear from me."

"Those people?" Miranda's eyebrow raised sharply.

I wanted to say, "She was an only child, just like me," but I just said, "Any people."

I could tell from Miranda's clinical stare that things were not going well for me. I looked over to Linda.

"Think I can have a drink of water?" I asked.

Miranda's face relaxed suddenly. "Sure."

"Let's take a break," she said to Mark and got up from her chair.

Mark turned off the bright light that shone on me—a relief. It took my eyes a moment to readjust to the room light.

Kelly brought me a drink of water.

"Here, Larry," she whispered, giving the glass to me as if I were a sick child. "And just take it easy. You knew that these are the kinds of things she was going to ask you about."

"I know," I said, taking a drink. "But when you're actually talking, it's a different thing."

Miranda and Mark were talking by the window, looking over at me with unfriendly eyes.

I had to make her like me.

Miranda walked back over to me and chirped with a wide, insincere smile: "Let's try it again, Larry."

"Good idea," I said eagerly. "There are some things I really want to say."

"And I'll let you say everything," she said, sitting down and checking her microphone. "In time."

The lights went on, and she started asking questions again. I did my best, trying to be a nice, positive, rehabilitated person. She let me go on about Lester Mantell for quite a while, but she was looking down at the index cards in her lap while I was talking. I did say everything I wanted to say about him—maybe too much. I didn't want to sound like a money-grubbing ex-con, but I did specifically ask people to call Mike Rathbun at the Westchester DA's, and I gave his number and email. At least I made that pretty clear.

Then Miranda suggested we go outside and "get some air into the story," so we walked down Martine Avenue with Mark walking backward in front of us with his camera. As we shot, Miranda tried to talk to me casually, but I was distracted by all the pedestrians who cleared out of our way while looking at us. I think Miranda liked the attention. In fact, someone yelled, "Mirandaaaa!" from behind us.

She seemed nicer, out in the open, and I tried to sound friendlier in my responses, all the while conscious that she might try to catch me in some way. She got me to talk about what it was like, to be out of prison. I answered her cautiously, and I didn't mention anything about Betsy, of course.

"So, Larry," she asked, "would you say that at this point in your life you're *happy*?"

She made the word seem like bait in a trap. I hesitated.

"That's not a word I would use," I stammered.

Tall, blond Miranda stopped—I stopped with her—and loomed over me.

"Well, Larry," she said, "maybe happiness isn't the easiest thing to achieve, no matter where you are."

How was I supposed to respond to that?

"I don't know what you want me to say," I said.

"Say whatever you want, Larry, but I remember what an old police captain friend of mine once told me." She turned straight to the camera and said dramatically, "Old murders never die."

She let that hang in the air for a moment before she said, "And cut!"

Mark cut the lights, Miranda relaxed, and it was over. They immediately walked away from me, conversing privately. I was left there, stunned and silent.

Linda and Kelly came to me with anxious looks on their faces. I could tell that I didn't come off as I wanted to, but at least I got in my pitch about Mantell.

"Well," I said with a sigh, "I did my best."

"I know you did," said Kelly sympathetically.

"Things came out of my mouth before I knew what I was saying," I explained.

"It's OK," said Linda whispered. "All that matters really is how they edit it."

Then she bolted toward Miranda with a happy "That was wonderful!"

I watched the two pretty blondes talk chirpily, hoping that Linda had some pull with Miranda to make the interview make me look good. But I couldn't leave it to chance.

I walked straight back over to Miranda. "Excuse me, Miss Jakes?"

She turned around, and I plunged right in.

"I want to thank you for letting me talk," I said. "I mean, have my say."

"Well, thank you," she said, appearing surprised.

"I just hope you can get that bit in I said earlier," I added quickly, "about Lester Mantell. It'd mean a lot if someone who's watching you knows anything."

"Hmm." She drew back from me. "I'll certainly try to get it in."

"It'd mean the world to me!" I said, knowing that I was pushing her but unable to help myself. "So many people watch you."

Why not try flattery? I had fucked up the interview so much that I had to get some Mantell action from it or the whole thing would be a waste.

"So thanks in any case, Ms. Jakes. You too, Mark."

I reached out and shook the hand of the surprised camera guy, who shifted the camera off his shoulder to reciprocate.

"No problem, man," he said.

Why not make friends with everybody? Better late than never.

We went back inside the building.

The way that Kelly said "Well, that wasn't *so* bad" made me realize just how badly it went.

I spent the rest of the day thinking about all the things I should have said, replaying the interview to make me sound smarter, wiser, and more compassionate. Instead, I said what I said. Why is everything so much clearer in your rearview mirror?

When Betsy picked me up after work, she waited about a minute before asking me, "Well? How did it go?"

I sighed. "I really don't know."

"How can you *not* know?"

"It really depends how they cut it together," I said. "At least that's what Linda Pirroux says, and that makes a lot of sense."

"Did you say what you wanted to say?"

"I think so," I said. "It all went by so quickly."

"Did you mention Mantell?" she asked. "That's what you wanted to do."

"Yes," I said. "I did."

"So then you're glad you did it?"

"I'll tell you when I see it on TV," I answered.

⌐

The next day, I waited until the afternoon to talk to Linda (she was in meetings; lots of meetings at Clemency), to ask her when she thought the interview would air and if she got any feedback from Miranda.

"I really don't know," she said, rushing back to her computer for something that was more important than me. "Sorry, Larry. I have a little emergency here."

I could see that I was yesterday's problem, and she was on to something else.

She sat down at her desk and typed something furiously, muttering to herself. Having no choice and not intending to leave her office without answers, I waited for her to finish. Patiently.

Linda stopped typing and sighed. "Idiots!" she said and looked up at me, suddenly bright and attentive.

"Yes, Larry," she sparkled. "What can I do for you?"

Despite how nice she appeared, I could see that she didn't want to deal with me, that I just meant trouble to her.

"I was just wondering if you've heard from Miranda Jakes," I said. "About when my thing is going to be on the air."

"I'll give her a call," she said. "I don't know how much control she has over the schedule. But you should watch Channel 11. You can see how much they're promoting it."

Promoting. The word made me squirm.

"OK," I said. "That's a good idea."

"And I'll tell you if I hear anything from Miranda," she said and went back to looking at the papers on her desk.

She suddenly yelled to her assistant just outside Linda's office, "Where are the RSVP lists?"

A meek voice from outside piped up, "They're coming!"

I could see that Linda was pissed off and preoccupied. I had gotten my message across to her, but I wasn't going to forget to remind her, just in case she forgot.

I was hoping that word had traveled throughout Clemency about my interview, that I was very cooperative, and it would somehow start to clear the air. I would go back to being nice, old Larry, just as I was before the article. But that didn't happen. People looked at me with the same air of suspicion and distrust. Maybe after the Channel 11 story was broadcast, people would change their opinions. I really didn't know.

I didn't watch much TV once I got out of the joint. When I was inside, TV—when I had rare TV privileges—was a way to get "out." But now that I was really out, I could see that what was on TV was mostly junk. Especially the news, which tried mostly to inflame people about little things and ignore the big things. And these depressing "reality" shows are nothing like reality. They make people look even worse—pettier, more devious and mean-spirited—than they already are.

But I started watching Channel 11's news to see Miranda Jakes and to see how they were "promoting" the interview.

"I suppose you have to watch that," said Betsy as she served me my dinner—soup and a sandwich—in front of the television in the living room.

"I have to see what they're saying," I explained.

"You know what they're saying: everyone is either stupid or crooked."

"Everyone *is* stupid or crooked," I replied.

"You don't really believe that," she said. "Most people are nice enough, if given the chance. It's no picnic, this life. And some people are *very* nice."

I watched a little more of the story that was on, about some little boy in Brooklyn who was beaten to death while in foster care. "Sometimes I don't know what I believe anymore. If I ever did."

Betsy leaned over and kissed my cheek softly. "Don't let them get you down."

"I don't," I said, trying to convince myself as well as Betsy that everything was going to be OK. As long as they let me get my message out about Mantell, it would be worth it. At least, that's what I kept telling myself.

I didn't see anything the first couple of days of watching, but then the main news people at the desk started to talk about Miranda Jakes' exclusive interview with "Laurence Allan Ingber, the Ivy League Killer," as if that were my entire name in one word. I always hated that.

I didn't like hearing their excitement about having the "famous killer" on their show soon, and "be sure to watch for it, folks." I guess that was the name of the game, getting people to watch something sensational to raise the station's ratings, but it made me very nervous. I thought back on what I'd said and hadn't said. I guess they could cut up my words any way they wanted. At least, I mentioned Mantell. What can I say? I did my best.

When the actual day for the broadcast arrived, I felt nervous and exposed. By now, it had been several weeks since the Derek article appeared, and the furor had died down a little. People still looked at me warily, but I was still hoping that things might get better over time. And now here I was, putting myself back in the public spotlight just when it had almost faded away.

I walked around the halls of Clemency, doing my regular chores for Rosemary, stopping into the kitchen to make tea, etc. No one said anything to me about the upcoming Channel 11 piece, but I was sure they all knew about it and would be watching.

Kelly dropped by my cubicle late in the afternoon.

"Nervous?" she asked.

She didn't have to say anything else; we both knew what she was talking about.

"It is what it is," I said with a sigh. "Anyway, it's out of my hands."

She smiled warmly. "That's a good way to look at it."

I wanted to ask her "Is there any other way?"—but I didn't.

My levels of worry and anticipation had gone up and down erratically in the previous days, but what really concerned me was one exchange that Miranda had with Brad Something, the hearty anchorman. The day before it was going to be on, as they were hyping her "exclusive," Brad asked her, "Were you scared of him?"

What kind of a question was that?

Fortunately, Miranda said, "No, but"—flirting with the camera—"well, you'll see. Watch tomorrow and you'll see why he's one of the most interesting people I've ever interviewed."

Did she really mean that, or was that just bullshit hype? In any case, it had gone on for *days*, trying to build some kind of freak-show curiosity about me. What had I gotten myself into?

⌒

I usually stayed late at work, doing whatever last thing Rosemary wanted, trying to stay in her favor, texting to Betsy when she could pick me up. But that day, I left at the crack of five, met Betsy in the Jeep in the alley behind the building, and turned on the TV to Channel 11 the moment we got home.

The news had already started. Local TV stations in New York run a lot of news. A lot of crazy stuff happens in New York.

"They've been promising your interview all afternoon," said Betsy as she took off her coat. "I was watching."

"Well, that's good," I said. "I suppose."

I sat down in front of the TV and gave it my undivided attention. Along the bottom of the screen ran a moving headline: "Coming up—exclusive—the Ivy League Killer." Just seeing it gave me the shivers.

What was worse was seeing the pictures of me; I looked so *old*. Funny, you see yourself in the mirror every day, but that is your face in reverse. To see your face the way others see you is a strange thing.

Betsy brought me dinner as one of their promotions came on.

Putting down the tray in front of me, she said, "You look good in that picture."

I smiled. "You're sweet."

"I'm serious," she said. "Tell me if the soup is hot enough."

"Just sit down," I said. "I want you to watch this with me."

"I will," she said, sitting next to me, smoothing my back. "Don't worry."

They kept promising, teasing the audience about "Miranda's fabulous exclusive interview," meanwhile giving time to the cute sports girl and the peppy weather guy.

Betsy clucked. "They really know how to stretch these things out."

"It's all about the ratings, right?" I said. "That's what they care about."

Finally, after what seemed like a dozen false introductions and even more commercials, the anchorman introduced Miranda Jakes sitting next to him. She looked more blond and more beautiful than ever.

"Brad," she began breathlessly, swinging to face the camera, "I had the most amazing experience going face-to-face with one of the most notorious figures from the 1960s: Laurence Allan Ingber, the Ivy League Killer. I'm sure everyone remembers the story."

She started to re-tell the whole Incident all over again as the screen showed some of the most famous photographs from the trial. The beautiful pictures of The Girl, the horrible pictures of me in custody—I was *so young*—and the unwatchable pictures of the crime scene. Fortunately, they blocked out the details of the dead bodies with squares of computerized colors; some things are even too gruesome for television.

"I've interviewed a lot of people in my time, but no one quite like Mr. Ingber. One look into his eyes, and you can see that he's been to some very dark, secret places."

Then they flashed to a close-up of my face, in tight super-focus, to make my eyes look absolutely crazy. Completely mad.

"Well into his sixties, Larry Ingber is quite a presence," Miranda purred. "He still talks freely about the crime he committed so many years ago."

Then, more of me in the conference room talking to Miranda about the Incident. I remember that the light was in my eyes.

"I look *so old*," I said.

Betsy shushed me. "Listen."

Watching myself was an out-of-body experience. What was I doing on TV when I was sitting right there in Betsy's living room in City Island? I tried to listen carefully, but it was hard to believe she was talking about me. Did I really look—and sound—like that?

Miranda was so much prettier than me, and larger onscreen. She looked so stern and judgmental, and I looked so—I don't know how I looked. Watching myself, I felt helpless. I hated that feeling; it was almost like being in the joint again.

Now the screen showed Miranda and me walking down the street in White Plains with her voiceover saying, "Larry is out of prison now. But whether he feels free is another matter."

Next I was talking in the conference room.

"I can't help what other people think," I said. "All I can do is take care of myself."

"But, Larry," Miranda's big face cut in, "have you made restitution to the surviving family members? Have you even tried to contact them?"

"Wait a second," I said to Betsy, "she cut out some stuff I said—about remorse and contrition. And acceptance of responsibility!"

"Ssshhh!" Betsy hissed.

We watched more. Miranda looked so blond, bright, and beautiful, and I looked so old, shifty, and shadowed. She seemed concerned, wise, and, ultimately, disapproving.

"The outside world can seem like an unfriendly place to him these days," Miranda said darkly.

Me again: "People think they know me but they don't."

The picture switched to Miranda alone: "Larry Ingber is trying his best to make it in the outside world. But it's a hard road when you've been known all your life as the Ivy League Killer."

Me again: "People think they know me but they don't."

"When is she gonna get to the Mantell stuff?" I whispered.

"Sssssh," Betsy hushed me.

Her voice continued dramatically, talking about my "fears" and "isolation." I remembered saying the things they were showing, but the way they shot it made me look suspicious and unhealthy. I guess TV can make anyone look like anything; nothing is real anymore.

"One of the challenges that Larry faces these days," Miranda began.

"Oh," I said. "This is the Mantell part!"

"Besides the burdens of a lifetime of notoriety—"

Suddenly, the picture switched over to anchorman Brad with a worried look and a "BREAKING NEWS" banner across the bottom of the screen.

"We interrupt Miranda's special report for breaking news," he announced thunderously. "There's been an explosion linked to terrorism in the subway station in Times Square and all subway traffic has been temporarily halted on all systems."

"What the hell?" I muttered.

"We'll get back to Miranda's story later," Brad said, "but now we switch to Luis Martin on the scene in Times Square."

Instantly, Channel 11 was in Times Square with their reporter, blinking police cars and closed-off streets in the background, as the serious situation unfolded.

"The victims have been taken to New York Presbyterian," Luis said, hammering on with the facts: a backpack, an explosion, a "robot cop," blood all over.

As he went on, I just sat back, amazed that my "moment" was over, and they were onto something else.

"Oh my," said Betsy. "This is terrible."

I know that she meant the explosion in the subway, but I couldn't help but feel crushed that I got cut off before any mention of Mantell, with no plea for help in finding him. All that public exposure...for nothing?

"And do they just forget about you?" Betsy asked, sounding as amazed as I felt.

"I don't know," I said. "I guess so, for now."

We kept watching Channel 11 for a long time. At one point, anchorman Brad said, "We'll rebroadcast Miranda's story that we had to cut off," but he didn't say when, and they went right back to the subway explosion story.

And I was suddenly old news again.

⌐

The next day at Clemency, everyone was talking about the explosion in the subway, and the trouble that some people had getting to work. Almost nobody was talking about my Channel 11 interview.

"Saw you on TV last night," said Dae in the kitchen, with no further comment.

"Yeah," I said. "That was weird."

I stayed in my cubicle all morning, away from any possible contact with people, until Kelly came in to see me.

"Hey," she said softly.

I could see that she knew the interview didn't go over well.

"That Miranda was much nicer when she was here," she continued. "I don't know why she had to make everything look so dark."

"Me neither," I said. "I thought that Linda was her friend."

"I don't think friendship has anything to do with it," Kelly said ruefully.

"But worse than that," I added, "it was cut off before I got to say anything about Mantell—*if* they were going to leave that in at all."

Kelly looked at me sympathetically. "Yeah, I know."

"But what do *I* matter?" I asked the air. "Think about those poor people in Times Square."

"Yeah," she said, nodding. "Times Square."

As if I weren't low enough, I got a text from Derek Ellison: *Wrong move, Larry—u should have sold your interview. why give it away??? think: reality TV.*

I deleted his message immediately. The last thing I wanted was advice from him.

And to make matters worse, I got a phone call from Fusco that night.

"You shoulda told me you was going on TV," he said without even saying hello.

"Why?" I answered. "Would you have tried to stop me?"

"No," he huffed. "But I should've."

Unfortunately, he might have been right about that.

"Next time," he barked, "tell me when you do anything that you think *I* would think is fucked up, or I'll drag your ass back in here for a revocation hearing. Understand?"

His ultimate threat, but it worked.

"Will do, Officer Fusco," I said, and we both hung up, not soon enough for me.

Betsy overheard the end of my conversation, and she could see the frustration and disappointment on my face. She came over, sat down next to me, and gave me a hug.

"You did the right thing," she said. "Maybe it didn't turn out as you wanted, but it was the right decision to make."

She was just trying to make me feel better even though she was against my doing the interview. I tried to believe that she was right.

Nonetheless, I had a bad premonition. Still, I told myself I can't stop looking for Mantell, no matter what happens. My father's voice echoed in my mind—"This is for you, your legacy from me"—and I resolved to keep going. What choice did I have? This is life outside prison, what I always dreamed about, where there is no escape.

THIRTEEN

Three weeks later, I was fired. No, make that "let go."

"This was never supposed to be a permanent job," Kelly said. "But you knew that."

Even though I had felt it coming, when the moment came, I was angry.

"I should never have done that interview," I said.

"It's not that," Kelly said.

"Yes, it is," I snapped back.

"Not entirely," she insisted. "The Gateway Program is to help launch returnees, not give them a permanent job. You know there are no other Gateway people working here. It's only 'cause we liked you so much that you got a job here. It probably wasn't a good idea in the first place."

"Don't say that, Kelly. But—c'mon! I'm still on *parole*," I said. "This will..."

"I talked to Ken Fusco," she said, trying to calm me. "He understands the situation."

The thought of Fusco understanding anything almost made me laugh.

"But how am I going to live?" I exclaimed. "I have bills. I have rent. I have a—whatdayacallit—a *phone contract* that goes for two years."

"I promise you'll get a good severance package," she said. "Fusco will give you time to get another job. And I'll give you a great reference and some leads for places to start looking for another position."

"Come on, Kel'," I said. "Who are we kidding? I have *felonies*."

The word—and the way I said it—might have scared her a little, so I changed my tone.

"You know what I mean: who's gonna give a job to an old ex-con, much less...me?"

Kelly looked at me sympathetically, but she didn't disagree.

⌒

Rosemary knew about it before I did since she was middle management. She came into my cubicle with a sober face, two glazed doughnuts, and coffee for both of us.

"The truth is," she said between bites, "it's the budget. And they want to make room to bring in some new interns. Interns don't get paid...*and* interns have parents who give money to Clemency. It's as much that as anything. It's not personal, Sonny. It's strictly business."

"Please don't call me 'sonny,' Rosemary," I shot back, pissed-off. "I think I'm almost old enough to be your father."

She flinched, almost jumping back from me.

"Wait a minute," she huffed, putting down her doughnut.

"I know I'm just a piece-of-shit ex-con, but—"

"No, no, Larry!" she cut me off. "Wait! That was a joke. A joke!"

That stopped me. "A joke?" I repeated.

"It's a line from *The Godfather*!" she said. "'It's not personal, Sonny. It's strictly business.'" This last bit she said in a tough street voice. "You never heard that? Sonny's the name of one of the—I didn't mean *you*, Larry!"

"Oh," I mumbled, feeling stupid. "I never saw *The Godfather*."

Her eyes widened. "You never saw *The Godfather*?"

"I'm sorry," I answered sheepishly. "But I wasn't...in circulation...when it came out."

"But still—" she said. "Not even since then?"

"I'm sorry!" I said, embarrassed at having taken offense at her innocent comment. "I never saw the movie. OK? Nobody's perfect...least of all, me."

⌒

Betsy and I watched *The Godfather* that very night. "To get your mind off everything, at least for a little while," she said. It was her suggestion when I told her about my misunderstanding with Rosemary and everything that had happened that day. Roland had an old DVD copy. (He had a little of almost everything in the store.)

What a great movie! Now I see why people make such a big deal out of it. I always loved Marlon Brando—I, too, "coulda been a contender" and "Stella!"—but this was very cool to see. And then, of course, I understood Rosemary's remark. Betsy said *The Godfather: Part II* was just as good.

"But the third one didn't even deserve the name 'Godfather.'"

The movie reminded me of Herb Perlov, the boyfriend of the mother of The Girl. Everyone always said he was in the mob, and he in fact turned out to be "Herb the Hebe," the lawyer for a Mafia family in northern New Jersey. Did I mention any of this stuff before? Maybe I did. I think I'm finally getting old. Dammit. The very last thing I had, the only thing they didn't steal from me, was my wits. And now...who knows?

The movie also made me think about all those goombahs I knew in Sing Sing. Those guys were the real thing; they kept me safe there and had privileges that no other prisoners had. I wondered, and not for the first time, if they were still around and operational. Of course, "associating with known criminals" is just about the worst thing you can do when you're on parole. But "getting fired" just changed my situation, big-time. The money Mantell stole from me was now more important than ever. One thing that *The Godfather* shows: sometimes revenge is necessary.

⌒

Can you believe it? They actually gave me a going-away party at Clemency. Just a small thing with a few people, not like the giant parties they have when someone goes on maternity leave or when a regular employee retires for real. But there was a cake for me with the design of an eagle in flight in the icing. It's amazing how they can transfer a photograph onto a cake these days.

Rosemary said, "I thought it fitting for you, Larry. You're just gonna take wing when you get out of here."

The other people—Kelly, Javier, Naomi, Dae, Linda, some of the new interns—murmured in agreement.

"Thank you all," I said, taking a sip of white wine. "I thank you for all your encouragement." Of course, I wasn't so sure about my wings.

Before the party, Kelly brought me the severance check from Human Resources, so I had it before I left: twelve weeks' pay, which Kelly assured me—and Rosemary agreed—was very generous for Clemency.

"It's time to push you out of the nest," Kelly said as she handed me the envelope.

Rosemary let me have an old printer they were going to throw away—mine at home was busted—and an old flat-screen monitor too. She also gave me a lot of cartridges for the printer, which cost as much as the printer itself. Betsy let me take the Jeep that day to carry these big things and a couple of boxes of stuff that I'd packed up from my cubicle.

Before I closed things up for the last time on the computer in my almost-bare cubicle, Javier helped me scrub all my personal data out of the computer.

"This will wipe your hard drive clean," he said, slipping a disc he brought with him into the drive. "Then I'm gonna download this app that actually shreds all your files and overwrites them multiple times."

"Great," I said, watching as his fingers started to work on my keyboard. I sipped at my second glass of the white wine, thinking it's amazing how some of these young people can play on a computer keyboard as if it's a piano or something. Javier's hands just *flew* over the keys. He even bobbed his head a little as he typed, like a jazzman.

"There. That should do it," he said, sitting back. "And I really have to thank you, Larry, for talking to me and keeping me going when I was taking that course at Pace."

"You mean when I scared you shitless about not dropping out?" I offered.

"Yeah!" He laughed. "Exactly. Scared me shitless."

Javier got up from my chair. "I'm gonna get my degree next year, and Jessica says to be sure to thank you."

"Well, tell her that's my specialty: scaring people shitless."

Of course, *I* was the one who was scared shitless—more scared than I had been at any time since my initial release into Four Winds. As I was driving away from Clemency for the last time, I cruised by a homeless guy, slumped in a doorway, stretched out on a bed of flattened cardboard. You see a lot of homeless guys on the streets these days. I know for a fact that some of them are ex-convicts. Ex-cons, Iraq War veterans, and the mentally ill. Don't we have a nice country?

At first and for a while afterwards, I'll admit that I was really angry: at Clemency for firing me, at Miranda Jakes and Channel 11 for the biased interview, at Linda Pirroux for talking me into doing it, at Kelly and Rosemary for not defending me, at Derek Ellison for opening up this old wound, and mostly at myself for not performing better during the interview, for not keeping better tabs on Mantell over the years, *and* for every other fucked-up thing that happened in my life.

Javier whispered to me, "So are you gonna get a lawyer and sue their asses?"

"Another lawyer?" I gave it some thought. "I think I've had enough of lawyers."

⌒

Betsy saved my life. At least for the time being.

"Roland will give you a job," she said, "until you can find something else. It might not pay so much, but—"

"How do you know he will?" I asked.

"He will because I know he will," she assured me.

"But how much more can he afford?"

"Not all that much," she said. "You know how the store is doing."

"But if I don't get a full-time job, Fusco is going to be all over me."

"I'm sure Roland can arrange something with Bob Jensen," she said. "You tell me how much income you have to show to Fusco, and we'll make sure you have a pay stub with whatever you need." She added, "Until you find another job."

"But what if I *can't* find another job? I have rent to pay. And bills. Bills don't stop."

"You'll *get* another job," she said. "You're a very good, smart man."

"You don't understand," I said, "I can't just waltz into a job, with my background, at my age. They probably wouldn't even want me flipping burgers at McDonald's! And my rent is so high. The Clemency severance is only going to last so long. I'll eventually run out of money. It's pure math."

"Let's see what happens," she said, putting her arms around me. "We'll figure out what to do. I promise. Now give me a kiss."

She tilted her head up for a kiss, and I kissed her, grateful for her support, her everything. But I was thinking to myself that, more than ever, I needed to find Mantell and my money.

⌒

At least Betsy was as good as her word. She said that she'd get Bob Jensen to generate a paystub that would satisfy Fusco so that I'd appear to be fully employed. She also said that if I'd watch the store a few days during the week, Roland could find another hundred dollars a week more for me until I found another full-time job.

But the math didn't lie. When I added up my expenses on a yellow legal pad and compared them against my money, I knew soon I would run out of severance. There would eventually be a gap between my expenses and my income that I couldn't bridge.

It was obvious I couldn't keep my apartment any longer. I simply couldn't afford it, and, truthfully, I wasn't spending much time there anyway. My home was now wherever Betsy was, if she would have me. Thank goodness I wasn't locked into a lease. But I had to ask Betsy if I could move in with her. It was one thing to have me here most of the time; it was quite another to have me here permanently. The thought of it scared me a little. I knew that I loved Betsy, but could she stand me all the time—full time? Would she find out how truly damaged I am? Didn't she know she deserved someone better than me? And what if she said no?

I walked into the living room, my fate in her hands even if she didn't know it.

"Betsy?"

She looked up from her book. She liked to read in this little armchair in the corner of the living room, her legs wrapped in a fuzzy purple blanket.

"Can I talk to you for a minute?"

I started to explain the math, that even with my severance and what Roland was paying me, there was no future in keeping the apartment. But she cut me off.

"So you're asking me if you can move in here with me permanently," she said. "Is that it?"

"Well, not necessarily *permanently*," I said, giving her an out. "Just until I can get on my feet. And I'll chip in on the rent, whatever you think is reasonable. And you can kick me out whenever you want."

She closed her book and put it down in her lap.

"What if I *don't* want to kick you out?" she asked, but it wasn't a question.

"I *promise* you," I said, "you won't regret it. I'll be so good to you—"

"Don't promise me anything!" she cut me off. "Just be who you are."

I knelt down and gave her one good, deep kiss and a long, grateful hug, all the time wondering if being who I am would be good enough.

⌒

It turned out that giving up my apartment wasn't as painful as I thought it was going to be, once I got back my security deposit and didn't have that big rent bill to face every month. I had to sell almost everything I'd bought at Ikea; there just wasn't room for it all in Betsy's apartment. At first I didn't think someone would want to buy an old guy's used mattress, but sure enough someone did. ("I can put a mattress cover on it, easy.") We kept a lamp and some of the kitchen utensils, but I sold some stuff on Craigslist, offered a good deal to this nice couple in the building on a few things, and the rest I gave to Javier and his family.

When I was cleaning everything out, I found all those little yellow pencils and tape measures I took from Ikea in the back of a drawer and threw them out, thinking how crazy I was to have taken them and how far I had come since then. Or had I?

Once I sold off the contents of the apartment, I really had very little: just my clothes, some toiletries, my computer, and a few books. I haven't had the kind of life that accumulates many possessions. All I have is experience...and memories I can never forget.

Betsy made some room in her closet for my stuff and gave me one of the drawers in her bedroom dresser as well as half a shelf in the medicine cabinet. I kept looking for any telltale signs that she regretted her decision to let me move in, any sighs or worried expressions, but there didn't seem to be any. She just seemed to accept me. Nonetheless, I remained nervous—about money, my next meeting with Fusco, how the store was doing, looking for another job, never finding Mantell. Even though I felt some temporary relief from the tyranny of my huge rent payment every month and even though Betsy gave me comfort, I still felt like I was living on unsteady ground.

No question: life after Clemency was going to bring me a whole new set of challenges, as if life outside wasn't hard enough. I had to have a plan. I won't lie and say I wasn't worried, and on several levels. I knew I needed Betsy to survive. Which made me suddenly even more worried: the last time I was so dependent on a female, it led me straight to disaster. I had to hope, trust, and pray that this was a different kind of love, and that Betsy wasn't anything like the crazy/beautiful girl from forty years ago.

FOURTEEN

The first Monday morning after Clemency "let me go," I put my plan into action.

After Betsy went to school, I waited until just after nine thirty and called Mike Rathbun to set up a meeting with him to check on what progress they were making. But I couldn't get Rathbun on the phone. All I got was his voicemail, so I left him a message, which I immediately regretted. He could easily ignore or delete it. I wanted to talk to him in person. Likewise, I thought of sending him an email, detailing all my recent internet searches. But I didn't do that; emails are easily deleted too.

Next, part two of my plan. I got out from my knapsack the list of job referrals that Kelly had given me, which she divided into "People I Know" and "Other Possibilities." There were some employment agencies and some individual companies. I figured I'd start with people who knew Kelly.

At first, I couldn't get anybody to talk to me. Two people recognized my name, and that was that. I didn't even use the triple whammy "Lawrence Allan Ingber." After a few calls, I started to think maybe Monday wasn't a good day to call people. I ran into a few delaying tactics from secretaries—"Does she know what this is in reference to?" I didn't want to leave a message, but I finally got someone on the phone: an employment counselor from one of the big agencies.

"So tell me about yourself," he said affably.

Happy that he didn't know who I was, I started off strongly, telling him about my associate degrees, though I didn't tell him where I was when I earned them. I told him about my work at Clemency, all my responsibilities and how much they loved me, especially Kelly and Rosemary.

"And before then?"

That's where I ran into trouble. I stumbled around for a few moments before I had to confess the truth: that I had been incarcerated but had been freed by Clemency's Gateway Program so that my whole debt to society was paid and I was "ready to work."

Dead air. For a moment, I thought the line had been cut.

"Well, I don't have anything right now," he finally said, "but if you want to send me your resume, I can keep it on file."

He couldn't possibly have sounded less enthusiastic. I took his email address even though I didn't have a resume to send him. And he ended the call as soon as he could, as if I could give him some fatal disease over the phone if he stayed on one minute longer.

I had started writing a resume many times before, but it was a joke. I went on this website for ex-cons to help with my resume-writing. (There are lots of websites, trying to help ex-cons, most of them looking to get your money.) And I learned about putting "action verbs" in my resume. But what kind of decent resume could I possibly put together? Sure, I had the associate degrees I'd earned in prison a long time ago, but I had no real job history, just helping in my father's furniture store, that camp counselor job for a summer, and several months as a glorified gofer at Clemency USA, separated by almost forty years of prison. Would it be better for me to list all the institutions I was in separately, to beef up my resume? To lengthen my credentials? What a joke.

I opened my laptop and looked at jobs on Craigslist, as I had a bunch of times before. I scanned the categories: "accounting + finance"..."admin/office"..."arch/engineering," all the way down to "TV/film/video"..."web/info design"..."writing/editing," and my eyes just blurred. I could do none of those things. There were people out there with real skills, real experience. *Young* people. How could I compete with them?

I looked in part-time jobs, and there were all kinds of weird things: "GOT SPERM?" and "Diabetes Research Studies." Did anybody really want my sixty-year-old sperm or my sixty-year-old body or blood? There were other things: restaurant busser/

runner. Did I have enough strength and endurance for a blue-col-lar job like that? Experienced bartender...hotel security...bike de-livery? Those were jobs for young guys. Where were the listings for "broken-down-but-willing, old ex-cons?"

Finally, by late afternoon, after a few more hours of futile calls to several possible employers who didn't want to hear from me, when I'd already given up on hearing from Rathbun, he called.

"Sorry, Larry," he said, talking loudly over the office chatter behind him. "We haven't forgotten about you. We want this guy too."

"Good," I said firmly, glad to hear that bit of information.

I told him about my unsuccessful internet searches, and he told me about their lack of success on various channels. But again, he told me to "be patient," something I hated.

"We thought all that stuff about you on the net might flush Mantell out, but no—no action."

"Oh," I grunted, "you saw all that?"

He didn't say anything. I guessed he didn't think I was asking a question.

"So," I continued, "what's the next step?"

"Keep watching the airports, keep watching the exchanges," he said. "See if he's using any credit cards we can trace. Check the banking records of people we know he's been involved with."

"What about the Nassau County cops?" I said. "Are you talking to them?"

"All the time, Larry," he said. "And the SEC, regularly."

"But time's going by," I maintained. "The longer he's gone, the colder the trail gets."

Again, he didn't disagree with me, so I guessed I was right. Unfortunately.

"Don't worry," he said. "He'll show himself. We've been do-ing all the right things. He's going to slip up someplace eventual-ly. He'll come up for air, and when that happens, we'll catch him."

"Good," I said, trying to echo his positive attitude. The question is," I concluded, as much to myself as him, "can I wait that long?"

He didn't answer me directly but told me very nicely to "get in touch" if I come up with anything, which kind of sounded to me like "Don't call us; we'll call you." And we ended the call.

I wasn't exactly surprised by what Rathbun said, but I was still disappointed. All these months and no progress? None at all?

I went back to my computer and searched "Lester Mantell" as I had a million times before. Sometimes I searched for "Lester Mantell thief" or "Lester Mantell investor fraud" or "Mantell embezzler." Sometimes I searched on Google, sometimes on Yahoo, sometimes on Bing. They all came back to the same few old listings from *Newsday, The Wall Street Journal*, and *Investor's Business Daily* about his disappearance and a whole lot of stuff about when he was my lawyer: the same old crap that told me nothing new.

I started to think of all the things I should have said to Rathbun, how I should have really pressured him to do something else. I should have gotten the name of someone at the Nassau County Bar Association from him. I tried to track Mantell through some of the creeps he used to work with. His firm—what started out as Bishop, Hosker, Finch & Mantell and became Finch & Mantell, then Mantell & Wishengrad, and finally Lester Mantell LLC—had dropped off the map, but I searched all the names again, looking for something new but getting the same results. Inadvertently, I brought up a picture from one of my appearances during the appeal phase of my trial, one with Mantell at my side—me, looking so young and scared, and Mantell, looking like some brave legal crusader protecting me, like Clarence Darrow or Atticus Finch. What a joke.

Lawyers! "Officers of the Court"! That's not to mention the first jerk who didn't let me testify at my trial and got me convicted in the first place. OK, I take that back: *I* got myself convicted because of what *I* did.

As I started to close my phone, I noticed where Rathbun's number was: at the very bottom of my "Recents," near that Bronx number. Sammy Zambrano's number. That was a path I was *not* going to go down. Even as a last resort.

For the next step of my plan, I had to talk to Betsy. I waited until she got home from school. I could hear the Jeep pull up and her steps up the clanky outside staircase.

She greeted me with a tired, sincere "Hello, how was your day, honey?" a peck on the cheek, and an offer of tea as she put her things down.

"No thanks on the tea. My day was fine," I lied.

She went to the kitchen and started setting up her teapot, telling me about the latest outrage by Croll. I waited for a pause before I made my request.

"Betsy, you think we can have a sit-down tonight after dinner?"

She paused for a millisecond and then continued to make her tea.

"Is that a prison expression?" she asked. "Because I thought that we always talked to each other. Do we need a special time to talk truthfully?"

"I don't know," I said, preoccupied with saying exactly what was on my mind and getting her to agree with my plan. "I guess not."

"We can talk after dinner," she said. "It's OK. Whatever you want."

"No," I said. "We can talk now."

"OK, then," she said cautiously. "Let's sit down and you can tell me what you want to tell me."

She brought her cup over to the table, and we sat down. She looked worried.

"I want everything to be aboveboard with you, Betsy," I said.

"Me too." Her eyes stayed absolutely level with mine.

"I appreciate everything you've done for me," I started slowly. "I appreciate your getting me this job in the store and everything...but this is what I want to do. It's what I *have* to do, really."

"OK," she said calmly, giving me time to frame my next thought.

"I can't wait any longer. I have to make one last effort, one last *big* effort," I said decisively, "me personally, to go after Lester Mantell and my parents' money. *My* money. It may take some time and some, uh, unusual measures, but I can't wait for the DA and the SEC and the FBI anymore."

"What do you mean 'unusual measures'?" she asked, trying to cover the note of fear in her voice. "You're not going to do anything illegal, are you? I don't want you to do anything that's going to endanger your parole."

211

"I won't!" I said. Which was technically the truth. I wasn't going to endanger my parole because Fusco wasn't going to find out about anything I did. "No," I vowed. "Absolutely not! Not by any plan of mine. I just want to get my money. My legacy from my father."

Betsy broke into a big smile and wiped a little tear from her eye. "Oh. Is that it? The money? I thought you were going to say you were *leaving* me."

"Leaving you?" I repeated. "Are you crazy? You're the best thing that ever happened to me. You saved my life! You're *saving* my life right now."

Tears came back to her eyes, but she controlled them with a sniff and a smile.

"OK...that's—I don't know what I was thinking," she said. "So, tell me your plan."

"I'm going to need to use the Jeep, a couple of mornings," I said. "And Roland's going to have to watch the store, or we can just leave it closed some mornings."

"Do you want me to go with you?" she asked.

"No." I laughed and took her in my arms. "This is something I gotta do on my own. But it's for us."

She didn't even know what I had planned, yet she wanted to go with me. How trustworthy she was. (And, to tell the truth, I had only half an idea myself of what exactly I was going to do, but I didn't tell her that.)

"I won't let you down, I swear," I said with conviction.

"Oh, pish," she said, nesting in my arms. "This is not about me."

But, as I was planning my next moves, I realized that I was trying to convince myself as much as I was convincing Betsy.

⌢

I approached Roland with some caution. I know that he had gotten used to me watching the store. Some afternoons, he'd go out to Gassim's or Buddy's, the nearest dive bar, leaving me with a smart-ass send-off like "I'll drink one for ya, kid" or "Sell something."

So when I asked him if it was OK if I took a couple of days off to do some personal things, he looked at me at first with suspicion.

"And you expect me to pay you for the days you're not here?" he drawled.

"You can do whatever you want," I said. "All I know is that I've got to take the Jeep and tend to some overdue business."

"And Betsy knows about this?"

"She knows," I confirmed.

He looked closely at me, wondering what I was up to, deciding whether or not to ask me about my overdue business, and finally said, "Then it's OK with me. I'll watch the place. I've done it once or twice before."

"Great!" I said and ran upstairs to get the stuff I had already gathered: a brown-bag lunch, an apple, my laptop, and my Mantell file. What I was going to do—what I should have done a long time ago: I was going to go to Mantell's old office in Mineola myself and see what I could find out. Sure, Mike Rathbun had assured me that they'd asked everyone everything, but I had to make sure for myself. Maybe they missed something. This time, I was going to leave no stone unturned, no question unasked.

I was actually excited to be out on the hunt for Mantell, doing something. I had left so much of the work to others—Nyquist and his people, Rathbun and Cuellar—that it felt good to be doing something for my own cause besides endless, futile internet searches.

I wanted to be absolutely thorough in my pursuit of Mantell. Obsessed, if you will. From then on, I wanted no one to blame for my fate but myself.

FIFTEEN

The Throgs Neck Bridge was silver and beautiful as I crossed it, with the surface of the water sparkling below me and the city clear in the distance. And when the Jeep touched down on the Long Island side, I hardly even shuddered. I felt great—strong and powerful, for a change—because I was doing something positive.

Mantell's last reported address was an office building near the Nassau County Courthouse, the same courthouse where I was tried. I found it pretty easily with my friendly GPS lady, but I changed the route to make sure I didn't drive by the actual courthouse, where my young life ended. I found street parking and approached the dowdy old building with cautious expectations. I got through security easily (old man, no weapons) and immediately checked out the building directory: some accountants, some investment brokers but mostly lawyers. Lots and lots of lawyers. And no listing for "Lester Mantell, LLC." No surprise in that; Rathbun said Mantell had cleared out. According to the letterhead, Mantell's office was on the third floor, but I decided I had to do the whole building.

I went from office to office asking about Mantell, methodically, with my little speech about looking for "Lester Mantell, the attorney, who used to have an office on the third floor." A few people recognized his name, but most didn't. I'm pretty sure a few people recognized me—damn Derek and damn that Channel 11 interview— which caused them to hush right up. I tried to show the most recent photograph I had of Mantell, which was quite a few years old, but it was all I had. Some receptionists were nicer than others. They let me show them my picture. Some weren't very friendly at all and refused to look at it, even when I pleaded with them to just take a little look. Maybe they'd remember something? Nothing.

When I was finished, I went back down to the lobby and asked the security guard, showing him my Mantell picture. A big black guy in a uniform, he knew nothing about Mantell and didn't seem to like me at all. I should mention that I looked very clean and presentable, dressed in a white shirt and sports jacket—not like a threat to anybody. I was trying to project "nice, old, harmless guy," but I guess it didn't work.

I walked outside and thought about going around to some of the local lunch joints in the neighborhood and asking there. But I knew that would probably be a waste of time, on top of the time I just killed in this damn office building.

But, of course, I *had* to do it, to satisfy myself. I tried two lunch places on Franklin Avenue—a sandwich place and an Italian place—and turned up absolutely nothing.

I sucked up my courage and self-respect and walked two blocks to the Nassau County Supreme Court building. Did I get shivers walking in? Damn right, I did. But I walked in a free man, and that felt good, good as I could feel in a place that fed the insatiable maw of the corrections-industry, prisons-for-profits beast. Of course, I had to pass through the ever-present metal detector and a phalanx of watchful security guards, all heavily armed, and have my bag searched. But I got in.

I wandered around the first floor for a while and scanned the building's directory for something—a familiar name—anything I could connect to Mantell. His former partners? Anyone?

Finally, I walked up to one of the security guards, one of the older-looking guys, with my Mantell photo and asked him if he'd seen him around the courthouse.

I got a very respectful, very certain "No, sir" from him. And when I asked him to look at the photo again, he just shook his head and said, "Sorry."

In desperation, I approached the oldest-looking guy in a suit with a big briefcase, figuring he had to be a lawyer, and asked him if he knew Lester Mantell.

I made my little speech, showing him the photograph, but he shook his head, waved his hand, and moved away before I could finish.

There was nothing else to do. I had come up dry, just as I had expected, even if I harbored deep inside the dim hope that I would find *something*. Wrong again.

⌒

When I got back to City Island, it was dark, and I was completely burnt out. It was after closing time, so I trudged up the outside stairs. As I walked in, I could hear the radio playing NPR loudly over the running water from the faucet—that meant that Betsy was home.

She pivoted from the sink and gave me a happy "Well, hello there!" over her shoulder.

I put my knapsack onto the counter and came up behind her, took her gently by the hips, and kissed her on the side of her neck. She liked it, and I liked doing it.

"How was Roland?" I asked her.

"Fine. Why don't you take a nice hot bath?" she suggested. "And then you can tell me what you found out."

"I can tell you right now what I found out," I said, plopping down on a kitchen chair. "Lester Mantell isn't in Mineola, and no one seems to know where he is."

"Does that surprise you?" she asked.

"No," I admitted. "But I'm stupid about things sometimes. Very stupid."

She looked at me with sympathy. "So what are you going to do now?"

I had an answer; I just wasn't sure about telling her right then. Since my release, I had strictly obeyed the first rule of parole: I will not be in the company of, or fraternize with, any person I know to have a criminal record, except for accidental encounters in public places, work, school, or in any other instance with the permission of my parole officer.

Every time Zambrano tried to get in touch with me, I should have reported it to Fusco, but I didn't. And don't think I hadn't thought more than a few times about Zambrano and his "easy green." His number was still in my "Recents," and, for some reason, I didn't erase it. I started to, a couple of times, but I never actually did.

I had obeyed that first rule of parole. But now it was time for some rule-bending.

⌒

The next day, first thing, I dropped Betsy off at school.

As she stepped onto the curb, she turned and asked with a note of suspicion in her voice, "Are you gonna be OK today? You're not gonna do anything bad, are you?"

"Of course not!" I lied.

She gave me a darkish look. Why did she have such X-ray vision? Or am I that transparent? If so, I hope it's only to her.

I took off without looking back. I didn't feel good about shading the truth from her. (It depends on your definition of *bad*, right?) But I had to do what I had to do. And this was something that had been in the back of my mind for a long time and only grew stronger as I grew more desperate.

I'll admit that sometimes when I was combing the internet for clues about Mantell, I had also done searches about some people I knew from long ago, people I thought might be able to help me in ways that Rathbun and Cuellar could not, if the time ever came that I needed them. And now that time had come.

I brought up Google and entered the name of one of the four guys I had been in Sing Sing with more than thirty years ago. The four guys from a certain group of people in northern New Jersey who helped me get through seven years in Sing Sing and not get hurt. From my previous searches, I knew that three of them were dead: two were murdered, one died in a nursing home. But one of them—the guy who was my cellmate for three years— was, as far as I could tell, still alive. Freddie Pooch.

His real name—I had actually forgotten it—was Alfredo Giacosa, but everyone called him Freddie Pooch because he had an enormously fat, bulldog neck that looked like some kind of a pooch. He had been a capo who ran a crew before he took the rap for loan-sharking and attempted murder. Granted I knew him a long, long time ago, but he just might be my best long-shot route to finding Lester Mantell. If the cops couldn't find him, maybe the robbers could.

Once again I searched for "Freddie Pooch" and "Mafia hangouts North Jersey." A whole bunch of articles came up. I clicked on the first one and started reading, with pen and notepad ready.

Sometimes, I still like to write things down—screw this "digital age." After a short while, I had a list of addresses in north Jersey—three restaurants, two waste management companies, and a social club—where I could start looking. I had to do this carefully and completely on my own. Just going out of New York State was against the terms of my parole, much less seeking out "a person I know to have a criminal record," so I had to be super careful. Stealth, as always, would be my ally.

I went and got some bills out of the cash envelope Betsy and I shared, hidden in the second drawer of her desk. I took two twenties out of the thin stack to add to what was already in my wallet. Then I remembered that just the toll on the George Washington Bridge was fourteen dollars, and I had to have some walking-around money, so I took another twenty. We were on a budget and watched everything we spent carefully, but damn, how money just evaporates!

I knocked on Roland's door and told him that I was going.

"Then get the hell out of here," he roared back agreeably. "Enjoy yourself! I will be more than fine."

Music to my ears.

With my knapsack, my list, and an apple for a snack, I went out to the Jeep and spent a good twenty minutes entering the places where I was headed into the Jeep's GPS. This was a huge pain in the ass on the little keyboard the navigation system had. But I knew it was the right thing to do in advance: I didn't know Jersey at all. Frankly I wish I had one of those old fold-up paper maps like my father used to get at the local Shell station where we got those prints of the New York Giants that we had taped to the wall in the basement, but I guess that paper is old-fashioned, just like me.

The sun was out, the Jeep was two-thirds full of gas, and I was eager to go, but I figured if I waited until after the morning rush hour, I would make better time overall. I planned everything out. In fact, I figured that I might have to wait until after the evening rush hour to come home, depending on what and who I found, but I could call or text Betsy about that later. As long as she had a ride back home from school—which I knew she had, from Larisha, her English teacher friend—then she would be OK.

Of course, I was wrong about the traffic: the Cross-Bronx Expressway was completely jammed. I turned on the radio and almost immediately turned it off. I used the silence to rehearse my moves in my mind. I might not be able to do it all in one trip. You couldn't just expect to waltz into New Jersey and find some old mobster simply by knocking on a couple of doors. I had briefly considered calling these places first, but I was right to dismiss the idea. The element of surprise was one of the best things I had going for me—and my physicality. I'm not the biggest guy in the world, but I have a way of imposing my will on people, when required. I just had to remember who I was and what I've been through.

Finally, traffic started to move, and I was over the bridge and into Jersey. Funny, I must have passed by the upstate thruway exit that I took with The Girl in her Mustang and the bodies in the Cadillac I was driving, but I didn't even notice it. I took that to be a good sign.

The navigation system cooed, "Stay left to continue on I-95," and I obeyed. A lot of the trucks seemed to veer off onto I-80, heading west across the country, but I was going south, into the bowels of Jersey. Suddenly I was re-stoked with energy, knowing that I was doing something good and worthwhile: taking my fate into my own hands, not waiting for the cops or Clemency to do my business for me. *Why did I wait so long?*

I'm not going to tell about all the places I went that day. It was an embarrassing day, even for me: going into the places I went into, saying what I did, getting the looks I got. All these people thought that I was some crazy old guy—or worse. And, yes, a couple of people recognized me.

One place at a time, I'd walk in, make a little small talk about the coffee or the room or the weather and then say, "I'm looking for the Pooch. Freddie Pooch." Sometimes I had to repeat it. I got a lot of cold looks and angry eyes.

I went to one restaurant, a real red-table-cloth, marinara-stained pizza joint, and got shooed away from two tables. At a waste management company, they threatened to call the cops unless I got out of there immediately. "I'm sorry! My mistake!" I pleaded and practically ran to the Jeep to get away.

After turning up nothing at the first five places, I got an inno-cent *How r u doing?* text from Betsy that I didn't answer. What could I say? *Am wasting my time—gas—money—life—xoxo.* What the hell was I thinking? The more I thought about it, I was on a wild goose chase, an exercise in futility. Call it what you like. Did I really think I could find Freddie Pooch after all these years, and even if I did, that he could help me? What century was I liv-ing in? What fantasy world?

I let myself be guided by the cool, unperturbed voice of the GPS lady, driving to the last place on my list, the place least likely to produce any results: Visconti's in Newark. I figured that a guy as old as the Pooch—he was older than me—*had* to have moved out of the old neighborhood to the suburbs. New-ark was a well-known, urban hellhole, right? Of course people still lived there, but a rich, old mobster like Freddie must have gotten out. Still, this Newark restaurant—in supposedly the last Italian section of the city—was on my list of Mafia hang-outs, so I found myself cruising around in the dark, looking for a parking space. Sure, it was a long shot, but my whole life was a long shot.

But the moment I walked into Visconti's, I felt my Prison Mind kick in, just like *that*. I was hit, in rapid fire, by the warm, strong smell of garlic. The sight of that famous poster of young Frank Sinatra's mugshot on a back wall, surrounded by a string of Christmas lights. And finally by the cold, unfriendly looks from the five old, heavy tough guys sitting at the back table in an al-cove at the far end of the restaurant. I felt my insides instinctively clench: I had entered someone's "territory."

I took a small table on the side with a view of the front door and the guys in the alcove then ordered an espresso from a surly waiter in a shiny black suit. I checked out the layout of the restau-rant. There was a doorway at the back of the alcove that they periodically disappeared into. Probably a private room.

Every so often, one of the goombahs would look over at me—and we would lock gazes. Sometimes a guy would look at me, hard, for a few seconds. Sometimes his eyes went right back to his plate of scaloppini. The men who looked back at me with dead eyes I could tell were true prison guys.

I sat there until the place was practically empty. I ordered one expensive espresso after another and sipped them, staring at the guys in the back as they talked and ate and checked their phones and went in and out of that back doorway. There were five of them at the table, with one fat fuck in the middle who seemed to be the head guy. I looked at him extra-cold, extra-hard. I saw him talking with my waiter and looking in my direction. That made me happy. Maybe, after a few hours of staring, I was starting to get under some Italian skin.

My waiter walked straight over to me and said in a most un-friendly way, "Can I help you with anything else?"

"No," I said, ignoring him, looking straight at the back table. "I'm fine."

"The kitchen is closing," he said, slapping my bill onto the table.

I said nothing, lasering in on the Fat Fuck at the rear table as he looked straight back at me. The waiter turned abruptly and walked away from me, but my gaze didn't waver. Not a flicker. Not an inch.

"Hey!" the Fat Fuck said, from across the room. "You got a problem?"

Great, I thought, laughing inwardly. I didn't even have to say a single word to get to him.

Slowly, I got up and walked across the restaurant. There weren't any customers left, but that didn't matter. All that mattered was the Fat Fuck, the four goombahs with him, and me.

I saw one guy start to reach for something in his pants pocket, so I slowed my pace. I wanted to show that I was coming in peace. But I didn't stop walking. My Prison Mind had taken over, and I was bulletproof.

I stopped square in front of the Fat Fuck, locked eyes with him, and said my line: "I'm looking for the Pooch. Freddie Pooch."

The Fat Fuck—in fact, all of them—seemed surprised. One guy on the end almost fell off his chair.

The Fat Fuck said, "And what makes you think you can find him here?"

"I don't think I'll find him here," I said evenly. "But I think I can find someone here who can get a message to him."

"And what's the message?" he challenged me.

"My message to the Pooch is"—I paused for effect—"Larry Ingber wants to see him. I'm an old friend of his. Larry Ingber. I guarantee you he'll want to see me."

A beady-eyed guy next to the Fat Fuck leaned in. "So who *exactly* the fuck are you?"

I turned to him. "I'm the guy who killed Herb the Hebe's goomah."

Everyone at the table stopped moving, maybe stopped breathing. Absolute silence. I saw a light of recognition in the Fat Fuck's dead eyes: he knew.

"You tell the Pooch that I want to see him," I insisted. "I'll be back here tomorrow night for an answer. Nine o'clock."

Then I turned, walked to my table, tucked three twenties into the leather billfold (which included a good tip for my undeserving hostile waiter), and went out the front door without looking back.

The night air hit me hard. I took my first deep, non-nervous breath in hours, and it felt great. There, in the middle of godforsaken Newark, I was finally, just maybe, making something happen.

⌐

The whole next day, working in the store, I was anxious and eager, waiting until nighttime when I would drive back to Visconti's. I had to be there at nine, just as I said I would. And I would go back there every night until I got an answer from the Fat Fuck or some kind of message. *Something.*

I went online and looked at the same web pages that mentioned Freddie Pooch, trying to remember specifics about him and the time in Sing Sing when our sentences coincided. He had been out and back in again (twice), but not for very long stretches. Nothing in any of the Jersey papers indicated he was still involved in family business, but that scene in Visconti's last night—and the fact that they didn't deny knowing the Pooch—gave me hope.

I needed hope. Betsy had her book club that night. She was very excited—"Alice Munro!"—so it was a perfect night for me to disappear. Better she knew nothing about my actions until I had real, positive results.

I walked into Visconti's at exactly nine o'clock—make that I *strutted* into Visconti's at exactly nine o'clock, looking like I belonged there. I let my gaze wander evenly, patiently around the restaurant before I directed it at the back table in the alcove. And there, right in the middle, exactly where I wanted him to be, was my new friend, the Fat Fuck. There were more guys at the table and a couple of leftovers from last night, but the guy I wanted to talk to was in the same place. This was a good sign.

I started to walk across the restaurant. There were other diners there, and some waiters moving around, but I kept my focus on my friend in the dark suit and dark shirt with the dark circles under his eyes. I knew that if I concentrated hard enough on him, he—or one of the wiseguys at the table—would sense my presence. Guys like that always have this sixth sense, this animal protectiveness. (I know; I have it.) And, sure enough, I wasn't halfway across the room before this skinny, bald guy sitting next to the Fat Fuck slapped him lightly across the shoulder to get his attention, then pointed to me.

I slowed down, wanting to show them that I was returning in peace.

"Hey!" the Fat Fuck barked.

I stopped short, not knowing what his play was.

"The guy is here," he announced.

All the goombahs at the table turned to me—and they didn't have that hostile look like last night. For a moment, my spirit lifted but cautiously.

"Pooch!" the Fat Fuck shouted.

I stood there as they all turned to the doorway in the alcove. Slowly the door swung open, and out came a little old bald man in a wheelchair, being pushed by a heavy guy in a Yankees jersey. The old man wore thick, black-rimmed eyeglasses and was hooked up to one of those oxygen tanks with a bag on the side of the chair and clear plastic tubes going up his nose. He looked shrunken in the wheelchair, almost deformed.

When all the guys at the table turned and gave him heartfelt greetings—"Hey!" "The man!" "Zu!" "Zio," some approaching him with kisses—I realized the old man in the wheelchair *was* Freddie Pooch. He wore a black short-sleeved shirt, with his bony arms and elbows protruding. But he was smiling and gregarious, accepting their handshakes and good wishes.

The Fat Fuck pushed his way to Freddie, leaned over, and whispered in his ear. As he talked, Freddie looked down at nothing, then over at me. I stood frozen and let things play out. Through his thick lenses, the little man in the wheelchair peered at me. I just looked back at him and smiled, but not too wide: a confident, made man Prison Smile.

"Hey, Pooch," I said. "Remember me? Larry." He looked at me longer. "From Sing Sing," I prompted him. "The pruno master."

A big smile grew on the little man's face.

"Is that you?" he said in a cracked voice. "You sonofabitch!"

He remembered me! I broke through. I approached him and could see in his eyes—through Coke-bottle glasses—the same guy who saved my ass in Sing Sing when I was a scared-to-death kid. His big, bulldog neck was now just a bib of hanging skin, but it was the same Freddie Pooch.

"Come 'ere!" he said, laughing as he pulled me down to kiss him on the cheek. As I leaned over, I made sure the big guy in the Yankees jersey, still standing behind the wheelchair, approved of my actions. I kissed Freddie's whiskery cheek, avoiding the plastic tubes.

Freddie held me tight for a moment, growling with pleasure, and then released his grip.

"This guy here has balls!" he announced. "Big fucking balls!"

All the goombahs around us laughed in approval.

"I haven't seen this Jew bastard in over"—he gestured in the air with his crooked index finger—"thirty fuckin' years, and he still looks exactly the fuck the same!" Freddie rasped. Everybody within earshot laughed uproariously: Fat Fuck, the skinny guy, Yankees Jersey, Pooch, me, everybody. We all had a big laugh together, and I was relieved beyond words—for the moment.

They set Freddie and me up in a back room was down the hallway from the alcove—a private room for parties, with a nice bar in the corner. It was used as their own clubhouse when it wasn't being rented out. After Yankees Jersey (whose name was Bobby) made sure Freddie was comfortable, he left us alone. Then a waiter brought us two small glasses of some golden-brown liqueur, and we drank a toast to old times.

I clinked glasses with Freddie and said, "Guys like us they can't kill."

That got a gruff laugh out of him that shook his whole body.

"Cent'anni!" he said and took a sip of the bittersweet liqueur.

"Cent'anni," I repeated heartily and drank a bit. "Tastes like pruno."

That got a big, hacking laugh out of him.

We talked about the joints we were in and the guys we knew in Sing Sing and what happened to them. (All dead.) Then it was time to get down to business. I told him I needed his help. I could tell he liked that I came to him with respect and humility. And the truth is, I *did* need his help. I told him everything about Mantell in a nutshell—how he ripped me off, the state of the investigation, the whole deal.

Freddie sat there and listened, nodding his head slowly. "Fuckin' shysters," he muttered. "What do you expect?"

"Pooch," I said, leaning toward him. "You still know people. I've exhausted all my other channels. Even the FBI can't find him."

"Fuckin' FBI!" he growled. "Where are they when you really need 'em?"

That broke us both up. Freddie started gasping for breath, so much so that Bobby had to come in and check the Pooch's oxygen.

"Get the fuck away!" Freddie said, waving his hand as the big guy adjusted the tubes, making sure there were no kinks. "He has hands like a buncha bananas!"

After we were alone again, I made my final plea for him to help me find Mantell.

"You know people, Pooch," I implored. "Or you know people who know the people."

He thought for a while, nodding, and finally said with consideration, "I can ask around."

"Great!" I said and held both his hands in mine, to seal the agreement.

I gave him the paper I had typed up that included everything I knew about Mantell: full name, date of birth, last known addresses, past business associates. I even had his Social Security number.

He looked at it very carefully, trying to get it into good light.

Finally, he said, "I'll get someone to read this to me."

He folded up the piece of paper very, very slowly. I was afraid that he would tear it and had to hold back from taking it out of his hands and doing it myself. But that would have been a sign of disrespect.

Eventually we returned to the main room, and I had the best Italian food I've ever eaten maybe in my life.

"Are you kiddin'?" said Fat Fuck, whose name was actually Carmine Natale. Apparently, he ran the neighborhood, or what was left of it, in this area of north Jersey. "This is the best food in the world, in this neighborhood. This is where Sinatra got his bread from his entire life!"

"It's where Frankie Valli came from," said Bobby, who was on the other side of the Pooch. "It's where fuckin' *Joe Pesci* came from!" (I blanked: I didn't know who this Joe "Pesky" was—another Thing I Had Missed.)

"Absolutely!" I nodded vigorously, pretending I knew the name. "So what's this about Sinatra's bread?"

"He used to get his bread. From Giordano's."

"On Whatchcallit Street."

"He'd have it flown all over the world," croaked Freddie. "His entire life."

"Flying bread?" I said. "I guess if anybody could do it, Frankie could."

That got a good guffaw from everybody at the table, and more wine was poured for all around. I was *in*.

I didn't get out of there until almost midnight. Pooch took me around the table one last time, making sure that everyone knew who I was.

"Remember dis guy. Dis is the guy who killed Herb the Hebe's goomah. A very big deal before you wuz born." Compliments like that.

I left him with one last firm handshake and his promise to see what he could do. That's all I really wanted to hear. Even Yankee Jersey gave me a bear hug before I walked out the door.

I felt like collapsing and dancing, both at the same time. I took a few deep breaths, to make sure I was sober enough to drive back to City Island, and got out my phone. There were three texts from Betsy, all sweet and supportive, and I sent back one of my own: *Everything super fine—coming home—xoxo.*

I got onto 78 East easily, just like last night, turned on the oldies station, and picked up speed to merge with traffic. I felt great. After all these years: Freddie Pooch! My hunt for Mantell *wasn't* dead. I opened up the window for some air and blasted the radio. It was the Temptations singing "The Way You Do the Things You Do." I had no idea that Jersey could smell so sweet.

⌒

And then...nothing. No word from the Pooch, nothing. All that work, setting it up and making it happen, and then not a word. Zero. Weeks went by. I called Mike Rathbun, but he had nothing new to say, and, to tell the truth, neither did I. I kept searching the internet and kept finding nothing new.

Nothing was selling on eBay. We would go whole days in the store and not sell anything. I read different business websites, looking for the key to creating a "sustainable business model." I put things up on the store's Facebook page: photographs I took with my phone of things in the store, little facts about naval history that were supposed to make people want to buy things, anything I could think of to generate sales. I got only a few insultingly lowball offers, which even Betsy refused to consider. Every customer who came into the store was subjected to my hard sell until Betsy had to tell me to relax. I think I was actually scaring the customers away. I know that I'm capable of that.

"Could you stop looking at that for a minute and come be with me?" Betsy asked me late one night.

I was sitting at the kitchen table, looking on Craigslist for a job I could do. I didn't have a TLC license. Maybe I could be an SAT tutor. I did well on my SATs, but I imagine the questions are different these days, and I'm sure they do math in a totally different way. There were so many skills I didn't have, things I couldn't do: bartender, bookkeeper, pharmacist, pediatric nurse.

Long ago, I could have learned to do so many things. Now I was just an old guy playing catch-up with everything. What did I really know how to do? All those associate degrees I got in the can were worth nothing, just busy work inside my cage. The main occupation of my life was surviving among criminals. And who did I know? Who was my best business contact? Sammy Zambrano, with his Medicare scam. *That's* a job I could get.

It took me a moment to resurface into the real world and defog my mind.

"What, honey?" I said.

She walked over and stood next to my computer. "You really have to give it a rest. Come to bed," she said. "All the world's problems will still be there in the morning."

She was right, but that didn't help me.

⌒

On one gray, drizzly Sunday, it was very slow in the store. Roland had disappeared into the back, and Betsy and I were in front in case any customers showed up. She was reading, and I was tense. I walked up and down the aisles, dusting things that didn't need dusting, rearranging objects that didn't need it.

"Are you OK?" Betsy asked me, and I replied reflexively, "Sure!"

I looked out the front window: steady, solid rain. A few cars drove by but mostly nothing. No people, no business today.

"You are as nervous as a rabbit," Betsy said, suddenly at my shoulder. "Why don't you go down to Gassim's and have a coffee? You like his coffee. It's quiet here. And you and Gassim like to talk."

Betsy didn't know it, but I was thinking of asking Gassim for a part-time job in his kitchen. Washing dishes or something. Anything I could do that would make me some money. Real money, right now.

"Take your time," she said. "I'll text you if a huge mob of shoppers suddenly turns up, but somehow I don't think you have to worry."

Not so reluctantly, I grabbed an umbrella from the barrel at the front of the store, an umbrella a customer left a long time ago, and walked down to Gassim's in the rain. I didn't get too wet, and I didn't really care if I did. I had my mind on something else I'd been thinking about for a while.

"No, my friend, of course not! Are you out of your mind?"

Gassim turned me down flat.

"You don't want to work in a kitchen!" he said. "Especially mine. I work my people too hard. I want you to remain my friend, Larry."

"How much do you pay your dishwashers?"

He told me, and it wasn't much. But it was something.

"You really wouldn't give me a job?" I asked him again.

"Larry," he put his coffee cup down with a clank. "You're too old."

I finally got him to tell me that Charlie Wagner, who owned the restaurant across the street—called Charlie's, of course—was always looking for kitchen help.

"And he pays people off the books," Gassim added reluctantly.

"Would you call him for me?" I pleaded.

Gassim made the call, and half an hour later I had talked myself into a job—"Just for tonight, to see how you do"—at Charlie Wagner's fish restaurant. I told him that I had experience with commercial dishwashers, which was the truth.

"A Noble," I said. "A double rack." I ran one at my next-to-last joint.

Wagner looked me up and down with his baggy eyes. "And you might have to bus some tables if we get busy."

"Whatever you want, Mr. Wagner," I said, obliging as a teenager.

I called Betsy and told her what I was doing and for how much.

"Are you sure about this?" she said. "That sounds like a lot of work."

"I just want to *do* something," I said. "And it's all cash, off the books. Maybe I can bring you back some food from the kitchen." Charlie's was a more upscale restaurant than Gassim's; I wouldn't be surprised if his food was better.

"I'll be fine. You just bring yourself back to me," Betsy said. "I'll wait up for you."

"Don't," I said.

"Oh, pish," she sniffed and hung up the phone.

⌒

I hadn't been in a big working kitchen in a long time and never in a restaurant kitchen like Charlie's. He had some spare whites in a back storeroom that he lent me.

"Let me show you what you have to do," he said. A squat, goateed guy, quite full of himself, Charlie led me through the noisy kitchen, spouting directions, rules, and names of people. He showed me the dishwasher I was to use, where I was to stack the clean stuff (dishes, flatware, glasses), and where to empty the garbage, another key part of my job. I heard most of what he said as my eyes skipped around, looking at all the equipment, the pots and pans, and the workers—some were looking at me and *all* of them seemed to be younger than me. Younger than me and, to tell the truth, darker than me.

"Hey," I said to everybody I saw, nodding respectfully. If I got any response, I waved my hand and said, "Hey, I'm Larry."

Mostly I got blank stares or looks that said *What is this old guy doing here?* So I just threw myself into the job—scraping and loading the dirty dishes, unloading the clean ones, clearing the garbage, and staying out of trouble.

The work was hard. I thought I was used to lifting heavy things around the store, but these racks of hot plates and steaming glasses were super heavy. I was sweating and breathing hard in no time.

"I need plates!" one of the cooks called to no one in particular, but I suspected he was talking to me.

Fortunately, one of the young Asian guys came over, scooped up a pile of plates, indicated that I should do the same, and helped me carry them over to the cooking island. He showed me where to leave them on the end and pointed to where the salad and dessert plates should go.

"Larry!" someone yelled.

It was Charlie, holding a mop out to me.

"You wanna clean this up?"

Someone had dropped an ice cream sundae on the floor.

"Sure!" I answered eagerly, taking the mop from him.

"And we need more stemware in the bar," he said. "Now!"

"Right, boss," I said.

An hour in, I told myself, *I can do this.* I got into the rhythm of how everyone was working. I scraped and loaded, unloaded and stacked, and in-between cycles I picked up any garbage I saw and generally made myself useful. Like most restaurants on City Island, Charlie's specialized in seafood—so the trash cans really stank from fish. Fish bones, fish heads, fish guts, shrimp shells, clam shells. A few times I had to breathe through my mouth to keep from gagging. And then, after a while, like everything else in my life, I got used to it.

Charlie came by to drop something into my trash can. "You're doing OK." He wiped his hands off on a towel and, walking away, said, "Tell Gassim that he owes me."

"Thanks," I said, not sure what he meant.

I *am* sure that all those plates and glasses and the silverware were hot and heavy, rack after rack. I almost scalded myself. Nothing serious but my hands were pink and raw after a couple of hours of washing, scrubbing, and scraping in hot water. I just kept reminding myself: that's why they call it work.

I didn't stop moving, except to go pee in the rank little toilet in a closet in the corner. I sent a quick text to Betsy: *Doing fine— don't wait up for me—xxx.*

Four hours into the night—I guessed it was night by then; there were no windows in the hot kitchen—I was asking myself, *What the hell have I gotten myself into?*

The kitchen was super noisy, and people did a lot of yelling. I got yelled at.

"Where the fuck are the clean fucking *forks*?" one of the waiters bellowed as I hustled some clean flatware into place. Some of the busboys laughed at me, I think. Fuck 'em. What did I care what they thought?

I slumped against the counter, waiting for a load of dishes to finish, when one of the Vietnamese guys came over with a plate of food for me, some fish, rice, broccoli. I took it from him with a grateful smile. Then I went to my corner of the kitchen and ate it quickly like a greedy, starving thief. It was Saturday night, and Charlie's was doing great business. Good for him, but bad for me, so I had to wolf down my food and get back to work. I wasn't the only one in the kitchen who was sweating, so I didn't feel so bad, but I didn't stop moving all night. The dirty dishes just kept coming.

Even after the restaurant closed and all the customers were gone, the kitchen kept working. I could see that the waiters and waitresses and some of the cooks had started to relax and hang around, but not me nor any of my friends here in the back with the dirty glasses, the leftovers, and the trash. I didn't see Charlie anywhere, and there was no one telling me to stop cleaning, so I kept working until I was the last man moving.

"Take a rest, pop," said one of the busboys, passing me on the way outside with an unlit cigarette between his lips.

"I will, kid," I said, and I did slow down. I had no idea how busy a restaurant gets on a Saturday night.

I then saw Charlie cruising around, talking to his staff, supervising as the kitchen wound down. I watched him—he was passing out money—and waited my turn.

One of the Vietnamese kids walked by me with a bag of trash on the way outside and said, "Clean up come last." I think that he meant *us*.

Finally, when I couldn't see anything else to do, I got my street clothes out from where I stashed them with my umbrella, went into the little bathroom, and changed out of the dirty, sweaty, fishy whites I was wearing.

When I came out, almost everyone was gone, and for a moment I thought Charlie was gone too, but there he was, across the kitchen, talking to the chef, a bully with a big beard and a big gut. I went right up to them; I was ready to go.

"Mr. Wagner," I said, "I left those whites you gave me in the bathroom, on the hook on the door."

The chef looked at me briefly, like I was a lower life form, and finished his talk with Charlie: "Think about it, Charlie!" Then he walked away.

Charlie muttered, "Asshole," under his breath and then turned to me. "You did good...uh...uh—"

"Larry," I helped him out.

"You should give me your phone number," he said, reaching into his front pants pocket, "in case I need you again."

"Great," I said, even if I wasn't sure how great I felt.

He pulled out a huge roll of money and started slowly peeling off bills.

"I'm not gonna charge you for the whites," he said, "though I usually do. But 'cause you helped me out and you're a friend of Gassim's, I'll let it go. Just make sure you leave 'em in the john."

"Thanks," I said. *Charge me for the whites?*

"But next time," Charlie said, "bring your own."

I wasn't sure if I wanted there to be a next time, but when he put the money in my hand, it felt good. It wasn't a lot, but it was better than nothing. And it was cash.

I couldn't wait to get out of there. When I got outside, it was cool, clear, and dry. The streets were still wet, but no rain was falling. I took off down the sidewalk, all alone. It was after two in the morning. I wasn't sure if Charlie would call me back to work there again or if I would want him to, but I had done something. I could do it again, if I had to. There had to be a better way to make money, though, short of Sammy Zambrano's Medicare scam. But what was I good for besides kitchen grunt work? I should have been happy for what Roland paid me. But it was still not enough.

I walked home with only the sound of my footsteps to keep me company, looking to the black velvet starless sky for a Moment of Grace and Thanks that just wasn't there. I climbed the outside stairs carefully and let myself in, trying to make as little sound as possible and not wake Betsy.

I took a carton of milk from the refrigerator, poured myself half a glass, and drank it down to try to calm my churning stomach. I was really too tired to shower but too fish-smelly not to.

As silently as I could, I took a fast, hard-scrubbing shower to wash the Charlie's off me. When I got out of the bathroom, I tiptoed back into the bedroom and noticed that even my clothes smelled like fish and were starting to stink up the room. So I gathered them all up to carry into the laundry room off the kitchen.

"Is that you?" Betsy mumbled, half asleep, as I cut back through the bedroom.

"Go back to sleep," I said.

"What time is it?"

"Time to sleep," I said and closed the door behind me. I hoped she wouldn't wake up. She needed to sleep, and I didn't want to talk.

I dropped my clothes into the hamper next to the stacked washer and dryer. Then I went into the dark living room, still damp from my shower, and sat there on the couch, bone sore, thinking about my night in Charlie's kitchen.

What a fiasco! What did I prove to myself? That I'm not seventeen anymore. I mean, I did it, but I feel like I was run over by a bus. But what else do I have going? Who is going to hire me, seriously? Should I buy my own set of whites and try to bring in money working full-time at night in Charlie's kitchen? Maybe I could get promoted and make more money. Off the books, of course.

Yes, I was very happy to have found Betsy and this home for me. *Home*: something I haven't had in a lifetime. But I sat there in the dark wondering how long I could keep it...and keep her. Nothing seemed sure anymore.

SIXTEEN

What happened next began a series of events that ultimately changed everything, for good and bad. I still can't believe some of it actually occurred. Certain things were my fault; other things just happened.

It started one afternoon when I was working in the front of the store. Roland was back in his apartment. We had lunch at the store counter, and he had left me with a classic Roland line: "What I need is a good crap and a good nap."

I hadn't sold a thing all day, and I was on my third time through Roland's *New York Times*—one of his last luxuries—when a customer finally walked in, the sound of door bells giving me a good jolt. It was a hefty middle-aged man with a goatee in a serious business suit—not your typical shopper, but I was OK with anyone.

I called out in a friendly manner, "Tell me if there's anything I can do for you," and let him wander among Roland's treasures.

He didn't seem to be looking at anything in particular, and I could tell he was mainly stealing glances at me. Occasionally, customers still recognized me from that damn Channel 11 interview, and I would cut them short. I was getting ready to do the same thing with this guy. I just waited for him to make his stupid move.

Sure enough, after a few minutes of pretending to shop, he walked up to me and said across the counter with a big smile, "You're Larry Ingber, aren't you?"

I sighed, keeping my temper in check. "Look, if you're interested in any of our merchandise, I'd be happy to—"

"What if I called you by a different name?" he burbled, smoothing his goatee.

I was getting ready for the Ivy League Killer razz I sometimes got, when he said, "What if I called you *Assistant Groinmaster*?"

I felt a deep jab into my trick memory.

"You're a hard man to track down," he said with great satisfaction. "You don't recognize me, do you?"

I was starting to remember—

"Harry Dornfeld. Camp Mooncliff. Run by the Marshak brothers. 1968!" he said. "You were my counselor."

This fleshy guy with a receding hairline looked at me with a wide grin. "We were the Doggies!"

That rang a bell. *It's what we called our campers, right?* I remembered The Girl, but other things were kind of fuzzy. As I mentioned, I took a couple of beatings, especially one in Oklahoma, that knocked out some of my memory.

He started to laugh and grabbed my hand, pumping it repeatedly. "You don't know how long I've waited for this! I *told* the guys I could find you."

I let him shake my hand—he seemed so happy to see me—but I wasn't so sure. I was suspicious: what did this guy want?

"So," I said, pulling my hand away, "what can I do for you, Harry?"

"Nothing!" He laughed. "You don't have to do anything for me. I'm just glad I found you."

"Why?" I didn't like how perfectly delighted he was.

"Well," he began, stumped for a moment, "we were all wondering what happened to you. I mean, besides what happened all those years ago. And then you were on TV and—"

"So?" I cut him off. "What does that have to do with anything now?"

That stopped him. I could see that he was surprised at my less-than-friendly response, but I didn't care. I didn't want attention from strangers—or comparative strangers. Forty years ago doesn't count.

"It doesn't have anything to do with anything, Larry," he said, miffed. "I don't know. We all *liked* you—"

"Listen, Harry," I said. "If you don't want to buy any antiques, I can't see that you have any business here."

"Wow." He sighed, pushing away from the counter. "I just dropped in for old times' sake and to—"

"Old times are over," I shut him down.

His expression hardened.

"*Hmff*," he grumbled. "I thought you might still be a nice guy. Y'know, you're *not* the most famous person from our bunk. You used to be, but Klein-o hit the jackpot. He runs a hedge fund."

"Klein-o?" I repeated with a laugh, vaguely familiar with the name.

"Jonathan Klein!" Dornfeld shouted. "The kid whose life you saved! With the red hair. He was drowning, and you pulled him up from the bottom of the lake."

"Oh, yeah," I dimly recalled. A few shadowy images started to form.

"You don't remember," he accused me.

"Sure, I do," I lied.

"Well, now he's one of the richest men in the—well, I don't know how rich, but he's in the billions, with a *B*."

"Well, good for ol' Klein-o," I said, trying to end the conversation.

Harry shook his head. "Wow. I came all the way out here on a friendly visit and—"

"I don't need any friends, Harry," I interrupted.

One shot from my Prison Mind, and he got the message.

"Damn," he said with a sigh, "you were such a nice guy," and turned, shaking his head again, and walked straight out of the store.

As soon as he slammed the door, I felt bad. I wanted to say, "*I'm still a nice guy!*" Except to curiosity seekers and old snoops. Maybe I shouldn't have been so hard on him. He came all the way out to City Island to see me.

It wasn't until dinnertime when I started to tell Betsy what happened that things became clearer to me.

"So this Harry person came into the store," said Betsy, "but he wasn't insulting or anything?"

"No, not really," I answered. "In fact, he tried to be nice, I suppose. I just wasn't in the mood for his nosiness."

But some things he said had started me thinking. And re-membering. I told her what Dornfeld said about Jonathan Klein and everything I recalled about saving his life, which wasn't all that much.

Betsy sat and thought for a moment. "So what are you going to do?"

"Well," I said, my thoughts unfolding as I spoke, "if I really saved this rich guy's life, maybe he feels that he owes me something. In fact, he *definitely* should feel that he owes me something. Maybe he can help me find Mantell. Rich guys have power, don't they?"

After a moment, Betsy agreed, "*Some* rich guys."

⌒

I spent the rest of the night googling Jonathan Klein. Betsy finally had to call me to bed after midnight. I spent a good deal of time trying to find out exactly what hedge fund managers do. The answer is complicated, but the short version is they make a ton of money. Sure, some guys bet big and lose big, but, on the whole, Klein Global Partners did very well. As Harry Dornfeld said, "Billions with a *B*."

There were lots of articles in different business publications depicting Klein as a successful businessman and secretive person with more enemies than friends, maintaining a flashy lifestyle and shady international connections to money launderers, but with a loyal and protective staff. There were also incidents of fisticuffs at some New York night clubs. Almost every article used the word *mercurial* to describe him and made some reference to his red hair and hot temper. As I read story after story about this deal or that, this fund or that—his homes, his cars, his divorces—I kept thinking, *He wouldn't have anything if I hadn't saved his life, right?* Maybe he would want to help me out. It was certainly worth a shot.

I fell asleep that night planning what I'd say to him. The tone I'd take. There must be a zillion people trying to get to a guy like Klein. I bet it wouldn't be easy to get through to him. But I would figure out a way. I got Betsy to turn on her side so that I could spoon up next to her and try to get to sleep. But I couldn't stop thinking about Jonathan Klein and his connections. This could really lead to something.

I got up the next morning, made a good breakfast for Betsy, drove her to school, and got back to my computer before I had to open the store. With a second cup of tea, I plunged back into the world of Klein. What a world it was: so different from anything I'd ever known. All this money, all this power, all these transactions in amounts that were like cartoon numbers. Betsy and I were trying to pay bills in the hundreds, and Klein dealt in the hundreds of *millions*. Did we even inhabit the same universe?

I had started a "Jonathan Klein" file, keeping everything I thought was essential, starting with the phone number and address of Klein Global Partners. I checked on MapQuest and noticed his office was all the way downtown, a couple of blocks from Wall Street and the New York Stock Exchange. Made sense.

Even though I knew things started early in the financial markets—hey, everything is twenty-four hours around the clock now—I waited until after ten to make my call. I figured that was a civilized time for a personal call. And my call was, indeed, personal. I was going to ask him—basically, a total stranger from long ago—for a big favor.

"Hello," I said brightly, "may I speak to Jonathan Klein?"

"Who may I say is calling?" a bright female voice responded.

"An old friend of his," I said, and I started my story. But before I could get much of anywhere, she said, "Can I please put you on hold?"

What else could I say but "Sure."

And on hold I stayed for quite a while. Maybe she was hoping I would hang up. She was wrong.

Finally, the line came to life, and the bright female voice said, "Mr. Inger? Could you please hold for Mr. Brian Halliwell?"

And before I could anything, the line went silent again.

Still, I was patient. They weren't going to get rid of me so easily. I just waited, unriled, remembering that I wanted to sound friendly and agreeable. An old friend, not a pain in the ass or a problem.

"Hello," a sharp, serious voice broke in, "this is Brian Halliwell. May I help you?"

"Ah, Mr. Halliwell!" I greeted him heartily even though I had no idea who he was. "Good to talk to you! My name is Larry Ingber—Laurence Allan Ingber," I even used the dreaded three-name version of my name for maximum impact, and I told the shortened version of my story, ending with my saving his life at Camp Mooncliff. "So I wonder if Mr. Klein would like to get together for coffee...or a chat...for old times' sake."

Dead silence. I waited him out.

From the other end of the line, I heard an exasperated but polite sigh.

"I think, Mr. Ingber," said Mr. Halliwell, "that you best put your story in an email."

"It's not a story," I countered. "It's the truth."

He quickly rattled out an email address. "That will allow Mr. Klein to give it the attention it deserves."

Could he have been snottier?

"OK." I took in what he said and repeated the email address as I wrote it down.

"Will that be all?" he asked on the edge of impatience.

"It's all for now, Brian," I answered in a calm, friendly way and ended the phone call.

As I suspected, getting to Jonathan Klein wasn't going to be easy.

⌒

It took me several drafts to get the right tone in my email to Klein. I wanted to seem friendly, and I was. Of course, there was a big favor I wanted from him behind my offer of friendship, but that could wait. I mentioned Harry Dornfeld's visit, hoping that his name meant something to Klein. In the back of my memory, I could hear them calling him "Dorny." I said nothing about helping me find Lester Mantell; I figured that would come later. I was uncertain about adding "Your Assistant Groinmaster" to the closing. It seemed so juvenile, but it seemed to tickle Harry Dornfeld. Maybe it would work on Jonathan Klein. I seem to remember that he was the Redheaded Doggy.

In some ways, I felt bad about sucking up to this rich jerk. *Wait*, I told myself, *he might not be a jerk. He might be a nice, generous guy.* But even if he is a jerk, I had to try everything I could think of. As soon as I clicked "Send," I regretted adding the Assistant Groinmaster part. Oh, well; I could only try to do my best.

Nonetheless, I continued my Klein research. He was an avid hunter and art collector, well known for bagging whatever trophy he was after. I found out where he lived. He had a few homes, but when he was in New York, he had a townhouse in the East Sixties: *nice.*

"Can you leave that alone?" asked Betsy with a yawn as she crossed the kitchen behind me. She wore her long purple bathrobe and was on her way to the refrigerator for some milk, which she would warm up in the microwave in my Mets mug.

"No, not really," I answered. I was sorry the moment I said it—at least the way I said it, as if I were angry. I wasn't angry; I was just...*resolute.*

"I'm just doing research," I explained. "I want to be prepared for when I meet him. *If* I meet him. No, *when* I meet him."

She watched the mug of milk go around in the microwave. I waited for her to say something like "You're wasting your time" or "Why are you obsessing over this man?"

Instead she let me say that to myself.

What Betsy did say was, "Turn out the lights before you come to bed. And please don't be too long. And bring waters."

⌐

Of course, I didn't hear a thing from my email to Jonathan Klein. I suppose I shouldn't say *of course.* He might have responded, either with just a "No, thanks" or "Sure, let's get together." Instead, I heard nothing.

I waited a week before I sent another email: a nice little reminder—"Remember me?" It went unanswered.

The next week, I tried calling Klein's office again. Sounding as nice as I could, I was rerouted to Brian Halliwell, who I could tell was putting up a wall between Klein and me. He apologized insincerely and assured me that he would "make sure that Mr. Klein was informed." Whatever that meant.

"Is Mr. Klein in the office today?" I asked.

"I'm sorry," he lied. "But we don't give out Mr. Klein's location."

He thought he could give me the brush-off. He had no idea who he was dealing with. I started checking the Klein Global Partners website every day and reading business-news sites, trying to track Klein's movements. I bet if I had the chance to talk to him, he might help me. I wasn't doing anything wrong; I just wanted a chance to make my case with him. Just to get an honest word with him, man to man. Maybe he wanted to do a favor for an old, not-quite-broken-down ex-con who once did him a favor. A fairly large one.

Twice, he turned up at big-deal financial conferences—once as a featured speaker, once as a guest panelist—but they were in Singapore and London, which did me no good. No, I was going to have to find him in New York. At his office, or maybe at his home in the East Sixties. Probably going to his office might be the better move. More businesslike, less personal.

"Larry?" Betsy inquired, looking over my shoulder. "Are you stalking this man?"

I angled the screen away from her. "It's not stalking. His people won't let me talk to him and he's not answering my email, so I have to figure a way to get through to him."

"Maybe he doesn't want to see you," she reasoned.

"Then let him tell me that to my face," I answered. "An email is simple. He could just write 'no' back to me. I bet this Brian guy gave me a phony email address or something."

Betsy sighed and turned away.

"OK," I relented. "Maybe it is kind of like stalking. But it's like an itch I have to scratch until it's gone. I have to do *something*. Nothing else is working. Rathbun and those guys aren't getting anywhere."

"Can't you just be happy here with me?"

"I'm doing this for you," I insisted.

She shook her head. "I didn't ask you to—"

"OK! I'm doing this for *us*...and because it's what my father wanted."

She stood there, not talking for a while, so I turned back to my screen and my Klein information.

"I'm just trying to help you," she said.

"Then help me," I said. "Don't work against me."

"That's not fair," she snapped, "and you know it."

Before I could turn around and tell her that I was sorry—she was right: I wasn't being fair—she was gone. I had never heard that tone in her voice. I should have gone after her and apologized. Instead I told myself I was going to make things right for her. I would reward her faith in me when I reclaimed my legacy.

I went back to my search, but I couldn't stop daydreaming about the things I would do for Betsy, the things I would buy for her, whatever she wanted. Hard-covered books, anything. She could stop working; I could make her life easier. She deserved an easier life. She gave so much to everybody.

⌒

Finally, by chance—or fate—I saw an ad announcing that Klein was being honored by the New York Public Library, presumably for some huge donation he gave them, on such-and-such a date. The black-tie dinner was at the Waldorf Astoria, not that far away from Klein's townhouse. Odds were that he would go home before the dinner to change into his black tie, and the rest of his tuxedo. Maybe I could catch him then. I knew I would have trouble getting to Klein in his office building: too much security these days. I would have a better chance in the streets. All I wanted to do was talk to him, man to man.

I cleared it with Betsy to take the Jeep downtown. I had grown to love City Island—I think I would have loved anyplace where Betsy was—but it was quite remote. The one bus out of City Island, the 29, which would have taken me to the subway to get to Manhattan, ran infrequently. It would have taken me almost two hours, each way, to get down to Klein's ritzy neighborhood. So it only made sense to take the Jeep.

I left Roland to watch the store, his store.

As I left, he called out cheerfully, "Hope you know what you're doing."

All I could say was "So do I."

243

I hadn't driven into Manhattan in half a lifetime: *more*. I remember how exciting I used to think Manhattan was. It's why I went to Columbia instead of someplace else, someplace that might have been better for me. But that's all blood under the bridge now.

As I got further into midtown, I remembered how scary it was driving in the chaos and confusion of all the traffic, and the crazy, anarchic, lane-defying stampede of cabs. I thought that driving in Newark was difficult, but this was nuts, a total free-for-all down Second Avenue. I got honked twice.

With the calm voice of the GPS lady guiding me, I homed in on Klein's East 63rd Street address. I set myself up to get there in plenty of time to find parking, so I could be in front of his townhouse to catch him going in—or out—before his fancy-ass dinner. I'd wait for him, not to scare him or anything, just to see him and say my piece.

It was a damn good thing I left early. I must have driven around for an hour looking for a parking spot. At one point, I pulled into a parking lot, but when I got a look at the price—almost forty dollars for just a couple of hours—I said, "*Fuck 'em*," and kept looking. The rip-offs in this world are simply unending. Who can afford these prices?

I got to know the blocks around Klein's townhouse really well. I kept circling around: down Fifth Avenue, across East 66th, up Madison, across another street, back down and across again. I pinballed around in different rectangles, looking for any parked car that looked like it was going to move. I found nothing. But I couldn't drive around forever or I'd miss any chance I'd have to see Klein. Just when I was about to bite the bullet and empty my wallet to park in one of those extortionate parking lots, I saw a car at the curb with back-up lights flashing: someone was moving. Saved!

I fast-walked to Klein's street, only a couple of blocks away. I approached slowly, counting down the townhouses toward Central Park at the end of the street. The people living inside these stone fortresses must be really rich to live this close to the park. Klein wasn't dumb; was it foolish of me to hope that he might be nice too? And charitable? After all, he was being honored that night for giving to the New York Public Library. Why not help the old ex-con who saved his life when he was a kid?

As I got closer to Klein's, I could see a gleaming black limousine with its parking lights on at the curb, right in front. And a big black guy outside in a driver's uniform, leaning against the passenger door. Like they might be waiting to take someone to the Waldorf.

I hung back around the corner of a building, just a few doors down. I didn't want the driver to see me and get suspicious. But the sidewalk wasn't very wide, and it wouldn't take more than a few steps for Klein to get from his front door to the limousine.

I had to be ready. I moved a doorway closer. I was glad that it was staying lighter later in the afternoon; I didn't want to surprise Klein in the dark. I didn't want to scare him. I just wanted him to stop and let me talk to him for one honest moment.

I waited against the corner of one of the limestone palaces, out of the driver's view, trying to look invisible. I was sure I was in the right place, at the right time. Wasn't I?

Then the driver straightened up suddenly as if he had been electroshocked. There was light from the opened townhouse's front door and then movement. Two men—one short, pudgy guy in a tuxedo followed by a taller man in a business suit—walked quickly across the sidewalk toward the limousine. I made my move.

"Jonathan Klein!" I stepped out calling in a strong, confident but friendly voice.

The smaller man—I could see now that his hair was wiry and red—stopped sharply and turned to me.

"It's me!" I said. "Larry Ingber."

We locked eyes. I could see him bringing me into focus.

"Larry...Ingber?" he mouthed.

I just stood there and smiled, presenting myself in the most nonthreatening way, making sure the younger guy with him, his assistant, who didn't seem to be packing, realized I was on a mission of peace. And, thank goodness, Klein slowly returned my smile.

"I tried to call you," I said. "And I emailed you too, but I never got an answer."

Klein swiveled and asked the taller man next to him, slick and sharp in his pinstripes, "Did you give him the fake email address?"

"He did," I cut in. "If this is Brian Halliwell."

Klein flinched and laughed out loud at the embarrassed younger man, caught in his transgression.

"Well, he got you." Klein chuckled. "Brian was just trying to protect me. That's his job."

"You don't need protection from me," I said simply.

Klein stood back and looked me over.

"Wow," he declared. "Larry Ingber. Talk about old times. Listen, I gotta go now. They're giving me some award. But Larry, I *definitely* want to see you."

He stepped toward me and took my hand in a warm, two-handed handshake.

"Really," he said, engaging my eyes. For a moment, I could see why he was such a successful businessman. This little guy had *force*.

He shot an order over his shoulder.

"Get his information, Brian," Klein said. "For *real*, this time." He grinned at me conspiratorially, turned sharply, and scurried into the backseat of the limousine.

The driver slammed the door and scooted around to his side as Brian Halliwell—Mr. Pinstipe—tall and handsome, peevishly entered my info in his smartphone.

"Thanks, Brian," I said. "I know you had his best interests at heart."

The limousine took off from the curb, blowing exhaust onto my pants, but I didn't care. I was right about where Klein would be, and I had made contact with him. Maybe my instincts weren't completely shot.

⁀

At first, I didn't hear anything from Klein. Zero. Days went by, and I started to think that, despite the firm double handshake and reassuring look in his eye, maybe I had wasted my time. The papers said he was "mercurial," and let's face it: who has time for an old convict with a famously bad past? Let me say that never once did Betsy throw it back at me. Roland made a couple of jokes, but they didn't bother me. What bothered me was doubting myself, doubting what I thought I saw. Was I still "all in my head," the way I was in the joint? I thought this repeatedly while I was scrubbing pots and hauling garbage in Charlie Wagner's stinking kitchen for cash.

Yes, I went back to working nights there and cycled just enough into my bank account to show Fusco. Sometimes Fusco would tell me to bring my bank statement to an appointment, so he could see how I was doing financially. But even when I had money to show him, he wasn't satisfied.

He scowled at my statement and shook his head.

"Where're you getting this money?" he growled.

"At the antique store," I defended myself. "You've talked to them. It all checks out. If you don't like it, come to City Island and see."

This was a calculated risk on my part. When Charlie started giving me cash, he told me to "keep it off the books." I figured there was no way for Fusco to trace me back to Charlie and get me in trouble with him. I knew that Fusco would never get off his ass to drive all the way to City Island.

"Dammit, Ingber, why don't I trust you?" he muttered. "You're doing something that smells bad." Little did he know.

"You're welcome to come down and see for yourself," I offered again.

"Maybe I will," he said.

I just smiled. Fusco was mean, but I trusted that he was lazier than he was mean. Still, I had to be careful: he was my parole officer for another year, and I knew that he still had me in his sights. Someday I would be completely free of him, but not yet.

Then I got what I hoped for.

A phone call.

"Hello, Mr. Ingber?" said a dry, businesslike voice. "This is Brian Halliwell, calling for Jonathan Klein."

"Yes?" I answered calmly as I felt this warm chill surge through my body.

I was invited to a dinner with Mr. Klein at such-and-such a time on such-and-such a date, and where would I like to be picked up?

I felt a tingle of joy as I gave Mr. Pinstripe my address. So I *had* gotten through to Jonathan Klein. For a change, I had been right about something, and it felt good.

⌒

The night of the dinner, Betsy helped me get dressed super nice. Or as super nice as I could get. It took me three tries to get my tie right so that it was even on the bottom. I had to borrow one from Roland, and I had to double it because he was so damn tall. None of us knew how narrow or broad ties were supposed to be these days, so Betsy went online and looked on some men's fashion sites, and we picked a dark one, medium width.

"So what do you think?" she asked me as I looked at myself in the dresser mirror.

"What do you mean?" I asked her. "About how I look? There's nothing I can do about that."

"Oh pish!" She laughed. "About *tonight*, silly."

"I don't know," I said honestly. "I'm just going to go and have a good time. I haven't really seen this guy in, like, forty years, but I got a good feeling from him. Hey, he *did* get back to me. He invited me *somewhere*."

"Where exactly are you going?" Roland asked as Betsy smoothed my collar down.

"You know," I said, "I don't even know. His assistant just said that I would be picked up at six thirty, so I'm going to be ready."

As Betsy lightly brushed off the shoulders of my jacket, she said, "Do you really think he can help you find Lester Mantell?"

"I don't know," I said, "but I'm sure as hell going to find out."

SEVENTEEN

I hadn't been in a limousine since my high school senior prom, so I felt both silly and ridiculously lucky as Betsy and Roland walked me out to see me off at the curb.

"Remember to sit in the backseat," Roland advised dryly.

Kissing me on the cheek, Betsy said, "You're going to have a wonderful time."

"I certainly hope so," I said. "I'll text you on my way home."

The driver—a serious thin black guy in a serious black uniform—opened the door for me, and I got in.

"Bye!" Betsy sang out as the door closed. "Have fun. And don't be nervous."

I waved goodbye, but they couldn't see me through the tinted windows. And by the time I found the switch to roll the window down, I was gone.

Rush hour traffic in New York is horrible, but it's definitely less horrible from the back of a limousine. There were little plastic bottles of water, dishes of red-and-white mints, and lots of fancy magazines in the pockets of the seatback, far in front of me. The driver asked me if I was comfortable.

"Definitely," I affirmed, sitting back into the soft black leather, adjusting my seat belt.

It was fun watching the world go by. People in other cars looked at the limo with envy, maybe, but they couldn't see me. I understand why rich guys like limousines: you feel really protected in one of these.

"'Scuse me," I prompted the driver, "but do you know where we're going?"

He pushed a button on the GPS gadget on the dashboard and said, "One five five, West Fifty-Fifth Street."

"Oh," I said. "Midtown....What's there?"

He answered in a light African accent, "Le Bernardin."

I took out my phone, looked it up on Yelp, and found out that it was one of the best, if not *the best* restaurant in the whole city. They mainly served fish. Lots and lots of fish. Good: I like fish. I never got enough of it my whole life, and now when you go into the grocery store, it's so incredibly expensive. I'm guessing it's going to be better than Charlie Wagner's...or Gassim's, for that matter. But they'll have to go some to top Gassim's lobster rolls.

"Here we are, sir," said the driver, stirring me out of my daydreams. "Comin' up here on your right."

By now, we were in the skyscraper canyons of Midtown. I hadn't been down here in a long, long time, not since I used to walk from Morningside Heights on mad, lost, endless rambles away from my life of hell at Columbia to buy an Orange Julius in Times Square.

A curved silver sign read "Le Bernardin," but the driver went past it, rolling down a little way to another doorway with a smaller silver sign.

"OK!" The driver grunted firmly as he slammed the car into park and got out in a flash. I had just enough time to check that I had everything I came with—keys, wallet, phone—when the door was magically opened for me, and the driver reached out his hand to help me.

"I'm OK," I said, getting out under my own power. I'm not *that* old yet.

The silver sign above me read "Les Salons Bernardin." Or were the letters cutouts *through* the silver metal? It was a cool effect.

"Mr. Ingber?" someone called to me. The driver was pointing me toward another man in a dark suit—a doorman who was holding the door for me.

"Thank you!" I said.

As I walked in, I told myself, *Don't be dazzled. It's just another night, in another place.*

"Mr. Ingber!"

There was a high level of noise in the restaurant—the intense buzzing of rich people—but I was sure that I heard someone call my name. As I turned around, I saw Mr. Pinstripe coming toward me.

"Finally!" He sighed, rolling his eyes.

In one smooth move, he thrust his business card in my hand— "Take this," he ordered—and turned me around by the shoulder, steering me up a little staircase.

"Mr. Klein has been waiting for you," he said, trying to sound welcoming, but I could tell from the tension in his voice that Mr. Klein did not like lateness. I snuck a look at his business card: it had gold lettering that said "Klein Global Partners."

At the top of the stairs, there was this little area with a bar and tables, and two beautiful, tall, unreal young women in the corner, whispering to each other. A waiter glided by with a tray of colorful drinks. I tried not to gawk, but I couldn't help myself. The whole thing was so ritzy, so glamorous—all wood and stainless steel, the high ceilings and windows—that I couldn't help but feel like a peasant, a complete outsider.

Another tall, beautiful woman—this one in a slinky black dress—called to Mr. Pinstripe.

"Mr. Halliwell," she sang out. "This way please."

He walked me across the bar area to where she was. I heard her whisper to him, "They got tired of waiting."

"*They*?" I asked.

Then, in the middle of a glass wall, another door opened, and Mr. Pinstripe pivoted to me and announced, "Mr. Ingber? Your party is waiting."

As I walked into this separate, little dining room, all shiny wallpaper and bright lights, a bunch of men's voices hit me— "YAAYYY!"—and four guys in dark suits and Jonathan Klein rushed toward me, it suddenly dawned on me: this was a party for *me*.

Klein had a wide, satisfied smile on his face as the four guys (Harry Dornfeld and three other guys, all bigger and fatter than me) crowded around, slapping my shoulders and back, spinning me around, taking turns hugging me. This wasn't just a one-on-one with Klein; it was a full-blown camp reunion.

"So you finally made it?" Klein said, pulling me to him for the last, big bear hug.

I think I've mentioned it before, but almost forty years in prison has given me a deep-rooted aversion to being touched. But I stood for all this touching, my arms tense, until they released me.

"He has arrived!"

"At last!"

"Finally! We can eat!"

Klein pulled me away from the crowd and "showed" me to the other men.

"Gentlemen," he said proudly, "may I present to you, your friend and mine, junior counselor in Inter Bunk Nine, your Assistant Groinmaster, the legendary Mr. *Laurence Allan Ingber.*"

The four men cheered too loudly, looking very happy. They were all middle-aged, all in nice-looking business suits, with huge smiles on their faces and drinks in their hands. Lively, cheerful men who seemed very, very glad to see me. And I had no idea who they were.

"Do you recognize any of these guys?"

"Um, besides Harry here, who came to the store, no, I really don't," I replied. Which got a big laugh out of everyone.

"OK, OK!" Klein said, shouting everyone down as they started to talk at once.

"This is Matthew Gold," he started pointing. "We used to call him Matty."

"We used to call him Pussy-boy," cracked someone, "but that's another story."

"This is Artie Sanoff. And Steve Dembicer. And Dorny, you know."

My friend with the weird handshake and goatee who visited the store raised his glass to me and smirked. We had a secret bond: he was the one who told me about Jonathan Klein.

"Do you remember *anything* about Mooncliff?" asked the very fat guy in the vest. (I think he was Sanoff.)

My mind was spinning, trying to remember all the way back and who these guys were as kids. It was so long ago.

"Sure," I said cautiously. "A little."

They all laughed uproariously again. Everything I said seemed to get a positive, almost jubilant reaction from the men. They had all obviously been drinking before I arrived, and with these lovely women and obedient waiters coming in and out of the room, serving them in this elegant, festive atmosphere, it *was* a party: why *not* be in a good mood?

"I can't understand it," said Klein dryly. "Who could possibly forget the Moon-shak?"

"Who could forget Sharon Spitzer?"

That name rang a bell, but I wasn't sure what it signified.

"*And* Dawn Fitzgerald!"

"Who's Dawn Fitzgerald?" I asked.

"I guess that was after your time," the thin, nervous one—Gold—said, leaning over my shoulder.

"Too bad," said Dembicer. "She fucked everybody."

"Everybody?" I repeated.

"Everybody but him!"

"Still, she had great cuppies."

"You and your cuppies!"

"I don't care if she pisses in my face, as long as I can see where it's coming from!"

"Hey," said Klein, clapping me on the back, "let's get this man a drink and something to eat."

One of the guys, the one with thick glasses and wild eyebrows—I think he was Dembicer—took me by the elbow, steering me toward the table.

"Yes!" said Sanoff. "Let's sit down and order. I'm *starved*. I haven't eaten since—"

"A half hour ago."

"Go fuck yourself, ya skinny bastard."

"Genetics, man. What can I say? I'm not going to apologize for my genes."

"No, you should apologize for your *suit!*"

"Wait till you taste the yellowfin tuna," Dornfeld said. "It's beyond belief."

He turned me to face the table. It was beautifully set: so many different glasses and silver utensils. And the flowers! Flowers all around. Like out of a magazine.

"I can't believe this," I said, sitting down in the super comfortable chair.

"Neither can we," concurred Dornfeld as the men started to take their places at the round table. Dornfeld leaned toward me and whispered, "Don't worry. He pays for everything," nodding in Klein's direction.

Just as I sat down, a waiter was at my shoulder, saying softly, "Sir, may I get you something to drink?"

"Let him see a drink menu."

Before I could answer, another waiter was on my other side, asking, "Do you prefer sparkling or still?"

I wasn't sure what he meant until I saw the two bottles of water he had, one in each hand.

"Uh...still," I said, thinking that was the right answer.

"Hey, Larry," a voice the other way said.

Dembicer thrust a little menu toward me, nicely printed with an elegant edging.

"Look at this," he said, putting the menu in my hand. "I think you'll find it quite engrossing."

"Thanks," I said, taking it, "Steve." I was trying to remember everyone's name. Dembicer, the crazy eyebrows. Fat Sanoff.

I looked at the menu and saw that the print was so small I was going to need my glasses. I dug into my inside jacket pocket.

"This chef has the most amazing imagination."

"Everything here is fantastic."

Taking out my glasses gave me a moment to catch my breath: this was *some* place. I remembered some fancy beach club when I was a kid, but this was much more than that.

I focused on the menu. It was a list of drinks, cocktails with all these weird ingredients: egg whites, fig puree, beet juice, black walnut liquor. I had seen Fusco recently, plus he hadn't tested my pee at the last couple of visits, so I decided to take a calculated risk and drink that night. It's not like I was doing heroin. It struck me that I couldn't escape thoughts of Fusco invading my mind time and time again, even at this fancy restaurant, but I only had myself to blame for that. What I couldn't forget was to ask Klein about helping me find Mantell. But I had to wait until the time was right and we had a moment alone.

I lowered the menu and said, "Ummm...how about a Scotch on the rocks?"

"There's a real man." Gold guffawed his approval.

"Said the Pussy-boy," someone cracked, to more laughter.

The waiter standing over me asked, "Is there any brand you prefer, sir?"

I hated that they were all watching me order my drink, like a child.

"Chivas Regal," one of them said. "Johnny Walker."

"Red, black, or blue?" someone added.

I couldn't think.

"What single malts do you have?" one of them asked.

"We have Springback," the waiter said unctuously. "And Glenkinchie."

"Give him the Scotch menu," said Sanoff. "They must have a Scotch menu."

As the men started arguing over the relative merits of different scotches, I looked straight across the table to Klein. He mouthed at me, "Get whatever you want."

"OK!" I said. "Johnny Walker...Black."

"Good enough," said Sanoff.

I was momentarily relieved until the waiter who wouldn't leave my shoulder said, "And how would you like that, sir? On the rocks? With soda?"

"Just rocks," I said.

"As I said," began Gold, slapping the edge of the table, "a real man."

"So we're all good?" asked Klein, making sure we were all set.

"We are *very* good." Dornfeld declared.

"Klein-o," said Gold, "I cannot believe you did this!"

"After all these years!" agreed Sanoff.

"You did it, man!" Dembicer toasted Klein. "You got him here!"

The others also raised their glasses in Klein's direction.

"The Scarlet Chicken gets what he wants," cracked Gold. "Nothing's changed."

"Master of the side pocket," said Dornfeld admiringly.

"*And* the Double Irish!"

They all laughed, but Klein visibly winced.

"Fuck that fat bitch from the SEC," said Gold, sniggering. "What kind of a name is Kassa-fucka-misian?"

"She's Armenian."

I assumed that *side pocket* and *Double Irish* were financial terms. I'd try to remember them and look them up when I got home. But the Scarlet Chicken?

"Nothing's happened yet, and it won't for a while," said Klein measuredly, and promptly changed the subject. "How about we have some food before Sanoff here starts to eat the silverware?"

Almost instantly, plates of food began to appear. Small, elegant dishes piled with artistic little sculptures of extremely tasty food. All the guys dug in ravenously, talking and eating at the same time. Klein ordered another round of drinks for everybody. Insults and jokes flew across the table like paper airplanes, pointed and hard, but they could really do no harm because the insults were jokes, and the jokes were insults.

"It's amazing how many different ways you can cut up food," said Sanoff, stuffing a little tower of something into his mouth.

"What a stupid fuckin' thing to say!" said Gold. "You don't expect to eat every piece of food *whole*! It has to be cut up!"

"You can't cut foam," said Dornfeld, referring to the empty glasses of flavored foam we had all just consumed.

"No, but you *can* cut cheese," Dembicer offered just before he sipped his wine.

"Who cut the cheese?" said three guys at once, and we all erupted into the most juvenile laughter you can imagine from grown men as they all started to argue over who said what simultaneously and what the penalty was for it.

More food and drinks came. I assumed that Klein had ordered everything in advance. I didn't care; everything was delicious. Even better than Gassim's lobster rolls. I'd never eaten food this good—or this fancy—in my entire life. I had the impulse to take out my phone and photograph each plate as it was placed perfectly in front of me, but I was afraid of looking like I didn't belong with these guys...even though I didn't. I looked around the table, at all the guys' happy faces as they ate, drank, and talked. They

were so relaxed with their old, *old* friends. They were prosperous
men who seemed so contented with their lives. I admit I wanted
to be friends with them.

I said, "I can't believe you guys have really stayed close all
these years."

"Well, *some* of us," said Dornfeld.

"Klein knows how to cut his losses."

Klein nodded and said, "Amen to that."

"Lubin is dead."

"Lipschitz," Gold said. "No one knows what happened to him."

"You mean Shit-Lips?"

"Simonson, but he never went back to Mooncliff."

"He was one strange kid. Remember? If he had been an
X-Man, his name would have—"

"OBNOXO!"

"He *annoys* people to death."

"And Adelman, but he died a long time ago."

"AIDS," Dornfield muttered to me.

"Bad meat in the can."

"Shut up, Dum-bicer."

"Asshole."

"His son is gay."

"I'm just telling him," said Dornfeld, pointing to me. "It's
nothing to be ashamed of, right?"

"Of course not!"

"Not that there's anything wrong with it," the three guys
said together and erupted into laughter, which I did not understand, and argued more about who said what first.

A look of confusion must have passed across my face because
Klein said to me, "Larry? You don't watch *Seinfeld*?"

"Another smart-mouth Jew from the Island," said Gold.
"Where's he from?"

"Massapequa, I think."

Through cupped hands, Dembicer announced, "Wantagh!...
Seaford!" and Gold, Sanoff, and I joined right in with, "Massapequa!...Massapequa Paark!"

And we all burst into the laughter of shared experience, lubri-
cated by very good food and very good wine. I couldn't believe I

remembered that series of stations on the Long Island Railroad, the famous conductor's chant on the Babylon line, but it's amazing what the mind chooses to remember...and what it forgets.

"Keeeeeep..." Sanoff started singing in a very low voice, "rollin', rollin', rollin'!"

And they all—me included—sang the theme from *Rawhide* as if it were 1960 forever. Some memories even prison beatings cannot erase.

"You see?" said Klein, slapping the table triumphantly when we finished. "This is why we get the private room. We could not sit in the middle of Le Bernardin *downstairs* and sing 'Rawhide.'"

Shaking my head in wonder, I said, "You guys are still the Doggies!"

They all raised their glasses, cheering, and toasted each other.

"And you get together a lot?" I asked, taking another sip of wine.

"Sometimes."

"Goldie belongs to Winged Foot, Dorny belongs to Sebonack, and the Scarlet Chicken of course has a box at the Stadium *and* courtside seats for the Knicks."

"Doggies are not stupid," pronounced Sanoff, followed by a deep belch.

"We gotta take some pictures."

Klein instantly snapped, "No! No pictures."

For just that moment, I saw a flash of the redheaded temper that I read about on the net. We all did. The host had spoken, and, after all, he was paying. I admit I was relieved too: I didn't like having my picture taken for a million reasons, starting with those stupid shots that Derek took of me, not to mention how I looked on Channel 11. I was hoping nobody would bring *that* up.

Dornfeld held up his glass and announced, "Hey, this is fuckin' amazing! Larry, you have no idea how often we've talked about this moment. Do you know how many times we've thought about seeing you again?"

"No," I said, hiding my suspicions, "how many?"

"You don't understand," Sanoff said fiercely, "you were a very influential figure in our lives."

"You were *definitely* one of our favorite counselors."

"And when you became *famous*—"

"After being such a *nice* guy— "

"It just blew our minds."

"We were just kids, and then, boom: it was all over the newspapers and TV and—"

"It was like you found out that your favorite uncle was—"

"Was *what*?" I cut them off.

Dornfeld leaned toward me. "Do you have any idea how much mileage we've gotten at dinner parties over the years telling people that the Ivy League Killer was our *camp counselor*? Are you serious? People love those stories!"

"What stories?" I said

"Poe!" Gold roared from the other side of the table. "You read us fucking Edgar Allan Poe! You read us 'The Tell-Tale Heart'! You read us the fucking 'Raven'!"

"I'll never forget that Jack London story you read us where the guy's breath forms this giant *icicle* of tobacco juice," Klein added, miming something big coming out of his chin.

"*The amber beard*!" Sanoff boomed. "In the cold, that keeps breaking off!"

"What's the name of that story?"

"And the guy wants to warm his hands in the *guts* of his *dead dog*! That gave me nightmares for years."

"'To Build a Fire.'"

"And all the other stuff! 'Hop-Frog,' where the jester burns up the guys who are tormenting him."

Good idea, I thought. The barrage of their memories, popping like flashbulbs, stunned me a little. But when I thought of it from their perspective—"My camp counselor, the famous murderer, who read us Edgar Allan Poe"—it did sound kind of creepy.

"I guess I did do all of that," I said.

"In addition to saving this guy's fucking *life*," said Gold, pointing at Klein.

"*That* I vaguely remember," I lied.

"And it's a damn good thing you did!" seconded Dornfeld. "Except for *you*"—he pointed at me—"the Chicken here is the most famous person to come out of the Moon-shak."

259

"So give this man another drink!" said Gold, filling up my glass.

"Yes," said Sanoff, "let's get the Assistant Groinmaster a very expensive *drunk*!"

Laughter from all, including me.

"I mean," continued Gold, "you're not driving, right? Klein-o got you a car, right?"

"Yes, he did." I nodded, picking up the newly refilled glass. "And for that, I am extremely grateful."

"We are all extremely grateful to our most generous host." Sanoff raised his glass in Klein's direction.

The others cheered and raised their glasses in agreement, as Dembicer added, "Even if all this is just the change in his sock drawer."

Klein took the zinger with a smile.

Dornfeld joined in, "Life is tough, going up and down on the *Forbes* list!"

Klein just smiled, looking down into his glass. Then he signaled to one of the waiters who was at his side in a millisecond.

"Larry," said Gold, pointing his glass and a finger at me, "you *used* to be the most famous person who ever went to the Moonshak. Until the SEC got curious."

"Klein-o likes his privacy," Sanoff trilled.

"Just like he liked the corner bunk," cracked Gold.

"Every fuckin' summer."

"Or else he'd *cry* like when his daddy hit him with a belt."

I saw Klein flinch at that remark.

"Now everyone knows everything about him." Dornfeld smirked. "CNBC, the Journal!"

"There's only one mystery left," Dembicer teased.

"Which is?"

"Are his pubes still red?" Dembicer concluded.

That brought huge laughter from everybody. We were so loud one of the waiters almost knocked over a glass as he poured more wine.

"Wait a second, wait a second!" Gold shouted down the laughter. "I happen to know the answer to this! I was in a *steam room* with Mr. Klein!"

"When was this?"

"Who cares?"

"And I can testify that the answer is—yes!" announced Gold. "The winner and still crimson—the Fire Crotch!"

Klein just sat there and took the abuse with a smile. Watching all of them gang up on him reminded me that men are the same all over, whether in a summer camp, a prison, or a super fancy New York restaurant. They can be cruel at any moment.

"Sue me," he said to me with an untroubled smile. "I like to play Winged Foot."

"You play golf, Larry?" Gold asked me mid-sip, almost making me gag.

"No," I recovered. "Golf was never my thing."

I couldn't tell them what my real sport was for my whole life: survival. I hadn't drunk this much in years—maybe ever. Oh, I had gotten fucked up on my pruno in the joint many times, but this was different. This was fine wine, and the room was buzzing just right. The guys made sure the waiters kept refilling my glass, and I kept drinking. I could tell that they were trying to get me drunk, but they were also getting drunk themselves, so I guess it was OK. Plus I had that limousine waiting for me downstairs. What was I scared of? Fusco? Life outside a cell? These guys— these self-satisfied "successes"? Everything that I never did and never achieved?

"'Scuse me," Sanoff called to a waiter, raising his almost-empty wine glass. "A little more of that fancy bug juice!"

Bug juice! The moment I heard those words, it came flooding back to me—that camp with the funny name: Mooncliff. I suddenly saw the mountains, the lake, the trails through the forest, all those people, that odd guy Stewie, who was my co-counselor, and all the kids!

"Of course!" I half yelled across the table to Klein. "I remember! You were the Redheaded Doggy." I started pointing around the table. "And you were the Fat Doggy. And you were the Doggy With Braces. And you were the Doggy Bully. And you—I don't remember you at all."

"Dornfeld has always prided himself on being invisible." Klein smiled.

"Yes, I guess I was the Invisible Doggy," Dornfeld shrugged.

"Yo, Larry," Dembicer called to me from across the table. "Do you remember when I ran into you on Central Park West with my mother after camp? In front of the Museum of Natural History? I thought you were the coolest guy in the world."

"I don't remember that precisely," I said honestly, reaching back into my battered and now wine-twisted memory, "but I'm reasonably sure that I was almost certainly...completely out of my mind."

"The thing is, Larry," Klein said, swirling the wine in his big, beautiful glass, "we all thought that you were a good guy, and we were all really surprised when the whole murder thing happened."

That word—*murder*—brought a brief silence to the table, even though we could hear the muffled, tinkling clatter of Le Bernardin all around us.

All I could say was "Me too."

"We all couldn't believe it," said Gold.

"I mean we really liked you, Larry," Sanoff said sincerely. "We all did."

"Then why didn't you help me when I was in?" I said.

An even dead-er silence.

I could have kept my mouth shut, but something made me go on, something I had been meaning to say. Maybe it was the wine.

"I'm very glad that you liked me, and you say how you all thought I was a nice guy and everything," I continued. "So why, during all those years, didn't you reach out to me? Write me a letter. Hell, write my parole board."

More tinkling silverware from behind the walls around us.

"Well," Dornfeld mumbled, looking down, saying nothing.

Klein spoke up. "We were *young* when it happened, Larry. And our parents completely freaked out."

"Everyone freaked out at Mooncliff!" added Gold. "I mean, the whole *camp* was suddenly connected to this huge scandal."

"They weren't exactly connected," I countered.

"You dumped the bodies there, Larry!" said Dornfeld. "In the *Quarry*, for God's sake!"

That, I admit, stopped me.

"We all read about it in the papers and watched on TV," added Klein. "We couldn't stop talking about it. We were completely surprised."

"We just never thought of writing you a letter. Besides, our parents would have stopped us."

"There was really nothing we could do, Larry," said Dembicer. "We were *kids*. And then there was the trial."

Mantell! I had forgotten, in all this blur of wine and talk, to bring up Mantell to Klein!

"What he's really trying to say, Larry," Sanoff said expansively, "is that we're like everybody else and really don't give a shit about anybody but ourselves."

Sanoff spread his arms out wide, knocking over three glasses, sending water and wine spilling across the table onto my lap and Dornfeld's too. I jumped back up from the table, but not before my pants got sprayed with water. I think Dornfeld got it worse.

"Shit, Sanoff!!" Dornfeld shouted. "You fat fuck and your stupid arms!"

Waiters with napkins came rushing to the table to blot the tablecloth and try to pat Dornfeld and me dry.

"I'm OK! I'm OK!" I said, not wanting them to touch me.

I took one of the big cloth napkins they were offering and rubbed it on the leg of my pants, trying to dry myself off.

"You've been a klutz your whole life," spouted Dornfeld. "You know that?"

"He knows it."

"Give him a cookie and shut him up!"

"You OK, Larry?" asked Klein from across the table.

"Yeah," I said. "Wet, but OK."

The waiters got things as dry as they could, and we all sat down again. I was only a little wet. We took a long pause and drank whatever we had left. By then, we were past coffee, past desserts beyond description, and into after-dinner drinks. I felt full and empty, both at the same time.

"Well, one positive thing," Gold announced, "I fucked the yoga teacher."

The Doggies all cracked up as Gold nodded and smirked.

"*You* do *yoga*?" Sanoff almost had to spit his drink into his snifter.

"He doesn't do yoga. He does yoga *teachers*."

"His *wife's* yoga teacher."

Gold grinned then sniggered. "You should see the positions she gets into. You can fold her up like a fuckin' Swiss Army knife."

"Goldie, you really are a dog!" Dembicer scolded over the laughter.

"Oh, come on!" Gold protested. "You know what I've been through."

Over the simultaneous shouting and counter-shouting, Dembicer said to me, "You can't imagine how much we hated his first wife. She was like a monkey with a cunt."

More laughter. I even saw one of the stone-faced waiters crack a smile.

"Honestly, I don't know what I was thinking!" Gold wailed.

"You were thinking her father had money," Klein answered for him, "is what you were thinking. And he *staked* you."

"Oh, shut up, Fire Crotch," Gold shot back. "No one had a worse father than you."

Klein's smile froze for a millisecond, then he said with a nod, "That is true. But it's like I keep telling you guys, your next wife...*Asian*."

That got more laughter and some breadcrumbs or something thrown playfully at him.

Klein was unperturbed. "Haven't you guys learned anything? You let your wife *think* she has all the power, but you're really in control. It's called Jew-jitsu!"

More laughter, more thrown food, and more over-shouting commenced.

Perfect little pieces of candy on perfect little plates appeared before us. Nonstop brandy kept disappearing from my large, beautiful glass. I was completely buzzed, but I was having a good time: these guys were all pretty funny and smart, if also a little mean and a lot privileged. As much as I could figure out, Gold was a lawyer, Dornfeld was in advertising, Dembicer was in commercial real estate, and Sanoff ran the family business. I think it was jewelry. They all seemed so satisfied, so fulfilled. Mooncliff, as I remember it, was a camp for rich kids, and rich kids seem to do OK. Almost all the people I met in prison—convicts *and* guards—grew up poor.

"He wasn't *in*-sulting you, schmuck," said Klein, calmly refereeing a small dispute. "He was *un*-sulting you."

"You just tell your friend the mayor," said Dembicer, "if he raises my taxes again, I'm—"

"What?" snapped Gold. "You're gonna move your buildings to Alabama?"

"I wish I could," Dembicer retorted.

"And then what would they be worth?" Gold cracked. "That far from the subway?"

"In shit-for-brains land."

"You tell him and all his amigos—'I got mine. You get yours.'"

"Well said!"

"He's not my friend," Klein finally answered, "and he doesn't control taxes. You have to go to Albany to fight that fight."

"And who do you know *there* you can buy, Klein-o?"

Klein just sat back, smiled, shook his head, and signaled for the check. The dinner was ending, and I think the Doggies were all fully stuffed, very drunk, and completely happy with themselves, myself included.

"You wanna split a cab with me to Penn Station?"

"Sure."

"Where are you going, Larry?"

Stirred out of my alcohol-food-and-chocolate-induced haze, I said, "City Island."

"Where the fuck is that?"

"Isn't that in the Bronx?"

"*Da Bronks*!"

"How the hell did you wind up there?"

All I could say was, "It's a long, *long* story, one that keeps telling itself." I heard the distant tinkling of glasses and silverware.

"The one thing I gotta know, Larry," began Dornfeld, "is really: how the fuck did you survive all those years in prison?"

They all got super quiet and looked at me with their complete attention, eyes shining and as alert as drunks could be.

"What?" I said, swirling the brandy in my glass. "Do you want me to tell you some scary stories, just like I used to read you Edgar Allan Poe?"

They didn't say anything, so I went on.

"Didn't I read you 'The Pit and the Pendulum'" I asked, "where the guy uses bits of meat to attract rats so they can chew through his ropes? Or would you rather I tell you how I killed rats for months and saved their teeth to make a weapon? What about 'The Cask of the Amontillado,' where the guy gets walled up alive? Or you want to hear about the four months I spent in solitary, naked with no toilet paper, no light, no nothing? Or how about the time I saw a guy gouge out another guy's eye with a spoon—and eat it?"

I saw a couple of jaws drop at that one, but I couldn't stop myself. What the hell was I doing here? I didn't belong with these people. I wasn't their plaything, but why not give them a thrill? Play with *them*.

"I've seen a guy burned alive," I stated simply. "A guy beaten to death with a lock in a sock. I've seen a bar put through a guy's skull, ear to ear. I've seen gang rapes. Gang rapes for money, gang rapes for drugs, gang rapes for fun. I've seen men devolve into a state of brutality, without any decent restraint, totally beyond the pale of any acceptable human conduct."

Their eyes were glued to mine, the fat, stupid schmucks. They didn't even deserve my stories. They didn't even know that the last thing I said was a direct quote from *Apocalypse Now*, this great movie I watched on DVD with Betsy a couple of nights before, a fantastic Vietnam movie with Marlon Brando.

"That's what you came for, right?" I concluded. "I hope I gave you your money's worth."

No one said anything for a while until the waiter asked if we wanted anything else.

"I think that'll be it, gentlemen," said Klein, getting up from the table first. And we all followed our host.

We thanked all the waiters and waitresses. No one reached into his pocket to pay; it was Klein's party. And we walked out of the little room as if I had said nothing at all.

I had to hit the bathroom. I think we all did. Four or five bottles of very expensive bug juice, plus coffee, plus that gorgeous medicinal brandy in crystal snifters as big as softballs—had to be pissed away.

We took turns in the one-person bathroom in the hallway, letting Klein go first.

"Thanks for the dinner, Klein-o," said Sanoff. "You're the most generous chicken I know."

We all heartily concurred as Klein went in, and the door clicked. As soon as he was gone, the talk instantly turned to Klein and his money.

"So how rich is this fucking prick?"

"Wasn't he supposed to marry that Mexican model after his last marriage crashed?"

"And have to split his money?"

"There are prenups."

"Did you see the bill?"

"I didn't dare."

"Besides taking his old friends out to Le Bernardin," Dornfeld said, "the only thing he has that I care about is a signed Springsteen guitar."

"Not his *five* homes?"

"Have you seen his gun collection? It's ridiculous."

"How much you think this was? With tip."

"What, are you gonna chip in?"

"I'm tellin' ya, it's the change in his sofa. The loose coins in his sock drawer."

"*Fock!*"

"Let's see: New York, Bridgehampton, Aspen...London...and someplace in the Caribbean..."

"How much was the Springsteen guitar?"

"I read it was seventy-five grand. And it was for a charity."

"More!"

"Hey, Springsteen gives a million of 'em out, I bet. He gets 'em free from the manufacturer."

"Nothing is free these days."

"OK, then he gets a discount."

"I'd give that for an Eddie Van Halen maybe. Springsteen? Never."

"Oh, you're an idiot. Go listen to Billy Joel."

"They say he's involved with Russian mobsters. And he's gotten guys killed."

"That's bullshit."

"I'm just sayin'."

Klein came out, and we shut up.

"You go next," I was ordered. It took me a while to get going in there, but I was OK. It was a relief, pissing all this high-shelf booze out of me. I stood there, hazily thinking about how—outside in the hallway—they were now all talking about *me*. And what were they saying? I couldn't worry about that now. I had to worry about aiming my pee in this elegant little bathroom.

When I was finished, I walked out and let the next guy—fat Sanoff—take his turn.

"They went downstairs," he said, pushing past me in a big rush to get to the toilet.

I walked down the stairs, hanging on to the railing, one careful, rocky, drunken step at a time, and the Doggies were waiting at the bottom of the stairs.

"He descends," announced Gold.

"His groin completely mastered," cracked Dornfeld.

I was happy to get to the bottom of the stairs in one piece. It was a good thing I didn't have to drive or try to find a subway and navigate my way back to the Bronx.

Klein, with a self-satisfied smile on his face, hands in his pockets, looked at me and said, "Once upon a midnight dreary, while I pondered, weak and weary."

"Over... over?"

"Over *what*?"

And it just spilled out of me: "*Over many a quaint and curious volume of forgotten lore. While I nodded, nearly napping, suddenly there came a tapping. As of someone gently rapping at my chamber door. 'Tis some visitor,' I muttered, 'tapping at my chamber door.' Only this and nothing more.*"

They applauded, and two guys clapped me on the back as I felt the room spinning unsteadily.

"I remember *some* things," I mumbled. Even after I had tried to pee away all the alcohol in my system, I was still pretty crocked.

"Where is Sanoff?"

"Where he always is—in the can!"

"Some things sure don't change."

"At least he's not beating his pathetic meat in there."

"I hope not! This isn't Red Lobster."

Dornfeld turned me to face him. "This was after your time, but you've never seen a person masturbate as much as Sanoff did at Mooncliff. It was a constant thing, under the covers, every night. Like a rabbit."

Dornfeld made a quick shaking motion with his right fist.

"He beat his dick like it owed him money!"

"It's amazing he can find it, under that gut!"

Just then, Sanoff tromped down the stairs heavily and announced, "I can't believe I ate the whole thing!" And as he got to the bottom step, he let out an enormous, unmistakable fart.

"Oh, Christ!"

It was a long, loud *blurttt*, and it resounded against the blond-wood walls of Le Bernardin.

"Some things don't change."

"Doggies are doggies."

"Let's get out of here!"

"Amen!"

Just as I was pushed out the door, I looked back and saw Klein whisper something to one of the black-suited restaurant men and slip something into the guy's hand. Maybe it was just a handshake, but I knew that Jonathan Klein took good care of everyone in the place, probably for more than my phone bill and Betsy's rent money combined.

The fresh night air hit me but had no effect on my drunken state. It only made me numb.

"Holy shit, it's cold!"

"Gentlemen!" said Klein, the last one to emerge. "It's been real."

"Klein-o, you really delivered—again!"

Dornfeld got in another line: "Great food, Klein-o. But remember: it's all shit in the end!"

"Thanks a lot, Dornfeld."

"You dick!"

"Oh, he loves it. We're the only people who don't treat him like a fucking king."

"You wanna drop me at Penn Station?"

"He has his new Audi."

"Better an Audi than an inny."

"Will you shut the fuck up?"

"I'm parked on Fiftieth. I'll see you, Dogs! Call me, Bobby!"

The party was breaking up right before my eyes.

"Let's do it again! Next time—Jean Georges!"

Klein was at the curb, about to step into a really long limo. He yelled out, "Stay in touch! I love you fuckin' schnorrers!"

I started to say something to Klein, but in my haze, I hesitated.

"Mr. Ingber!" someone shouted out.

I called out to Klein, "Jonathan!" But his door had been slammed shut, and his driver was around the side, getting in.

"MR. INGBER!"

I looked around, almost dizzy, and noticed everyone was gone—except my driver, who was at the door of my limo, calling to me.

He smiled and held open the door for me. "You ready?" he seemed to say.

And I was. I walked straight across the sidewalk—or as straight as I could—to the waiting backseat of the black limousine. Nothing could have ever looked more welcoming.

I almost fell into the backseat, trying to turn around and sit at the same time. As I settled in, I carefully checked for my wallet, phone, and keys, confirming that I had everything I came with. As soon as we got going, I would take out my phone and try to text something to Betsy about this incredible night.

And the moment the limousine pulled away from the curb is when I realized, to my sudden, abject, dizzying, drunken horror, that I had forgotten to ask Klein to help me find Mantell!

EIGHTEEN

The next morning, I slept in, which I almost never do, but I had reasons. Usually I try to get up before Betsy to get the tea kettle going. But not this morning. Forget about the kitchen: I barely made it to the bathroom. Till the very last moment, I wasn't sure which end of me last night's dinner was going to come out of.

When I did stagger into the kitchen, in a semi-presentable state, with my teeth well brushed—though I could still taste the garlic or something spicy on my tongue—Betsy was at the stove, cooking.

"How're you doin'?" she greeted me in an affectionate, rueful tone.

"OK." I sighed, finding my way to a chair at the little two-person table by the window in the kitchen.

"You're just not used to all that rich food," she said.

"You're right about that," I admitted. "But it was worth it."

"What did you have?"

"Oh...fish."

"That's it? Fish?"

"Yeah, but fish like you've never seen. I mean, tasted."

"I saw some of it," she said. "On the internet, on their website. It looked very fancy."

"It *was*," I said. "You would have liked it. It was very"—I remembered the whole evening—"elaborate."

"You want some tea?" she asked, holding up my Giants mug.

"How about some...dry toast?"

"My poor boy," she said sympathetically, putting down the mug. "In a 'dry toast' condition."

271

I watched her take out a piece of bread and pop it in the toaster, hoping she wouldn't ask me about last night and if I got Klein to agree to help me find Mantell.

"So, tell me," she said, "is your Mr. Klein gonna help you find Lester Mantell?"

Did all women have that radar, that X-ray, or only Betsy?

"I think maybe I'll have that tea," I said.

"OK," she said, getting my mug and methodically making my tea as I'd seen her do so many times before. "So...*is he?*"

She was relentless.

"Well, I didn't exactly ask him," I muttered.

"Why *not?*"

She spilled a little of the boiling water on the counter.

"Well, I guess I kinda got a little carried away with the whole evening, the place, the food and everything, and I was going to ask him when this idiot spilled water all over me, and I'm really not used to drinking so much—that I forgot to—"

"You forgot?? Oh, Larry. How could you?"

"No!" I countered. "I was thinking that it's actually *better* this way. Not to ask him for a favor, the first time."

"But you had him right there, face-to-face. How do you know there'll be a second time?"

"I'll call him," I said, getting up to take her hands. "He liked me. I know it."

"But you were in the same room!"

"OK, what can I say?" I confessed. "I blew it."

"Oh, Larry."

"But I'll make it right. I promise, and you're burning my toast," I said.

"Oh, pish!"

Thank goodness for that distraction, changing the subject if only temporarily. And, as it turned out, the carbon in the burnt toast was good for my stomach, even though nothing could really help what was going on inside me—the sense of disappointment in myself, the feeling of failing Betsy.

We didn't talk much on the ride to Thomas Paine. I could have made more excuses, but they were exactly that. I couldn't keep out of my mind how royally I had fucked up, memories reeling back to this fuckup, that fuckup. My whole life's been a series of fuckups. OK, I stayed alive in prison, but now that I had gotten out, it had been nothing but a struggle. Betsy was taking such a chance on me—I had to find a way to make it right.

Traffic was always heavy around her school. Didn't kids walk anymore? Everyone seemed to be waiting in an endless drop-off line, policed by crossing guards with orange vests and handheld stop signs.

"You'll see," I said as I inched up in the line, "I'll give Klein a thank-you call and ask him to help me find Mantell *then*. Everything'll be fine. I got a very good feeling last night."

Right as I pulled up to the curb and Betsy was about to get out, she tapped herself lightly on the forehead and said, "And I forgot to tell you: Ken Fusco called."

"Fusco? When?"

"Last night," she said, pushing the door open, "at the store. Just after you left."

"What did he want?"

"To speak to you."

"But he has my cell!" I said, as she swung her legs out of the Jeep to step down.

"Great. What else could go wrong?"

She turned back to me and said with deadly calm, "That's entirely up to you."

Making one last stab at humor, I reached into my pocket and presented some red-and-white candy. "You want one of my limousine mints?"

"No, thanks," she said, looking down at my open palm. "I have my Altoids."

And as she closed the door, I saw a crestfallen look on her face—or did I imagine it? But I had to keep moving. The drop-off line couldn't wait for another heartfelt apology from me. I didn't think disappointing her would hurt so much.

⌢

When I got back, I did my usual routine of straightening up the apartment before I opened the store. I would wait for the right time to call Klein's office to thank him for last night—I didn't want to trust his email, that's for sure—and to ask him about Lester Mantell. In that order. But first I had to call Fusco.

I could hear Roland was awake downstairs. It was the day for Nurse Debbie to come see him. (By now, I even knew *his* routine.) I was glad that Roland was being well taken care of. He wasn't getting any younger, and more attention from Debbie meant less responsibility for Betsy...and me too, I guess.

I rehearsed my call to Klein. I would tell him what a great time I had (true) and how good it was to see all the Doggies again and relive old times (again, strange but true) before I got down to business. I couldn't call too early, though go-getters like Klein are probably up at dawn, getting reports from the Chinese stock market or something. But I didn't want to wait too late in the morning, in case he was going out to an early lunch.

But before anything else: Fusco. I had to keep him out of my life. I didn't have that much more time to go. I bet that I was doing better than the other skeeves he had to supervise, like those losers from Four Winds. Why was Fusco bothering me? Because he liked to—it was just his nature.

Fusco got into his office early, so I knew I could get him out of the way early. I set myself up at the kitchen table with my tea and dialed him on my cell phone.

"Yeah? Fusco. What?" he barked, picking up after the second ring. What a pleasant phone manner he had. Especially early in the morning.

"Hello, Officer Fusco," I said fake-pleasantly. "This is your easiest case, Larry Ingber. I understand you were looking for me."

"Yeah, I was," he began, but I cut him off.

"Then why didn't you call me on my cell phone?" I asked him. "Why did you call at the store? You can always get me on my cell."

"I called there on purpose," he said, "because I wanted to see if you was there."

"Oh, I still work here, if that's what you're asking. You know you can always come down and see for yourself, Officer Fusco," I said, just barely keeping the sarcasm out of my voice. I knew that he would never get off his fat ass to come down here and check for himself, even though New Rochelle was just a few miles away.

"Don't be so fuckin' smart," he sneered through the phone.

"I'm not smart," I said. "If I were smart, I wouldn't have someone like you in my life."

"Smart-ass," he muttered. "You woulda been out ten years earlier if not for your big mouth."

"Maybe so," I said. "And maybe it's my big mouth that's kept me alive all those years."

"I want you to come to my office next week," he said. "Next Wednesday, at three thirty."

"Why?" I protested. "That's not my regular day."

"So you can tell me why I shouldn't recommend to the board that they put you back in Four Winds—or worse," he snarled. "That's why."

"For what reason?"

"Because we found your name in Sammy Zambrano's phone, and he's told us that you're involved in his Medicare scam."

"Bullshit!"

"He told me you were in on the ground floor," he continued. "That you were one of the masterminds of the whole operation."

"That's crazy!" I shouted. "You can't trust Zambrano. He just threw you my name because he knew that you wanted to nail me on something!"

"Now *you're* the one who's crazy." He laughed and snorted because I told the truth and hit a nerve.

"You can't prove I had anything to do with something I had nothing to do with," I insisted. "Zambrano wants to make a patsy out of you."

"*Says you*," he barked. "You just be here in my office when you're supposed to and prove me wrong. That's...next Wednesday at...three thirty. Next week, big mouth. And please: miss it! *Don't* show up and give me an additional excuse to throw your ass back where it belongs."

And he hung up the phone. Hard.

I hung up too but slowly, then realized I was sweating heavily. I shouldn't alienate Fusco—in fact, just the opposite. And not with this sudden Zambrano bullshit to contend with. Sammy

Zambrano fingering me? That's ridiculous. Fusco couldn't have any real proof. Sammy might have given him manufactured proof, but I would deal with that when I saw Fusco.

I told myself that I better not forget that appointment with him: next Wednesday at three thirty. I could tell this was not the time to cross Fusco. He sounded serious about wanting to tie me to this Zambrano nonsense before my parole was over, and I was beyond his control. Then I'd really be free. I was just about to write down the new time when I heard an enormous crash from downstairs. It actually made the walls tremble. It sounded like something heavy fell. Something or some*one.*

I dropped everything and ran downstairs to the store, holding the bannister with two hands so I didn't fall myself. When I got to the bottom, I called out, "Roland!...*Roland*?"

Nothing.

Then, I heard a faint "*In here*" from the utility room. That's where we kept stepladders, tools, brooms, and shelves of boxes of "unsalable junk worth keeping"—Roland's term. I dashed to the utility room and pushed the half-open door to see Roland lying on the floor under a big pile of boxes and wooden crates.

"Oh, shit," I said and squeezed in.

"'Oh, shit' is right!" he grunted, trapped under the weight of all the stuff.

"Roland!" I said, setting my feet and carefully lifting off the box on top. "Why didn't you ask me to help you with this?"

"Because I thought I could get the damn thing myself!" he answered with maximum annoyance.

"Are you hurt?" I asked as he tried to rise, unsettling the pile and shifting more things onto him. "Shit!" I said catching a slipping box.

"You mean besides my pride?" he said, his voice gravelly and angry.

"Wait a second!" I said. "Don't move!"

I got enough off him for him to struggle out.

"Dammit!" he said as he took my hand and got unsteadily to his feet. "It was my damn fault," he said, rubbing his forehead.

"What happened?" I asked him.

"'What happened?'" he grumbled, moving away from me, finding his balance to stand alone. "I got old!"

⌒

I helped him back into his room and made sure he was OK. I hadn't been back in Roland's apartment but a couple of times. It was such an old man's habitat: dusty books on all the shelves, ancient photographs on the walls, stale cigar smell in the air, and a big, well-used lounger across from a large TV. Next to the chair on the right sat a lamp on a side table holding a whole lot of tiny bottles of medicine, and on the left a TV tray with a half-empty bottle of Jim Beam and a glass.

Roland finally admitted that one of the boxes "grazed" him on the head, so I got him to sit down in the lounger while I filled a plastic bag with ice. By the time I got back to his living room with the ice, I could tell Roland was depleted.

"You sure you're OK?" I asked, handing him the bag of ice, which he put right on his forehead.

"Yeah," he said disgustedly. "Oww!"

"Next time," I said, "please call me. I'm just upstairs."

He looked up peevishly. "I told you—I thought I could get it myself."

"OK. No problem," I said. I could see that the old guy's feelings were hurt as much as his forehead. "Let me go back and restack that stuff in the storeroom."

I started to walk out when he said one more thing.

"Larry?"

I turned back to face him.

"Thanks," he said, looking me right in the eyes. He didn't like to show weakness, and I respected that. He was significantly older than me, but I thought, *This is where I'm going to be soon: old, and on the inevitable road to helplessness.*

I went back into the utility room and restacked the mess, getting a splinter from one of the crates along the way. I really wish he had asked me to help him, but Roland was stubborn. Just like me. In fact, the whole utility room needed straightening, and I was in there for a good twenty minutes before I remembered I wanted to call Klein at eleven.

I ran up the stairs, two at a time. Even though I had no actual deadline, I felt this pressing need to call him *now*—before he forgot all about last night. Of course, it took me a good five minutes to find my phone. I was on the verge of calling it from the house phone in the kitchen when I saw it, half hidden under a pile of papers for recycling. Then I got my wallet and picked out the elegant business card that Brian Halliwell gave me. Klein Global Partners. I rubbed my finger over the embossed gold type on the cream-colored card, telling it to *Count me in.*

Pressing in the phone number, I rehearsed what I was going to say. I *had* to do this right.

"Klein Global Partners!" a crisp young female voice answered. "Mr. Halliwell's office."

I went into action: "Hello. May I please speak to Mr. Halliwell? This is—"

"Hold please!"

I waited until another bright voice spoke.

"Klein Global Partners!" she said. "Mr. Halliwell's office."

"Hello. May I please speak to Mr. Halliwell?"

"Who may I say is calling?"

"Larry Ingber. *Laurence* Ingber." I don't know why I corrected myself.

"And does he know what this is in reference to?" she said in a friendly but suspicious way.

"I'm a friend of Jonathan Klein's," I said, "really...we had dinner last night."

"Oh," she said. That stopped her. "Would you hold please?"

Great. I was getting through. While I was on hold, some light classical music played. Nice touch, but the problem was that I waited listening to that damn music for more than five minutes. I was wondering if she had forgotten me. Did Mr. Pinstripe say, "What the hell does that jailbird want?" Was he making fun of me with his minions? Would he even tell Klein that I was calling? All those negative thoughts coursed through my mind as naturally as water flowing downhill as I waited...and waited...and waited.

Then the line clicked to life: "Hold, please, Mr. England!" the bright girl said.

Great! Close enough. But then she was off, and I listened to five *more* minutes of classical music. Just when I was despairing of ever getting through, the line picked up again.

"Mr. Ingber? Brian Halliwell here."

"Brian!" I said cheerfully. "Nice to hear your voice. You think I can I speak to...Jonathan? About something from last night?" At the last moment, I decided to be informal.

"I'm sorry," he shot back, "but Mr. Klein is in meetings all day."

All day. Damn.

"Well," I said, stalling for time, "he asked me to call him." That was only a slight lie. He said, "Stay in touch," didn't he?

"Is there anything *I* can help you with?" Mr. Pinstripe asked, sounding very insincere.

"No," I answered. "When is the best time to call back?"

"It's hard to say. Mr. Klein is very busy. Why don't you put your request in an email instead? Jay dot Klein at Klein Global Partners dot net. That really will get through to him, promise," he purred.

No question he was getting rid of me. I knew from that first time I met him that he was going to be trouble.

"It's OK, I'll call again," I said. "It's really better if I explain it to him in person. I mean, on the phone, talking."

"He does read his email. I promise," he advised me. "I really don't know when he'll have time for you."

"Hmm," I said. "Maybe I'll try his email. But can you be sure to tell him I called?"

"I shall. Now can I help you with anything else?" Pinstripe snapped, polite but impatient, obviously wanting to get rid of me so I took a different, desperate tack.

"Thank you, Brian," I said. "And just one more thing," I added. "I want to thank you and tell you how much I appreciated last night. I can see how much you do for Mr. Klein."

That stopped him momentarily. Flattery almost always works.

"It's simply my job," he replied.

I snickered. "It's more than that, and you know it."

He paused and said, "I'll be sure to tell Mr. Klein that you called."

"I'd be most grateful," I said. "And thanks again." Might as well try to befriend him now—better late than never.

And I hung up. Well, that didn't go exactly as I planned. Again, I cursed myself for not nailing down Klein last night and *making* him help me find Mantell. A guy like him had to have resources that even the FBI didn't have.

Mentally I began to compose the email to Klein and went back downstairs to Roland's apartment to see how he was doing. Fortunately, I found him sitting up in his armchair, reading a book while watching CNN at high volume, eating something from a bowl.

"Nuts?" he said, offering me some.

"No, thanks."

"And let's not mention my little tumble to Betsy," he said. "No reason to worry her."

"Good thinking," I agreed, happy to see that Roland was alive and himself.

I went back upstairs, got my laptop, reheated my tea, and came back down to watch the store from the counter. There, I sat and composed my email to Jonathan Klein.

This is exactly what I wrote (as saved in my Sent mail):

Dear Jonathan—

I tried to call you at your office, at Brian Halliwell's number, but I couldn't get through to you. I guess I'm old-fashioned, but I wanted to thank you PERSONALLY for last night. It was great: the food, the place, the Doggies—everything. You are a very generous person.

Amid all the fun last night, I forgot to ask you something: I've been having trouble locating my former attorney, Lester J. Mantell, of Mineola, L.I. and St. Croix, U.S. Virgin Islands. I was wondering if I could talk to you about using some of your resources to help me find Mr. Mantell.

This is a matter of the greatest importance to me.

Thanks for everything,
The Assistant Groinmaster

I sat there for a minute, reading it over, and then clicked "Send." As soon as I hit the button, I regretted signing it "The Assistant Groinmaster." That was stupid and juvenile. What was I thinking? That it was casual and funny? Did it undermine the seriousness of my message, or did it show how relaxed and trusting I was? Maybe I should stop overthinking everything so much. Or isn't that what got me into trouble in the first place? *Not* thinking.

And anyway, if Klein didn't answer my email, I knew where he lived.

When Betsy finally got home, she didn't mention a thing about Klein. Was she waiting for me to bring it up, or was she just a forgiving person? Actually, both. She was serving dinner, leftovers of a nice casserole she had made, when I couldn't wait any longer.

"I called Jonathan Klein today," I said offhandedly as she set down a plate in front of me.

"Oh?" she said noncommittally.

"He was in meetings all day, so he couldn't talk, so I sent him an email," I said. "That's what his assistant said to do....I didn't hear anything back."

Betsy sat down with her plate and started eating, saying nothing more.

"Klein Global Partners," I said tartly.

Betsy picked at her food, not looking at me. She said, reasonably, "Someone like that is probably very busy with important things."

I pounced right on that: "What? And a convict like me is completely unimportant?"

She looked straight at me. "I didn't say that. And you're not a convict anymore, right? Do you think you're acting like one?"

That pushed me too far.

"I don't know what you expect of me!" I had raised my voice, startling her, but I didn't care. "I'm trying my hardest! I help downstairs, I help with Roland. I'm trying to get other work. Maybe I'll go back to Charlie Wagner's tonight and—"

"You don't have to do that," she shook her head. "You burned your hands."

I stood up from the table. "What do my hands matter? Nothing is working like it was supposed to. Yeah, I'm out of prison, but I still feel trapped. I just can't find a way to feel free....And this is not about you; it's about me. Not everything is fixable!"

I finally got to her; she broke into tears. She dropped her fork on her plate and fast-walked out of the room.

"What?" I yelled after her. "Did you expect anything else?"

I heard her run into the bedroom and close the door behind her, *click*. I was angry with myself. I didn't want to feel weak. I thought that surviving all those years in prison had removed all the weakness from me, but I was wrong. I had screwed up the Klein connection. After all she had done for me, I let her—let *us*—down, and I couldn't take the blame.

And it broke my heart even more when she didn't *slam* the door like a regular angry person. She closed it calmly and precisely, as if she were closing the door on us.

Of course, I couldn't eat much of the dinner. My stomach was all knotted up with tension and regret. So I went downstairs to escape my bitter, rueful thoughts, check on Roland's condition, and give Betsy some time alone in the apartment, away from me. She definitely deserved it.

Even though it was late, I didn't hesitate to knock on Roland's door because I heard his television. I knocked loudly though. Roland's hearing always dodgy; after all, he was well into his eighties. I was about to knock a third time when he ripped open the door, wild-eyed and wild-haired.

"What's the matter?" he demanded. "Is everything OK?"

"Yes!" I had to laugh, to defuse him. "Of course, everything is fine. I was checking on you. Because of what happened."

"Oh," he grunted. Stopped in his tracks.

Eyeing me suspiciously, he considered the situation, then opened the door a little wider. "You want to come in?"

"Sure," I said, walking in casually but respectfully. In all the months I'd been living there, I had hardly ever "invaded" Roland's private sanctum, and here I was again, for the second time in a day.

The TV was on loud. It looked like he was watching the History channel. And there was an open book on the table next to his lounger, the one with all the medicine bottles.

"Here, let me turn this down," he said, striding back to his chair on his stiff leg to pick up the remote. He pointed it at the TV and pressed down with his thumb. "I hate these things," he said, working the remote until the sound went down. "Thank goodness! They make these things so loud... the commercials."

"It's to wake people up who were sleeping through their shows," I said.

"I wasn't sleeping," he said, somewhat defensively. "Not exactly. This is one of my favorite shows. Hitler gets his ass kicked—again."

"Who doesn't love a happy ending," I agreed, looking around at the crammed bookshelves and walls full of photographs of young, strapping Roland on different boats of different sizes.

"You want a drink?" he asked.

"No, thanks," I said, thinking of my sensitive stomach and last night's debauchery.

"No problem," he said, putting down the remote and picking up a bottle of Jim Beam. "I'll have yours."

He poured a couple of fingers of whiskey into a glass, sat back down in his lounger, and hoisted up his stiff leg on the ottoman with an *ufff*.

"Come on in," he said. "Take a load off, Annie. Or Fanny."

I sat down on the couch perpendicular to Roland's chair-TV axis after moving a pile of old *New York Times* aside to find a clear spot.

Sinking back into the old couch, I tried to get comfortable, feeling that something metal had sprung deep inside the couch's cushion.

"You read all these books?" I asked. I've seen prison libraries with fewer books than Roland had.

"Most of 'em," he said absently. "You have a lot of time to read at sea. Dead time."

"I know what you mean," I said. "Books kept me alive, sometimes for years."

"How long were you in the joint for?"

"Too long," I said.

He looked over at me sharply, as if seeing me for the first time. Then he poured a little more into his glass.

"I always drink just enough," he said, taking a sip from the glass. "And not a drop more. I'm actually in great shape, outside of that stupid fall today. Considering everything."

"What is 'everything?'" I asked, unable to contain my curiosity.

He snickered. "You want to know the full catalog? Arthritis. Bum, unfixable knee. A broken back when a two-ton boom dropped on it, three vertebrae fused."

"Wow," I said. "That must have all been painful."

"Painful?" he barked a laugh. "What exactly is *painful*? There're all kinds of painful." He took another sip and looked thoughtful. "Painful is when you're in the middle of the Indian Ocean, and you can't get home for unexpected funerals. This is before cell phones, when you'd be out of touch for weeks. Months, sometimes."

He took a second sip and put down the glass. I figured if I kept quiet, he would talk more, and he did.

"Didn't Betsy tell you? I had a wife and daughter died in a car accident. It was a very long time ago. It was outside Boston when I was half a world away," he stated, trying to keep the emotion out of his voice. "They were in the ground three months cold before I even knew about it. Didn't Betsy tell you all this? To explain to you why I'm the way I am."

I shook my head.

"She doesn't know that I was this way to begin with," he said. "Always was. People don't change. They just become more of what they already are."

"Unfortunately," I concurred.

"Sorry for getting personal," he said. "But it's the anniversary. I try not to live in the past, but the past has a mind of its own."

"I know what you mean about pain," I said. "Some kinds of pain never go away. Scar tissue may form around it, but the wound is always there. Hell, it becomes a central part of you."

He laughed mirthlessly, and his eyes moved from his glass to meet my gaze.

"So," he said for a second time, "how long were you in the joint for?"

This time, I told him the truth.

"Shit," he said. "That's longer than I was in the Merchant fuckin' Marines! You sure you don't want a little Jimmy?" He clinked his glass against the nearby bottle of Jim Beam.

"Maybe just a short one," I said.

He got up from his chair with only a little struggle, said, "Then let me get you a clean glass," and shuffled over to the TV table with his bar setup. "Forty years in prison, a man deserves a clean glass."

"Not too much," I said, my stomach still in knots. "Don't waste it."

"Here," he said, handing me the half-filled glass. "Shut up and drink it. It'll make you feel different."

"I *want* to feel different," I said. I took the glass and toasted him, "Your health! And a better sense of balance."

"That's as good as anything," he grunted and raised his glass toward me as he sat back down heavily.

I sipped the whiskey and looked around at his lair. (There was really no other word for it.) His books and the photographs from his life surrounded us, dark and full of memories. Admiring all the pictures of the ships he was on and the places he had been, I said, "Looks like you've been all over the world, Roland."

"*Twice* all over," he wheezed. "Make that five times."

"You're lucky," I said. "I've seen so little." There was no point in hiding my regret: facts are facts. "You're a real citizen of the world."

"Nah, I'm an American, clean through, bone deep," he said. "No matter where I went, I always felt like a real American and nothing else, and I always came home. Always *wanted* to come home."

"Good for you," I said.

"You'd think so, wouldn't you?" He sighed, looking thought-fully into the bottom of his glass. "Except that every time I'd come home, little by little, I'd see my beloved country get just a little bit, bit by bit...worse."

"You know, Roland," I said deliberately, "I hate to say it, but I've seen the *same thing*, but for me, it was one big jump. OK, when I went in, people were fighting about the war—the Vietnam War—and civil rights, and women's rights and a bunch of other things, but there was never the level of *viciousness* you see now. What the hell happened? Why is there all the *hatred* you see in people? You see it everywhere—in the stores and in the streets, on TV. In the way the people *drive*. Even with all these great phones and wireless everything, everything seems just... uglier. And dumber. And nastier. It's not the America I remember. What the hell happened?"

He looked at me gravely and stared down at the floor. He seemed to be reaching deeply into himself.

"Well, my son, it's like this," he began, "there are two Americas: the Good America and the Bad America, always have been. And they've always been at war, on and off. But now the centrifugal force and stress of modern life have separated them out, and now the Bad America seems to be winning."

"What do you mean?" I asked him. "Exactly."

"I mean that Christopher Columbus was an amazing sailor, and he slaughtered tens of thousands of Arawak men, women, and children for gold that didn't exist. The Founding Fathers were very brave men who risked their lives, fortunes, and sacred honor to increase the freedom of men, and forty-nine percent of them, including George Washington and James Madison, owned slaves. Saint Thomas Jefferson wouldn't even free the sons he had with Sally Hemmings—his own sons! The Constitution as it was originally written designated four classes of people: free persons, those bound to service, Indians, and other persons, in other words: slaves. And this doesn't even include *women* who weren't technically people anywhere, a condition that still exists today in many places, but that's beside the point."

"Keep going," I urged.

"All you have to do is read about it," he continued, waving at his vast library, "if you have the stomach. If you're willing to see the truth. Which most Americans aren't. Whoever called us the United States of Amnesia was absolutely dead on-target."

"The truth is dangerous," I replied.

"It certainly is," he said, nodding. "And it is an increasingly rare commodity because it is purposefully, systematically being obscured. But it's hard to admit the truth about your country. It's much easier to lie. Lies give you freedom; they give you room to maneuver morally. We don't like too many hard facts in the USA, especially when your fact gets in the way of what *I* want to do. *My* money, *my* rights. Forget the Land of the Brave, Home of the Free, e pluribus bullshit: this country is about nothing but conflict. Conflict and pushback. Always has been, right from the beginning. Settler versus Indian...North versus South, East versus West, black versus white...native-born versus immigrant, boss versus worker, city versus country...Democrat versus Republican, rich versus poor...smart versus stupid. 'I got mine, you get yours!' versus 'promote the general welfare.' Bloodthirsty, bloodless, and never looking backward."

He was really going now, pitching forward in his chair, eyes ablaze.

"The contradictions have always been there, but the country used to be big enough to hold 'em all. Then the good times got all used up, but, of course, profits must still be made. And when companies found people in other countries who would work for pennies, well, forget it; that was it. They killed the unions who were protecting the workers, and the whole middle of the country got hollowed out. The jobs all went to China or Malaysia or Mexican robots, and the damage was done. That America ain't ever coming back. And people are mad. They don't know what's gone wrong, but they're mad, and they have every right to be because they've been fleeced by the owners of the U.S. of A. They're mad and looking for someone to blame, someone to hate, and most importantly – someone they can feel superior to. Everybody needs someone to look down on. No matter how shitty their lives are, 'At least I'm not a nigger-faggot-chink-beaner-kike-towelhead'" He sighed deeply and shook his head "Honestly? I think it's worse than it's been since, well, since the Civil fucking War. I don't know if this country will ever come back, but I know that I won't be here to see it."

He took a long drink after that, and I took one too.

"Is that what you learned at Harvard?" I asked him.

"Betsy tell you I went there?" he answered, somewhat irked. "Yeah." He sighed. "I got my Preparation-H in Cambridge."

"I like that," I said. "'Preparation-H.' I thought that telling someone you went to Harvard is like dropping the H-bomb."

He sniffed at that. "That's good too. Except sometimes the H-bomb drops on you."

I could see him think for a moment, a wistful look in his eye.

"College used to be a place where you got an education," he said. "Now it's a place where you learn to get rich *or else*."

"Did *you* get rich?" I teased him.

"Obviously," he answered, deadpan. "I probably could have. It's what my father and mother wanted for me, but it was not my choice. I made my choice: I wanted to be free."

"Free," I repeated, thinking what that word meant to me for so many years. "I just don't understand what the hell happened to everything while I was gone. That good old imaginary America; *some* of it was real, wasn't it?"

"Aww, they let everything get out of whack!" Roland sat back and took a drink. "They let the greed get all out of control. Greed is like any vice: it must be controlled for the sake of the general population. There used to be a balance. OK, there were always rich people and poor people, but now it's just ridiculous. It's like the fuckin' middle ages."

"No kidding."

"It's all about money now," Roland spat out. "America isn't a country anymore; it's a fucking corporation. The Supreme Court said that the government is officially for sale and can be bought like a street whore, an expensive street whore. This country used to be a decent place to be nobody in. You could still have some dignity as an average American, walking down the street. You could be poor but you still felt like somebody, even if it was a lie. Hell, we were happy to be duped. The difference is that now the lie has been exposed, the greed is just boundless, and nobody can stop it. Nobody. Boundless and shameless, predatory capitalism. Screw the customer, screw the employee, make the profits and keep them all. Greed never sleeps. What can you say? The bad guys won, and they have their own well-oiled lying machine, pumping out the hate every day. People think it's raining, when they're just getting pissed on."

"Amen!"

"Never trust people," he grumbled. "Hitler was a vegetarian, and Nixon was a Quaker."

"People don't know history," I commented. "They don't want to know."

"And all this ignorance and denial have made us into a mean country. Flat-out mean," he declared. "Yep, the bad guys are winning. People are giving in to stupidity and cruelty. We don't deserve this country."

"Maybe we're getting *exactly* what we deserve," I said darkly. No matter how smart Roland was, how much of the world he had seen, where he went to school, a person who has not been in a U.S. prison doesn't understand the depths of American cruelty.

Roland looked at me with softer eyes.

"Why aren't you upstairs?" he asked. "Everything OK with you and Betsy?"

"I guess so," I said. "Except for that I'm not good enough for her."

"What man is 'good enough?'" he scoffed. "Women are the superior sex. That's why we have to dominate them."

I laughed at the sorry truth of that.

"You better be good to Betsy," he said measuredly. "Treat her wrong, and I'll cut your heart out." Then he gave me a big smile as he finished his glass.

"Don't worry, Roland," I said. "I have no intention of treating her wrong, at least not intentionally. I'm not stupid; I know what I've got."

"Do you?"

"I think I do," I defended myself. "After what I've been through? What I've seen?...Betsy is a genuinely good person. I didn't think people like that existed. She's so upbeat all the time."

"She's a good faker," he said.

"You think she's faking?"

"You didn't know her husband," he said. "She had some difficult times."

I waited for him to continue, but he said nothing. Finally, I had to prompt him.

"You gonna tell me about 'em?"

"There's nothing to tell," he said. "Steve Hull was a good-enough-looking guy, I suppose, but he wasn't very nice to her. I think he was afraid of her."

"Afraid of Betsy?"

"Afraid of her brain," he corrected me. "Afraid of her strength and her goodness. She's a tiny thing, but she's strong. And she is honest."

"And she's not pretending," I insisted. "That's the way she really is."

"I'm not talking about little lies," he said. "Everyone has to lie a little to get by, to be polite and be able to live with yourself, but it's the big lies that you gotta avoid. The big lies are the ones that'll kill ya."

I thought about how positive Betsy almost always was. But was she really covering up some deep unhappiness, something I didn't recognize? And was that why she was involved with me, a broken-down ex-con, because there was something sad and troubled inside her? What was I missing? There was so much she didn't know about me, but I didn't know about her either: her marriage, the darkness inside that Kelly first told me about. Is everyone unknowable and alone?

"The other thing," he said, looking down into his glass, "is that I think I might be losing the store."

"What do you mean?" I asked.

"I talked to Jensen. The numbers just aren't adding up anymore, kid," he said.

"So what are we going to do?" I wondered out loud.

"I don't know about you," he said, getting up from his chair, "but I'm going to bed."

I left Roland's apartment, closing the door very quietly behind me. My mind was spiraling downward. I felt like everything was going wrong—with the store, with my country, and with myself.

I liked Roland a lot and didn't want to let him and Betsy down. What if I couldn't ever get any of the money that Mantell had? What then? I had to come up with some way to help save the store, or some way to get money. It wasn't just a place of business; it was where we lived. This was a real home for me, living with Betsy. I couldn't stand by and watch it disappear. America seemed to want to crush everyone who wasn't rich or privileged these days. It was turning out that the world outside was cruel, just like prison, only you were your own guard, and you watched yourself, trapped in your own *celf*, twenty-four hours a day.

I walked back up the stairs, feeling an emptiness I thought I would never feel again outside of a jail cell. I thought that when I got out, my problems would be over, but I knew now that I was kidding myself. As I opened the door to the apartment, I went in as quietly as I could, as if I didn't exist at all. Maybe I had finally bottomed-out. I didn't think I'd ever feel anything as bad as prison, but this was damned close. Maybe it wasn't the cage, after all; maybe it was me.

NINETEEN

The next Saturday, Betsy and I went to Kelly's house for grand-niece Emily's birthday. I told Betsy to get her some Legos, but she said she already had a book for Emily, and besides, Legos are expensive. We were just going to drop in, say hi, leave the present, and go, but it stretched into a much longer visit.

We had left Roland in charge of the store on a Saturday afternoon, when we had our peak traffic (for what it was worth these days), so I didn't want to be away all afternoon. It was simply getting to be too much effort for him. But Betsy started helping with the party, and she seemed to enjoy the kids. Even though she was with kids all week—well, older kids—she really liked watching these little ones. I did too, seeing them run around, wasting their manic energy, mixing uneasily with one another, pretending things. Just like grown-ups.

I made myself useful and invisible, throwing away the garbage that piled up (paper plates, plastic forks, and paper napkins—all *Little Mermaid*), and staying out of the way. Kelly was thankful that I pitched in, and I told her it wasn't anything special.

In a very solicitous way, she asked me how I was doing. I told her that I was fine, working in Roland's store. I didn't know what exactly Betsy had told her, and anyway, I like to play my cards close to the vest.

"Did you hear what happened?" she asked me, picking some icing off her sweater. "Remember Derek Ellison?"

"Remember him? No!...Of course, I remember him!" I huffed. How could she even ask me that?

"Well," she said, eyes going wide, "he had this terrible accident, and now he's paralyzed. He's in a wheelchair."

"Wow," I said. I almost added, "Serves him right," but I didn't. I did, however, think it. Instead I asked, "What kind of an accident?"

"I think he was water-skiing," she said.

I pictured Derek, that handsome young kid, in a wheelchair, and it made me sad, despite my hard feelings about what he did.

"You think it would have been snow-skiing," I said.

"Why is that?" Kelly asked.

"He went to Dartmouth," I replied.

She was about to say something, when there was a crash of glass breaking from the other room.

"Oh no," she said, pivoting away from me and fast-walking out of the kitchen.

I went back to work wiping the counters, thinking about Derek—that rich, good-looking kid, that fortunate son—and about how life fucks everybody. Absolutely everybody.

⌒

As we drove home, the news about Derek put me in a pensive mood. I didn't want to feel sorry for someone I didn't like. Betsy was humming happily; she had a good time at the party and was so great with the kids. I had to ask her something I'd been meaning to for a long time.

"You're so great with kids, honey," I said. "Why didn't you, you know—?"

"Have kids of my own? I couldn't," she said simply. "I tried, believe me, but it was physically impossible. Anatomically, I mean. I suppose today, with all the new science, something could have been done, but that was a long time ago."

I looked over quickly to see if I was upsetting her, but she seemed OK.

"So why didn't you adopt?" I asked.

"He didn't want to," she answered.

"Why not?" I probed.

"He didn't want to do *a lot* of things," she said, ending the conversation.

I knew enough to keep my mouth shut until we got home.

With Roland's blessing, we did a big Memorial Day sale, which generated a lot of foot traffic and some money. The free sugar cookies that Betsy baked and handed out were perhaps more successful than the sale. I went to meetings of the City Island Chamber of Commerce, a group that Roland had long ago offended and alienated. I scoured websites for articles like "Eight Steps to Save Your Small Business." On one of them, the last step was "Recognize Reality."

I had a very unpleasant conversation with Bob Jensen after he had yelled at Betsy over the phone the day before. She might have been wrong about some numbers, but he had no right to yell at her. *She* was the client, *she* was the customer. Still, with Roland less engaged in the business, we were more than ever beholden to Jensen and his advice.

The very next Monday, something happened that slowly set in motion a great many changes. I had dropped Betsy at school and was back cleaning up the apartment when my cell phone rang. I saw that it was Kelly's number. That surprised me; she never called me on my cell anymore.

"Hi...Kelly?" I shouted into the phone, just in case I lost her.

"Hey, Larry!" she said, sounding very happy and enthusiastic, which made me a little suspicious.

"What's up, Kelly?" I listened as she began to tell me once again about Derek Ellison's accident.

"You told me that, Kelly." I waited for more.

"OK." She sighed. "Here's the deal. This isn't the first time they've approached me about you."

"About *me*?"

"Sylvia Lemaire," she continued. "You remember her. She asked me again."

"Again?"

"As a favor to Mr. Blackburn. You know that he's close to Charles Ellison, Derek's father. And he asked Blackburn to get involved."

I didn't say anything. I just waited for her to go on. As if the name *Blackburn* was going to open any doors. He wasn't my boss anymore.

"It seems that Derek isn't doing very well since his accident. By that, I mean psychologically. He's depressed."

"Who wouldn't be?"

"No, I mean seriously," Kelly said.

"Why don't they give him some antidepressants?" I suggested. "That's what they do to depressed people." (They tried to give me all kinds of drugs—antidepressants and stronger stuff—to control me in prison, but I never took them. They had my body, but I never surrendered my mind.)

"No, really," she insisted. "They're genuinely worried about the kid."

"That's too bad," I said. "Get him a therapist."

"No, he wants to see *you*."

"Me?"

"The thing is that Derek feels guilty about that article he wrote about you."

"Good. He should be."

"And he thinks that that's what somehow caused his accident."

"What?" I paused, genuinely surprised. "He thinks that I *jinxed* him? That it was, what, some kind of existential punishment for betraying me?"

"I don't know what he thinks," she said, "but he wants to apologize to you in person."

"Wait, it wasn't a jinx, Kelly," I corrected myself. "It was *karma*."

"In any case," she continued, "he really wants to see you, and maybe it'll change how he's doing. Would you see him, Larry?"

"Let me think about it," I said. "But I really have no desire to do anything for those people. Why should I?"

"No reason," she replied, whether she agreed with me or not. "Just think about it, OK?"

That night, Betsy waited until we were in bed before she asked me, "So, Larry—are you gonna see Derek Ellison?"

"You know about this?"

"You know that Kelly and I talk," she said, defending herself. "And we also talk about things that have nothing to do with you."

I told her my first reaction straight out. "Why should I do anything for the Ellisons? That article got me fired."

Peter Seth

"But now it's about the boy," she pleaded, "in a wheelchair for the rest of his life."

"How can you feel sorry for him?" I said, raising my voice even though I didn't want to.

She froze and said warmly, "How can you *not*?"

⌒

Of course I decided to go see Derek, but only for Betsy so that she would think better of me, that I wasn't a hard-hearted, vindictive ex-con. I really had very little sympathy for Derek, no matter how young he was or how much he had fucked up. I called Kelly back and got the Ellisons' phone number.

"You have no idea how much this means," Kelly said.

"You're right," I replied tartly. "I don't."

She thanked me again, and I hung up and punched in the phone number before I changed my mind.

I must say that Mrs. Ellison couldn't have been nicer, sounding both gracious and desperate. It was arranged that I'd drive over there that afternoon and "just chat" with Derek.

"I'll watch the store, no problem," Betsy volunteered. (Thomas Paine was closed that day.) "You're doing the right thing, Larry. I'm proud of you."

"Yeah, right," I mumbled, my feelings still divided between doing the right thing and fuck 'em.

I took the keys to the Jeep and said goodbye to her from the back door.

"You know that I'm doing this for you!" I said in one final, clear protest.

"Thank you, Larry," she said, ignoring my negative mood. "See you later. I'm baking some chocolate clouds."

"You can't bribe me with baked goods," I responded.

She smiled. "Yes, I can."

⌒

So I drove to Scarsdale when a good part of me wanted to drive down to Manhattan and camp outside of Jonathan Klein's town-

296

house to see him face-to-face. Instead I did a favor for people who did me wrong.

It wasn't hard to find Derek's house. Everything is easy to find with the GPS lady giving me directions. Driving into the Ellisons' neighborhood was like going into The Girl's neighborhood. You went from ordinary suburban streets to—*Oh!* This *is where the really rich people live.* Suddenly the houses got bigger and farther apart, the lawns spread themselves out wider, greener, and thicker. Cars were more expensive. There were long walls and tall hedges, and almost no people. They were all hiding.

"Your destination is on your right."

I turned in at the bottom of a long, blacktop driveway that led up past a broad lawn to the top of the rise and a very substantial two-story, whitewashed brick colonial house, sheltered by enormous trees and perfectly trimmed bushes. Though it was still afternoon, the porch lights were on, on either side of the front door: big, black iron sconces. There was a big white car at the end of the driveway, just in front of the garage on the side of the house, and a large minivan behind the car. Lamplight glowed through the lacy curtains in the front room. Obviously, people were home.

Before I even got to the front door, it opened. As I stepped up onto the porch, a tall, thin, blond woman in a white silk blouse and slim black pants emerged from the house and welcomed me with an extended hand and a weary, sincere smile.

"Mr. Ingber?" she inquired elegantly.

"Mrs. Ellison?" I returned, looking into her eyes. They were light blue and twinkly: she was clearly a very pretty woman, with perfectly coiffed hair and just the right amount of jewelry.

"Call me Catherine," she insisted. "Please."

"Only if you call me Larry."

"Agreed!" she said, shaking my hand firmly with her bony grip. I walked into the house, and was just overwhelmed. I mean it was fucking perfect. The center hall glowed with low lamplight, reflecting off the silvery antiques, honey-colored walls, and polished oak floor. There was an enormous mahogany cupboard filled with treasures from generations of the Ellison family. A wide, carpeted staircase curved gracefully up to the second floor around a brass chandelier that glittered with a dozen little candle lights. Soft classical music was playing somewhere. The air was warm and smelled like cinnamon. It was, quite simply, the most beautiful house I had ever been in.

"Is this the house Derek grew up in?" I asked.

"Yes," she said. "Mostly."

I couldn't help but feel sorry for her. When I was down, who was sympathetic to *my* mother?

"Derek speaks so highly of you," she chirped nervously, leading me further into the house. "I'm so glad you could come to see him."

I didn't say anything, following her down the hallway, past photographs of their happy family, playing golf, sailing, and vacationing in exotic places. It seemed that Mr. Ellison wasn't home. I wonder if that was on purpose. Probably. These did not appear to be stupid people.

"I can't tell you how happy I am that you're here," she said in a softer voice. "He's been rather devastated by the accident."

"Well, I guess that's pretty understandable," I said offhandedly.

She stopped and turned to me. "Of course it's understandable," her voice suddenly reduced to a serious whisper. "But he just can't live this way."

I wanted to reach out and give her a hug, she looked so helpless and on edge.

Instead I just said, "Don't worry. He'll be OK. You'd be surprised: people can survive almost anything."

She led me into a large, sunny, open space: a huge family room with high windows, a large flagstone fireplace, and a view of the long backyard. The room was dominated by a big hospital bed in the center, and there was Derek Ellison, sitting up in the bed, strapped in tight by his sheets. His eyes were closed. It looked like he was sleeping, but for some reason I thought he was pretending.

"Come in," Catherine beckoned me softly. I walked farther in, looking at everything: the fancy bed, the computer on a stand next to the bed, the big TV screen at the foot of the bed, the table full of medicine bottles, the oxygen tank next to the bed, the way the whole place had been transformed into a sick room.

She whispered, "He was awake just a little while ago."

"He's awake now," I said in a normal voice, walking toward the foot of the bed.

I looked at Derek. His face was different. He was still handsome, only his cheeks were hollowed out and his hair was cut short and ragged. He looked like a dying poet in a painting by Goya.

Quietly I said, "Hey, kid. How are you doing?"

He opened his eyes and looked at me. I was right; he was awake the whole time.

"I'm doing shit, Larry," he said. "What does it look like?"

In spite of myself, a shudder of pity went through my body. He looked at me with the saddest eyes I'd ever seen on a kid except when I looked at myself in the mirror when I was first locked up.

"Boy," I said, "did *you* ever fuck up! Looks like you ain't gonna be Organ Morgan no more."

And then he did what I hoped he would do: he laughed—so hard he had a little trouble catching his breath. He started to take gulps of air, and Catherine was about to get the nurse—Derek needed twenty-four-hour care—when he recovered his normal breathing and ordered his mother to come back. I could see that Catherine was scared of everything, and she had every right to be. It was unnerving to see what used to be a normal, healthy young man in his early twenties struggle to breathe.

"Sorry about that. No more jokes." I moved closer and pointed to the turned-off TV opposite the bed. "That's a huge screen. Been watching the Yanks lose?"

"Sometimes," he said. "Not much."

"You've got a nice computer there," I offered positively. "An Apple."

"Can't you see, Larry? I've got everything!" he replied with a bitter finality that quieted the room.

Catherine, who was watching from the background, finally whispered, "Sweetheart, I think Consuela has just finished a batch of those soft cookies you like. I'm going to go see if they're ready." And she left us alone.

I pulled up a chair next to the bed, and it wasn't long before I got Derek to talk about his accident. As I listened to him, I couldn't help but hear echoes of myself, how I made alibis and excuses for the Very Stupid Thing I did when I was young. Even younger than Derek. He was at least in his early twenties. He should have known better than to try to water-ski between two boats, just like I should have known better than to give my heart and link my life to that beautiful, unstable girl.

Derek then moved his head and looked me in the eye. "Larry? You know why I think this happened to me? It was because of what I did to you. I should never have written that article and exposed you to—"

"Oh, that's ridiculous!" I overruled him. "One thing had nothing to do with the other. You did one stupid thing, writing that article. And then you did another stupid thing, with the water-skiing. But that doesn't mean that they were *interrelated* stupid things."

"I got carried away," he insisted, "and tried to write you like this great character."

"Forget about that," I told him. "It doesn't matter anymore. Sometimes shit just *happens*, and you gotta learn to live with it. Believe me, I know this. It's just the way life goes. You were born into this rich, nice family. Sometimes, luck just evens out."

I saw so much despair in his face it was like looking in a mirror.

"My father can't stand to be in the same room with me," he said. "He's in here for five minutes and then finds some reason to leave. I can't blame him. This is fucking crazy, me being like this."

His eyes started to tear up.

"I know it is," I said. "But crazy things happen in this world. You just have to accept them and play the hand you've been dealt. How much were you drinking when you had your accident?"

I could see that touched a nerve in him. He didn't answer immediately, which meant "a lot."

"It's OK, kid," I said, trying to soften my voice with a little forgiveness. "Everybody makes mistakes, everybody fucks up. But now that you're here, *don't make things worse*."

It felt so strange yet so right using one of my father's sayings—something he must have said to me a hundred times. But I said it because it's true. Bad things *are* going to happen in life. Anybody can deal with good times. It's how you respond to adversity that's the key. Of course, this is theory, and all theory is gray.

"You'll see," I continued. "Life does go on. Bad shit happens, but life goes on, and it can surprise you. And you're still alive, man! You're still alive. You can be in the worst of situations and yet good still manages to exist, if you can find it."

He closed his eyes and seemed to travel into himself.

"I'm such an asshole," he said, sobbing.

I had no choice but to get a Kleenex from the nightstand next to bed and wipe his tears.

"You're not an asshole," I said, comforting him, "you're a pussy."

Which made him laugh hard, perking him up a little bit as I dried off his face.

After some prodding, I got him to show me how all his fancy, specially-designed-for-the-handicapped computer gear worked. It wasn't easy for him, tapping the screen with a pointer held in his teeth, but he could do it.

"You're pretty good with that thing." I encouraged him, watching him move his head deliberately to make each tap, watching him make mistakes, mutter a curse, and try to hit "Delete." But I didn't help him; I let him do it himself, as tough and time-consuming as it was. Face-to-face with all this tragic, youthful waste of life and energy—if I wasn't sorry for him before, I was now.

"You're gonna have some great neck muscles," I said.

"Thanks a bunch," he growled through clenched teeth.

Once he got us on YouTube, for the rest of the afternoon we watched funny videos on his giant screen. I couldn't believe he had never seen some classic Marx Brothers bits...and Woody Allen monologues...and Mel Brooks' *The 2000-Year-Old Man*: all stuff from before I went into prison, what I recited to myself from memory to keep myself sane when I was in the SHU. (That's the Special Housing Unit: solitary confinement.) Maybe the stuff that kept me sane in the SHU would keep Derek sane in his personal SHU. He didn't even know who W.C. Fields was!

"What kind of an education did they give you in Buttfuck, Vermont, or wherever the hell Dartmouth is?"

"It's Buttfuck, *New Hampshire*. Please!"

He showed me some funny things too, all these wacky skits on Lonely Island and Funny or Die, and some raps by Eminem with the lyrics written out.

It turned out that Derek was a big golf fan. Apparently, that was the only thing he had in common with his father. So Derek showed me a bunch of famous golf shots by Jack Nicklaus, Ben Hogan, and Tiger Woods, who was amazing. Derek seemed to really enjoy watching them.

When I got up to leave, he apologized to me again, as if that would make me stay longer.

"Honestly, Larry," he insisted, "I wouldn't have written that article if I knew they were going to fire you."

"Yeah, well," I stalled, putting my chair back where I found it. "I just wish you wouldn't keep talking about it. That ship has sailed."

"Sorry," he mumbled.

"It's OK, Derek," I said, coming back to his bedside. "And don't worry. You're gonna be fine. You have a great support system here. And, honestly,"—I drilled this into him—"life is a very precious thing. You'll be surprised at how little you can live on."

He looked back at me with his sad, handsome eyes. "Thanks for the honesty, Larry."

I think it was good for him to talk to me. As I was leaving, Catherine, who had drifted in and out of the room the whole time I was there, not wanting to get in the way, told me that Derek said things to me she hadn't heard him say to anyone. Not even the therapist they had brought in to talk to him. As she walked me out to the Jeep, she asked me if I would come back. I lied and said I would think about it, even though in my mind I was already on my way back to the store to help Betsy.

But leaving Derek, I had a real "count my blessings" Moment of Grace and Thanks. I'd had a hard, unfair, cruel life, but at least I have my legs. When it came time for me to leave prison, I could walk out.

I drove back to City Island, resolved to do everything I could— starting tomorrow—to get my money back from Mantell, to help Betsy and Roland and me. That afternoon with Derek retaught me one thing, as if I didn't know it already: carpe fuckin' diem.

When I got home, Betsy asked me how it went, and I told her.

"The kid is pretty much screwed," I said, "unless some major medical miracle occurs. But at least they have the money to take care of him. He has a full-time nurse."

"Such a young man," said Betsy darkly. "He had his whole life in front of him."

"Yeah," I echoed. "Such a young man."

"And now he's in his own kind of prison," she murmured. "For the rest of his life."

Yes, I felt sorry for him, but I feel sorry for a lot of people all over the world. I feel sorry for the millions of guys—and women—still in prison, some of them actually innocent, and all deserving better conditions. I feel sorry for the families of all those prisoners, and their kids, just trying to live a decent life in this hard, cruel country of ours. I feel sorry for the homeless people (and they *are* people) you see all around our glorious city. I could have easily been one of them; lots of ex-cons are. Derek, even with his horrible accident, is lucky: he has money. If you don't have rich parents or are rich yourself, you've got a long, hard road in America today. We've allowed things to get completely out of hand: the rich are too rich, the poor are too poor, and now we're all paying the price.

PART III
WHAT HAPPENED THEN

TWENTY

After getting out of prison, I thought I'd never complain about anything anymore, but the next weeks were pretty tough. In addition to working at the store all day, I started working Thursday, Friday, Saturday, and Sunday nights in Charlie Wagner's kitchen. Betsy didn't want me to do it, and I didn't particularly like the work, but it was ready money, right there.

Jonathan Klein didn't contact me despite another email and two more phone calls to Brian Halliwell. I wasted an entire day and an evening on a visit to Klein's townhouse in Manhattan. It took me forever to find street parking—I just couldn't afford the highway-robbery rates of the parking lots on the Upper East Side—and once I got there, I never saw a trace of Klein. Not even a light in a window. I rang the bell but no one answered. The Doggies said Klein had other houses in other places.

I spent time searching the web for Mantell information, looking for other victims who knew something. I figured that new information had to come to light. I found nothing.

"Can you just look up for two seconds?" Betsy asked me.

"Sure." I snapped back to the present. "What can I do for you?" I tried to be cheerful for her, even though it was a lie.

"Can you watch the store while I go to CVS?" she asked.

"I can do anything you want," I replied, "but don't you want me to go?"

"No," she said. "I know exactly what I want. Do you need anything?"

I could have thought of a million things to say. Instead I just said, "I'm fine," and went downstairs to cover the store. I tried to do everything right, trying to be like Betsy, trusting that something good would happen.

Walking the straight and narrow was a good plan because one afternoon, Fusco made a surprise visit to the store. Thank goodness I was there. He walked in unannounced and at first didn't say a word to me. Frankly, I was surprised he got off his fat ass, but parole officers are supposed to make unannounced visits to their clients, to see if they're lying.

"So whatduhya know," he said after strutting unhappily around the store for a good three minutes, "you were telling the truth."

"I always tell you the truth, Officer Fusco," I replied genially.

"Is your boss here?" he asked unpleasantly.

"He's asleep in the back," I said, which was the truth. "But if you want me to wake him up—"

"No!" Fusco waved me off. "Don't wake him...for the time being."

I couldn't resist giving him a quick tour of the store. "If there's anything you'd like to look at, Officer, I'm sure we have a few things that would interest Mrs. Fusco. Maybe a tea cup? Or a lobster trap?"

Fusco was at the door by the time I finished. "You got lucky this time, Ingber," he growled. "But we're not finished."

He slammed the door closed, the sleigh bells rippled, and I took a big, deep, relieved breath. He never even mentioned anything about Sammy Zambrano, so I guess he never got anywhere down that dead end. But he clearly still had me in his sights. I had to stay on the straight and narrow or stay out of his way.

Later that day, I got into a fight with Bob Jensen on the phone. I never liked him and liked him even less when he was mean and condescending to Betsy. But, unfortunately, he was the accountant that we had to deal with. No one knew the finances of the store—the taxes, the mortgages—like he did. Roland had taken out a second mortgage a couple of years ago.

"I don't know what I have to do to get through to someone over there!" Jensen snarled. "You tell that stubborn old man."

"Why don't you think of some ways to actually help Roland," I countered, "instead of always complaining?"

It devolved from there until I finally told him to call back later and hung up the phone. He was just about to hang up on me too.

The night before, Betsy had dropped a small bomb. She came home from school, took off her things, and sat down at the kitchen table without saying anything. I could instantly tell that something was wrong.

"They're pushing me out at Thomas Paine," she said in a plain, unemotional voice. "They're going to make me take early retirement after next year."

"You're kidding!" I said.

"I thought I had at least three more years," she said, "but I had a feeling this was coming. I make too much money."

"What?"

"They can hire a kid out of college for half what I make," she said. "And Croll's never liked me. I stand up to him too much."

I walked over and put my arms around her. She had told me about recent staff meetings to deal with budget cuts. They had eliminated teachers' aides' and fired two janitors and a gardener. The school was looking dirty for the first time since she'd started working there, almost twenty years ago. She had taken it upon herself to keep the ladies' faculty bathroom neat. But I don't think she was expecting this.

"Well." She sighed deeply. "This is going to change some things."

I couldn't help but say, "You don't mean *us*, do you?"

She gasped. "No! Don't be silly!" she said. "Of course not. Unless you—?"

I embraced her. "Now who's being silly?"

She stayed in my arms for a while and finally said, "It's just that I thought I had a couple more years."

For the rest of the night—dinner, cleanup, some reading and TV—she seemed preoccupied.

"Do you want to talk about it?" I asked.

"No."

I'd never seen Betsy so downhearted.

"Just hold me," she said in bed that night, under the covers with the lights out, as I spooned up next to her, listening to the sound of a boat offshore in the distance blowing its sad horn. It felt good, holding her. She was small and delicate but warm, and I loved her so. She deserved a better man than I could ever be.

I lay there unmoving, and I felt my heart beat inside my chest. Something about the beat didn't seem right. Was I having heart palpitations, or was it my imagination? All the years inside, I held on to my health as best I could, and now that I was out, was I losing it? Just when I wanted more than ever to live, was it all slipping away from me?

I held on to Betsy and tried to get myself to sleep, counting backward from one hundred, thinking about ways to get money, but I knew that I had to do more than just that. Much more.

⌒

It started on a dark Monday. The store was closed, Betsy had taken the Jeep to school, and the rain was coming down like nails. Even though I had given up on the thought of Jonathan Klein ever calling me, I kept following him on the internet, looking for any news. It had been many weeks since the dinner at Le Bernardin, and I couldn't help but return to my daydream. I really thought Klein liked me. That's why I was so surprised he never got back to me. It just goes to show you how much I know about people. With the rain pounding against the windows, I grabbed my phone—what the fuck—went into my contacts, and called Jonathan Klein one last time.

I waited for the call to go through and looked at the clock. It was after four. Maybe it was late in the day, but maybe that was the best time to get him.

"Klein Global Partners!" chirped a bright female voice.

I went into my spiel, asking to speak to Mr. Klein, telling them who I was, and getting put on hold.

When the line came back to life, it was Mr. Pinstripe. *Shit*.

"Hello, Brian," I said, consciously trying to sound calm and friendly. "This is Larry Ingber. Think I can I speak to Mr. Klein *this* time?"

He said nothing.

I added a distinct "Please?"

After a long moment, he sighed. "Could you wait?"

He put me on mute or the line went dead, I couldn't tell which. I hated waiting on the phone, hated it my whole life. I waited during precious, expensive prison calls while Mantell put me on hold, then bullshitted me about my case, my money, and, as it turned out, *everything*. I waited on the phone for hours for The Girl too, a zillion years ago, and felt just as stupid, just as used.

I thought I heard the line click back in.

"Hello?" I said, but there was nothing there.

Damn!

"Mr. Ingber?"

"Yes, Brian?" I said eagerly.

"He'll have to call you back," he snapped and then the line went dead. Call ended. That was it. The absolute dead end with Klein.

"So that's it," I said out loud. Once and for all, I knew that I had blown it. Finished. Kaput. End of story.

Klein owed me nothing. Sure, I saved his life when he was a kid, but that was a long time ago. Even if I needed help finding Mantell and Jonathan Klein had all these resources, there was nothing about this outside world that entitled me to fairness. When I was in prison, at least I knew what was what: everything was in its place. This life of freedom was a more difficult, more unpredictable, more insecure life. I honestly didn't know what I was going to do.

Just at that moment, my cell phone rang.

Thank goodness! I figured it was Betsy telling me she was on her way home and that traffic would be slow in this pouring rain. It certainly couldn't be Klein calling me back. But when I looked down at my phone, it wasn't either one of them: it was a number I didn't recognize—a 201 area code. That was New Jersey. Caller unknown.

I pressed the green "Accept" button and cautiously said, "Hello?"

There was a pause, and an equally cautious, low voice said, "Hello?...Is this you?"

"Depends who this is," I replied, unable to identify the voice. "*You* called *me.*"

"Isn't dis my old friend from that shitbox on the river?"

"Pooch?"

"Why ya using names," he said affably, "ya stupid prick?"

"Sorry," I said, "but I didn't expect to hear from you."

"Whutayamean?" he said sharply. "I don't forget friends. You should know that."

His voice was raspy: did *I* sound that old? "So listen," he went on, "dat party ya wanted some information about?"

"*Mantell*?"

"Yeah. Well, that ain't his name no more," he said. "His name is now—write this down—Avery, Brandon Avery...Brando like the actor but with an *N*. And then, Avery. A-V-E-R-Y."

"Brandon Avery," I repeated.

"And he's living in the Bahamas," he said. "In—"

"*The Bahamas*?" I exclaimed.

"Yeah, Nassau in the Bahamas," he said. "Ya want his address?"

"Damn right I want his address!" I sputtered. "Only one thing," I said, stalling while I looked for a piece of paper and something to write with, "how do you know all this? Are you *sure*?"

"Look," he huffed, "ya asked me to find out about dis Mantell piece o' shit and now I'm tellin' ya."

"I *asked* the FBI guys here about other islands, other places," I said. "The FBI couldn't find him."

"Ya don't understan'," said Pooch. "Dis guy has some kinda protection. Regular law enforcement ain't gonna find him."

"And you're absolutely sure about this?" I asked. I didn't want to offend him, but my mind was spinning back to everything Cuellar and Rathbun told me, how hard they were working to find Mantell. Was it all a pose? Or was Mantell's protection beyond even Rathbun and Cuellar's jurisdiction?

"Hey," he grunted, "I still have a few teeth in my head and a few friends in Miami."

"*Miami*," I echoed. That was close to the Bahamas; maybe it made sense that Pooch had some connections there.

"So ya want the address or not?" he said, starting to sound impatient.

"Damn straight!" I said. "Shoot." I laughed inwardly at the double meaning of the word as I wrote down the address for a certain Brandon Avery in Nassau, the Bahamas, not Long Island. Maybe that's why they couldn't find Mantell: he changed his name *and* his island.

"Ya want his phone number too?" croaked the Pooch.

"You're shittin' me!" I said, almost dropping the phone.

"Eh! Ya wuz always a good cellie," he rasped, sounding sincere. "And I never forget. People forget things dese days, but it's up to guys like us to remember."

"You're right," I said, looking down at the strange address on the paper. "And thanks for this, man. This means a lot to me."

"Glad I could help yuz out," he said. "It's the least I could do, for plugging that kike bitch—ha-ha-ha-haa!"

Some lies never go away, which, in this case, was a good thing.

"Yeah, right," I muttered, "and thanks, Pooch!"

The line went dead.

I turned off my phone, feeling a rush of excitement that made me almost dizzy. I couldn't believe it: this was my first real lead on finding Lester Mantell! I mean *Brandon Avery*. Brandon Avery of Nassau, in the Bahamas. Could he have picked anything WASP-ier? And it wasn't the Nassau I grew up in: it was *another* Nassau. Maybe that was a good omen.

Wait until I tell Betsy! I started to text her, but then thought, *Wait a second: this kind of news deserves actual talking.*

I tapped her name on my "Recents" phone page and waited. I was just busting to talk to her; it had been a long time since I had such good news. But it went to her bright, cheerful recording, and I hung up. I felt as if there was something incomplete within me until I told her.

Then the phone rang again, vibrating in my hand, scaring the shit out of me.

Betsy! At last!

But no, it was a 917 number—"Caller unknown."

I hit "Accept" and ventured a "Hello?"

"Larry Ingber?" said the voice. "Jonathan Klein here."

"Jonathan Klein!" I half shouted into the phone. By now, he was the last person I expected to call. "I never thought I'd hear from you."

"Well, I've been traveling lately. But Brian told me that you called, more than once, in fact," he said. "So I assume you *wanted* to hear from me at some time."

"Of course, I did!" I said, racking my brain for what I wanted to say. "Yes! I wanted to say—yes—thank you! For that great dinner at Le Bernardin and everything."

"Oh yes," he said as if recalling an event that had happened a hundred years ago, "absolutely. Eric does a fine job. Best fish in the city."

"Best fish I ever had," I agreed, stalling, trying to focus and spit out what I was dying to talk to him about.

"Let's do it again sometime," he said. "But maybe without all those other schmucks. You like the Yankees?"

MANTELL!

"My lawyer!" I shouted in relief as I found my tongue, and the whole story spilled out of me. "I meant to mention it to you at the dinner, but I forgot to, with all the drinking and the Doggies and the fish. I sent you an email. Did you get it? But that doesn't matter. I'm just glad you called me back so I could ask you directly."

"Wait a second," he said, "slow down, Larry. Ask me what?"

"The FBI, the Westchester DA, and the SEC haven't been able to find him," I said. "But they were looking in the Virgin Islands and the Caymans. Now I've just found out on fairly good authority that maybe they *weren't* really looking for him. And now, now his name isn't even Mantell anymore—it's Avery, Brandon Avery, and he's in the Bahamas."

"Where in the Bahamas?" Klein calmly asked.

His question stopped me momentarily. I got out the piece of paper and read him the address.

"Hey, I know exactly where that is," he said. "I have a house just outside of Nassau. Jamboree. I'm going there tomorrow for a couple of days. You want a ride?"

"W-what?" I sputtered, not sure that I heard him correctly.

"I fly there all the time, when I can," he said. "I'm going there tomorrow. I have a plane. I can take you."

I vaguely recalled one of the Doggies mentioning that Klein had a home in the Caribbean.

"In fact, I'll help you find this guy," Klein continued brightly. "It'll be fun! I'd love to catch a crooked lawyer."

I was dumbstruck but finally stammered, "W-what did you say about—"

"I have some very good people down there," he cut me off. "We'll find your Mr. Mantell or Avery or whoever he is."

"Wait a second, Jonathan. Are you serious?"

"Larry...?" he said with a slight but unmistakable change of tone. "I'll tell you when I'm joking, but mostly—and you should know this—I am an *extremely* serious person."

That was the impression of Klein I took away from the dinner.

"Decide what you want to do and call me back," he said crisply. "I'm going to Nassau tomorrow, but just for a day or two. I have a couple of appointments on Wednesday morning, and I don't know when I'll be going back after that. Maybe months. It's hard to say. This is my first trip there in almost six months."

What a life.

"I fly into a private airport," he continued. "Customs and immigration are not a problem. They know me. I'll just walk you through. If you come with me, everything will be fine."

I was stunned. Dazed and amazed.

"Come with me, Larry," he cajoled. "C'mon! I can use the company."

"Gee"—I think I actually said *gee*—"I don't know what to say. It's very tempting."

"A free trip to the Bahamas on a G5?" He chuckled. "And how long did you say you've been looking for this guy? I'd say it's tempting."

"Well, yeah," I said. *Was this my real chance to catch Mantell?* My blood and mind were racing. After all this time, this is what I'd been waiting for. I could pay off Roland's debts, which would allow us to stay in the store. It wouldn't matter if Thomas Paine was giving Betsy the heave-ho.

"Well, you decide for yourself," he said, switching back to that business voice of his. "Use this number I called you on. It goes directly to me. This number *I* answer, not Brian."

I couldn't help but say, "Good."

Then it hit me hard: I had *Fusco* on Thursday!

"Damn!" I said. "I have to be back by Thursday afternoon. In Westchester. In New Rochelle for"—I didn't want to say a meeting with my parole officer that I couldn't afford to miss—"an appointment I have."

"Perfect!" he said. "I have to be back in the city before next weekend because I have to be in London. You say you need to be in New Rochelle by Thursday afternoon? That should be absolutely no problem. Hell, I fly out of White Plains, and it's only three hours to Nassau—"

"But I *really* have to be back," I cautioned him...and myself, thinking of the risk I'd be taking. Leaving the country would be a major parole violation, and if Fusco found out—I really had to think this one through.

"If I get my meetings done early, I'll get you back by *Wednesday night*," Klein said with assurance. "Really. It's my plane!"

"You promise?"

"What are you, a Doggy?" he cracked. "You want me to say, 'Cross my heart and hope to die, boil in oil, stew in lye, stick a needle in my eye?' OK, I *promise* I'll have you back by Thursday by noon at the latest, *no sweat*. Just bring your passport."

"I don't have one," I confessed.

He paused for a moment. "That's OK. You have some ID?"

"Sure," I answered.

"That should be enough," he said. "I leave tomorrow morning from White Plains. You tell me what you want to do. Either you're in or out. Call me back on this number. I gotta go."

"OK, Jonathan," I said. "I'll call—" and the line clicked off.

⌢

Can a person be energized and paralyzed at the same time? I was. My mind was flooding with contradictory, dangerous thoughts— *Go! Don't go! Go!*—when I heard the door open. I turned around as a drenched Betsy walked in, shaking off the rain from her coat and hair.

"You won't believe what's happening out there!" she said, winded. "It's insane."

"You're not going to believe what's happening *in here*," I said. "It's *completely* insane."

I don't think she heard me as she folded her dripping umbrella and hung up her raincoat.

"I would have texted you that I was going to be late," she said, somewhat flustered, "but my battery went dead. It just won't keep a charge anymore."

"What if I buy you a *new* iPhone?" I said excitedly. "What about a new *gold-plated* iPhone, with the biggest screen they make?"

"What are you talking about?" she said as she walked away from me and went toward the bathroom.

"I'm talking about that you're not going to believe what's just happened," I said.

"And the 'check engine' light is on in the Jeep," she said as she came back with a towel around her neck, drying the tips of her hair. "We're gonna have to get that looked at."

I took both her hands away from her head and held on to them so she would listen to me.

"I've found him!" I said. "I know where he is."

"Larry, you're squeezing me!" she squealed, twisting away.

"Didn't you hear me?" I shouted joyously as I released her. "It's Mantell! We know where he is! We can find him and get my money!"

I think it took her a moment to comprehend what I was saying.

"Really?" she whispered. "After all this time?"

"Finally, I know where he is!" I said. "And I know how I'm going to get him. You're not gonna believe how it happened."

I sat her down and told her the whole story of both calls—Pooch and then Klein—how they came one right after another. Betsy sat there, wide-eyed and silent.

She waited a long moment and then asked me, "So what are you going to do?"

"What do you mean what am I going to do?" I replied. "I'm going to go after him!"

"Why don't you let the FBI or the police get him?" she asked.

"I told you why. Mantell has protection. The FBI is *never* going to get him. That's why he's stayed free."

"But if you leave the country without asking," she said, "won't it violate your parole or something?"

This, of course, was the Big Question facing me.

"Klein says he'll have me back before I have to see Fusco on Thursday."

"And you're willing to take that chance?" she asked gravely.

I hesitated—but only for a moment.

"Betsy? It's my best chance to get my money back," I said decisively. "Maybe my only chance. It's like it fell into my lap:

where Mantell is *and* a way to get to him. I can't wait any longer. In six months, who knows where Mantell will be? Klein says he'll help me *right now*. He's a rich man with a lot of influence. I won't get caught. When you think about it, I'd be crazy *not* to do it."

"Oh, Larry," she said, a disappointed look on her face. Had she been listening to me?

"What?" I asked her, but of course I knew what she meant.

She touched me on the knee. "I know things are tight financially, especially if I'm not going to be at Thomas Paine much longer, but is the money so important that you'd risk your freedom for it? After all you've been through?"

I couldn't deny the truth of what she was saying. I just looked at the situation in another way.

"I'm telling you that I'll be back," I insisted. "Klein promised we'd be back, maybe even by Wednesday night. He says it's only three hours from White Plains to the Bahamas. It'll be in and out, just like that. And he has *ways* to help me. Hell, he has his own plane, for God's sake!"

She looked down, then up, then right in my eyes.

"Larry," she said softly, "I'm going to say what I say to the kids who come into the office when they get in trouble: the easy way is the hard way; the hard way is the easy way."

Her eyes were so sincere. She was trying to help me, I knew it, but I didn't want her help right then.

"I'm not one of your kids, Betsy," I said.

"Then don't act like one!" she snapped. I think that was the first time she ever raised her voice at me like that. "If Fusco finds out you've left the country, isn't that a violation? Do you really want to risk going back to prison just over some money?"

"It's not just the money!" I said. "It was my legacy, what he stole from my parents and me. The betrayal of trust. It's being stabbed in the back—and then suddenly being able to turn around and get revenge on the guy with the shank in his hand. It's a way to take control of my life, for the first time, maybe *ever*."

I could see that she didn't believe me, but I felt it settle in my mind: I would go to the Bahamas with Jonathan Klein and reclaim my rightful legacy from Lester Mantell, once and for all.

I called Klein back and worked everything out. He told me where to be (the airport in White Plains at a place called, if you can believe it, Million Air under a big maroon overhang that I "couldn't miss") and when (tomorrow morning, 7:00 sharp). I didn't have the nerve to ask him for a limousine to pick me up.

I went into the kitchen, where Betsy was drying her hands after washing some dishes. She turned to me just as I walked in.

"Do you think I can borrow a suitcase from you?" I asked her.

She just looked at me, her eyes filled with tears, and threw the towel she was holding onto the dish rack. Without looking at me, she walked out of the room. I heard her go into the bedroom and shut the door, hard. Part of me knew she was right, but I knew that *right* was no longer the sole controller of my actions. I was beyond that now.

I went downstairs and rapped on Roland's door. I could hear the loud TV inside, so I knocked again.

"Yeah?" he said when he ripped open the door. "What's wrong?"

"Nothing's wrong," I said. "Think I can borrow a suitcase from you?"

I went inside and told Roland what had happened—the phone calls and everything—and what I was planning to do.

Roland smiled. "You *do* like to live dangerously, don't you?"

"I know it's a roll of the dice, but I think I'm doing the right thing," I countered. "The way it's all coming together, maybe I'm doing the *exact* right thing, at the *exact* right moment in my life."

Roland chuckled. "I hope so. For your sake."

So did I.

I went back upstairs with an old suitcase of Roland's, walked through the living room where Betsy was sitting, coiled tightly, reading in her chair, and straight into the bedroom, saying nothing. As I've said, I don't have a lot of clothes, but I put three days of clean underwear, socks, a couple of shirts, pants, and my one good sports jacket out on the bed. Then I went into the bathroom, got my bottle of aftershave, and sprinkled a couple of drops into Roland's stale valise. The dry, old leathery suitcase with an outside pocket wasn't so bad; it had character, just like Roland himself.

"You're really gonna do this?"

Betsy was standing in the doorway, with her arms crossed.

"I just want to get a few things," I non-answered, starting to put my things into Roland's bag. "I thought maybe I'd sleep downstairs tonight at Roland's. He said it was OK. So that I can leave super early in the morning and not bother you."

She stood there for a moment, then sighed.

"Do whatever you like," she said. "It's what you're going to do anyway." And she turned and walked away.

Silently, I finished my packing. I tried to think about what I would need in the Caribbean—as if I would know—all the while thinking about Betsy's disapproval...and how she was going to react when I took some money from our cash envelope. I was going to need some money to travel with, right?

I walked into the living room, where she was reading. "I'm gonna have to take some money from the envelope."

She didn't say anything, or even look up.

"Can I?" I asked.

She sighed and said evenly, "Do you want me to get it for you *myself*? If you're going to do something stupid and reckless, does it mean that I have to *help* you do it?"

"Thanks," I said glumly. Sure, she gave me the OK to take some money, but the way she did it made me feel lower than ever.

I took some twenties from the envelope. I figured Klein would pay for everything, but I had to carry some cash, just in case something happened. When I had all the stuff I needed, remembering my phone charger at the last minute, I went to the door with the suitcase and my knapsack.

"OK," I called to Betsy who was still in the living room. "I'm going down to Roland's now. ...I'll be in touch."

She didn't respond, and I didn't go into the living room to say a proper goodbye, maybe because there wasn't a proper goodbye to say. I didn't want to see her face-to-face once more so that she could try to dissuade me from going. And I didn't want to face the possibility that she might be right.

"Bye," I called, trying to sound cheery and positive as I closed the door behind me and went downstairs. The store was always a little spooky at night, with just a few lights on, throwing shadows against the darkness. It was never more so than that night, when I wondered when I'd be back.

I slept on Roland's living room couch. Or *tried* to sleep is a better description. He had tried to make me comfortable, with his fuzzy sheets, a granite pillow, and an ancient blue woolen blanket that I kicked off all night. But I had too much churning in my sleepless mind: what I'd find in the Bahamas, what I'd do to Mantell—excuse me, Brandon Avery—once I found him, and the all-important timetable for getting back for Fusco on Thursday. Sleep was a joke as I waited in the dark for the alarm on my phone to go off.

I woke up even before it went off. It took me a moment to realize where I was. Then I remembered what I was about to do and went into action. I splashed some water from the faucet in Roland's kitchen on my face to wake up and got dressed silently, trying not to wake the old man up. I figured when I got outside Roland's door, I'd call a taxi and blow a bunch of money on getting to the airport in White Plains. After all, what choice did I have?

Quietly I folded up Roland's blanket, stacked the Pillow of Gibraltar on top, and got my things together. Silently I let myself out of Roland's door, reminding myself to turn off the burglar alarm first thing—even before I called a taxi.

But when I turned around, Betsy was standing there in her jacket with her car keys out, ready to take me to the airport.

"I must really love you a lot," she said unhappily, "for me to do something I'm against."

"Thanks, Bets—"

"And don't you *dare* make me visit you in prison," she cut me off.

I said nothing else. I just followed her out to the Jeep with my things and was grateful for the ride, if not her approval.

It wasn't far to White Plains, and the roads weren't crowded this early. Somehow she knew the way to Million Air. I didn't ask her how she knew where I was going; I guess she overheard me on the phone and looked it up. We were there in minutes.

"Million Air," she jeered as she approached the fancy red marquee, looking for a place to stop. "Isn't that just perfect?"

"Just drop me off anywhere," I said, surveying all the parked cars in diagonal rows.

"Don't worry," she replied as she found an open stretch of curb. "I have no desire to meet your Mr. Klein."

And she pulled the car to a final stop.

"I'll try to stay in touch if I can," I said. "But I don't want to run up any big international roaming charges or anything. My phone bill is already killing us." *Besides*, I thought to myself, *it would probably be a good idea not to leave any telephone record of my trip out of the country.*

She reached into the pocket of her jacket and pulled out something for me.

"Here," she said, handing me a jumbo silver paper clip with a bunch of twenty-dollar bills folded inside.

"But that's your emergency money!" I protested.

"I think you're gonna need it more than I will," she said flatly.

Reluctantly I took the money, stuffed it deep into my pocket, and it was time for me to go.

"Can I kiss you goodbye?" I asked her.

"If that's what you want to do," she answered.

I leaned over and she turned her face so my kiss landed on her cheek. It was OK: I didn't want to force her into a kiss she didn't mean.

"Thanks a lot for the ride. I'll see you Thursday night, or maybe even earlier," I said with confidence.

"Just come back in one piece," she said, looking straight ahead through the windshield. I think a tear was starting to run down her cheek, but I didn't want to think about that. I wanted to tell her that I was doing this for her—at least, partially—but I didn't think she would believe me even if it was the truth.

"I'll be back," I assured her. "You're not getting rid of me that easily."

I got out of the Jeep, pulled my things out of the backseat, and slammed the door. Then she drove off without a moment's hesitation, without looking back at me even once.

I started toward the maroon overhang that read "Million Air." When I turned around to see Betsy one last time, the Jeep was gone. And I was on my own, about to embark upon the Adventure in Paradise that would change everything.

TWENTY-ONE

I'm not going to go into everything about my time in the Bahamas, how I got there and what happened. My troubles—and specifical- ly, my actions—I am fully responsible for, and I don't want to get anybody else in trouble. To this very day and for the rest of my life, I deeply regret some of the things that happened. What did I call them once: "unfortunate consequences"?

But let me begin with the good part of my trip with Jonathan Klein to the Bahamas. As I've said before, I'm not used to being treated nicely. And ever since I've gotten out, I've seen how a great many people are these days: angry and on-edge and ready to strike out. My reflexive position is to think that people know who I am or are suspicious of me anyway. So when I'm doing something on the farthest edge of legitimacy—like leaving the country in violation of my parole—I'm extra jumpy. Ultra-watchful.

But nothing is more suspicious than a person not wanting to look suspicious, right? So when I walked into Million Air with my jailbird attitude—trying to conceal my jailbird attitude—thinking that everyone knows exactly what I'm doing, I have to say that I was shocked by the welcome I received. With the first thing out of my mouth, telling the brightly blond young woman at the re- ception desk that I was there to meet Jonathan Klein, it was as if I had said, "Open sesame!"

Before I knew what hit me, I was sitting in a comfortable armchair with a café mocha in my hand. But before I could sip off the foam and look at my *Wall Street Journal*, Jonathan Klein walked into the waiting room.

He wasn't alone; right behind him was a young Asian wom- an in a dark business suit, and behind them was Klein's driver, pushing a trolley full of luggage, with more bags hanging from his shoulders.

Immediately, I got to my feet on nervous legs: it was beginning.

"Jonathan," I said in a slightly raised voice, just to make sure he heard me.

He had been walking quickly, his head down, as if he were burrowing through the air, his mind on other things. But when he heard my voice, he stopped and looked my way. A big smile broke across his face.

"Larry!" he shouted back. He walked straight toward me. "You made it!"

"I certainly did," I shot back as I took a few steps to meet him.

As we shook hands, he grabbed me on my elbow with the other hand for a firmer grip.

"This is going to be *fun*," he said.

"Well, I hope so," I answered, eager to agree with everything he said but a little worried about how he said the word *fun*. After all, I was pretty much in his hands from here on.

"Larry, this is Janet Ko, my assistant." He stood aside to reveal the young Asian woman who was standing slightly behind him. She was taller than Klein, quite pretty and slim. She wore a sharp-looking, dark suit and held a stainless-steel attaché case in her tight little hand as if it contained the nuclear codes.

She thrust out her other hand to me, smiling just enough. "Pleased to meet you, Mr. Ingber." She had very confident, knowing eyes.

"Call me Larry," I said. "Please."

"Shall we keep moving?" Klein summoned us, and as soon as he spoke, Janet Ko moved.

I kept up with them both, the driver behind us with the luggage.

"Can I help you with those, sir?" the driver said, calling ahead to me.

"No, I'm good!" I said, with my knapsack over one shoulder and Roland's valise in other hand. I could have added, "*In fact, I'm pretty fucking great! This is really happening.*"

How Klein moved through the airport—how people treated him and how he *expected* to be treated—was a source of wonder for me. I just trailed behind as he fixed everything, or rather, everything was fixed for him in his way. There was this tall, lovely young woman with a blond ponytail and an iPad walking alongside Klein the whole time, making sure that everything was going smoothly for him and his party, chattering and flattering. Later Janet told me that she was called a "handler." And indeed, everything was being handled.

I only had to show my ID once, and that was after Klein said, "Don't worry about him: he's my Assistant Groinmaster!" and everybody laughed out loud and let us pass. Just as easy as that. I watched Janet's face as we walked away from that encounter. She had a composed, pleasant non-smile on her face, staying quietly behind Klein and right next to me. I looked over at her once, and she looked back at me as if to say, "Isn't my boss cool? Which makes me cool too."

Just keep smiling and look relaxed, I told myself as we moved past the uniformed security guards and checkpoints. Once outside on the tarmac, I saw rows of small planes that looked like beautiful, giant toys. They gleamed in the brightening morning sun. I wondered which one was Klein's, but it really didn't matter to me. They all looked spectacular. I hadn't been on a plane since 1966, and that was a big jet down to visit some long-lost relatives in Miami. And I've never been on a little plane in my life—only in my craziest hallucinations of escape.

I never went to Disneyland as a child—or Disney World, for that matter, which wasn't even open when I went into the joint—but when I stepped into Jonathan Klein's big/little jet plane, I felt like a kid getting onto some futuristic space ride at an exclusive millionaires-only theme park. There was an actual *stewardess* and big lounge chairs and a whole office set up, and what looked like a separate little bedroom at the back. Everything was colored a warm beige or in dark, exotic woods. And there was a full kitchen with food. Tons and tons of food.

The stewardess's name was Barbara, and she couldn't have been nicer. She was pretty and blond in her powder-blue uniform. Not quite as young as Janet Ko, but very attractive and attentive.

(Klein was not stupid.) She asked me if I wanted anything, and I said by reflex, "No, thank you. Not now." I didn't need anything extra; just being onboard was enough.

As I made my way farther into the plane, I couldn't stop staring at everything: the lush leather chairs and the sleek, molded plastic surfaces; the four clocks in a row on the wall displaying the time in New York, London, Tokyo, and Los Angeles; the big screen with a world map showing where the plane was; and the little oval windows letting in the golden morning light. It was like something out of a movie, except that I was in it.

Klein rushed by, bumping me with a heavy black briefcase.

"Take good care of him, Barbara," Klein said, adding with a sly smile, "He's a very fragile old man."

That got a laugh of agreement out of me, knocking all thoughts of Hollywood out of my head.

Klein shouted another instruction, "And tell Carlos I'm ready."

"Absolutely!" Barbara answered, crisply turning and walking to the front of the plane.

"Make yourself at home, Larry!" Klein shouted from the back office area as he hoisted his briefcase onto the desk.

"Have you ever been on a G5 before, Mr. Ingber?" asked Janet, who had taken one of the big loungers facing the rear of the plane, presumably so she could keep an eye on Klein and be ready to serve his needs.

"No," I said as I contemplated which chair to sit in. "And it's Larry, please. This is the first time I've ever been on a private plane."

"Really?" she said, just a little too innocently.

"Oh, come on, Miss Ko," I called her on it. " I bet you know all about me. You don't have to hide your competence."

From the back of the plane, Klein laughed loudly, having overheard us. "He got you there, Janet!"

I looked over and saw embarrassment tightening Janet's blushing cheeks as she turned away from me, placing her carefully guarded stainless-steel attaché case in a safe place next to her seat.

Klein continued, "She doesn't miss much, Larry. She went to Columbia, just like you did."

"Columbia?" I said to her. "Really?"

"And an MBA from Wharton," Klein added.

"Another good school!" I said, taking the lounger across the aisle from her, facing the front of the plane, to give us both plenty of room. "Very impressive."

I could see that I was making her feel self-conscious, and I was instantly sorry. I wanted Janet Ko to like me. Besides the fact that she seemed like a perfectly nice young woman, I got the sudden, strong feeling—almost a premonition—that I was going to need her help before this whole thing was over.

Through an intercom, a deep male voice purred, "The tower's given us the OK, Mr. Klein, so if you'll buckle in—?"

"Thank you, Carlos!" Klein said.

I looked around at Klein in his big lounger as he released the button on the armrest that let him talk to the pilots in the cockpit. I think he could control almost everything on the inside of the plane from his throne. Everything about this whole setup was cool.

"Buckle up, Larry," he said with an undeniably self-satisfied smile. "Time to escape."

Escape. That word had lost its meaning for me long ago, and yet, here I was, on a private jet heading to the Caribbean to do something I've been obsessed with for years. I clipped myself into the seatbelt of my very comfortable, very soft lounger when the plane lurched and started to move. My heart began to beat faster. I suddenly realized I was sweating like crazy.

In a moment, the excitement and glamour vanished, and it really hit me: what the fuck was I doing? Leaving the country in violation of the terms of my parole? Risking my freedom? For *what*? Betsy was right. No amount of money, even to save the store for her, was worth the risk of going back to prison. Legacy or no legacy, my father wouldn't want me doing this. For a milli-second, I felt like ripping off the belt and telling Klein to stop the plane and let me the hell off.

I almost said it, but I didn't. Instead, I grabbed the ends of the armrests with both hands, held my words, and gave myself an inner pep talk. I had never done anything remotely this adventurous, this daring—OK, this *foolhardy*—in all my sixty-plus years, except, of course, for that time I helped The Girl clean up those two bodies.

But to be brutally honest, for most of my life I've hardly lived like a man; I lived like a *surviving animal*. And now, here I was in this super-deluxe private plane on my way to the Caribbean, a place I'd always dreamed of going, to do something that might actually help the woman I love—as well as getting the money that was rightfully mine——*and* a little revenge. That wasn't such a bad play. It was worth the risk. And besides, the dice had been thrown.

"You OK, Mr. Ingber?" asked Barbara, checking my seat belt.

"Yes, ma'am!" I answered her directly. "I am completely fine."

The experience of taking off in the plane—how often had I dreamed of this kind of feeling?—was thrilling. We went up into the air at such an angle that I was pressed back hard into my seat. I slowly leaned over and looked out of my oval window at the earth below me. I couldn't see the airport anymore, just the green trees of Westchester and some bluish hills in the distance. At that moment, I wished Betsy could see all this. She works so hard—at that ungrateful school for that jerk Croll *and* for Roland *and* the store *and* me—she should have a taste of this fancy life someday.

"Enjoying yourself?" Janet asked me from across the aisle.

"Some," I said nonchalantly, which made her smile. Just slightly.

Barbara walked up to me carrying a tray of food for Klein.

"Mr. Ingber, can I bring you something like this?" she said, showing me the tray. There was a delicate white china cup of coffee topped with dense foam with a capital *K* drawn on top in darker foam. There was also a beautiful plate of cut-up fruit. And it wasn't just that the fruit looked perfectly sweet and ripe – it was the way that Barbara had fanned them out artistically in graceful arches of strawberry, cantaloupe, honeydew, and some little, round green fruit with tiny seeds that I wasn't familiar with.

"What are those?" I pointed to the green things.

"Kiwi."

"Kiwi," I repeated in wonder, like a kid learning a new word. "Maybe later."

She walked on. So that's what kiwis are. You learn something new every day, especially if you've been in Rip-Van-Winkle-suspended-animation for forty years.

Not long after, I was enjoying a huge plate of kiwi and a second cup of *K* coffee, when Klein called out, inviting me to his private sitting area in the rear of the plane.

As soon as I sat down on the couch opposite his throne, he swung around to me and said with a wolfish smile, "OK, Larry, tell me all about this crooked lawyer of yours."

"Mantell?" I exclaimed, happy and grateful he remembered my reason for being there. "Wait a second."

I dashed back to my chair and got the knapsack, where I had my Mantell file. My legs felt a little rubbery moving about the plane. By the time I got back to Klein, he was sitting there with an open laptop.

"Imagine that," he said as he typed, "a lawyer who stole from somebody. What a shock."

I flashed on the cocky little redheaded kid from that camp, the Redheaded Doggy, and it threw me for a moment.

"Uh, OK," I stammered out as I gave him my ancient manila envelope filled with all my Mantell information. Klein looked through the papers, seeming to vacuum in all the information at one glance.

"Based on what I know now, he's living under the name of Brandon Avery, using that address in Nassau. With this phone number." I pointed to the piece of paper on top. "And he uses that post office box number."

"I know *exactly* where this is," he said slowly as he read.

I watched him as he started typing in quick bursts, concentrating intensely. Was this the power of mind that made him his zillions?

"And he was your lawyer for how many years?" he asked, still typing away.

"Forever," I said. "From my first appeal, right up until before my release."

"Maybe you should have changed lawyers sooner," he muttered.

"Well, yeah," I mumbled.

"Janet!" he called out.

Before I could turn around, Janet was standing next to me, waiting for Klein's orders.

"I just sent you an email. Please forward it to Myles Pritchard," he said. "Tell him that he is to locate this Mr. Brandon Avery. All the information is right there."

"No problem, sir," she chirped and started to walk away.

"And tell him to make sure that all inquiries are absolutely confidential," Klein added with a wink. "We don't want to alert our Mr. Avery that we're on his trail, right?"

"Absolutely!" I said. "This is great. I really want to thank you for doing this, Jonathan. I really had no other—"

"Forget it," he said, waving off my gratitude casually. "It'll be fun. Catching a bad guy...right?"

He shot me a sly, mischievous smile that made me feel confident and a little uneasy too. After all, this was my *life* we were playing with.

"Right," I said.

⌒

The rest of the flight was so enjoyable, it was like a joke. I felt like a cartoon. Barbara kept offering me Wi-Fi and movies and video games and different kinds of food and drinks until it was embarrassing, so I finally had to take something: more kiwi. It's really an incredible fruit, even if it is green.

At some point, I turned around and Klein was gone.

"Hey!" I whispered to Janet, who was working on her laptop. "Where is he?"

"Oh," she said. "Probably napping in the bedroom."

I had to laugh at that: this captain of commerce, monarch of money, *napping*.

"Don't laugh," she corrected me, "he power-naps all the time. Sometimes for fifteen minutes, sometimes for a half hour. He says it's because for many years he slept in two four-hour shifts, monitoring different financial markets, and it destroyed his normal sleep cycle. But then again, I've also seen him go eleven straight hours at a negotiation and never go to the bathroom once."

"Wow," I said. "A financial genius *and* a camel?"

That got a shy laugh out of her.

I continued, "So how long have you been working for him?"

"About...four years," she answered cautiously.

I didn't want to pry into her business—I was treading carefully—but I had other questions to ask her.

"You know what I was thinking?" I floated out to her. "Why isn't Brian Halliwell here?"

She straightened up in her seat and looked at me with more interest. "Oh, you know *Brian*?"

"Not well," I demurred, not sure if Mr. Pinstripe was an enemy of hers. "But I know him."

She nodded in slow judgment of me. "Well, generally I travel with Mr. Klein, but Brian is his senior aide—senior to me. He's been with Mr. Klein for a very long time."

"I see," I said, pretending to understand more than I did. "But this is still a real good job for you, right? Even with Klein's famous redheaded temper."

"Even with his famous temper," she said with a smile. "Jonathan Klein doesn't forget a favor, or a slight."

Hmmm.

I decided to throw myself on her mercy.

"You know, Ms. Ko, this trip is a very big deal for me," I said sincerely. "Mr. Klein helping me and everything. I can't tell you how much it means, for someone who has so much to help out a guy like me, when he doesn't have to. You know what I mean?"

She looked at me carefully, likely deciding what she should say, what she should conceal.

"I think I do," she slowly said. "And please, call me Janet."

That made me feel better, thinking that I was getting through to her.

She turned back to her laptop, but then added something else.

"One thing I'd remember, Larry: Mr. Klein is very generous and likes to help people. No one has connections to the venture and tech communities as he does. But he's been under a lot of pressure lately, and sometimes has—what's the best way to put it?—a short attention span."

She made sure that I heard those last three words clearly.

I nodded. "OK. I appreciate your honesty."

"No problem at all." She waited a moment for her message to sink in, then turned back to her laptop and resumed her furious typing.

Short attention span. Those words echoed in my mind, for the first of many times. I reminded myself once again that I had until Thursday to find Mantell/Avery and get back to Westchester for Fusco. Three days to do everything. Three days without Betsy. I could do it. I could do everything.

I took out my Mantell file and looked it over for the millionth time. I stopped on an old photograph of Mantell standing in front of the Mineola courthouse, answering questions from reporters about my appeal, that made him look like some crusading young lawyer, a champion of the underdog. I wondered what he looked like now, now that he was Brandon Avery. He was a good ten, fifteen years older than me, so he must look pretty damn old, unless he got plastic surgery. That would be just like him, especially if he's on the lam. But no matter the passage of time, I would recognize him—his suspicious brow, his shifty jaw, his "vulture eye"—when the time came.

I started to doze, thinking about that old Edgar Allan Poe story I read to the Doggies, "The Tell-Tale Heart." I guess it did scare the shit out of some of them. I never thought of that at the time. I always loved Poe, and not just because we have the same middle name. I thought that I was giving them some classic American literature, the stuff I loved when I was their age. But I guess that "vulture eye" stuff, that old black Poe magic, does open impressionable young minds to the multitude of horrors that man is capable of. Dungeons and devices. Revenge from the grave. Burnt-up bodies. Such sweet horror. Poe had no idea...no fucking idea.

"Mr. Ingber?"

I jumped in the air, still strapped down.

"Can you bring your seat up?" cooed Barbara, leaning over me. "We're landing in about ten minutes."

"Landing?" I mumbled, coming out of my fog of dreams.

As my eyes adjusted to the light, I saw that Barbara was going back to Klein's private room, carrying a tray with a dark red liquid in a large tumbler.

"Did you get some sleep?" Janet asked, closing her laptop.

"I guess I must've," I confessed, my mind still fuzzy. "No, sorry, not sleep," I corrected myself, "a *power nap.*"

She appeared to like that I remembered her term.

Barbara came back past me, on her way to the front of the plane.

"'Scuse me, Barbara," I said politely, "but what was that he was drinking?"

She started to answer me when—

"*Barbara!*"

Klein's sharp voice on the P.A. system froze her in fear.

"Tell you later," she whispered to me and went right back to Klein's room.

I was impressed by the instantaneous response he got. Maybe it wasn't fear; maybe it was loyalty. Did it matter which? Whatever it was, I felt the plane start to sharply descend—or rather, my stomach *ascend* in my gut—and I tightened my seat belt and held on to the big armrests.

Janet leaned toward me and said, "Hang on. Carlos's landings are sometimes a little sudden."

As the plane slowed down in the air, I closed my eyes and the noise became tremendously loud. We then evened off. I looked out the window and saw the runway going by very quickly. I felt myself being pulled forward as the wheels finally bumped down and we rolled down the tarmac. Carlos applied the brakes, and we slowed, safely back on the ground. We were still moving as Barbara got up and walked toward the back of the plane.

"Welcome to the Bahamas!" she said as she passed me. "Tell me if I can get you anything. A water? I'll be right back." And she was gone past me to wait on Klein.

Janet said helpfully, "You have to drink a lot of water down here. It can get very hot."

"I bet," I said, looking out at the flat, dry, sandy land with tall palm trees and thick greenery in the distance. Now that we were back on earth, I realized my heartbeat had slowed down to a reasonable rate, but I had practically sweated through my shirt.

"But you'll see," Janet said matter-of-factly, "this *is* paradise," as she picked up her silver attaché case and put her laptop back inside. "At least the way that Jonathan Klein does it."

I'm going to be a little vague about deplaning in the Bahamas: the security and how we got through customs and immigration and beyond. I don't want to get anyone into trouble, least of all myself. I don't mind telling you I was scared. All I had was my driver's license for ID. No passport. No visa. I didn't even have a ticket.

But Janet said, "Don't be worried, and don't *look* worried. That's even worse."

She was right about that. So I tried to look cool and follow Klein invisibly as part of his entourage. His posse. His baggage.

In retrospect, I don't know why I was afraid: getting off the jet with Klein was like walking with royalty or the pope. I guess when you have a fancy private plane, normal rules don't apply. There was a handler on this end, just like there was in White Plains, only this beautiful young woman was black. It seemed like just moments after we landed, we were walking—completely free—toward Klein's waiting car. Actually, there were two vehicles waiting for us: a long black Mercedes sedan and a big black Range Rover SUV. I didn't even have to carry my own stuff.

"Larry!" Klein called to me to walk up next to him. "So how'd ya like the flight?"

"Pretty amazing," I said.

"It actually saves me time and money, the G5," he said walking quickly across the hot tarmac. "It gives me one-stop range so I have global reach. It can fly at over fifty thousand feet so that I can fly over bad weather on the most direct route."

Keeping up with him, I said, "The fact that it's this great big *toy* has nothing to do with it."

He snickered. "Of course not."

There was a driver—a smiling, young black man in dark slacks and a short-sleeved light blue shirt—holding the door open for us.

"Welcome back, sir!" he said.

"Thank you, Joseph," Klein snapped back cheerfully. "Everything good with the baby?"

"Baby is fantastic!" the young man said gleefully in one of those cool Caribbean accents as Klein ducked his head and scooted into the backseat of the Mercedes. I followed him in.

"Where's Janet?" I asked.

"She'll go with the luggage," said Klein, taking a plastic bottle of water from a holder in the door and cracking it open.

"The luggage?"

"It's part of her job." Klein shrugged. "Nothing to worry about."

"She's a very smart young woman," I said.

Klein grunted a laugh. "That's why I hired her."

"And nicer than Brian?" I suggested.

"You could say that." Klein nodded again. "But that's how I like my people. Sweet and sour."

He seemed very pleased with that comment, and himself in general. I mean, why shouldn't he be? He seemed to have the world by the balls.

⌒

The drive from the airport to Klein's place was a convict's dream. Even the name—*Ba-HAAA-maaz*—was full of languor and romance. The fact that the main city was called Nassau only made me laugh inwardly. This wasn't anything like the Nassau I grew up in: *my* Nassau County on Long Island, the place that hated me, the home I could never shake.

I couldn't stop gawking at the scenery. The flat land...the palm trees...the perfect sky...and the blue ocean, going forever toward the horizon. Everything was open and free and clean. I pressed down the window button and drank in the salty air. One whiff, and a warm tropical tingle ran all through my body.

"Pretty damn nice here," I said.

"Yes, it is," he said, as if taking credit for the entire island's existence.

I turned and asked, "Why the Bahamas and not a million other islands?"

"Why?" he repeated. "Because it's not too far away. What was that? A little over three hours? And from here, it's only eighty miles to Miami."

I couldn't resist asking, "And it has nothing to do with the banking laws down here?"

Straight-faced he replied, "What banking laws?"

That made me laugh.

"And you drive on the left," I said. "That's cool."

"The Bahamas used to belong to England, and we're still part of the commonwealth," he said. "The English stole it from the Arawak Indians."

"Same as Columbus, right?" I said. "Didn't he also steal Florida from the Arawaks?"

Klein's eyes widened. "As a matter of fact, I believe he did."

"Well," I said, "Happy Columbus Day."

⌒

Even though this was paradise, Klein had extra security. There was a guardhouse at the gate at the entrance to the neighborhood where he lived, and the guard who lifted the gate for us was wearing a machine gun. Once inside, we drove past one enormous house after another, with big balconies and wide patios and colorful awnings, lush trees and vast lawns, explosions of pink-flowered bushes, and the pure blue sky above everything.

"Do all these houses go down to the beach?" I asked.

"Yes," he said. "I believe so."

"Damn," I whispered. I reminded myself once again not to sound like a peasant, but I couldn't help myself. That's what I am.

After a few minutes, we got to a high whitewashed wall that had another guard at the gate. Here we turned into the driveway. The driver lowered his window and waved as we cruised past the guard.

Gates within gates, I thought. *Jonathan Klein likes to be secure.* In a way, that was good for me. A very rich man who likes to be in control of things? He really could be the man to help me.

The car crunched down the gravel driveway until it stopped right in front of a huge, white two-story house with tall windows and large dark green awnings, surrounded by big shade trees and verandas.

"This is it," Klein crisply introduced me to his mansion. "... *Jamboree.*" The way he said the name showed me how much pride he had it in. And why not? It was like a house you'd see in a fancy travel magazine. Imagine the ultimate oceanfront mansion, then make it even nicer.

Before I knew it, I was in my own spacious bedroom on the second floor that had a big, lazy overhead fan; a giant bed; its own bathroom, complete with a Jacuzzi tub; and a long sliding glass door that led to a private patio overlooking the spectacular ocean. Everything in the room was a different shade of white, if there is such a thing. You could see the water from the high and fluffy bed if you kept the drapes open. There were flowers on the dresser in a big vase, and flowers on the patio. Flowers: for me.

I kept saying to myself, *Betsy should be here; she deserves something this nice.* But I was the one who was here, so I resolved to remember everything for her. I'd make sure she wouldn't regret that I took this trip. Especially when I came home with the money.

Let me just say a few words about that first night's dinner. Lobster. Wine. Ocean. Stars. Brandy. Klein held court at the head of the big glass-topped dining room table—the glass must have been five inches thick. It wasn't much of a court: just Janet and me.

"This is the only place I can really relax," he said, making a wide gesture with his wineglass. "It's where I can read, where I can think."

"You can't think in New York?" I asked.

"Not the same way," he said, shaking his head. "In New York, there's pressure. There's noise, people shouting. There's the competition, the media. Here, I can let that all go. I have space to imagine. To let loose."

He was so full of himself that I couldn't resist teasing him. "And you never think about your competition while you're down here?"

Janet across the table stifled a small laugh.

"But I get it," I continued. "Thinking under a palm tree is a different thing."

Klein smiled, took another long sip of the smooth white wine from the beautiful crystal goblet, and said, "So you *do* get it."

We let Klein talk. He was an expert on everything: how lobsters are caught, varieties of wine, how to fix the Knicks and the Yankees, the history of glassmaking. I was busting to ask him about when we were going after Mantell, but I kept quiet. I didn't want to pressure him, no matter what pressure I felt within. I could tell that Klein was a guy who didn't like to be pushed. Instead, I maintained good rapport with Janet while we listened to Klein pontificate. I could see why Klein liked to have Janet around: she was smart, pretty, and agreeable. I wondered if he was sleeping with her.

"Your next wife...Asian." That's what he said at Le Bernardin. Of course, Klein was about twenty years too old for her, and a "Beast" to her "Beauty," but that doesn't seem to matter if you have a couple billion dollars, a private plane, and a place in the Bahamas.

"Let's have dessert on the terrace," said Klein, pushing away from the table. He turned to one of the servants—have I mentioned the ever-present servants, all in uniform?—"Tell Gregory that dinner was superb. As usual."

Klein rose from his seat. Janet and I did as well.

What can I say about dessert under the stars, with the waves crashing in the background? The multiple joys of Klein's life were undeniable. I sat in an impossibly comfortable chair on the terrace overlooking the ocean and inhaled deeply. The salty air was sweet and mild. I had gotten used to the smell of the sea, living in City Island with Betsy, but this ocean air was different. Warmer, with nothing that smelled like rotting fish. Everything here just smelled...in bloom.

"How often do you get down here?" I asked Klein.

"Whenever I can," he said casually. "A couple of times a year, when I can."

"If I had a place like this," I said, "nothing could pry me away."

"We do the best we can," he said, fake-modestly.

"Hey, you're a busy man," I conceded. "Sometimes you can be here, sometimes you can't. Luck evens out."

"I like that," Janet said dreamily. "'Luck evens out.'"

"It's an old expression," I said. "I wish I really believed it."

"Janet?" said Klein, clearing his throat and changing his tone. "I think you can ask Myles to come in now."

"Absolutely," she said, switching suddenly to her business self, getting straight up out of her chair.

Out of politeness, I started to get up, but she stopped me with her extended palm. "No, please." I froze as she turned to Klein and said, "And if you don't need me anymore, I think I'll go upstairs after I send Myles in."

"I always need you, Janet, but yes, you should go up now," Klein said, sitting back. "And sleep well." He turned to me and added, "There's nothing like the ocean for sleeping. The air, the sound of the waves, the white noise. It beats any pill, anytime."

"I'll send him right in," said Janet. "Good night, Mr. Klein. Good night, Larry. Don't get up, please."

We both said good night and watched her walk away. She was far too young and attractive for old guys like us. Klein was a few years younger than I was, but I was in better shape, except for a couple missing teeth in the back. He was pudgy and a little rumpled, no matter how expensive his suits were. But, still, I wondered if he and Janet ever—

My train of thought was interrupted by the arrival, clicking onto the patio, of a tall, sharply dressed black man sporting a business suit, briefcase, and serious black-rimmed glasses.

Klein called, "Myles!" and got up from his chair with an *uff*. The man picked up his already rapid pace and extended his hand to receive Klein's handshake.

"Very good to see you, Mr. Klein," he said in one of those cool, clipped Sidney Poitier accents. "I trust you had a good flight."

"Perfect as usual," Klein replied. "Myles, I'd like you to meet someone." Turning to me, he continued, "This is Larry Ingber. Larry, this is Myles Pritchard."

I got to my feet and extended my hand to Myles. He was quite broad-shouldered.

"Myles," I greeted him.

"Mister Ingber," he said my name carefully as he locked my hand briefly in his massive grip.

"Gentlemen? Please?" said Klein, inviting us both to sit down in these big cushioned wicker chairs around a low table made of teak or some other beautiful wood.

"Larry," Klein said to me in a slightly different voice, his more business-like voice, "I asked Myles here to look into our Mr. Brandon Avery, and he's here to tell us what he's found."

"Great!" I straightened right up, almost spilling my wine.

Klein looked at me sharply. "Isn't that what you're here for?"

"Yes!" I said. "Of course."

"Then let's listen to the man," Klein said, directing my attention to Myles, who had removed an iPad from his briefcase and was clicking it on. "Myles?"

Myles started to speak, reading the information from the screen. "According to public records, Brandon Avery is an exporter of local crafts, though he apparently does none of the manufacturing himself. He uses several names for his various enterprises: Futurity Corporation, Essence of the Islands Corporation, and the Fair Justice Institute."

I had to snicker at the last one, which caused Myles to look up at me.

"He has an office on one of those alleys off Bay Street, near Cumberland—"

Klein interrupted. "Near the Hilton?"

"Yes." Myles nodded. "A few blocks away. In the back, there is a set of offices on the second floor. But he does not go there on a regular basis, and he does not receive his mail there. He gets his mail at the general post office."

"I know *exactly* where this is," Klein interjected.

"But," Myles said, shifting his big body forward in the chair, "he is also a money-launderer, a fence, and a banker for one of the local street gangs."

"Wait a second, Myles," I broke in. "You found all this out between the time I told Mr. Klein on the plane about Avery *this morning* and now?"

Myles looked at me with dark, serious eyes and said nothing.

"I told you I had good people, Larry," Klein said.

"Sorry," I muttered, properly chastened. "I didn't mean—anything."

"Go on," Klein prompted Myles.

"I've sent Miss Ko a copy of all this information," he said. "Do you want any further surveillance, to locate Mr. Avery? We can watch his office and the post office for when he picks up his mail. My men can follow him—"

"No, Myles," Klein held up his hand. "This is fine for now. As long as you sent Janet all the information."

"Already done, sir," Myles replied crisply.

"Good then," said Klein. "I'll call you when I need you."

Myles shot to his feet, swiftly put his iPad back into his briefcase, and practically stood at attention in front of Klein, ready to be dismissed.

"It is very good to see you, sir," he said with a confident smile, briefcase tight in his grip.

"And how is Diana doing?" he asked.

"Very well!" Pritchard said, happy to be asked the question.

"I'm glad to hear that," Klein said.

"Isn't she sending you letters?" the big man said, sudden irritation clouding his face, his whole body seeming to tense and actually grow inside his suit.

"Oh yes, yes!" Klein tamped down his concern. "All the time. Every week. I was just asking you as her father. To get your view of things."

"Oh," muttered Myles, immediately calmed by Klein's answer, "I just want to be sure that she's—"

"Go home, Myles!" Klein said good-naturedly.

"Will do, sir," said Myles, "and call me anytime. For anything."

He smiled slightly and then turned with an almost military about-face.

Klein watched him go with a look of pride. He took another sip and clinked the glass down on the tabletop, all finished.

"Very impressive guy," I said.

"He's a top man," Klein declared. "He used to be second-in-command of the Central Detective Unit for the Royal Police Force."

"And now he works for you?" I asked.

"Mostly for me. But I'm sure he has other irons in the fire. Myles is not a stupid man. I send his daughter to George Washington. She's studying criminology," Klein said and then abruptly hollered, "Joseph! More cognac!"

"Really?" I replied, watching Klein look into the bottom of his glass for one last drop. "I guess Myles *really* isn't a stupid man."

That got a self-satisfied grunt out of Klein as another white-jacketed servant came hustling out of the house, with the bottle wrapped in a linen napkin, to refill his glass.

I wondered if Jonathan Klein was going to take care of me the way he seems to take care of everybody in his orbit. I sipped my cognac, looked up at the impossibly gorgeous night sky, and wondered if, here in paradise, my luck was finally going to even out.

TWENTY-TWO

The next morning, I woke up startled and disoriented, in a large, strange bed—a bed as big as some of the cells I lived in—in a huge white room, on clean sheets as smooth as polished steel. And then I slowly remembered where I was...and grinned. But then I got nervous all over again. No matter how smooth the sheets were, how perfumed the air, I was still living suspended in a state of danger until I got back on U.S. soil and made it to my appointment with Fusco.

To calm myself down and focus, I took one of my James Bond showers in the nicest shower I've ever been in, in a white marble bathroom half as big as our apartment. Then I got out some clean clothes—did I mention that someone unpacked for me?—and went downstairs, fresh and rested. And still nervous.

Janet was sitting at the giant table on the patio, where an enormous breakfast had been laid out on the sideboard. Looking up from her laptop, she gave me a big hello, told me to help myself, and informed me that I probably wouldn't see Mr. Klein until sometime that afternoon.

"Fine with me," I said, hiding my disappointment fairly well I thought. Recalling last night's meeting with Myles Pritchard, I was hoping that Klein might want to get to my business right away. Of course, I was wrong; Klein was down here to do other things. Business things, financial things. I had to remind myself that I was just a sideshow and suck up my impatience. Even if I knew what Mantell's address was from Myles's report, I couldn't find it by myself. I was not in control of my own situation and had to trust Klein to do the right thing.

So after breakfast—perfect eggs, thick bacon, freshly squeezed orange juice, and these delicious things called "Freddiecakes"—I took a walk on Klein's beautiful, very private beach, killing time until he was ready for me, whenever that would be. I walked alone on the impossibly powdery sand, counting the rolling blue waves and the passing minutes. I should say that I was alone except that I was constantly being watched by one of Klein's roving band of security guards.

All morning long, I saw men in suits, two or three at a time, arrive to see Jonathan. They came in expensive cars and carried briefcases. They were escorted by Janet to Klein's wing downstairs, stayed for a while, and then left. One group after another. This was the main business that Klein came down to the Bahamas to do.

I realized that the best thing to do was stay out of the way and wait my turn. I decided to go to my bedroom so that I didn't vibrate away all my energy and concentration. As soon as I closed the door, I got down on the floor and did fifty push-ups. I could still do my "jailhouse workout," no matter what. I wanted to be fully prepared to do what I had to do to get my money back from Mantell. It was so close, I could taste it.

I didn't go downstairs at lunchtime. I decided to stay out of sight until we were ready to move. I didn't want to have to make small talk with anyone or suck up to Klein anymore (or any more than I had to).

I guess someone noticed when I wasn't around because there was a knock on my door, and when I opened it, another uniformed servant—a teenage boy, really—stood holding a tray of food for me.

"Miss Janet said to bring your lunch up here, sir," he said super politely.

It was a perfect sandwich of something, with the crusts cut off, with some kind of sweet potato–looking side dish, and a glass of iced tea with lots of ice cubes and a sprig of mint. And a cloth napkin alongside the plate, wrapped artfully around the silver knife, fork, and spoon. It was fucking beautiful.

On the one hand, this was great, being served fabulous food in my own gorgeous room in this fairy-tale place. But on the other hand, I couldn't wait to get the hell out there, once I had done what I went there to do. Get my money, get home in time to see Fusco, run to Betsy, fall at her feet with the money, and, in triumph, win her forgiveness.

It was another two nervous hours with Janet's words about Klein's "short attention span" echoing in my memory before I got the knock on the door that I was waiting for.

"Mr. Klein is ready for you now!" a voice called from the hall.

"I'll be right down!" I called back, scrambling around to make sure I had my wallet, my keys, and my useless phone firmly in the pockets of my jeans. I had texted Betsy once before the plane took off—*Miss you—u ok?*— but I didn't want to turn on my phone down here. I'm sure the roaming charges would have been extreme. I don't know why I didn't check with my phone company about the international rates before I left, but I was sure they were ridiculous and didn't even bother. I also didn't want any calls to appear on my phone bill anyway, proving that I was out of the country.

Klein was waiting for me at the bottom of the stairs wearing a flowered shirt and baggy shorts, and clunky sneakers: casual, even for him. He was there with Janet, finishing what looked like an angry exchange with her.

"Klein-o!" I called out to him as I walked down.

"Larry!" Klein's attitude changed suddenly from furious to friendly. "There you are!"

I could see that Janet was upset about something, but Klein was happy to see me.

"So what have you been doin' all day?" I couldn't resist saying as I landed on the marble floor next to him.

"Working," he replied curtly. "With varying degrees of success. And you?"

"Hanging around, waiting for you," I said. I wasn't going to lie to him, or sugarcoat things, even though I could tell that something had already put him in a contentious mood.

"Good," he said, seemingly oblivious to my comment. "So now, you ready to pay a little visit to your lawyer friend?"

Without waiting for my answer, he started for the front door, knowing that I would go right with him.

Janet, walking along with us, asked, "Are you *sure* you don't want Myles to go with you, sir? Or one of his men?"

"Not a bit!" Klein said, waving her off with the flip of his hand. "Larry and I can handle this ourselves, right? We have the address. Let's go find this guy."

"Absolutely," I concurred.

We walked briskly out of the house, down the front terrace and into the sunshine. A black showroom-floor-new BMW convertible with the top down was waiting in the sparkling white gravel driveway, with a driver standing guard. As we approached the car, I realized that Klein was heading for the driver's seat, on the right side.

"Wait a second." I stopped. "*You're* driving?"

"I know how to drive," he said with some annoyance. The car was a sweet little coupe, really meant for two people: him and me. There was barely space in the back seat for packages, much less passengers.

"Get in, Larry!" he commanded. "We can do this, the two of us. I don't need a staff for every fucking thing in the world."

He got in, and I obeyed. I think he meant that last comment for Janet, who was standing there watching us.

It was weird being a passenger in the left front seat as Klein started the car and then revved it twice. He moved deliberately like a teenager in the early throes of Driver's Ed, adjusting the mirrors and checking his angles.

"Goodbye, sir!" Janet yelled as he put the car in gear, and we took off, spinning gravel. "Call if you need anything!"

Klein just looked ahead, focusing on his driving.

"What happened back there?" I asked him.

"Nothing," he answered, obviously still pissed off. "*Two* blown deals. Wasted my fuckin' time. Sometimes you just want to do something real. With real people. This will be real."

He floored the gas and tore down the driveway, throwing me back in my seat. The gate was already opened for him as we drove through. Klein waved to the security guard. "Thank you, Julian!"

And in a moment, we were out on the open road along the shore, speeding under the cloudless blue sky, breathing in the sea air, making our own breeze in the open BMW.

"God, I love driving here," he said.

"Even if it's on the wrong side?" I asked him.

"*Especially* because it's on the wrong side!" he shouted over the sound of the engine and the rushing wind.

Klein picked up speed, moving his head, checking the mirrors in the light afternoon traffic. This driving-on-the-left was disorienting for me, but Klein seemed right at home, driving this sweet, flashy car. Another toy, another Beemer.

Slowing down on a curve, we passed an old black woman in a colorful headdress, sitting in a lawn chair at the side of the road under two big, rainbow-colored umbrellas. Next to her was a large red ice chest with a sign in fluorescent Magic Marker letters: "BEST ICES ON THE PLANET."

Klein lightly beeped his horn twice and shouted, "Wilhelmina!"

"Hello, mistah!" the old woman shouted excitedly, waving both hands, as we whizzed by.

"She has the best shaved ice on the planet," he declared. "Really."

He clapped me on the thigh twice and laughed. He seemed to be having a good time, but I could tell he was under some stress: his deals didn't go right, and inside he was fuming. Where was the famous Klein temper? He seemed to be a pretty in-control so far, but I was going to have to watch him carefully.

In just a few minutes, we were in downtown Nassau, a strange mix of buildings: ritzy and grungy, side by side. Some two- or three-story office buildings, a few fancy stores and rows of brightly painted little shops and cafes. A Holiday Inn and a Hilton. There were also a lot of banks with names I'd never heard of. In the distance was a row of cruise ships, one after another, as big as apartment buildings. And beyond them, there was some giant resort hotel. Fast-driving Klein had to slow down; there were plenty of cars and tourists walking around, jamming things up, not to mention a few horse-drawn carriages.

When he stopped for a traffic policeman in a fluorescent yellow vest, Klein reached into his shirt pocket, took out of a piece of paper, and gave it a quick read.

"I know exactly where this is," he said with precision in his voice, and he sped up going through the intersection. "These streets get crowded," he muttered, watching in all directions for cars and pedestrians. "But I know the back alleys," he said, turning suddenly—that weird *wide* right turn—into a narrow passageway between two buildings. He did seem to know his way.

He rolled carefully down the alley, watching for trash bins and downspouts on one side, a big chain-link fence on the other. He turned again, down an even narrower alley.

"Are you sure this is for cars?" I finally asked him.

"Of course, it is," he said. "This is completely right."

We emerged into a wide, sunny area where there were lots of parked cars and a dumpster. Facing us was a big gray building with a long gallery of offices on the second floor, just the way Myles Pritchard described it. Klein pulled the car over to the side in a clear space by a wall, stopped, and firmly put on the parking brake.

He turned to me and said, "OK, Larry: let's go get your money."

Together we climbed the rickety outside stairway to the row of offices, Klein leading the way. We worked our way down the row, checking every door, until we came to the last one. And, sure enough, the nameplate on the last door bore the tarnished brass name: AVERY LLC.

We looked at each other and smiled a mutual *So far, so good.*

"Would you like to do the honors?" Klein asked. And I did.

Knock-knock-knock. My heart was almost pounding through my shirt. After all this time, was this going to be it?

After no response, Klein said, "Knock again."

There was a dirty window, its blinds drawn, next to the door, and Klein tried to see in.

"I think there's a light on in there," he said, shielding his eyes, trying to peer through the reflection.

I knocked again. Harder.

"Shit," I muttered. Myles said that no one was in the office on a regular basis.

Just when I thought we were at a dead end, there was a noise from inside the door. I heard the clicking of locks being unlocked.

"Hey!" I whispered to Klein just as the door slowly opened.

An old man, very tanned and wrinkled, with frizzy white hair combed back stood there looking at me suspiciously. By *old*, I mean older than me. He had to be in his seventies. He wore one of those white lacy Caribbean shirts with all the pockets in front. He had a sparse white goatee and an unlit cigar butt hanging out of the side of his mouth.

"Hello!" I said crisply. "We're looking for Brandon Avery."

The old man's eyes narrowed. "He's not here."

Klein pushed in front of me and moved in on the old man.

"Excuse me," he said, "my name is Jonathan Klein, and I need to talk to Mr. Avery right now, about a business proposition."

The old man was practically pushed back by the force of Klein's personality, and suddenly we were inside the dark, musty office. There were two large old wooden desks and some ancient furniture: a couch, a coffee table with some magazines on top, some gray file cabinets, stacks of dusty cardboard boxes, and a hallway that went somewhere toward the back. An air conditioner hummed, but the office was warm and had the smell of old cigars and slow decay.

"Nice place," said Klein.

The old man adjusted the blinds, trying to get some light into the room.

"I'm sorry, fellas," he croaked, "but Mr. Avery isn't here today."

"When will he be back?" Klein said.

"Not for a week, at least," the old man said in a raspy American voice. He stood back against the edge of a desk. "What do you want him for?"

"We just want to see him," I said strongly. "That's all." I didn't like this old guy's manner.

"This is a serious matter," said Klein, "about a financial opportunity for him."

"What do you mean 'opportunity?'" the old man repeated skeptically.

Klein leaned into the old man. "Do you know who I am?"

The old man looked Klein over, moving his head side to side slowly like a searchlight.

"You're one of those Wall Street guys, aren't you," he said sourly, "with one of those big houses out on Bay Street?"

"No," Klein corrected him. "I'm the Wall Street guy with the *biggest* house on Bay Street."

Then the old man looked at me carefully.

"But how do I know *you*?" he asked, inspecting me with an evil eye.

"My name is Larry Ingber," I said. "And don't worry: Mr. Avery knows me very well."

The old man looked startled for a moment, then turned away to retrieve a legal pad and a pen from the desk. Keeping his head down, he put out the pad and pen to Klein and said, "Why don't you write everything down, exactly as it happened—"

Then the bolt of lightning hit me.

"Wait a second," I confronted the old man. "*You're* Avery! I mean, you're not Avery—you're Lester Mantell!"

The bent old man straightened up a little.

"No!" he protested. "What are you talking about? My name is Delaney. Harry Delaney."

But he couldn't fool me. I saw through his wrinkled, leathery skin and his crappy little white beard. I saw through all the years.

"You son of a bitch!" I spat out. "It *is* you!"

"No!" the old man stood back from the desk. "You're wrong! I just work for Mr. Avery!"

"What, you don't recognize me?" I moved in on him. "Larry Ingber, the guy you screwed!"

Shrinking back from me with his hands half raised, the old man pleaded, "You're wrong! I'm telling you Mr. Avery isn't here!"

"You goddamn thief!" I grabbed the old man by the throat, but Klein caught my arm and pulled me off him.

"Wait a second, Larry!" Klein shouted. "Maybe this isn't the guy."

"I swear to God, I don't know what he's talking about!" the old man squealed, moving around the desk.

"You fucking liar!" I zeroed in on his fearful, deceitful eyes. No matter how many years had gone by, I *knew* it was Lester Mantell. "You didn't think I was ever gonna find you?"

"He's crazy!" the old man yelled, moving to the back of the office. "You keep him away from me! I have a bad hip!"

I grabbed Klein, spun him around, held him tight by his shirt-front with both hands, and looked him right in the eye.

"I'm telling you, Jonathan," I declared flat-out, "it's the same guy. I *know* it!"

That's when the old man made a break and ran for the back hallway, knocking over a chair to block our way.

"Come on!" I yelled as I released Klein.

As I jumped over the chair to follow the old man, who was already out of sight, I heard a thud and a crash. When I turned left at the end of the hallway, I saw a big pile of cardboard boxes in our path. And at the end of another hallway there was a half-open door to the outside. It took me a few seconds to climb over the boxes and get outside, onto a back staircase. Klein was right behind me.

"Shit!" I gasped, looking over the railing and down the side. "He's gone."

"No!" Klein shouted. "There he goes!"

He pointed across my chest at another alleyway that I didn't see. There, at the end of the alley, was Avery/Mantell running away.

"Let's go!" I yelled, and we thundered down the rattling metal staircase. I held on with two hands, making the turns so I didn't fall and break my neck.

When we got to the ground, Klein pointed to two different alleys and shouted, "You go this way—I'll go around!"

"One of us will cut him off!" I concurred.

I took off in Avery's direction as fast as I could, and Klein went around the building, the other way. I ran down the alleyway only to run into another alleyway...and another parking lot with *three* ways to get out of it. Which way did he go? I took a guess and ran to the farthest part of the lot, figuring he would try to get as far away from us as possible.

I found myself out on the open street, suddenly dodging pedestrians. I looked in all directions, but no Avery. Where was that frizzy white head? I ran back toward Avery's building, hoping that I'd run into Klein coming from the other way. I fast-walked quickly down the pavement, darting around pain-in-the-ass tourists, my eyes looking in every direction, but I didn't see anyone. No Avery, no Klein. *Shit.*

"LARRY!"

I looked around and it was Klein—in his car.

"Get in!" he yelled. "Come on, he's getting away! He got to his car!"

I ripped open the car door and was barely in my seat when Klein floored the gas. I slammed the door closed, just in time to miss hitting a light pole.

"Where'd he go?" I quizzed him.

Klein was driving too intensely to answer, but I could see he knew where he was going.

"Fuck!" he hissed, swerving around a slow bicycle rider and picking up speed.

"What is he driving?" I asked Klein. "What am I looking for?"

Klein shot back, "A dumpy little dune buggy!" He passed two cars, fast. "I just lucked into seeing him coming out of this garage," he continued. "Prick almost ran me over."

"Where do you think he's going?" I asked.

"South!" he yelled.

"Why south?"

He took one hand off the wheel, pulled something out of his shirt pocket, and gave it to me. It was a matchbook that read, "Aviva—Albany House."

"I picked this up in his office," he said. "That's a restaurant on the south side of the island, so I'm guessing he lives down that way and that's where he's heading."

"Great!" I said, impressed that Klein found the time to pick up this clue. I didn't even see him do it. "Let's find this bastard!"

"Hunt this dawg down!" Klein shouted joyously.

He floored the BMW, and we surged forward, throwing me back against the seat. These German cars can move.

"Fortunately," Klein said, changing lanes again, "his car is a piece of shit and he's burning oil, so he shouldn't be so hard to trail...if I guessed right."

Klein drove super fast and semi-recklessly. He bobbed his head, checking the mirrors or looking over his shoulder before he switched lanes and surged ahead. He raced around another two cars, causing someone to blast a car horn at us. But I didn't care.

"There he is! Son of a bitch." Klein pointed ahead of us. "That's him!" He craned his neck, trying to see around the cars in front of us.

By now we were out of the city of Nassau and on some outer road: a two-lane blacktop with—you're not going to believe this— all these crappy American fast-food places, one after the other: KFC, Wendy's, Domino's fucking Pizza!

"Look on that side!" he ordered. "Is anybody there?"

The road was narrow, and there were some street vendors down the way.

"Yes!" I shouted. "Too crowded!"

Klein swerved the other way and passed the car in front of us.

"Shit!" I gasped, gripping the car with both hands: one on the door, one on the dashboard.

I looked over at Klein. He was having the time of his life.

"I knew it!" he muttered triumphantly. "He *had* to take this road."

"Are you sure it's him?"

"I *know* this area," he said, concentrating on his driving. "Some schmuck tried to talk me into investing in a golf course down here. Near Bonefish Pond."

"'Bonefish Pond!'" I repeated the name.

"Where'd he go?" Klein shouted. "Shit!"

Suddenly Avery wasn't there.

"Fuckin' piece of —!" Klein said, slowing down a little. "He must've turned off onto one of these—*wait*!"

Klein whipped the car into a U-turn, crossing traffic that— thank goodness—wasn't coming toward us.

"I *know* this area!" he told me, looking from side to side, to see where Klein's dune buggy could've gone. "Not all these roads go down to the beach," he said, slowing down a little.

"So what does that mean?"

Klein explained, "A grifter like Avery couldn't afford beach-front. He must be down one of these dead-end roads....Let's try in here!"

And he sped up and pulled another U-turn, whipping the BMW off the main road street and onto a side road through a break in the trees that I hadn't even noticed. Suddenly it got bumpier, with potholes and uneven patches in the asphalt. As we rumbled along, I saw tumbledown houses on either side, back in the trees. Some were no more than shacks. This was a different, poorer part of Nassau than I had seen.

"There he is!" he shouted. "Look! Puff of smoke!"

He pointed almost right across my face and there, through the trees, was a faint cloud of black smoke on a street parallel to ours.

"That's him," he said firmly.

"Great," I said, trying to keep sight of the dune buggy as Klein sped up and cut quickly across on a side street.

"Shit-shit-shit," he muttered, driving faster as the houses flashed by. He made a tight left onto another road where the houses were even shabbier and more spread out. Far down at the end of the road, it seemed to dead-end in a forest.

"You still see him?" I asked.

"Yeah," he said. "Let's go around once." He let the car slow down a little as we went past where he saw the dune buggy go.

"Good idea," I said. "Circle around. Let's see what the layout is."

Klein drove slower, going up the block and swinging left, looking across the yards to see which house the dune buggy belonged to. Down at the end of this sleepy lane, everything looked even poorer. Some houses were almost completely hidden by big tropical plants; others had rusted cars and junk in their yards. There were some low fences that made it difficult to see what was what in the long shadows from the setting sun.

Klein turned the car down an even rougher track, past another couple of shacks, toward what looked like a dead end. We rolled slowly down the path over the uneven, worn asphalt.

"This is a weird place to live," I said, looking around at the hardscrabble surroundings.

"Yeah," Klein said, "but a good place if you want to disappear and still be near some banks. You say he's a scam artist? A lot of islands have beaches, but we have beaches and *banks*. I hate to say it, but we have more than our share of these old con artists."

"Pirates of the Caribbean," I said bitterly.

"Wait a minute," Klein said as we slowed almost to a stop in front of what seemed to be the last house on the street, a shabby yellow bungalow with a separate garage in the back. Beyond that, everything looked like a dead end and dark trees.

"Let's stop here," Klein said carefully, turning off the motor.

Suddenly it was very quiet. I couldn't hear anything except for some insects and perhaps the sound of the ocean in the distance.

"Where's the dune buggy?" I asked.

"I think he drove it around the back," Klein said, not taking his eyes off the house.

We sat there for a moment.

"What should we do?" I asked him. It was his turf, his island.

He sat there for a moment, looking straight ahead. Then he turned to me.

"Why don't we just go get him?" he said firmly. "You saw him. He's a little old man."

"You're right," I said. "This is what we're here for."

It was time to act. We opened our car doors simultaneously and got out. For a moment, I stood there, scoping out the shabby house, its faded yellow paint and empty little white front porch. Big overgrown plants obscured the windows, but I couldn't see in anyway. The blinds were drawn, and there were no lights on. I didn't see the dune buggy anywhere, but maybe it was behind the house. Did he have time to stash it in the garage? All in all, it was an unfriendly scene.

Klein looked at me across the hood of the BMW and asked, "You think we should call the cops?"

Cops? That was the *last* thing I needed.

"No," I said. "We can do this. This time, *we're* the cops."

"OK," Klein said. "I'll try the front door. You go around the back, in case he tries to run."

Klein walked steadily toward the front door, slowly and quietly, while I went across the sparse lawn, around the side of the house. There was no movement by the window shades or anything.

When I got around to the back of the house, I saw the dune buggy parked in front of a run-down, wooden two-car garage in the dusty, empty backyard. But the back of the house was quiet: nothing but a door with a simple wooden step.

From the front porch, I heard Klein's loud *knock-knock-knock* on the door.

"Mr. Avery?" he called out strongly.

Nothing. Then *knock-knock-knock* again.

"Avery!" Klein pounded on the door again. It seemed to shake the whole shanty, rattling the windows. I heard him turn the doorknob roughly, back and forth, back and forth.

Just at that moment, the back door flew open, and Avery came running out into the backyard, making a break for the dune buggy. Fortunately, he didn't see me at all. I took a run at him and hit him with a hard flying tackle that sent us both crashing to the ground. I landed on him heavily and heard him groan with pain.

The fall knocked the wind out of me, but I was on top and recovered first. I got onto him firmly, straddling his body. He was woozy, and it was easy to grab his wrists and pin him to the ground.

Just as I took a deep breath and settled my weight squarely on top of him, Klein came up behind me and pulled my arm.

"Not here!" he hissed. "Let's get him inside. Someone will see."

It was dingy inside Avery's kitchen, and it stank too. Avery. Mantell. I didn't even know what the hell to call him anymore.

"Goddamn!" Klein coughed as we moved the old man, each holding an arm. "It smells like shit in here."

With one hand, I pulled a kitchen chair into the middle of the floor, and we sat Avery down square in it and stood over him. As he started to come around, I pushed him back against the chair.

"Sit there and don't move!" I ordered. "You crooked piece of shit."

We all were breathing pretty hard. I know that my adrenalin was rushing like crazy.

Avery looked up at Klein and me. His hair was standing up, and his cheek was streaked with dirt and blood. Suddenly he started to cry.

"What is wrong with you guys?" he asked, weeping. "Why are you after me?"

"Oh, shut the fuck up!" I told him, grabbing him by the shirt.

Klein restrained me, pulling me away, and talked straight to Avery.

"Listen," he said directly into the old man's fearful face, "we know where you live. We know where your office is. We know your fucking post office box number. There is no more getting away. *Do you understand?*"

Klein got closer and spoke more softly. "Now this is what I want you to do. I want you to turn over this guy's money—"

"The money you *stole*!" I added.

Avery trembled in the chair, looking back and forth, not knowing who to fear more, and said, "What money?"

I wanted to smack him.

Klein said, "You know what we're talking about!"

The old man stuttered, "Y-y-you mean...the money his *parents'* had?"

"What do you *think* we mean, you thief?" I snarled.

"That money?" he cried out, "That money is *gone*! Long gone."

"What do you mean *gone*?" Klein grabbed Avery's shirt from the other side.

"I MEAN IT'S GONE!" Avery said, sitting up straight in the chair. "Spent! Used up! A long time ago! To legal fees, and appeals, and custodial and executor fees—*expenses*! You think the law is free?"

For a moment, I was stunned.

"You were in jail a long time, kiddo, and I'm sorry, but that money got spent. And don't forget," Avery continued, "your parents were not wealthy people to begin with."

"Shut the fuck up!" I refused to believe him. "There was way too much money there, even for you to steal. And the FBI is after you. You stole from other people too. And don't call me 'kiddo,' you thieving prick."

"Look around!" Avery shouted. "Does it look like I have any money?"

Klein and I did look around. The place was a fucking mess: no other words for it. Unwashed dishes were piled up in the sink. We could see into the main room, where there was just a big TV, a low sectional sofa, and some mattresses against the far wall under the front window. The walls were drab gray, and there were no pictures, no anything, on the walls. There was hardly any light or air in the whole place, only dust and stink.

I looked down at the old man's face, tight and rabbity with fear. Somehow still I didn't believe his explanation.

"I know lots of crooks who have money but don't like to show it," I said. "Sick fucks like you."

I looked over at Klein. I could see that he didn't know who or what to believe. And frankly, for the moment, neither did I.

And then all hell broke loose.

There was a banging noise in the front of the house, and the back door burst open. From nowhere, a bunch of teenage boys ran into the kitchen from both sides, yelling and screaming, and before we could do anything, they grabbed Klein and me. We tried to wrestle away, but there were too many of them and a couple were really big. Bigger than either of us. Instantly they had both of us tightly, one kid on each arm.

"Hold on to them, boys!" yelled Avery, who was out of the chair, his strength suddenly recovered. He was obviously in charge of these street kids. Didn't Myles mention something about Avery and some street gangs? "Don't let 'em go!"

"Wait a second, Avery." Klein started to bargain with him, even as he struggled in the grasp of two big teenagers. There were six of them, all dressed in dark clothes and flashy sneakers, even the two littler ones. One of them, wearing wraparound sunglasses, was really fat. The kids who held on to me—all of them reeking of McDonald's—were damned strong. The more I tried to struggle, the tighter they held me.

"Wait a second *nothing*." Avery laughed in Klein's face. "It's a different thing, isn't it, when the shoe is on the other foot, and *you're* the ones outnumbered."

"You son of a bitch," I muttered, not surprised that he had faked that pitiful, harmless-old-man act.

"Don't be stupid, Avery—" Klein began, but Avery cut him right off.

"*I'm* not stupid! *I'm* not stupid!" he screamed into Klein's face. Klein flinched. Avery got spit on him he was in so close.

"You and your jailbird friend are the stupid ones," Avery continued, "for coming to look for something that should have been forgotten about a long time ago. A *long* time!"

Avery took a deep, heavy breath, looking at each of us, and smoothed his white hair. Then he barked an order to the biggest teenager, who was wearing an oversize Bob Marley T-shirt: "OK, take them out to the garage...and keep 'em quiet."

Before I knew what was happening, I was being hustled, carried, and dragged across the backyard, with one teenager's grubby, greasy hand tight over my mouth. Klein was right next to me, fighting as hard as I was, but there were too many of them, too strong and too young. In a matter of seconds, they had opened the side door to the garage and thrown us hard onto the packed dirt floor.

"Fuck!" Klein yelled in pain. "What the hell is wrong with you?" he screamed at the teenagers, who had all crowded into the garage and closed the door behind them.

I rolled over and scrambled to my feet, helping Klein get up too. I scoped out the situation as we retreated to a corner, the teenagers moving in to surrounding us.

Klein put up his hands to the biggest kid. "Stop right there! You: Bob Marley. Whatever he's paying you, I'll *triple* it."

The kid paused for a moment as the others looked to him.

"I'm not kidding," Klein pleaded. "Look at my car. It's right up the street!"

"Shut up, you!" he yelled back.

Klein persisted, "It's a BMW!" He reached into his pocket, pulled out his car keys, and jangled them in the air. "Take my car. Really—take it. Only let us out of here."

"Shut up, shut up!" shouted Bob Marley T-shirt, holding up his hand as if blocking out Klein's offer.

Klein enticed him. "I can give you much more money than that old man—"

Suddenly one of the smaller teens, a squat kid in a green headband, whipped out a gravity knife, and slashed the air twice, inches in front of Klein's face.

"SHUT THE FUCK UP, HE SAID!" he shrieked.

That's when I knew we were in real trouble. These kids were young, excited, scared, and stupid, all at the same time. I've seen kids like this all my life, coming through the system, and they are dangerous. They had to be handled properly, or we could be really fucked.

Calmly I held up my hand in a peaceful gesture to the knife wielder. "Wait a second. You. Let me talk to your boss." I indicated that I meant the big kid in the Bob Marley T-shirt.

Bob Marley T-shirt looked over at me. He seemed to like that I sounded less hysterical than Klein and called him the boss.

"Let me tell you about your Mr. Mantell," I said smoothly. "And I'll—"

"Who you mean?" he asked sharply.

"See?" I responded. "You don't even know the old man's real name."

"And what is *your* name?" he said, stepping up right to my face, challenging me.

Using my best Prison Mind, I answered back, "My name is the guy who's going to make you more money than you've ever seen in your life—tonight, right now, right here—if you do things smart. If you do exactly what I say. Now go get me the old man."

That stopped him. He looked at me, and I looked back at him, just like I faced down a million punks in eight of the toughest prisons in the land of the free, the home of the brave.

"OK," he said, nodding very slowly, wary of being taken advantage of. "So you want to see the old man?"

"Yeah," I said. "I do. Now. If you want to make some serious money."

Bob Marley T-shirt took a moment, looking at me and then at Klein, who was still holding the BMW keys.

Then he nodded. "OK, I'll get him."

Great! I thought. *I'll get them to leave us alone in the garage, and then we'll find a way out of here.*

The big kid turned slowly and started to go toward the garage door, but then he had one last thought.

"Bwoy!" he commanded. "Tie them up first!"

Shit.

TWENTY-THREE

Two kids tied Klein and me up, sitting back to back on wooden chairs, looping rope around us a dozen different ways, giggling like children.

"You're making a big, *big* mistake, boys," Klein said.

"Shut up, fatty!" one yelled in his face.

"Tie 'em up tight!" the other one said as they wound the rope around and around.

"Hey!" Klein squirmed.

That got a jeering laugh out of the teenagers. I knew enough not to say anything. I was busy looking around for two things: a possible way to escape and a weapon.

Klein leaned his head back and muttered over his shoulder, "I'm sorry, Larry. It was stupid not to bring anybody with us. It was my fault, my stupid, arrogant—"

"Shut up, fat red man!" the other teenager shouted in Klein's ear, and he shut right up.

I looked around. The garage was bare, and it was dingy inside. The sun was almost totally down, and there was only a bare bulb overhead. We were on one side of the two-car garage; on the other was a rusted pickup truck on blocks. And there was a long worktable in the back, but I couldn't see if there was anything useful on it.

Just then, the door opened, and I turned my head to see Avery walk back in, followed by Bob Marley T-shirt and the other teenagers. He stood in front of me, his white hair slicked back, arms crossed in front of his chest, looking triumphant.

"Larry, Larry, Larry," he said, shaking his head. "*Bubeleh!* Look at the mess you've gotten yourself into. You and your fancy-ass Wall Street friend. You were never very good at controlling your impulses."

He looked like an old, suntanned hamster.

"And who the fuck are you, *Lester*? Look what you've come to," I countered. "With all these kids hanging around you? Who the fuck are you? Fagin?"

"Fagin?" He coughed a raspy, cigar-smoker's laugh. "I like that. That's very...literary. No, Larry, I like to do favors for young people. I always have. Like *your* case."

"Fuck you, thief," I said.

"That's funny," he said, "coming from the Ivy League Killer!"

Klein interrupted, trying to bargain. "Listen, Mantell or Avery or whatever—"

But Avery/Mantell wasn't finished with me.

"How dare you come after me!" he yelled in my face, cigar-stink and all. "After all the favors I did for you and your family!"

"Favors? Are you kidding me?" I shouted back. "So why was it that what Clemency got me released on was *inadequate counsel*?" I wasn't taking any of his shit. "If you're such a paragon of goodness, why are you down here hiding, holed up like a rat in this shithole? You can change your name, but you're still the same cheap shyster—"

That's when he backhanded me across the face, hard. My ears were still ringing as Avery walked around to Klein and said, "And *you*. I know who you are, big man over here. Well, some things you can't buy your way out of."

And he slapped Klein hard across the face, so hard it rocked both of us in our chairs. Klein let out a cry of pain.

My eyes were still blurry as I turned my head to see Avery, rubbing his hand, giving the teenagers his orders.

"OK," Avery barked, "we gotta move them. I'll get the boat. You watch 'em. I'll be right back." He walked to the door and stopped. "Hey, did you check their pockets?"

Bob Marley T-shirt said, "No."

"Schmucks!" Mantell/Avery barked. "Do I have to teach you everything? Empty their pockets, and put everything over there." He pointed to the work shelf by the door. "You two"—he indicated to Bob Marley T-shirt and Green Headband—"Watch these pricks. The rest of ya, come with me."

He walked out of the garage, followed by most of the teens. The door slammed behind them.

"You OK?" Klein whispered to me over his shoulder.

"Shut up!" Bob Marley T-shirt yelled. Then he ordered the other kid to check our pockets.

Immediately, Green Headband was on Klein, reaching into his pockets and pulling out his wallet.

Klein yelped, "Hey! Be careful!...Wait a second, I have a lot more money than that, if you just let us go."

Bob Marley T-shirt laughed. "I bet you do, fat boy! Get the other one."

I felt the kid reach into my pants pockets, one after the other. I twisted as best I could, but he managed to pull out my wallet and phone.

"Hey. Look at this old phone," Green Headband said, playing with it.

"Don't turn that on," I said. "The roaming charges are—"

"Fuck you!" he said, slipping the phone into his pocket. "It's a piece of shit. And where is *your* phone, fat bwoy?"

"I don't carry a phone down here," Klein said.

"Bullshit!" Green Headband said, almost spitting his reply into Klein's face.

Opening Klein's wallet, Bob Marley T-shirt whistled low. "Ooooh, look at this." He flashed open Klein's wallet to his buddy, showing off a big wad of cash.

Green Headband whooped a loud laugh. "Somebody gonna get some puss-puss tonight!"

"I gonna get everyting!"

They both broke into wild laughter, just like the stupid kids they were. Except these were *dangerous* stupid kids.

Klein tried again: "Listen to me, guys. You can take my car if you let us go! You're going to get into big trouble if —"

"SHUT UP!" Bob Marley T-shirt yelled, echoing in the empty garage. "You just sit there, fat boy! And wait for de boss."

Green Headband came up to my face, "And you, old man, you should start to pray." Then he laughed, still stinking of McDonald's.

"Come on," Bob Marley T-shirt said to his buddy, "let's get a puff."

He then turned to Klein and me. "And don't you two move!" As if we could. I was tied so tightly I was losing feeling in my left hand.

They laughed very hard at that one and put the two wallets on the shelf where Avery told them. Together they walked out the door as Green Headband pulled out a pack of cigarettes and a lighter.

"I love BMWs!" Bob Marley T-shirt said. "You know BMW stands for Bob Marley and the Wailers?"

As soon as the door was closed, I turned as best I could and whispered to Klein, "Are you OK?"

"No!" he said, fierce and hurt. "That old prick is going to pay for that."

Klein didn't sound good, but I couldn't worry about him. I started to shift and move within the ropes.

"What are you doing?" Klein asked over his shoulder.

"Don't move!" I whispered harshly. I started working my left arm and pushing out with my back. "I have a loose shoulder. I think I can dislocate it and maybe slip out of this."

I jerked my arm and, with a silent scream, pushed hard and popped my arm out of its socket, causing an incredibly sharp pain to shoot down my arm.

"We gotta get the fuck out of here," Klein said.

"No shit," I muttered, wiggling my body as I rocked and squirmed to loosen the ropes, finally getting my shoulder and then my arm out. The pain was indescribable, but I was free. Strange, the residual benefits of imprisonment.

"When do you think they're coming back?" Klein whispered.

I ignored his question as I worked to free my other arm, with my left shoulder throbbing. I looked around for a weapon; there had to be something here. As soon as I had both arms free, I popped my arm back in its socket and reached down to loosen the ropes around my legs. I felt something very deep in my pants pocket, on the side.

"Get me out of these!" Klein hissed. Somehow he was still tied up tightly.

I could hear the teenagers just outside the door, talking and laughing, about to come back in at any moment.

"Hurry!" Klein begged.

I pulled out what I felt buried deep in my pocket: the wad of twenty-dollar bills that Betsy gave me right before I left—what now seemed like light years ago—with that big-ass metal paper clip around them. *The paper clip!* I quickly stuffed the twenties into my pocket, took the paper clip, and straightened it out with a few hard twists, making a small loop around my little finger so I could hold it firmly.

"What are you doing?" Klein asked.

"Just shut the fuck up," I whispered. moving into the shadowy space beside the doorway. My Prison Mind had completely taken over.

Green Headband walked in first, still looking behind him, talking and laughing. *Perfect!*

Immediately I grabbed him tightly, swung him around, held him from behind, and smashed his face into the wall. With my hand firmly around his neck, I thrust the straightened paper clip right up into his throat, as deep and hard as I could, and I jammed it there as tight as I could.

He instantly went stiff and started gasping.

"Ssshh! Stay still," I whispered into his ear. "I don't want to kill you, kid, but I will."

"Larry," Klein hissed.

"Don't move!" I held the kid tightly, driving the metal prong hard up into his neck. Thrashing in my grasp, he started to make gurgling sounds, but I held him firmly by the neck and shoved the shiv in deeper. I could feel blood trickling down over my fingers. I reached down with my other hand and felt his knife in his back pocket, where I saw him stash it. As I clamped him around the throat, I managed to take out the knife and slip it into my back pocket.

He started fighting me harder, his green headband slipping off. I drove the paper clip sideways through his throat as best I could and almost climbed onto his back as he tried to spin away from my grip. I kept jabbing it into his neck as he choked and bucked, but I would not be denied. Not by this punk kid.

"Larry!" Klein called to me, warning me that the door was opening. "Watch out!"

Bob Marley T-shirt walked in, and I shouted to him, "You! Don't move!"

I held Green Headband up against me as a shield, blood pouring from his neck.

"Stand over there!" I ordered the big teenager. "Or I'll cut his fucking head right off!"

He couldn't see that all I had was a straightened paper clip, but there was enough blood pouring from Green Headband's neck, and I was acting so crazy, that Bob Marley T-shirt stepped back, fright across his face.

"Move over there!" I told him. "Or I'll kill him right now!"

Green Headband was whimpering and getting heavy to hold, but I kept jamming the metal in. The kid was shaking and crying.

"Wait, mistah! No! Don't!" Bob Marley T-shirt held out his palms, telling me not to cut any deeper.

"Stay right there!" I ordered them.

I knew the paper clip wasn't going to deter them much longer. With my free hand, I reached into my back pocket, pulled out Green Headband's knife, and snapped the blade out.

"There!" I growled, putting the knife blade back up hard against Green Headband's neck. Now I had a real weapon.

"Larry!" Klein pleaded, rocking back and forth in the chair. "Cut me loose! Before the others get back," I could also see that Avery had hit him really hard and left a red mark across his cheek.

"Kendry," Green Headband croaked to his friend, but I pulled back on the knife blade, holding him closer.

"Don't you move, you little bastard," I growled into the kid's ear, and I began to inch him backward across the floor to where Klein was tied.

"Come on!" I snarled in his ear as the door burst open. Avery came in with the other teenagers before I got to Klein.

"Larry!" Klein called desperately. "Watch it!"

I had no choice but to back up against a wall, holding Green Headband by the throat with the knife pressing against his neck, holding him hostage.

"Stay right there!" I yelled to all of them. "Don't move—or I'll cut his fucking head off!"

Avery stood still for a moment, stymied.

"Wait a second, boys!" He stopped the kids behind him, who were all keyed up and yelling. I couldn't understand half of what they were saying, their Island accents were so thick.

"Stay there!" I yelled to them, holding the knife tight as the blood soaked my grip. "Or I'll kill him!"

"OK! OK!" Avery/Mantell's hands flew up into the air. "That's enough!" He silenced his gang and was, what? Surrendering to me?

"OK," the old man said to me with a calm, sinister smile. "Kill him. Cut his fucking head off. Do it. You've got the knife."

Green Headband wiggled like crazy when he heard this, but I held him tightly, drawing still more blood.

The teenagers protested and cried for their friend, but Avery stood firm in front of them.

"Go on!" he ordered me. "Kill him! I don't give a fuck."

There wasn't a sound in the garage except the soft crying of the kid whose life I held on the edge of a knife blade.

"You see?" he said with this weird, joyful look on his face. "He won't kill him. He won't kill him because he's a fucking little faggot! Look—he's shaking! Ivy League Killer, my ass! He never had the guts to kill anyone himself. His *girl* did the killing for him. You weak piece of shit, you *deserved* to be stolen from."

"OK!" I hollered. "Who wants to catch his *head*?"

Green Headband struggled, forcing me to cut him deeper.

"Go on!" Avery shouted. "He won't do it. He's too fucking weak."

They started to come forward.

"Get him!" Avery/Mantell bellowed. "NOW!"

Taking different angles, all four of them moved in on me, with Avery behind, urging them on. Time slowed down, like in one of my prison fights, when Myles Pritchard and three other big guys—maybe the sweetest sight of my life—came busting in the door. *Wham slam, crash*: punches were thrown, nightsticks and gun butts came down onto skulls, and bodies went flying.

In a matter of seconds—*whack-whack-whack-whack*—all the teenagers were facedown on the garage floor.

"Stay right there!" Myles commanded. "Get down on the floor, now! You too! All of you!"

I let Green Headband fall to the floor, where he grabbed his throat, gurgling.

"Don't make a move!" Myles roared, pointing his gun at each teenager on the floor, one at a time. "Put your hands behind your head!"

Wiping my bloody hand on my shirt, I ran over to Klein with my knife and started to cut away his ropes.

"Myles!" Klein gasped. "I can't believe you're here."

"No problem, sir," he said, keeping his eyes directly on the teenagers. "Just glad that we could find you."

"Stop moving, Jonathan," I implored. "I don't want to cut you." Finally, I sliced through the ropes without cutting Klein or myself.

"Goddammit...to fucking...hell!" shouted Klein as we pulled the tangled rope off him. Klein grabbed me by the shirt and looked me in the eye.

"Where's Avery?"

Fuck!

We looked around, but the old man had slipped away in all the commotion.

"Where'd he go?" I asked, feeling like an idiot for not noticing his escape.

Klein turned to Myles and spat out an order: "Give me your gun!"

Before he could protest, Klein grabbed the gun out of Myles's hand. "You keep these punks here," Klein said.

"Please! Mr. Klein!" Myles tried to stop him, but Klein turned away, jammed the gun into his pants pocket, and grabbed me by the arm.

"Come on. Let's get him," Klein said.

Klein and I burst out into the night: it was dark, but the air was still daytime warm. I was a little stunned to be free and still buzzing from all the blood, the throbbing pain in my shoulder, and the adrenalin rush of my *am-I-about-to-die?* moment.

"Which way did the old fuck go?" he demanded, looking around frantically.

"He said something about a boat," I said.

"A boat?" Klein shouted. "Then it's *this* way!"

And he took off, running away from the house across a field at the edge of the trees.

"Come on!" he called to me, and I sprinted after him.

"Where are we going?"

"He said he had a boat!" Klein panted as we ran. "The only place that could have a boat around here is the canal!"

It was hard to see in the fading light. I stumbled over the uneven ground.

"What the fuck is this?"

"An old cricket pitch," he said. "Come on!"

I kept up with him, but I was fading and my bad knee was starting to throb. I thought I was in better shape, but I guess I spent all my strength, wrestling for my life in that garage with that kid *a quarter* my age.

"There he is!" Klein shouted. "That's him—in the white!"

We kept running, but I couldn't see what he was talking about. I did get a whiff of the ocean air. We were getting close to the water.

Just then, I tripped in some hole or something and fell. I tried to catch myself with my right hand, but I hit the dirt hard. I was stunned for a moment, and my shoulder felt like it was on fire, but I scrambled to my feet and took off after Klein.

"Jonathan!" I shouted into the darkness.

By the time I caught up to him, I saw that Klein had the gun out and was running along the top of a concrete wall above a long channel of water, maybe thirty feet wide, going a long way in both directions, beyond where I could see. There were big houses on the other side, some of them with boats tied up to docks.

"What is this?" I shouted to him.

"Seabreeze Canal!" he yelled back, with the gun still in his hand. "It's the only way to the ocean. If he has a boat, it has to be someplace around here."

Klein stopped and took a breath, leaning over, gasping for air. I caught up to him as he straightened up. He said fiercely, between breaths, "Bastard hit me...across the face...my old man... used to hit me like that."

Suddenly the loud gunning of a powerboat engine broke the night silence. We looked up the channel. From nowhere, the big white motorboat shot through the water, right past us. There, at the controls of the open boat, was Avery, standing there, his white hair blowing in the wind.

"That's him!" I yelled. "He's getting away!"

"No, he isn't!" Klein yelled back, raising the gun, tracking the moving boat.

"DON'T SHOOT HIM!" I shouted. For some reason, at that very moment, something inside me detonated: I didn't want him killed.

Klein stood stock-still, aiming carefully with both hands as if he were target-shooting. "I won't. I'm only going to shoot the motor."

I reached out to stop him, but I was too slow. He expertly fired off two rounds—*blam-blam!*

I saw the shots hit the outboard motor, making the boat swerve sharply. It careened into the canal's concrete wall, sending off a spray of sparks, then rebounded to the other side, churning white water behind it. Avery struggled to maintain control over the boat, but it lurched and scraped the opposite wall, trailing fire and flames in its wake in the dark.

Klein and I were running along the edge of the canal in pursuit when the boat finally crashed at a turn and burst into full fire. It was like a bomb going off. I could see Avery screaming as the flames engulfed him and the entire boat. Fire and fuel spread all over the surface of the water as the boat started to capsize, lighting up the whole canal.

Then I couldn't see Avery in the raging flames. Had he gone under?

I took a step to the edge of the channel, but Klein screamed, "Don't! Not for him." And he held me back as the boat slowly flipped over.

We looked down at the black water, covered with fire, and there, for a moment, next to the flaming hull, Avery resurfaced. Fire engulfed his face as he struggled with some netting that was pulling him down. He screamed one desperate "Help me!" but before I could move, he disappeared under the water.

Klein held onto me and wouldn't let me go. He grabbed my shirtfront and looked me straight in the eye. "Fuck him. He was a piece of garbage. We are more important."

Everything about Klein—his power, his money, his confidence, his heartlessness—came together in that moment. And I thought *I* was tough?

Before I could do anything else, Myles Pritchard was standing there with one of his guys.

"Mr. Klein," he said urgently. "Quickly. Please, sir. Where is my gun?"

Myles took charge. It seemed like only a matter of minutes, and Klein and I were in the backseat of a car being driven back at super-speed to Jamboree. And, of course, you can guess who was driving.

"Janet," Klein said with a gasp, "how in hell did you find us?"

"Larry's phone," she said. "We kept scanning and scanning. There was no signal, and then suddenly there it was. The GPS took us right to you. Myles wanted to follow you as soon as you left, but I said not to. I guess I was wrong—oh, I picked up your wallets."

She tossed them to us from the front seat, one at a time. My shoulder was still throbbing with pain, so I didn't reach out to catch them in the dark. But the second wallet fell into my lap; it was Klein's.

"Here," I said, holding it out to him, "this must be yours. It's heavier."

He took it with a grim smile. "Thanks."

I looked at Klein's face as we sped through the flickering light, from streetlights, stores, and oncoming headlights, and saw that he was bruised and shaken up. I was too, but I was accustomed to violence; I spent my whole life around it. Klein looked completely shattered.

"We'll get you home soon," said Janet confidently.

Home. I painfully recalled the past few hours—finding Avery in his office, chasing him back to his house, almost dying at the hands of those fucking children, that crazy run along the canal—and I was numb. And scared. What happened was beyond anything I could have feared...or that Betsy could have warned me about.

"Myles and I will take care of everything," Janet said firmly. "Don't worry."

But I did worry, big-time. Here I was, out of the country illegally, having to be back at Fusco's tomorrow or risk my parole—and now I'm an accomplice in *another* fucking murder that I didn't commit. It didn't seem possible.

Klein was slumped in the corner of the back seat, his hand partially covering his face. I wondered what he was thinking. I hoped he was thinking about how to get us out of this incredible fuckup. I was on *his* island, in *his* car, going to *his* house, under *his* protection. He'd better have a way out of this. *I* didn't shoot anyone. Sure, I got him involved with Avery and this whole thing, but I didn't pull any trigger. I would have to tread carefully, more carefully than ever around Klein, who I needed now more than ever, to get me back home. More than ever, I would have to watch out for my own interests, or else I might have to answer for that burning corpse in Seabreeze Canal.

We didn't talk for the rest of the ride. As soon as the three of us walked into Jamboree's cavernous front hall, Janet finally broke the silence.

"Mr. Klein," she said. "I'm going to tell Carlos to get the plane ready to take off in the morning. Unless you'd like to go right now."

She said *exactly* what I wanted to hear. Let's get off this fucking island right now, before anything worse happened. I released a sigh and started to say a big, relieved "Yes" when Klein spoke.

"No," he said simply. "I have to stay here."

"What?" Janet and I said simultaneously.

Klein looked very troubled. "I have to take care of this myself," he said.

"Please, sir, think about it," she pleaded. "You should fly out *tonight*. Right now."

"No," he said. "That wouldn't be right."

I couldn't believe what I was hearing: the last thing I expected from Klein was a conscience!

I started to speak up for myself, when Janet did it for me.

"Larry has to be back in New York tomorrow," she said strongly. "And I think you should go with him."

I tried to catch Klein's eye and said seriously, "You know I have to get out of here, Jonathan."

Klein pulled down at his lower lip and didn't respond.

His eyes couldn't meet mine, and I knew why. He was a murderer now, and everything he did from now on would be to protect himself. He was rattled. He touched his face and felt the red welt that Avery left on his cheek. I knew that Klein had all the cards, all the control, but I had to press my case.

"You said you'd get me back to New York on Thursday and not to sweat it, remember?" I said. "Well, Jonathan, I'm sweating now. I have to be back for my meeting with my *parole officer—* you understand? Or I'm screwed. Whatever the hell happened tonight, I have to be in New Rochelle at four o'clock tomorrow afternoon, or I risk everything. My freedom, everything I have."

He looked down and mumbled, "Let me just think about this."

"Don't think, sir!" Janet implored. "Go back to New York. Let Myles and me handle things down here."

"No." Klein shook his head. "That wouldn't be right."

"Right?" I echoed with a short laugh. "It's a little late for that tonight, man!"

I looked over at Janet for help. I didn't want to ask this nice young woman to help cover up her boss's crime, but that was the deal. Too much was at stake for Klein, for me, and for her.

"Let me call Carlos," Janet implored. "Please don't be...!" But she left her sentence unfinished. What was she going to say? *"Don't be responsible for your own actions."* That was the wrong way to go.

Klein stood there. I was pretty sure he was in shock. He was bruised and caked with dirt and sweat. His eyes were wide, but they didn't seem to be focusing on anything.

I stood there for a moment, with blood caked on my hands. Blood, if you don't know it, is sticky. I decided not to push Klein, at least for the moment.

"I'm gonna go wash up," I said wearily to Janet. "*You* talk to him."

I started to walk up the big staircase, careful not to touch anything, then turned back. "You might think about getting that car washed. Inside and out. And the BMW too. If you happen to know where it is."

Janet looked worried, and she had every right to be.

I started back up the stairs, one heavy step at a time, bone-tired physically, mentally, and emotionally, not knowing what the future held but knowing that I had certainly fucked up the present, when I heard footsteps behind me, running up the stairs.

I turned as Janet caught up to me and whispered in my ear, "Get your things packed, Larry, and be ready to go."

As sincerely as I could, I said, "Good luck, Janet."

She smiled at me gamely. I could tell she was on my side. With Klein in the shape he was in, she was my best hope of getting home.

I continued back up the stairs to my beautiful white bedroom with the private balcony overlooking the perfect ocean, went into the shower, and washed all the blood off my hands and body as best as I could. (Who knows what would show up if someone shined a black light on me.)

When I got out, I checked my clothes for blood. There was quite a lot on my shirt and some on my pants too. I thought about throwing them out, but maybe this wasn't the right place. I'd dispose of the bloody clothes somewhere else. For now, I folded them up carefully, making sure any bloody areas were turned inside out, and slid them in the outside pocket of Roland's valise.

It took me about five minutes tops to get dressed and get all my stuff together.

Then I sat on the edge of the bed, waiting for Janet to tell me that we were leaving. I looked out at the black nighttime ocean, wishing I could call Betsy. I wondered what she would say about all this now that I fucked up royally. Avery, Mantell, whatever his name was, was gone, and my money along with him. I was a thousand miles from home, not in control of my own destiny, with an appointment that I just *had* to keep in jeopardy, and, yes, involved in another murder that I didn't commit. Betsy wasn't an I-told-you-so kind of person, but the truth is, she did tell me so.

A knock at the door jolted me with hope. Was it Janet?

I ran over and ripped the door open. Big Myles Pritchard was standing there with a grim smile on his face. He looked like he'd just been through hell too.

"Hello, Myles," I said warmly. After all, he was the guy who just saved our asses a few hours ago. "What's up?"

He held out his open palm, and there was my phone, looking battered and dirty.

"Well, thank you, Mr. Pritchard!" I said, taking it from him. "Never thought I'd see this again."

"I'm not sure if it'll work," he said. "Boy threw it at me, and it hit me pretty hard. Right in the chest."

I couldn't resist asking: "What happened to the kid?"

"He'll live."

"And what about Avery?"

Myles's look hardened. "Do you *really* want to know, sir?"

"No," I corrected myself. "I *don't*." I was already in deep enough.

He turned to walk away, but I said one more "Thanks, Myles."

"No problem, sir," he replied. Then he walked away down the hall and down the stairs very fast.

I closed the door behind me and tried to turn on my phone, but it was dead. I wish I could have called Betsy right then, no matter what she would have said—screw the roaming charges—but thank goodness I had it with me. And thank goodness that stupid kid with the headband had turned it on.

I sat on the edge of the bed, using my stay-awake tactics from prison—state capitals and the order of the presidents—hoping someone would come knocking, telling me that we were going to the airport right then.

When that didn't happen, I walked out onto the balcony and listened to the *rush-pound-rush* of the waves and the high trees whispering in the breeze. I'd never been to a place this beautiful, *ever*. Even when I was a kid, my parents never had the money to take me someplace like this. This was a different kind of life from what ordinary Americans experience, and I was sure I'd never see anything like it again. This was a one-time-only deal, but I had blown it royally because right now, as beautiful as it was, it was the wrong place to be.

TWENTY-FOUR

I guess I had fallen asleep in my clothes, sitting up on the bed, when *knock-knock-knock* on the door jolted me awake..

"Larry?"

I rolled and fell off the bed, then walked to the door on unsteady legs. I had no idea what time it was as I swung the door open.

Janet was standing there, crisp and awake, dressed in the same business suit that I first saw her in.

"Let's go!"

I could have kissed her or hugged her or something. Instead I just smiled. "Let me get my things."

As I followed her down the stairs, I saw Klein talking with some servants as his driver stood by with all the luggage, ready to go.

"What did you do?" I whispered to Janet, walking slightly behind her.

She whispered back, "I talked sense to him."

I saw that Klein was looking up at us, so I just gave Janet a quick, hidden thumbs-up.

"Ready, Larry?" Klein called. He was back wearing his uniform: expensive sports jacket, white oxford shirt, schlumpy jeans, thousand-dollar shoes.

I could've said so many things. Instead I just said, "Yes, I am."

"Then let's go back to New York," said Klein grimly. It didn't look like he got much sleep that night either. And his cheek still had the red mark from Avery's backhand.

The ride to the airport wasn't long in minutes, but it felt like forever to my nerves. Dawn was rising, ridiculously beautiful with purple clouds building in the east. Still, I was crawling inside my skin: Klein and I were as "hot" as any two perps could be. We should have left last night.

The closer we got to the airport, the greater the sense grew in the pit of my stomach that somehow I wasn't going to get off that island. And my time window was tightening. It was only a three-hour flight to White Plains, and New Rochelle wasn't that far from the airport. If I went straight to Fusco's from the plane, I would have a little time to spare. Still, on several levels, I was as tense as I could be, thinking of what was ahead of me—and what was behind.

We drove right onto the tarmac, next to his plane. The SUV barely stopped moving when someone opened my door for me while other people started to get the luggage out, just like that.

Klein and Janet were ahead of me, walking up to the plane. Barbara the stewardess was already standing at the top of the steps with a silver tray bearing little glasses of orange juice. Talk about a sight for sore eyes.

At the foot of the stairs, there was a different beautiful handler, and a uniformed official with a clipboard.

Immigration! I just followed Klein and hoped for the best.

"Make sure you have everything," said Janet over her shoulder to me. "'Cause we're not coming back anytime soon."

That's when Klein stopped in his tracks. Stock-still. Janet and I stopped too.

"No," Klein said decisively. "I can't go."

My heart froze.

"No," he repeated firmly. "I have to stay." I could see his face was set in a mask of resolve. "If I go now, I won't ever come back."

He seemed sure of his decision, sudden as it was, but that wasn't good enough for me.

"Wait a second, Jonathan," I challenged him.

"You take the plane, Larry," he cut me off, "and go back to White Plains now, by yourself."

At first, I couldn't believe what he was saying.

"Sir," Janet put in, "I really wouldn't do that if I were—"

"No, Janet," Klein said. "I've got to stay here and fix this thing right now. If I run, it'll look worse. I'll stay here, and I'll make the problem disappear, once and for all."

It was obvious that Klein had made up his mind. All that was left was for Janet to sigh and say a resigned "OK, sir."

"But be sure to send it back, Larry," he said with a rakish smile. "Don't steal it."

I gripped his shoulder and looked in his eyes. "You know I'm not a thief, Jonathan; I'm a killer." I could easily have added, "Just like you"—but I didn't have to. He understood my message. We now had this bond: a blood bond.

He nodded and told me to get my ass moving. I complied.

⌐

Within five minutes, Klein got me through "immigration" and the plane was in the air. In ten minutes, Barbara was serving me Klein's special red energy drink made of pomegranate and guava juices mixed with two kinds of protein powder—the most refreshing drink I've ever tasted. Of course, I had no reason to feel good. I still had to get to Fusco's by four o'clock. And I was going home with absolutely nothing, just myself and no money. Plus I almost got myself killed *and* got involved with another murder. But at least I was going home alive, and it looked like I was going to make my appointment. No harm, no foul—except for that dead body. But Klein was going to take care of that little matter, right?

Energy drink or no, in twenty minutes I was dead asleep, dreaming that I was flying back to Betsy, soaring through clouds of fire, in slow motion, carrying an armful of bloody palm fronds, turning over gradually, in loop after loop.

Someone touched my shoulder gently.

Were we landing already?

"Mr. Ingber?" purred Barbara in my ear. "Just checking to make sure that your seat belt is on. We're coming into a little turbulence, but Carlos is going to try to fly over it."

Coming out of the mist of sleep, I managed to ask her, "So when are we getting into White Plains?"

"I'm not sure," she said. "We might have to land in Teterboro—"

"No Teterboro!" I shouted, waking straight up. "We *have* to land in White Plains!"

She was startled, and I was instantly sorry for giving her what sounded like an order. I mean, who the fuck was I?

"I'm sorry, Mr. Ingber," she said, "but there's some weather over Westchester, and things are stacking up."

Just then, the plane took a little dip. Barbara grabbed the back of my chair, and she and my stomach both said, "Whoa!"

"Stacking up?" I asked, swaying and holding on to my armrests. "For how long?"

"I'm really not sure," she said as the plane dipped again. "But we're going to lose a little time, I know that. I'll tell Carlos you'd like to land in White Plains, but I can't guarantee anything. Some things we don't have control over."

Raindrops started to splatter against the little oval windows. Barbara excused herself, went back to her seat, and buckled herself in. After that, I just closed my eyes, hung on to the armrests, and felt the plane moving erratically in the sky. More things out of my control! We could be up in this stomach-turning air, flying around for hours, then landing in fucking New Jersey. Then I would miss Fusco, which would mean hell to pay. He'd definitely slam my ass into a revocation hearing, fast.

And what was I going to do when we landed? I didn't have any passport, just my New York State driver's license. More to the point, I didn't have Jonathan Klein to walk me through the airport and make all obstacles vanish.

I checked my wallet: I had only seventeen dollars left. I wish I had those three twenty-dollar bills that Betsy gave me. Of course, it was that big, nasty *paper clip* that proved to be priceless.

The plane took another dip, and I almost lost my pomegranate juice. So I closed my eyes again, hoping for the best, and hung on. There was nothing I could do; I was in suspended animation, powerless in my own life, from another bad decision I had made.

Over the intercom, Carlos's voice said, "Excuse me, Mr. Ingber?"

I sat straight up, tense and fearful.

"Looks like we're going to be on the ground in about fifteen minutes," he announced proudly. But where were we landing? I closed my eyes and hoped.

"We'll be touching down in"—my breathing stopped—"White Plains. Only about twenty minutes behind schedule. Sorry for the rough ride, Mr. Ingber."

I exhaled. I could have told him that I was used to it.

I checked the New York time on the wall clock and—*yes*! I still had time to make my Fusco appointment, provided I could get past immigration and customs. If I got that far, I would figure out a way to get to New Rochelle. My phone was dead, so I couldn't call a cab. Maybe I could get Barbara to call me one. But the seventeen dollars I had left probably wasn't enough to get me to New Rochelle. And it certainly wasn't enough to get me from New Rochelle back to City Island. I definitely didn't want to call Betsy to pick me up. Maybe I would have to crawl back to City Island on my hands and knees.

We started to descend. For a moment, the rain let up, the gray clouds outside my window broke, and I could see everything: lakes and hills and big houses, spread out over the rolling green landscape of northern Westchester like pieces on a Monopoly board. Briefly, it was beautiful. Then we went back into gray clouds and spattering rain, and the plane began to buck and tip.

"Hang on, please," said Carlos over the intercom.

"Whoa!" I said, gripping the armrests tighter. We dropped through the thick gloom, and I got this sudden picture in my mind of Fusco waiting for me on the tarmac with a couple of bullnecked cops ready to throw me into the back of a black-and-white, take me to some lockup, beat the shit out of me, and send me back to prison.

I shut my eyes and told myself to take some deep breaths and count backward from one hundred (as I had done a million times before, in so many horrifying situations that they can never be counted). I was halfway to fifty when I felt the wheels scrape down on the ground. Westchester! I was home...almost.

The noise of the engines caught up with us as we rolled down the runway, going from very fast to slow. I looked out of the windows as best I could but I saw nothing. No Fusco, no gang of cops. Just rain.

"Are you OK, Mr. Ingber?" Barbara said, standing next to me, looking concerned. "I'll have your luggage up at the front."

Shit! *My luggage*! It still had those bloody clothes tucked into the side pocket!

"I'm fine," I said. "I mean, yes—I'm just glad to be back."

Why didn't I throw them away at the airport in Nassau? I know why I didn't: because I was afraid of being seen. But I still had them on my person. What should I do? Leave them on the plane? But that would provide a definite link from Klein to the clusterfuck in that garage in Nassau. Could I do that to him? We were coming to a stop—I saw the tarmac rolling by, slower and slower—and I had to make a decision about the bloody clothes.

"Please stay seated, Mr. Ingber!" Barbara called out.

And I did. I decided to keep my bloody clothes with me and risk the consequences. I couldn't add to Jonathan Klein's problems. After all, he lent me his G5.

When the plane had finally stopped, the door opened, and the glare from outside rushed in. The moment was here: all I had with me was the ID in my wallet. Would that be enough to get me through? There was nothing for me to do but get up and walk out and see what was going to happen. Ex-con or no ex-con, I was still an American citizen, and they had to let me into my own country—even if it was just to arrest me.

I picked up my knapsack and walked to the front of the plane where Barbara waited for me, a warm smile on her face, directing me down and into the afternoon light.

"Goodbye, Mr. Ingber," she purred. "Sorry for the bumps."

"Me too," I replied uncertainly.

"Everything's ready for you," she said as I turned to walk down the steps and into the unknown. But instead of Fusco or immigration cops or regular cops, it was—can you believe it?— Brian Halliwell. Mr. Pinstripe himself, stood there on the tarmac, absolutely stone-faced, under a big umbrella as if he was there to meet Klein. Instead he was there for me.

"Ah, Mr. Ingber!" Brian called to me. "I knew you were in there somewhere."

Standing next to Brian was, yes, another tall, blond handler with an iPad (no ponytail), helping Brian help me.

Stunned and grateful, I walked into the rain and floated down the steps.

"Mr. Klein told me to take good care of you and that I was to take you wherever you want to go."

"He said *that*?"

"But," he said, "let's process you first."

Someone had even put Roland's valise on the luggage trolley for me.

⁀

Some things were done—that's all I'll say—and in five minutes I was in the back seat of a limousine with Brian, drinking from a little bottle of ice-cold water and speeding to Fusco's office in New Rochelle. Somehow no one looked inside Roland's valise and found the bloody clothes. I still have no idea how that happened.

I checked the clock on the limo's instrument panel. If we didn't hit traffic on the Hutch, I would be OK, but it would be close. The whole ride there, I devoured myself from the inside out with nerves, thinking about what I left behind me in the Bahamas and what I didn't leave behind. Nonetheless, I wished that Fusco had been waiting outside to see me pull up to the front of his dumpy office in that big black limousine, a good seven minutes before my appointment time. Can you believe it? The Hutch was easy, and I got there early.

Before I could make a move to get out, Brian put out his hand and touched my arm.

"You can leave everything here," he said. "We'll wait for you. Mr. Klein said to take care of you and make sure that you got home safe and sound."

"Mr. Klein said that?" I asked. "Safe and sound?"

Brian replied with utmost dryness, "Words to that effect."

"In that case, Brian," I said, thinking of one last embarrassing thing that I had somehow forgotten in all the madness, "you think you can lend me thirty bucks? I left all my cash in the Bahamas. I promise I'll pay you back."

Along with everything else, I was late paying my supervision fee to Fusco.

Brian smirked, dug into his pocket, pulled out a gold money clip, extracted a twenty and a ten, and handed them to me with his perfectly manicured fingers.

"I will pay you back, man," I said.

"Don't worry about it," he sniffed.

By then, the driver had run around to my side of the car and opened the door for me. "I really owe you, Brian," I said sincerely, "in more ways than one."

"No problem," he said with a pure note of disdain. "Whatsoever."

I got out of the limo and went toward Fusco's building, five minutes early. I didn't even have to close my own door.

I ran up the steps two at a time into the building and went through security, grateful that I didn't have to carry my suitcase of bloody evidence in and out of there. I was at Fusco's office and in the door, two minutes early. Funny thing was that *he* was running behind schedule and kept me waiting for a long time in his dingy outer office with two other guys, two other "cases," my peers. One huge black guy in a hoodie who seemed to be stoned on something and a little Latino guy with a goatee who looked like he spent his entire life in some weight room. No one said anything, but both of them stared at me with this look that said, "What is this old white guy doing here?" All I would have said to them is "You don't want to know."

I sat there wondering whether Brian would still be waiting there with the limo when I got out, whenever that was. I decided to try to be like Jonathan Klein and assume it would be there. And whatever happened, happened.

When Fusco finally called me in, I walked straight to the chair in front of his desk, sat down, and slapped the thirty dollars I owed him on the desktop.

Fusco didn't look at the money or at me. He just stared at his computer screen for a minute, making me wait a little more, just to make me suffer a little extra. But I recognized his game and wouldn't play.

Finally, he broke the silence.

"You like to live dangerously, don't you, Ingber?" he said scornfully.

"I don't know what you mean," I said as neutrally as I could. Did he know about my trip to the Bahamas? Could he possibly know what happened down there? I said nothing and waited for him to make his move. If I've learned one thing in this life, it's that sometimes the best thing you can say is nothing.

Fusco turned to me. "Sammy Zambrano says you're shit-hip deep in his new scam."

Cool as anything, I replied, "Sammy Zambrano is a born liar, and you know it."

"He has your number on his phone with *multiple* calls to you," he charged.

"So does Verizon Wireless," I said. "That doesn't mean anything. Zambrano is just giving you my name 'cause he knows you hate me and you want to revoke me, so maybe he can cut a deal with you if he flips on me. But there's no proof of anything I did with Zambrano because I didn't *do* anything with Zambrano. Zilch."

I was a little cocky because what I said was true. And I felt great that it was this Zambrano stuff that Fusco was talking about, not the disaster in the Bahamas.

Fusco smirked with disappointment. I think he knew that I was telling the truth about Zambrano, and it irked him.

"I don't hate you, Ingber," he lied.

"I don't hate you either, Officer Fusco," I said, returning the favor.

"It's just that no matter how many times I see you," he said, facing me, "I think of all the advantages you had and how you wasted them. A white guy! You had no business doing what you did. Even today, after all these years, the sheer waste of human life disgusts me."

"Yeah," I shot back, "me too. Now if you give me my receipt, I'll get the hell out of here. The last thing I need from you is a sermon, not when I'm so close to being finished with all this—" There are no words dark enough to describe the System.

He printed out my receipt, but as he gave it to me, he held it for a moment and said suspiciously, "Wait a minute: why do you have a *suntan*, Ingber?"

"It's not a suntan," I said, concealing my sudden panic, "it's the high blood pressure I get from you. Thank you, Officer Fusco." And I took the receipt.

"You're not welcome, convict."

I ran downstairs through the empty stairwell; I had no patience to wait for the elevator. And, sure enough, when I got to the ground floor, I could see through the plate glass that Brian and the limousine were still at the curb, just where I had left them, just as he had promised.

"Thanks for waiting, Brian," I said once inside the warmth of the limo.

"I'm sorry that took so long."

Brian ignored my apology, looking up from his phone. "Where to now?"

It was just a shot to City Island. Brian stayed involved with his phone. I really didn't want to make small talk with him. I could have asked him, "Did your boss tell you about his latest killing...in the market?" Instead I was just grateful for the ride as I sat there in silence, thinking about how I risked so much and still came home empty-handed. No legacy, no nothing: just another Very Bad Incident to haunt my days and jeopardize my future.

⌒

When we got to the store, it was after closing hours. Usually, there was still some light on in the back by Roland's apartment. Instead, the store was all dark and no lights in the apartment. I had Brian drive me around the back so I could go up the outside stairs. But when we got there, the Jeep was gone. *Was it in the repair shop? Had Betsy gone somewhere?* I didn't think it was her book club night.

"Thanks, Brian," I said. "And thank you," I said to the driver, but he was already out of the limo.

"And thank Mr. Klein," I said. "This was a big one."

Brian purred, "I imagine it was."

But somehow I don't think he knew what had really happened. I bet our adventure in the Bahamas might have put a few wrinkles in his pinstripes.

I got out and took Roland's valise from the driver with a smile. "Thanks, man."

"My pleasure, sir," he said, nodding a little, and turned to go back to the limo.

And thank you for not looking inside.

I ran up the outside stairs and let myself into the apartment.

"Betsy!" I called out, but there was silence and darkness; no one was home.

I put my things down in the kitchen and went back downstairs through the store to ask Roland if he knew where she was. But when I knocked on Roland's door and called his name, he didn't answer. I knocked again. *Could he and Betsy be out someplace, maybe at Gassim's?* I could have walked down there, but I decided to call her first.

I ran back upstairs. I'd call Betsy from the phone in the kitchen—my cell died a hero's death in the Bahamas. I had a lot to tell her, and a lot to conceal. But at least I was home in one piece.

I started to dial her number when I heard the door open. Betsy came in, unaware that I was back. I waited until she closed the door behind her.

"Hello, Betsy," I said.

"Ohmygod!" she cried out.

"I'm back," I said simply. I honestly didn't know how she would react to seeing me.

"Where have you been?" she asked plaintively. "I've been calling and calling!"

"My phone broke, and—"

"Roland had a stroke," she said, taking off her coat and putting down her purse. "He's been at Bronx-Lebanon since Tuesday night. I'm trying to get him transferred to Albert Einstein, but the system's just impossible to deal with."

It took me a moment to comprehend what she was saying.

"Roland?" At first, I could just say his name. "Is it really bad?"

The way she looked at me said everything.

I walked over to her and took her in my arms.

Shuddering, she said, "Where have you been?" and burst into tears. "Oh, I wish you had been here. I needed you."

I let her cry and cry, saving my story for later.

The next days were spent in and out of the hospital. Betsy was on the phone a lot, talking to doctors, talking to nurses, talking to Bob Jensen. There was no one else to do it.

I never saw Roland again. I mean, I never saw the real Roland again, talking and joking and giving me his opinion on things. I saw his body lying in a hospital bed, but Roland wasn't there anymore. The doctors didn't know how much longer his body would stay alive. I'd never seen Betsy sadder.

"What can you say?" she said, sighing, sitting in the hospital cafeteria, drinking the worst coffee in the world. "Everybody dies sometime, but still, it was kinda sudden."

Everything that happened in the Bahamas seemed like a distant nightmare, but eventually I had to tell her something. How much I would tell her, I was still not certain.

We were driving back from the hospital when Betsy finally brought up the topic that hung over our heads.

"So are you ever going to tell me what happened in the Bahamas with your friend Jonathan Klein?" she asked delicately.

"There's nothing to say," I said with such nonchalance that I'm sure I sounded unconvincing.

"What do you mean 'nothing to say'?" she countered. "Did you find Lester Mantell?"

"Yes."

"And did you get your money back?"

"No."

I didn't elaborate, which said more than words could.

Betsy drove on a bit and finally asked, "So it was that bad?"

"You don't want to know," I told her truthfully.

"That bad," she concluded—correctly.

I didn't want to tell Betsy exactly what happened in the Bahamas. If she didn't know anything specific, she couldn't be called as a witness in any trial. What she didn't know couldn't hurt her, or me. Did I lie by omission to Betsy? Yes, I did. But it was for her own good and, to be honest, to conceal actions that would diminish me in her eyes.

She sighed sadly. "I wish you had been here."

All I could say was "Me too."

⌒

When we got home, we trudged up the stairs in silence. When we got inside, I asked her, "Can I run you a hot bath?"

She smiled. "Thanks, you're sweet."

I could tell she was disappointed in me. Even if she didn't say anything more, I saw it in her eyes. There was no denying it; I had let her down. My big roll of the dice came up craps, *and* I wasn't here when she really needed me.

As I went to the bathroom to start filling the tub for Betsy, I thought about Klein and how fucked up things got, and how lucky I was to be back home, still alive. And I thought about poor Roland, the store, and what could happen.

I adjusted the temperature of the water until it was perfect. As the tub start to fill, I contemplated my sorry finances, wondering exactly when to tell Betsy that I needed a new phone. I couldn't even tell her why. My brilliant trip to the Bahamas was supposed to solve all our problems.

Wrong again. Dead wrong.

I reminded myself to throw Roland's suitcase into the dumpster in the back when Betsy wasn't looking. Or, better yet, when I was running an errand, chuck the whole thing off a bridge into the ocean. Mustn't keep incriminating evidence around. The memories were more than enough, and they were here to stay.

TWENTY-FIVE

We had no idea how long Roland would hang on. Recovery, we were told, was out of the question; the stroke had caused too much damage. His brain was essentially dead. The doctor, this young Indian guy, told us to prepare for the worst. I thought that "the worst" was hanging on, hooked up to tubes, in a vegetative state, in a depressing hospital room, but apparently there was something worse than that. I couldn't imagine what. Even in my long stretches in the hole, as close to death as life gets, despite it all, my brain was still alive and working.

The doctor told us to go home, and a nurse would call us if anything changed.

There was nothing to do but wait...and start planning for the inevitable.

Nurse Debbie came by on her regular day. She was sad but oddly detached about Roland. I guess you have to be when all you do is take care of sick, old people. There are no happy endings. She sat there and told us how Roland was one of her favorite patients, how strong he was, how much she liked to argue with him. We had a laugh about Roland's famous quirks, as if he were already gone.

Then she did the strangest thing. She said that Roland was a few weeks behind in the co-payment he was supposed to give her and could she have the money that she was due because she would have a harder time collecting it once he was dead.

Betsy had no choice but to write her a check from the store's account. She should have said no, but I think she was so shocked at Debbie's cold-blooded request that she just wanted to be done with her.

389

"Gee," Betsy said to me, closing the door behind Debbie when she walked out of the store, "you think you know a person."

But I know as well as anybody that when it comes to money, people can become strange, unpredictable creatures.

⌒

Between vigils at Roland's bedside and the hours I had to keep the store open to sell something, anything, I kept looking on the web at the few Bahamas news sites—*The Nassau Guardian, the Bahamas Press*, and something called *BahamasB2B*—for anything about what happened that night in Seabreeze Canal. But there was absolutely nothing—nothing about Avery, nothing about any murder or disturbance that night or even about the fire. Maybe Klein did have the power to hush things up.

Betsy and I spent hours in Bob Jensen's office going over Roland's finances. Jensen was also his lawyer—wouldn't you know it? Roland left everything to Betsy. That wasn't surprising; Roland often said that he had no family. But the situation wasn't pretty: Roland was in more debt than we knew.

"Three antique stores in City Island have closed in the last five years," Jensen said. "But you know that."

Betsy started to name them, counting on her fingers: "The Sea Chest...Teddy's Navy Barn. Teddy was there even longer than Roland—"

Jensen interrupted, "It's just a fact of the economy. It's amazing the old guy's kept it going all these years. Y'know, Ed Dempsey offered him four hundred grand for his entire inventory three years ago. He should have taken it."

"But Roland loves the store," Betsy said. "Despite how he might grumbles sometimes, it's his home."

"Doesn't matter," Jensen said, looking again at the computer screen and clicking his cursor up and down. "Your finances change? *You* have to change."

Then he turned to Betsy and added, "Of course, if Roland had charged you more rent all these years for your apartment, he might be in better shape now, but that's neither here nor there."

I could see what he said hurt Betsy. Betsy, who did nothing but care for Roland.

We talked a little more about different options and taxes, but I could tell Betsy's heart wasn't in it. We were finished with Bob Jensen, for that day.

As soon as we left his office, she had to choke back her tears.

"He's not even gone." she said with a sigh, "and all we can talk about is money."

⌒

It was a mixed blessing when Roland died three days later. The initial shock of the stroke, that a man as tough and vital as Roland could be cut down and silenced so completely and at once, had given way to the realization—and Betsy's acceptance—that he was never coming back mentally, and the physical part of him nothing but an afterthought.

When word got out that he had died, the parade of people from the neighborhood who came by the store to pay their respects (and tell stories about him) was steady. All kinds of people too. Mostly old, but some young. All races too. A lot of old black guys, old Asian guys, old Italian and Irish guys, and quite a few women came by to say how much they liked Roland.

Liked? Funny that a guy as salty and opinionated and extreme as Roland, who told the world exactly what he thought of it and all its inhabitants, should wind up being liked by so many different, ordinary people. But it was because he was *real* in a world sinking in bullshit. He left a lot of good memories behind him. I'm just sorry I didn't get the chance to sit around and shoot the breeze with him for a hundred more hours, sharing his beloved Jimmy and listening to him talk the night away.

We had the wake at Gassim's—Gassim insisted—with Roland's ashes on display in a beautiful brass navigation lantern, the finest we had in the store. We made a shrine for the ashes behind the bar, lit with candles and surrounded by flowers, saintly medallions, shells, and many empty bottles of Jim Beam (everybody seemed to know what Roland's favorite poison was). According to Betsy, since Roland was part Irish, it was declared an Irish wake, which meant there was a lot of laughter and drinking and stories about Roland. A few guys from the Cornerstone, a bar in Woodlawn that Roland liked, brought some musical instruments—a guitar, a fiddle, an accordion, a little tin whistle—and played some Irish music: sad, lilting, soulful music that seemed to fit the occasion to a T. They sang "Danny Boy," and it made Betsy and a lot of other people cry. I didn't keep count, but way more than two hundred people came to pay their respects to Roland. How many people will mourn when I die?

At the end of the wake, after Gassim's closed in the late night/early morning, the hardcore few of us joined together at the end of the parking lot at the water's edge at the very tip of City Island to dispose of Roland's ashes. It was eerily beautiful, with the lights on the Throgs Neck Bridge and Manhattan in the distance sparkling like the Emerald City.

Different people spoke. I can't remember everything that was said, but I remember someone said, "Roland had a great, big laugh. He loved to laugh, and you know what made him laugh the most? Stupidity." Someone else said, "He saw things clearly, the way only a madman can."

Betsy said how much she loved Roland, "even his moods," which got a laugh of recognition. "He wasn't perfect," she continued, "and he wouldn't like me to say this, but he was one of the nicest, most kindhearted men I've ever known."

Someone recited the Lord's Prayer, which almost everybody joined in saying.

"Larry?" Betsy addressed me. "Do you want to say anything?"

For a moment, I was lost in my memories of Roland and his glorious anger. As I moved to the front of the group and held the brass lantern full of Roland's ashes, I gathered my wits and knew exactly what to say:

> Do not go gentle into that good night,
> Old age should burn and rave at close of day;
> Rage, rage against the dying of the light.

I remembered a lot of the poem, but not all of it. As I was saying it, I was flashing back to Derek's full recitation of it—every word!—at my parents' grave on Long Island in that incredibly depressing, flat, brown cemetery. I might have made up some words—sorry, Mr. Thomas—but I got to the end somehow.

> And you, my father, there on the sad height,
> Curse, bless, me now with your fierce tears, I pray.
> Do not go gentle into that good night.
> Rage, rage against the dying of the light.

When I finished, I heard a few people sniffing away tears.

Everybody—at least everyone who wanted to—dumped a big, heaping spoonful of Roland's ashes from the lantern into this very obscure finger of the Atlantic Ocean. But at least it was Roland's beloved Atlantic.

Betsy and I poured out the last of the ashes and watched them float away with the last of the rose petals from the shrine at the bar. Then I closed the top of the lantern and helped Betsy climb up from the water's edge. There was nothing else to do but go home, get into bed, and count our blessings.

But of course I couldn't sleep. Even scooped up next to Betsy, I couldn't stop thinking about Roland and his long, good, sad life...and the future of the store...and what happened in the Bahamas...and the sight of Mantell burning up in black water...and Fusco on my trail...and failing Betsy...and failing myself.

The Mantell money, my money, was gone, for good. Everything that I had been hoping for, for so long, was lost.

I was lucky to be alive, which is more than I can say for Lester Mantell. Or Roland, for that matter. Lucky to be alive and out of prison. I was crazy to risk my freedom for money. What was I thinking? That it was more than just money?

I moved even closer to Betsy, hoping to absorb some of her goodness. She tried to tell me not to go. I should have listened to her.

It's still not too late for me to straighten out, right?

⁀

In the days after Roland's death, people came into the store to reminisce about the Great Man and wish us well, but they didn't buy anything. They looked around and said nice things about Roland and his stuff, but few wallets were opened.

Worse: word came in the following weeks from Bob Jensen about the status of Roland's estate. After all the taxes were figured out and what Roland owed on top of that, it didn't seem like there was any way to keep the store going.

"He was going under, and he knew it," said Jensen. "Retail is dying all over. He should have taken the offer from King's Cargo, three, four years ago. Ed Dempsey gave him a fair price for his inventory."

"You think he'd be interested now?" I asked.

"OK," said Betsy, "but then what would we sell in the store?"

I turned to her and said gravely told her the truth: "We're not selling much of anything now."

We did a "30% OFF—Life Goes On SALE" the following weekend. I figured Roland would appreciate the sentiment. Betsy made a banner for the front of the store with some art supplies from Thomas Paine, and I pushed the sale on every internet site I could find: Craigslist, the store's Facebook page, everywhere. And it got us some action, but Betsy and I both saw the writing on the wall.

Two weeks later, she went over to see Ed Dempsey at King's Cargo Antiques, to feel him out about a possible sale.

"What can I say? He has a very nice store," Betsy said when she got back. "And it's not just nautical. He has furniture and paintings and some very nice smalls. *And* he runs a decorating business."

"Good for him," I said.

"But he's gotten a big head ever since he was on that show," Betsy said.

"What show?"

She stopped setting the dinner table for us. "I thought I told you. He was on *Antiques Roadshow*," she explained. "He was one of their experts."

"Oh." I shrugged. "Good for him."

⌒

We tidied up the store before Dempsey was supposed to come over. I was just hoping there'd be some customers when he walked in. And when he swaggered in—an hour after he said he'd be there—a couple of French tourists were browsing. But we sucked it up and were nice to him.

"Ed! Good to see you!" Betsy greeted him like a long-lost relative and offered him tea and cookies. The porky, plaid-vested slob accepted, of course. (He wound up eating seven of Betsy's cookies before he left. Not that I counted.)

Meanwhile, I walked over to the French couple and made some nice small talk with them, hoping they would buy something, anything.

"Roland always had some of the most wonderful scrimshaw," Dempsey pontificated as he strolled around the store, looking everything over semi-disdainfully.

"Yes, he did," Betsy said. "It was his pride and joy."

"My father always coveted that powder horn with the Battle of Lake Champlain," Dempsey said, peering into one of the glass cases with some of Roland's best scrimshaw and rarest brass instruments. Dempsey was a third-generation antiques dealer. That's one of the reasons he knew so much: he was born into it.

Meanwhile I used what was left of my high-school-and-one-year-of-college French to try to charm the tourists. I practically sang "La Vie en Rose" on my knees, but they walked away with a City Island brass key ring, just about the cheapest thing in the store.

The next day, Dempsey called with an insulting offer of two hundred and seventy-five thousand dollars for the entire inventory—lock, stock, and scrimshaw. It was barely enough to cover the first mortgage.

After postponing the task several times, Betsy and I went through Roland's "effects," his stuff. It was mostly old clothes and shoes. No hidden treasure in the back of his closet, no pirate treasure. We didn't find the letter from Nelson Mandela that Roland showed to Betsy once. If we had found that, we could have sold it for some decent money—at least a couple of hundred dollars; I checked on eBay. Of course, Betsy would probably have wanted to keep it had we found it. She did keep his walking stick, one of his hats, and some photographs of young, happy, healthy Roland. I kept the tie that he lent me for the dinner at Le Bernardin. Everything else we gave to a local thrift shop.

⌒

Against Betsy's wishes, I went back to working every night in the kitchen at Charlie Wagner's

"You don't have to do that," she pleaded. "It's too hard for you."

"No, it isn't," I half-lied.

The work was hard, but I couldn't get anything else. I had looked for a job to add to what we made from the store. Of course, when you check off that "Have you ever been convicted of a felony?" box on any job application, the chances of landing said job go down to just about zero.

I scoured the classifieds of *The Island Current*, the local newspaper; The PennySaver; on bulletin boards; on Craigslist; and anything I could find on the internet for "Bronx handyman." Only I wasn't really a handyman. I could do things around a house, but I didn't have real tools or real experience—or real skills, for that matter. I spent my whole fucking life in jail! That's what I knew how to do: survive.

Even basic heavy labor jobs I couldn't do as well as younger guys, stronger guys; the groups of Mexicans and Dominicans— whoever I'd see hanging out around the Home Depot on Gun Hill Road. All those guys were probably better workers than sixty-plus me. And probably cheaper too.

Still, there had to be a way forward.

"Could you please stop that for a minute?"

Betsy's voice jolted me out of my trance. I had been looking through Monster.com and LinkedIn, worlds that were foreign to me.

"You can't just keep looking at that stuff all the time," she said, standing in her bathrobe by the doorway.

"Just a little while longer," I said.

She took a step into the kitchen and raised her voice. "You don't think I'm worried about things, the way you are? You don't think I have the same concerns that you do? I just don't let it control me every minute of every day. At least, I try not to."

"Come on, honey," I said, reaching for her affectionately. "You're always so cool and composed about how you deal with—"

"Please!" she cut me off. "I am not always cool and composed! Please stop saying that. You put too much pressure on me sometimes, when you keep seeing me that way. You can be so—I don't know—*obsessive*. You have to let me breathe sometimes."

She took a step back and crossed her arms in front of her. I didn't know what to say because...because she was right, I guess.

In a softer tone, she continued, "Look, you can stay up and do whatever you want—"

"No, I —" I tried to make peace with her.

"Or come to bed," she said. "Or go out for a walk."

"You know," I said, standing up, "that's a good idea."

"What?"

"Go out for a walk," I said. "Stop looking at this damn computer and put some oxygen into my lungs."

"OK, take your time," she said in a sad, distant voice, walking back to the bedroom. "But don't be too long."

I could tell she felt bad about yelling at me, but I didn't really mind since what she said was the truth.

⌒

She was right about taking a walk. It was good to breathe the fresh, salty air and try to change things in my head and maybe find a Moment of Grace and Thanks. Just being free to walk wherever I wanted: at one time not so long ago, this was an unthinkable dream come true for me. Now I can walk wherever I wanted, but unfortunately, I had no place to go.

So I walked for the sake of walking, just like I walked all through Manhattan during my one Year of Hell at Columbia. I walked to the far north end of City Island Avenue until I found myself in front of a bar, a dark, little neighborhood dive, one that I had passed by a million times but had never gone into. I guess that was freedom too: the right to walk into any bar I wanted, anywhere in the U. S. of A. I thought being around people might help me feel normal.

Some things don't change, even in forty-plus years. The stale beer smell of bars is one of them. And even if you couldn't smoke inside anymore—there were a couple of puffers near the front door—the patrons themselves smelled like smoke. They stank of cigars and pipes and the cigarette stench in their clothes.

When I walked in, I got the expected evil eye once-over from the patrons. This place was as segregated as a prison. Maybe more so. These were all mostly fat white guys, and they were all watching a bunch of mostly fat black guys play football on the TV over the bar.

I walked slowly to the far end of the bar, checking out the patrons as they checked me out. Even the young guys looked old with their beer bellies, their scowls, and their grizzly beards. It could have been a bar in Anywhere, USA, except for the numerous Yankee caps: this *was* still the Bronx. The bar that was near that summer camp—Bailey's—at least had a jukebox, but I didn't see one around here. What's a bar without a jukebox? This was strictly sports and shots.

I got to the second to last stool and sat. I didn't look at anybody in particular, but I saw everything in the mirror over the bar and over my shoulder. One thing I learned in prison is how to size up the danger factor in a room in about two seconds.

The bartender—bearded and plaid like a lumberjack—made me wait a while. Or gave me time to get settled and make my choice. Depends on how you look at it.

I hadn't been in a bar like this in a long time. A beer in a bar cost more. Sorry, but I had to think of every penny I was spending. It was my constant habit now. I knew exactly how much cash I had in my wallet, how much we had in the bank. Funny, I never had to worry about money when I was in prison.

I thought about what Betsy had said, about how obsessive I was and the pressure I put on her. Did I depend on her too much, just as I did on The Girl so many years ago? Was I making the same mistakes all over again? Hadn't I learned anything in forty years? Was I still the same idiot, unable to make my life work?

Finally, Paul Bunyan came up to me, pulling me back from my twisted thoughts, and asked me what my pleasure was tonight. *Pleasure* seemed like a funny word to me.

I really hadn't thought of anything and was about to ask what they had on draught when I remembered the beer that Derek ordered at the place we got steamers in Freeport.

"OK, how about..." I ventured, "a Stella Artott?"

Laughter burst out around me. I heard some derisive muttering, no actual words. But I could tell, especially when I looked at Paul Bunyan's gnarled smile, that I had said something wrong. I had fucked up the name of the beer.

"Sorry, bud," he snickered. "Just what's listed on the board." He jerked his thumb over his shoulder, showing me the blackboard that listed all the beers.

"OK," I mumbled. "Whatever you have on draught."

He turned away with a smile and a sneer for the benefit of everyone who was watching us. I could see in the mirror behind the bar—and I could *feel*—people looking at me: the new guy, the old schmuck who couldn't pronounce the name of his beer. OK, they were right.

So I sat there alone, embarrassed. Alone is what I was used to being. That didn't bother me. But I could feel the resentment vibrating all around me. I glanced down the bar and noticed sidelong looks coming my way that were decidedly unfriendly.

One guy tried to catch my eye, tried to stare me down. By then I had done a million stare-downs in a thousand prison yards, and no one intimidated me. Certainly not this pig-eyed, punk-ass drunk in his Yankees cap. Like he was Derek Jeter.

But I turned away from him and back to my beer; I didn't engage. I didn't need any more trouble.

But why the knee-jerk hostility toward me? Why was everyone suddenly everyone else's enemy? I was used to it in prison, but why out here? Why is everyone so angry all the time? Roland's words echoed in my mind: the Bad America won. We used to have such hope and optimism in this country. Now everybody in America hates somebody else, and hate makes people stupid. All sense of the common good is gone because your enemy might get something out of it. Everybody just tries to save themselves, and the whole thing has gone to hell.

I kept going over our financial situation and I couldn't help it: maybe it was years of living with criminals, but the thought of arson crossed my mind. Just burn the store down and collect something on the insurance policy, enough to start another place. I knew a couple of arsonists when I was inside. They were actually pretty smart guys, good prison businessmen.

Then I felt ashamed the thought had even occurred to me. It was my Prison Mind that I hoped would never reappear, and here it was. It only took a moment to shake the notion out of my head. I couldn't burn down the store, not only because of Betsy, not only because of all Roland's precious stuff. I couldn't do it because I wasn't a criminal anymore. I never really was one. I just had to pretend to be one in order to survive.

The thought of Sammy Zambrano's promised thousands involuntarily crossed my mind, but the image of Fusco, still on my case, stomped that idea right back where it belonged. I had enough to think about with what happened in the Bahamas and Jonathan Klein.

I finished my beer and, despite the animosity in the room, left Paul Bunyan a decent tip. Then I walked out, looking at no one, and tried to leave all those feelings behind me.

I made the long walk home, got into my pajamas as silently as I could and into bed with sleeping Betsy. I was cold and I spooned up against her warm, small body.

"Is that you?" she mumbled. "I'm sorry about before."

I shushed her and whispered, "It's OK. Go back to sleep."

Then I moved even closer to her and lay there in the dark, fitfully following her into another night of bad, twisted sleep as I pictured Lester Mantell on fire going under the black water and heard his cries echo in my memory.

TWENTY-SIX

The next meeting with Bob Jensen was even worse than the last. The numbers were just not good for the store. Jensen urged Betsy to make the deal—lock, stock, and sextant—with Ed Dempsey. That would give us just enough to pay off the first mortgage until we sold the building.

"Sell the building?" Betsy responded darkly. "Then where would we live?"

Fat and bland Jensen sat back in his chair and shrugged. "That's entirely up to you."

Afterward, we were sitting in the kitchen when Betsy, who was looking at the figures in our big Jensen file, came up with a plan so we could keep the store: we'd sell the inventory to Ed Dempsey and rent out the downstairs space for income. Then we could still live in the upstairs apartment.

"Depending on how much we rent it for and what kind of business it is," she said, "this could work. We're going to need some more income to not fall behind. But we'll still have a place to live."

"You think it's possible?" I asked.

"I think we have to at least try and make it work."

Betsy wanted to stay here, in these little rooms above the store, and I couldn't blame her. It had been her home for almost twenty years. And here I had found the normal life I wanted after prison, or as close as I was ever going to come. Even with all the financial worries (and worries about Fusco and that body in the Bahamas), this life with Betsy was all I had, and I wasn't going to lose it without a fight.

"I'll just have to figure out a way to make extra money," I said.

I worked at Charlie's almost every night as it was, but the wages were so low, the money didn't go very far. I thought about trying to work my way up in Charlie's kitchen, but once I asked him about a job as a prep cook, and he just laughed at me and told me to clean up a spill.

"Why don't you go into the living room and read for a while?" I asked. "Don't you have a book club meeting soon?"

"It's better when I keep busy," she answered. "There are things to do downstairs. I'm too distracted to read."

"That's what reading's *for*," I replied.

So after I set her up with tea in the living room, I went back downstairs to the store to check our website and eBay pages (no action), sweep the floor, and look around before setting the alarm.

As I tidied up, I couldn't help but see how nice the store looked. We had made it look as good as it could, but business was still impossibly slow. I guess it was just the economy; people didn't need nautical antiques. They needed food money, rent money, and forget it if you got sick or wanted to send your kid to college. If I were going to Columbia these days, with what my father made, I'd be totally screwed, with thousands and thousands of dollars in debt by the time I got out...if I ever got that far.

I was sweeping up when my (new, cheap) cell phone vibrated in my pocket. Who could be calling me? I hoped it wasn't Fusco. No, it was some 914 Westchester number. Probably some damn sales call.

"Hello?" I ventured.

"Hello, Mr. Ingber?" said a cautious female voice I didn't recognize.

"Yes?" I answered suspiciously.

"This is Catherine Ellison," she said, her voice a little clearer. "Derek's mother."

"Oh," I said with relief. Mystery solved. "How are you, Mrs. Ellison?"

"Hm. Not really so good, to tell you the truth," she said. "I mean, *I'm* fine, but Derek could be doing better."

"I'm sorry to hear that," I said neutrally.

"I was wondering," she said, going back to her quiet voice, "would you perhaps consider coming over to see Derek again? Just for a short visit. To cheer him up."

I paused. That was the last thing I wanted to do. Besides I had larger financial worries—

"I'd pay you," she quickly added.

"How much?"

To quote *The Godfather*, she made me an offer I couldn't refuse.

⌒

I went the next day. I took the Jeep while Betsy covered the store. If there were some emergency, she could call or text me or, worse comes to worse, call a cab (although that was money).

"How long are you going to be at Derek's?" she asked me just before I closed the back door.

"Honestly?" I replied. "I really don't know."

But this could be a good thing. Bills don't...you know.

It wasn't far to Scarsdale, and I drove to the Ellisons' house without having to look at a map or program the GPS. It was such a beautiful neighborhood, with flowers in bloom, even more perfect than the last time I was there.

Catherine Ellison welcomed me into her house as if I were the pope who had also just discovered a cure for cancer. She must have offered me four kinds of food and drink before we even got to the big back room that was now Derek's.

He was in a wheelchair watching the big TV while his bed was being remade by a small, dark-haired woman.

"Derek, sweetheart?" Catherine said as we walked in. "Look who's here."

I walked into the room, big and sunny yet remarkably sad, filled with all kinds of medical equipment and the hospital bed. Derek looked tired and shrunken in his wheelchair, a ghost of that cocky, self-possessed kid who drove me around Long Island in his BMW. A *young* ghost.

"Hey, man," I said, moving closer to him. I saw there was some device on a tray up close to his mouth. "Can you change channels with that?"

"Yeah," he said. "With this straw."

"Cool," I said. "How does it work?"

Reluctantly, he said, "You blow into it." He moved his head and put the plastic straw into his mouth. "It's a pain in the ass. See?"

"You got an ass in your *mouth*?"

"Douche," he called me with a snicker.

Behind me, Catherine quietly sighed with relief.

⌒

Derek and I spent the next couple of hours watching different things on his computer. And I got him to show me the fancy joystick and controller for his mouth, with four sip and puff sensors and a push switch.

"This is incredible technology," I declared.

Catherine, who was always hovering around, listening and offering us food, said, "It's all set up so that he can make phone calls and play video games. He likes video games, don't you, Der'?"

"Come on," I said. "Let's play something."

We played some video games, which I was terrible at but Derek seemed to like. Apparently, he had played these games when he had use of his hands, and it was hard for him to accept playing with just his mouth and breath. But it was kind of incredible that he could do it at all. Either way, hands or no hands, he beat the hell out of me.

I got him to let me take him outside in his wheelchair. The Ellisons had all these ramps built around the house and backyard, to make it easier to move Derek around. We sat in the sunshine on the back deck—well, *I* was in the sunshine; Catherine made sure that Derek was in the shade. It's a shame his ritzy neighborhood didn't have sidewalks, or I would have pushed him around the block.

"Are my parents paying you to hang out with me?"

"What do you care?" I non-answered.

"I'm just asking you," he said.

"Sure, they're paying me," I said. There was no point in lying to the kid.

"How much?" he asked.

"None of your business," I said.

"Well, whatever they're paying you," Derek said, "ask for more."

That got a good laugh out of me. And for a while, he almost forgot about his problems, and I almost forgot about mine.

By the time I left, Derek had had an afternoon full of laughs and fresh air, and I had a pocketful of cash.

⌒

"How was it?" asked Betsy when I walked into the apartment.

"OK," I said wearily. "I feel sorry for the kid."

I didn't realize how tiring it was, hanging out with Derek, trying to cheer him up without being too obvious about it.

"I don't know why," I said, "but the kid seems to like me."

"You're a very nice person, Larry. That's why," said Betsy with an amused shake of her head.

"They want me to come back tomorrow."

"Will you?"

"You bet," I answered. "If you'll cover the store alone. I mean money is money."

"You're doing a good thing," Betsy insisted.

"It's purely by accident. Hey," I said, suddenly energized by the cash in my pocket. "Let me take you out to dinner. Please? Let me do something nice for you. Tonight."

I was finally realizing that life is all about doing nice things for the people—or person—you love. Nothing more, nothing less.

⌒

Since it was summertime and Betsy was off from school, I spent as much time as I could at the Ellisons because she could cover the store. More time at the Ellisons meant more money. I think my visits were doing Derek some good. At least that's what Catherine kept telling me. Derek was a smart kid, but he got a bad break. One misjudgment altered his life forever. I can identify with that.

I even made my peace with Charles Ellison. I don't think I ever saw Derek happier than when I beat his father with my shitty jailhouse chess on an antique chessboard made of black-and-white marble, with hand-carved, hand-painted Civil War pieces. The smile almost split the kid's face.

"Good game, Larry," said Charles Ellison, shaking my hand after the game.

"Thank you, Charles," I said, returning his firm grip.

"And thank *you*," he said with his best sincere voice. "For everything."

The money from the Ellisons was oxygen for our financial health, but it was only temporary. The more I calculated and re-calculated, I wasn't sure there was going to be enough money. Even if we sold off the inventory, that would take care of the first mortgage, but what about the second mortgage? And if we fixed up the bottom of the store and got a tenant, would that be enough for us to live on? Even with the money from the Ellisons? But it was the only choice we had.

⌒

I made one last sale before the Ed Dempsey deal was sealed. I was sitting at the counter, checking on my laptop for news about Jonathan Klein—his company had suffered some losses lately—when the sleigh bells on the door rang.

Instantly, my gut tightened as I recognized Sammy Zambrano. Same skinny, shifty-looking punk, but now he was wearing a slick suit and matching hat. He strutted in like he was the prince of cool. I think he looked like the same asshole, only better dressed.

"Hey, cellie!" he called out as he came up to the counter.

I stood up. "I'm not your cellie, Zambrano, and what the hell are you doing here?"

He snickered in his snotty way. "What? Isn't this a store? Isn't all this junk for sale?"

He turned away from me and picked up a ship's bell from the display table behind him. He held it up and rang it with a laugh. "Hey! Maybe I should buy this!"

I moved out from behind the counter and reached for the bell. "It's not a toy!" I said, taking it from him.

He didn't fight me. He just laughed in that stupid *who-cares?* laugh you get from a lot of young guys in love with themselves and their ignorance.

"Don't have a fucking heart attack! I wasn't gonna break it," he said as I put it back on the table.

"I know you weren't," I said, standing in front of him. "So what can I do for you to get you out of here?"

"Nothing!" He laughed, turning from me and wandering away, pretending to look at the merchandise. "I was just in the neighborhood and thought—"

"No one's just in this neighborhood, Zambrano," I cut him off. "What do you want?"

He smirked at me and muttered, "Fuckin' guy."

"I don't need your compliments." I shook my head. "Say what you want to say and get out of here."

I waited for him to say his piece.

He lowered his voice. "OK, you missed out on that Medicare gravy, and, lemme tell you, serious bank was made. But I'm going have something very soon with reverse mortgages that's gonna be even bigger. You know what they are? I need old *white* guys to apply for—"

"Don't tell me about your fucking scams, Zambrano!" I shot right back in his face. "The last thing I want to do is be involved with a loser like you."

"Loser?" he took offense. "You calling *me* a loser? Look at you, a shitty clerk in this shitty store. I drove here in my new *Camaro*, you know what I'm talking about?"

Angrily he reached into his pocket and pulled out a large roll of bills. He made sure that I saw the size of it.

"I got a kid," he said. "How much for the bell?" He picked up the ship's bell he was playing with and put it on the counter.

"Sixty bucks," I said. "But it's not a toy."

"Fuck you. He'll like it anyway," Zambrano scoffed, finding three twenties in his roll of bills and dropping them on the counter.

I didn't like selling him anything, but a sale was a sale.

"You want me to wrap it up for you?" I asked him.

"No," he said. "I'll just take it like this."

He picked the bell up rudely so that it clanked as he walked away from me. Then he turned back with that smart-ass attitude of his.

"I was just trying to do you a favor, old man," Zambrano said. "Me? I'm offa parole! You understand? No more Fusco for me, asshole! I am free of Fusco!"

And he did a little dance, ringing the bell and shaking his butt. I won't deny that it hurt me a little, to think that this punk was off parole, and that he had a huge pocketful of cash—and a son too, for that matter—but I had an answer for him.

"Why don't you free yourself from here, Sammy? And from me?" I told him. "I got your message, and the answer is no. It'll *always* be no. No matter what you think, no matter what anyone thinks, *I'm not that guy.*"

It felt good to say it straight to his face, and it stopped him cold.

"OK, old man," he said. "I get it, I get it. You're a free man, and you don't want nothing to do with operators like me."

"Operators." I snickered as he strutted toward the front door, looking around once more.

"Well, good luck with all this shit," he sneered as he jerked open the door. He held up his purchase and yelled, "Nice bell!" as he shook it.

I watched the door close and said a silent goodbye. I think he got my meaning, and I hoped that I was finally finished with Sammy Zambrano.

The day that Ed Dempsey moved all the inventory out of the store was a sad one for Betsy. And me too.

"It's like Roland dying all over again," she said to me quietly as we watched Dempsey's movers take everything, piece by piece.

"Be careful with that!" Dempsey yelled, followed by something in Spanish that I didn't understand.

He seemed so triumphant, especially when he got his hands on that scrimshaw powder horn engraved with the Battle of Lake Champlain.

"It's not Roland," I said to Betsy. "It's only his stuff."

Dempsey was so happy about the acquisition that I wondered if Jensen got a kickback for maneuvering Betsy into the sale. But at least we'd have a better chance of keeping the building. We'd fix up the downstairs and get a good tenant, and with Betsy's salary for the year and what I'd be able to contribute, we'd have a chance of staying here.

I had only three months of parole left. I was going to ask Jensen for a pay stub that I could show Fusco just for these last months, but I was pretty sure he wouldn't do it. I knew Charlie Wagner wanted to keep me off his books. I bet that I could get Catherine Ellison to write me a kind of letter of employment that Fusco would buy. In fact, if I told her my situation and asked for a letter, that might guarantee me a certain number of hours with Derek each week. It could be something I could count on.

Everything, except for my feelings for Betsy, now seemed uncertain. I kept having nightmares about Mantell/Avery burning up in the water, and about trying to pull Klein back, not wanting him to shoot. Funny, I never dreamed about Mantell when I was in the joint, yet I was dreaming about him all the time as Brandon Avery. For weeks, I checked the few Bahamas websites I knew and saw nothing about his death or even the boat fire. After a while, I stopped checking, and nothing happened. No one knocked on my door.

During this whole time, I never contacted Jonathan Klein—by email or phone—doing us both a favor, I thought. But my mind was uneasy. I couldn't leave it behind me, what happened in the Bahamas and the remorse that I had participated in another murder, even if it was a scumbag like Avery/Mantell. But at least I had tried to stop this one. *I* wasn't a murderer. I went to the Bahamas to get the money my father left me, but I didn't go down there to kill anybody.

Maybe that *was* my father's true legacy to me: finding out, once and for all, who I really am.

TWENTY-SEVEN

Few things are sadder than an empty, out-of-business store.

Ed Dempsey took almost everything: all the display cases, tables, and bookshelves. Everything that wasn't nailed down except for the three old stools that sat in front of the counter, the cleaning supplies in the closet, and the stuff in Roland's office that we didn't clear out yet. He even took Roland's antique brass National Cash Register.

"It's in the contract," Dempsey had said, and I'm sure he was right. The deal was for everything.

Dempsey and his men were gone by late afternoon, but Betsy kept sweeping the empty floor, making these piles of almost invisible dust and scooping them up with a dustpan.

"Come on, Bets, would you stop?" I said, taking the broom from her. "You'll take the finish off the wood."

"We're probably going to have to refinish this floor before we get a tenant," she said.

"We *definitely* have to refinish the floor," I concurred, "but not tonight."

She leaned on me, looking over the empty space and sighed. "The end of an era."

Her expression was sad and drawn. I had never seen her looking so old.

"You'll see. This will make things easier for us now," I said. "It'll give us a little breathing room and time to plan the next step."

She didn't say anything.

I tried another topic: "Dempsey has a nice store. He'll treat all of Roland's things very kindly. They'll have a good home." (I had been to King's Cargo, and it was indeed a beautiful store.)

410

She still looked downhearted.

"Hey!" I said. "How about this? Let's go down to Gassim's for some lobster rolls."

"Lobster rolls are your answer to everything." She rolled her eyes.

"Come on, Miss Elizabeth!" I said. "You only live once. Carpe diem. Carpe this diem with me."

She half resisted as I pulled her to me for a kiss.

Then I saw something through the front window, something I didn't expect: a long black limousine pulling up to the curb. Jonathan Klein's limousine.

"Holy sh—" I whispered as I watched the driver run around from his side and open the passenger door in the back. Sure enough, rumpled Jonathan Klein rolled out of the back seat.

"What is it?" asked Betsy, noticing the change in me, the tension that surged through my body.

But Klein didn't walk straight into the store. He watched as the driver closed his door and popped open the trunk.

"Is that who I think it is?" Betsy asked. "He looks smaller in his pictures."

"How do you know what he looks like?"

"You think you're the only person who looks on the internet?" she answered.

I watched the driver get some big boxes out of the trunk and wondered out loud, "What could he be doing here?"

"I don't want to meet him," said Betsy decisively and turned away to go upstairs. But I grabbed her arm. "Stay—please?"

I should have let her go upstairs. I never told her the specifics of what happened in the Bahamas, although she knew it was something bad. Keeping her and Klein apart would probably be a smart thing, but somehow I wanted her to stay, to have her meet Klein. In retrospect, I think I wanted to show him that I had something wonderful, something that he, even with all his billions, didn't have.

Before Betsy could say anything, the door burst open and Klein came in first, holding the door open for his driver, who was carrying two big boxes, one on top of another. On the bottom was a white Styrofoam cooler, and on top was a wicker picnic basket.

"Jonathan Klein!" I shouted fake-happily. "What a nice surprise!" My voice echoed in the open space.

Klein stopped stock-still when he saw the empty store.

"What the hell happened here?" he asked.

All I could say was "Things change."

Klein looked more disheveled and amped-up than ever, even if his sports jacket cost ten thousand dollars and his loafers were alligator. He seemed distracted by the empty store. Then he appeared to remember something.

"Oh," he said, turning to his driver. "Henry, you can put those down here and wait in the car?"

The driver said a sharp, "Yes, sir!" and put the boxes down on the floor with a grunt.

With a mischievous, confident look on his face, Klein said to me, "Wait till you see what I have for you."

Henry was out the door when I finally remembered to introduce Betsy.

"Oh, Betsy? Honey?" I turned to her, beckoning her, finally pulling her gently forward. "This is the famous Mr. Jonathan Klein. Jonathan?" I turned to him. "This is Betsy Hull. *My* Betsy."

She gave me a quick, pleased look before Klein moved in on her, with his odd, forceful charm. He took her hand in both of his.

"I'm honored to meet the famous Betsy," he purred.

"I'm not famous." She actually blushed.

"Oh, you should hear the way Larry talks about you," Klein countered. "He just lights up whenever he mentions your name."

"Lights up *what*?" she joked, pulling her hand away.

"Hmff!" Klein snickered. "You *said* she was funny."

Freed from Klein's grasp, she turned to me. "I'm going to go upstairs."

"Please stay," Klein said.

"No," she said definitively, "I'm sure you two have a lot to talk about. Maybe I'll see you later."

"Very nice meeting you!" Klein called out as she went quickly up the stairs.

When she was gone, he said soberly, "She doesn't like me."

"Don't say that."

"She doesn't know what happened, does she?"

"No! Of course not!" I said, miming locking my lips. "I'm not completely stupid. I mean, she knows that something bad happened. I'm not that good an actor."

"Women have that fucking radar," Klein grumbled.

"But she doesn't know *exactly* what happened," I clarified.

"So she just dislikes me on general principles?" Klein asked.

"What can I say?" I sighed. "Women have instincts."

"Shit," he muttered glumly, shaking his head.

I could tell that behind this happy surprise visit Klein was nervous about something. When he was holding Betsy's hand, I noticed a bad rash on the back of his neck, and he seemed generally twitchy and tense from the moment he walked in. I had read on the web about his recent reversals, but he still had his limousine. I wondered, *Was this the same Jonathan Klein I left in the Bahamas?*

"Oh!" Klein suddenly was animated. "Wait till you see what I have for you!"

From his pocket, he pulled out a key ring with a gold Swiss Army knife and squatted down next to the Styrofoam cooler Henry had left on the floor.

As he unfolded the blade and sliced through the packing tape, he said, "Remember that stretch of Bay Street, by that bank of yellow trees? Remember Wilhelmina, sitting under the umbrellas?"

Klein stripped off the packing tape and removed the cover from the big box, and I saw what he had brought. Of course I remembered at once—"BEST ICES ON THE PLANET"—five large plastic containers packed in dry ice.

"Klein-o!" I smiled. "You are insane."

"No, I'm not," he said directly. "I just like what I like and have the ability to get it."

What message was he sending me? Klein definitely looked older and edgier than he did in Nassau, even though it was just a few months ago.

"Look!" commanded Klein, pointing at each big tub of colored ice. "That's mango...that's coconut...Persian lime. And that's my favorite," he said, pointing to the last, the darkest tub. "Scarlet plum. I get doubles of that. Wilhelmina makes it from all native plants."

"I repeat," I said. "Insane."

But in two minutes, we were sitting on the stools in front of the counter, eating the best ices on the planet. Really. Klein had brought this whole picnic setup in a wicker basket with bowls and spoons and even an ice-cream scooper. Whatever else, this guy knew how to live.

We ate in silence for a good five minutes; silent except for "Yummm" and "Ooo-ee" and "Damn!"

Klein said, "You ready for seconds?"

"Not yet," I said. "But soon."

Klein finished his bowl, hopped down from his stool, put his bowl on the counter, and paced around the store a little.

Finally he said, "Larry, I bet you've been wondering where I've been."

He had a look of pride on his face. He knew he had surprised me, dropping in like this, and he liked it, having the upper hand, the advantage.

"Well, Jonathan," I said, "now that you mention it...I was thinking that I would probably never see you again."

"I know!" He nodded emphatically. "I know it, and I respect it. You didn't try to get in touch with me, in any way. I really like that about you, Larry."

"One thing you learn in prison," I replied. "Keep your eyes open and your mouth shut."

He came back and sat on the stool next to me. He put his hand on my shoulder and held it firmly, fixing me with his gaze. I didn't twitch a muscle, wondering what he was after.

"After what happened," he said, "you didn't call me, you didn't email me. You sat tight, and you waited."

"Sometimes doing nothing is the right move," I agreed.

"Larry?" He cackled. "Maybe you shoulda been on Wall Street. I coulda used you."

"I think that ship sailed a long time ago, Jonathan," I said. "Besides, white-collar prison never appealed to me."

He snickered and shook his head. "I know some guys who might disagree with you about that."

"Some guys are soft," I responded.

He grunted in appreciation, liking the implication that the two of us were *not* soft. He reached around to the counter, picked up his bowl, and went back to the Styrofoam tub to scoop out a whole second helping but just the scarlet plum.

"You know that big field that we ran through that night?" he asked me, licking his fingers. "When we were chasing Avery? Avery, Mantell, whatever the fuck you want to call him."

"Yeah?"

"Some guys wanted me to invest in a golf course there," he said. "That's why I knew the area so well."

"Well enough," I said, thinking back to that wet, uneven field where I tripped and fell so hard on that night of insanity.

As he shoveled the ice into his mouth, Klein mused, "I like golf, but that was the wrong place for a course."

"'A good walk spoiled,'" I quoted. "Isn't that what they say about golf?"

"Who?" he asked, licking his spoon.

"Mark Twain," I answered.

"What?"

"I think Mark Twain said that," I clarified.

He barely finished his mouthful, burbling enthusiastically, "That's what I love about you, Larry!"

"What?"

"The fact that you read us fucking Edgar Allan Poe and Mark Twain and Jack London!" Klein said. "And even though I was a kid, I remember thinking, *This is really good stuff.* For the first time in my life."

He got up from his stool and put down his bowl with a clatter. "And when I passed my swimming test into Area Three and you read us 'The Raven,' I thought that was the greatest, scariest, most awesome thing I'd ever heard. And you know what? The first thing I did when I made a little money was to buy a first edition of 'The Raven,' from the issue of *The Evening Mirror* it first appeared in, in—what?—1840-something. I now have one of the largest collections of first edition Poes in the world. You see how impressionable young minds are?"

"You're right," I said, getting the last spoonful in my bowl. "The scarlet plum is the best. When it's melted, it looks just like blood."

Klein laughed and then said nothing. I knew there was something on his mind and if I waited long enough, he would tell me everything.

"So," he finally said, "you want to know what happened after you left Nassau?"

I thought for a moment. Did I really want to know what he did to get him/us out of this mess, presuming that he did? Then again, I couldn't be any more of an accessory to Avery's killing than I already was, so why not hear his story?

"Jon?" I said. "You can tell me nothing, or you can tell me everything. You know that I'm not gonna tell anybody anything, ever."

"Not even Betsy?"

"*Especially* not Betsy."

He nodded. "Deal." He licked his lips. "OK, I did what I said I'd do. I handled things right there and then."

"Which means?" I prompted him.

He turned his palms out. "I paid everybody off," he said as if that should have been obvious to me.

"Everybody?"

"Maybe six people," he said, "but I'm sure that some of the money filtered down. Fortunately, Avery, Mantell—whatever the fuck his name was—was a complete piece of shit, and nobody was unhappy to see him dead."

"Cops call it 'a public service homicide,'" I added.

"I love it down there," he said, "and I wasn't going to let it be ruined by this one little thing."

Wow. So murdering another human being was "one little thing"? Klein was cold. Colder than me, and my heart was on ice for forty years.

Klein chuckled. "Thank God for that trick shoulder of yours, or we might never've gotten out of there."

"You never know what comes in handy from your past experience." I laughed bitterly.

Klein nodded. "Hah. And I don't think I've ever seen anybody almost decapitated with a fucking *paper clip*."

All I could say was "I have."

He looked at me for a long moment. He seemed tense and troubled.

"There is an unfortunate thing in all this." He sighed. "Janet's left me."

"Oh," I said, feeling genuinely sorry for him. "That's too bad. You think it had anything to do with the—?"

"Oh no!" he waved me off. "It's really OK. It was time for her to go."

I could see that he was lying. Janet was a good team player, but would she help cover up a murder forever, even if the victim was a piece of human trash? Did Janet Ko grow a conscience?

"What is she going to do?" I asked.

"Go to law school, I think," he said.

"That's, what, *three* years?"

He dismissed my comment. "I gave her enough severance for *four* law school educations! And the best reference I could write. She'll be fine, once she decides what she wants to do."

"Doesn't she want to be a lawyer?" I asked.

"Maybe." He shrugged. "I think she's just going back to school because she's good at it."

"She'll be hard to replace."

"Everyone is replaceable," he countered. "The main thing is that she signed an NDA."

When he saw my blank look, he clarified: "A non-disclosure agreement. A confidentiality document."

So he bought Janet's silence about what happened on Seabreeze Canal that night and everything afterward.

He got up from the chair and hitched up his pants.

"You know what?" he continued. "I'm thinking of setting a scholarship fund for kids on the island."

"Good for you," I said firmly.

"Yeah,"—he adjusted his belt—"so that the kid whose head you almost cut off can maybe get an education and learn to be something other than a street punk."

"That's really nice of you, Jonathan," I said, wondering if he was telling the truth. I hoped he was.

"You know," he said, "speaking of things we never asked each other, I never asked you exactly how much Avery actually owed you—I mean, exactly how much he stole?"

"Exactly? Well." I sat back against the counter. "For a long time, I knew the exact amount in all the accounts. I even tried to keep track of the interest that I should have been making, but after a while, I lost count of that. So I don't have the *exact* amount—"

"OK!" Klein cut me off with a flick of his hand. "*Generally* how much? In round numbers."

"Ohhh," I stalled and then estimated. "About two hundred and thirty, two hundred forty thousand dollars."

Klein froze right in front of me, his eyes wide, his mouth open.

"Is that *all*?" He winced.

"Well," I huffed. "That's a lot of money to me. That's all the money that my folks saved for me for all the years I was inside. And that's not counting the inflated fees that he charged me all those years that I probably should have gotten back."

"But a lousy two hundred and forty thousand dollars..." Klein said the amount as if he had a mouthful of dirt. "To risk your life for? To risk *my* life for! *That's* insane."

"I'm sorry, Jonathan," I said, "but that is a lot of money to *normal* people."

That stopped him.

"You have no concept of money, do you?" I said.

"*I* have no concept of money?" He laughed at me.

"No, you don't," I shot straight back in his face. "You have no idea what real people go through every day, paying bills, trying to survive paycheck to paycheck, worrying about money every single day. It's all just paper to you. But every day out here in real America, not Wall Street, it's tough if you're not super rich. You wonder why there's so much hatred out there in the streets? It's because everything's out of whack, and guys like you have everything, and everybody else is left with nothing, and we've all been driven crazy from the pressure. The greed at the top is just out of control and is choking the whole damn country to death."

I didn't mean to say all of that. It just came out. Klein had been good to me, and it was foolish to unload all my frustrations on him.

He stood there for a moment, looked down, and smiled. Then he looked me straight in the eye.

"Greed?" he repeated. "You know what I came up here to do, don't you?"

"You mean it wasn't just to bring me the best ices on the planet?"

He smiled with a little nervous twitch in his eye. I wondered if he was on pills or something. And the rash on his neck was pinker than ever. Something was going on inside Klein, and I wasn't sure what.

He looked up at the ceiling and let out a sigh. Then he walked over to the counter, drew out a long wallet from his inside coat pocket, and tossed it onto the counter.

"I almost never do this," he said. He took a pen from his shirt pocket, wrote out a check at super-speed, and handed it to me.

"Here," he said simply. "That'll also pay the gift tax. I wouldn't want you getting in any trouble with the IRS."

The check was from his personal account. For three hundred thousand dollars. Made out to me.

"Maybe Betsy will like me now," he said wryly.

Now I've seen some crazy things in my life, but this really stood me still. I had to refocus my eyes on the number twice, to make sure that I saw what I thought I saw.

"You don't have to do this," I said. "You know I'll keep my mouth shut. I'm not gonna blackmail you."

"Maybe," he said with a tight smile. "But this is a little insurance. Look at it this way: if you hadn't'a saved me from drowning in Area Three at Mooncliff that summer, I wouldn't be here at all. So maybe this is a roundabout way of finally paying you back for saving my life in 1968."

My mind flashed back to that summer camp that led me to so much tragedy—and forward to I-don't-know-what. Maybe my luck had, at last, finally evened out.

"And this is good?" I asked, holding up the check to the light.

He snorted once, that I would even joke about such a thing. "If anyone asks, you say you won it playing cards. Go Fish. Just like we used to play during bunk games."

I carefully folded the check and put it in my shirt pocket.

Klein put his hand on my shoulder. "You, my friend, were the last loose end."

He packed up the bowls and put everything together in the wicker basket.

"Keep the ices," he said.

"But there's too much," I protested. "Take some."

"Nah," he said, waving me off. "I can get 'em anytime."

He picked up the basket, and I escorted him to the front door before he changed his mind and took his check back. Wasn't *mercurial* the word people used about him? I could feel my heart beating in my chest under the check in my pocket.

"Tell Betsy goodbye for me," he said.

"Will do," I said, holding the door open, when I thought of one more thing. "Oh, dammit, Jonathan. I forgot: I still owe Brian Halliwell thirty bucks."

I reached for my wallet, but Klein stopped me.

"Please! Don't sweat it," he said, touching my arm gently. "I think I can cover it for you."

I held the door wide open. "Thank you again, Mr. Klein."

He took a step onto the porch and then turned back to me. "You know, Larry, I think it's probably a good idea if we never see each other again."

I could see in his eyes that he had made up his mind. It was a cold-blooded business decision: pay me off—the last link to the killing of Avery—and cut everything off after that.

"Good idea," I replied. "It's not personal, Sonny. It's strictly business."

"Take care, Larry," he said with a big smile. "You know, I think we should have promoted you to full Groinmaster a long time ago."

I laughed and responded, "Is it true that you only pay fifteen per cent in income taxes?"

"Go fuck yourself, jailbird!" he shot back jovially as he stepped out onto the porch.

"Got you covered," I shot back, "killer."

We shared a last ironic laugh, and I closed the door. Then I turned that lock as tight as I ever did and felt the biggest Moment of Thanks and Grace since I walked out of prison. My mind raced like mad: this was going to save the store, this was going to save everything! I would "have something" and maybe "do something" after all.

I ran around, turning off everything and setting the alarm, bursting to get upstairs and tell Betsy of our good fortune. With my brain about to burst, I practically floated up the stairs, thinking, *This is so much more money than I've ever had in my life.* I felt like a character in a Dickens novel, an orphan who comes into sudden fortune—OK, a very old orphan—except that this was *real.* I thought about what other jailbirds would do with it. Go to Vegas and run it up to a million? Go to Freddie Pooch and have him put the money to work on the street with his loan sharks? Or just go away and disappear forever onto some island—like, say, the Bahamas, but one of the cheap outer islands—and live out the money in a haze of rum, sunshine, and young women.

But that wasn't me.

Betsy's eyes filled with tears when I showed her the check. I couldn't hide the big smile on my face. I finally could make good on all my good intentions and inner promises to pay her back for all the love and trust she had given me. Talk about Grace and Thanks.

"Don't cry," I said. "It's only money."

She refolded the check and handed it back to me.

"My goodness," she said sadly. "What did you do in the Bahamas that he has to give you this much money?"

I blanched for a moment: I still didn't want her to know what happened, but I couldn't say, *"Be happy for me! I didn't kill anyone. I was only an accomplice...again."*

"No, you don't understand," I said, forming for an explanation. "He didn't *have* to give me any money."

She didn't like that answer. I had to clarify things.

"You don't get it," I said. "He's a generous guy! I saved his life when he was a kid. I told you that."

"Yes," she admitted. "You did."

"There you go," I reaffirmed. "This is just payback. He does lots of charitable things for people. He's an extremely rich guy, you know that. I guess he just wanted to do something for me."

Taking the check out of my hand and looking it again, she said, "You really think it's good?"

"Don't be silly," I replied, taking it back from her, folding it and putting it into my shirt pocket, then patting it for safety. "I'm going to put in the bank *tomorrow*! And I have an extremely strong feeling—no, make that a certainty—that it's going to clear."

She paused and asked me, "So what are you going to do with it?"

"What do you mean, what am I going to do with it?" I laughed. "You know what I'm going to do with it."

"No," she said with honest, open eyes. "I don't."

I took her gently by the shoulders. "This is what I'm going to do: I'm going to pay off everything on the store, everything that Roland owed, and then we'll own it free and clear and be able to fix up the downstairs all nice and rent it out and still live up here for as long as you want, even after you stop working at Thomas Paine. Isn't that what you want?"

She didn't say anything at first. I don't know if she believed me. She blinked a few times and looked away for a moment. Then her tears started to flow.

"Don't cry!" I said. "Why are you crying? You should be happy."

When she could talk, she said, "When I saw the check, my first thought was *Now he's going to leave me.*"

And she started crying all over again, and I had to hold her tight and kiss her hair and rock her.

"Are you kidding?" I said. "*I'm* the one who's lucky to have *you!*"

She suddenly pushed me away at arm's length.

"That's a lot of money, Larry," she said. "You can't just give me three hundred thousand dollars to buy the building. You'll have to become my partner or something. Something legal."

I laughed and took her by the hands. "I don't want to be your partner, Betsy Hull. I want to be your *husband.*"

The words were out of my mouth before I knew what I was saying because it was the obvious, the right thing to say.

"That is—if you'll have me," I added. "If you want to think about it—"

"Don't be ridiculous." She laughed, her eyes filling with new tears. "Of course I'll say yes! I've given my life to you, or haven't you noticed?"

I took her hands and kissed them and said warmly, "I noticed."

"But—" She shook me off and turned away.

"What's wrong?" I asked. "Do you want me to kneel? I'll kneel."

But before my knee could hit the ground, she caught me and straightened me up.

"No!" she said. "It's not that."

I could see that she was preparing to say something that had been on her mind, so I stood back and let her have her say.

"OK, let me put this right. I love you, Larry," she said. "I know I do. I love you more than I ever thought I could love a man."

She paused.

"But—?"

"But I won't marry you until you do one thing."

"Which is?" I asked.

She took a long moment. "I want you to say goodbye, once and for all, to that dead little bitch from Long Island."

That stopped me, cold. I think it was the first time I ever heard her curse.

"How do you think I feel," she continued, "looking at that thing on your arm all this time?"

I guess I haven't mentioned it before—why should I have?—but I have this bad prison tattoo on my right bicep of The Girl's name in wavy, dark blue letters that sag badly now.

"I want you to get that thing taken off your arm. And I want you to go to her grave on Long Island and say goodbye to her. She's dead, but you haven't buried her. I'm just not going to play second fiddle to a corpse anymore. And then I'll marry you. But not before."

TWENTY-EIGHT

We went the very next Sunday. It wasn't hard to find where The Girl's gravesite was. I googled it, and it came right up. I wasn't surprised where it was, in this ritzy cemetery near her hometown.

We didn't say much on the drive there. Betsy talked a little. Just crossing the Throgs Neck Bridge, driving onto Long Island, still gave me the creeps, especially on a mission like this one. But I think Betsy knew that it would be weird if we didn't talk at all.

"What a clear day!" she said. "And such little traffic, even for a weekend. There'll be no rush hour. This was definitely the right day to go...and when we get home, we have some leftover turkey meatballs and spaghetti for dinner. I know how much you like that. And I think there's a game on."

She was trying to keep my mind off the past. Of course she failed, but I couldn't blame her for trying.

"How's your arm?" she asked.

"Fine," I said. "I can hardly feel it."

I had had my first session of laser tattoo removal the day before. It would take a few treatments, spread over a few months, but it wouldn't be long before there would be pink, empty skin where there had once been ugly, blue ink. It was the right thing to do. Now that I think of it, I don't know how she tolerated seeing that crappy thing on my arm all this time.

Once we got to the cemetery, I knew it was going to be fairly easy to find the grave. She was a famous dead girl. According to Wikipedia, she is "a pop symbol of tragic, young love in the Sixties." A beautiful creature who was too sensitive and fragile for this star-crossed world—like Juliet, or Catherine from *Wuthering Heights*, or Bonnie of Bonnie and Clyde, or Princess Diana, or

424

any other ill-fated celebrity you can think of. There were actually websites devoted to her, and, supposedly, lots of young girls on Long Island were obsessed with her. Gorgeous pictures of her still floated around, with that Natalie Wood/Audrey Hepburn thing of hers. Fans would leave flowers and love tokens, especially candy hearts, on her grave, just like people left bottles of Jack Daniels on Jim Morrison's grave in Paris. That's another thing: people adored her because she never grew old. She was always young and beautiful, even in death.

And sure enough, after we looked up the exact site of her grave at the Visitors' Center and made our way slowly through the maze of headstones to the far corner where she lay, there were bunches of wilted flowers and a little vase filled with white roses right there, leaned up against her gravestone, along with quite a few cellophane packages of candy hearts. I walked closer, looking at all the flowers and pretty paper and sympathy cards that people had written to her as if she could still read them. It looked like a party had just ended and now there was nobody left to clean it up.

Betsy said, "Just when you think you've seen the saddest thing ever..."

There was a simple granite headstone, polished on the front and sides but rough on top. Engraved on it was "RACHEL LOU-ISE PRINCE—1952–1969—Gone too soon."

I finally said her name. It was Rachel.

Next to hers was a bigger, double headstone for her parents: "EMMANUEL BENJAMIN PRINCE" and "ELEANOR ROSE PRINCE." Poor, rich, fat Manny. And cursed/accursed Hell-eanor. We called her Hell-eanor with good reason. Still, she didn't deserve what happened to her. No, make that *what we did*.

I guess it made sense that both of her parents were gone, just as both of mine were. I did some quick math and realized that Manny (*Emmanuel!?*) outlived his wife and daughter by only twenty years. Not surprising: Manny wasn't a healthy man, not with those cigarettes, that huge gut, and all his inner rage, which I'm sure I added to. Interesting that he wound up being buried here and not with some new tootsie he acquired later in life. He always had girlfriends, but in the end, he remained true to his hateful, ugly wife and his crazy, beautiful daughter.

From behind me, Betsy softly asked, "You OK?"

"I'm fine," I said, surprising myself.

"Take your time," she said, moving back by some trees. "Just say your goodbyes, once and for all."

Once and for all is a tall order when you've been thinking about something your whole life. But that's what I was here for. Betsy was right: it wasn't fair to her to drag my sick, lost, misguided love for another girl into a marriage. Especially since The Girl had been dead for more than forty years.

"Well, Rach," I said, "looks like you've still got a lot of fans. I guess I'm not the only one who couldn't forget you. ...See all this junk they leave you? Where'd they get the candy hearts thing? People have the most fucked-up ideas."

I know that it was weird, talking out loud to a dead girl under the ground who wasn't really there anyway, but it felt right. It made it more final.

"See what a freak show we are?" I continued, looking down through the grass. "Nothing's ever gonna change that, except that now I'm old...and you're...you're long, long gone. All these years have passed, so many things have changed out here in the world, but you're still the prettiest girl in the room, right? I mean, just look around!"

Nowadays, I guess they would have called her bi-polar. I just thought that she was the most beautiful, exciting girl I'd ever known. And she seemed to really like me. But for the millionth time, I saw in my mind the things that happened that night. The accidental carnage, the moving of the "things," the drive upstate, the "Psycho" ending. I still don't remember the car crash clearly, but I think that's where she told me that she loved me too.

"One good thing," I said. "They filled up the Quarry. Now it's just for clean water and sewage treatment. Pretty appropriate, don't you think?"

I thought back to all the time I spent with her, all the years I thought and dreamed about her, and all the life I lost on the way to this moment.

"You know the Zone we talked about all the time," I continued. "Our Zone of Love? Well, it wasn't really real, was it, because it wasn't really truthful. It was all just juvenile desire, raging hormones, and the need to escape—you from your parents and me from the pressures that were on me. We were so young and stupid. What I have here with this woman is *real*. If you and I had had anything real, we would have worked out your problems with your parents and gotten you some help, and maybe all that horrible stuff wouldn't have happened. We would have done something different. I know that *I* would have done something different. I *should* have done something different...and that's where the story should have ended."

I crouched down and talked right into the earth.

"We were just kids, Rach," I whispered. "Well, I'm not a kid anymore, not by a long shot. And this is where I have to let you go—forever. She doesn't like you, even the thought of you, and I love her more than I love you. More than I *ever* loved you. A *real* love, this time. So let me go, OK?"

That's when it hit me that I hadn't been thinking or dreaming about Rachel for a very long time. For months and months—ever since Betsy came into my life.

There was only one last thing to say.

"But I do forgive you, Rachel. So why on earth should I moan? I guess I'll have to forgive myself too."

A shudder ran through my body, filling me with a sense of relief. It was like an anchor lifting from within me with a force greater than my love for Rachel, maybe even than my love for Betsy. A feeling that maybe everything was going to be OK washed over me. And not just for me, but for *everybody*.

I stood there for I don't know how long in that Moment of Grace and Thanks when it faded, becoming part of me. I turned and walked away from it all.

I put my arm around Betsy as we walked the gravel path back to the Jeep.

"Are you OK?" she asked in the gentlest possible voice.

And I said sniffling actual tears, "Yeah. I'm OK...in fact, I feel good."

I hugged Betsy, and we walked away from Rachel Prince's grave and all that it meant, once and for all. At long last, I was maybe, *finally* free.

⌒

Make that *almost* free. I still had two appointments left with Fusco, and I knew he still had it in for me. He didn't know that Roland was dead and the store was out of business, but I wasn't going to tell him. I had just six more weeks of parole to go, and I didn't want to call attention to myself. If I could just stay under Fusco's radar for a little while longer, I'd be out of the system forever.

I sat in the chair across from him in his dingy New Rochelle office while he looked at my file on his computer screen, searching for something to use on me, I'm sure. I said nothing.

He shook his head slowly.

"I see you're up to date on your fees," he said sadly.

I continued to say nothing, controlling the bitter smile that I felt inside.

He turned to look at me with his piggy eyes.

"You might get away from me this time, Ingber," he said, "but you're gonna fuck up eventually. I just know it. I've seen a million convicts like you. Sooner or later, you'll do something. I don't care how old you are. Maybe I won't be around to see it, but someday you'll fuck up and you'll wind up back where you belong."

I left his office without telling him that I had already fucked up, royally—in the Bahamas.

By the way, Klein's check cleared. You should have seen my regular bank teller's face when I made the deposit. After she saw the amount on the check, she seemed to look at me with much more respect than usual, which was both amazing and slightly disappointing. I guess money means that much to people, no matter who you are.

I kept seeing Derek on a regular basis because it was the right thing to do and because the money was too good. Once we paid off everything, fixed up the downstairs, kept back some for taxes the way that Klein said we should, and put aside money for the wedding and the rest of my tattoo removal treatments, most of the money was spoken for.

But by then, Derek and I had become good friends, so it was more than just the money. I never had a son of my own, but if

I did, he'd probably end up like Derek and like me: smart but fucked-up in some fundamental way.

So I thought that I could really help him. Derek didn't get along with his father, and Charles had trouble dealing with his son's misfortune (even though he tried to put on a good face and spared no expense in providing for his son's care). So I spent a lot of time with Derek.

Much to Catherine's approval, I did exercises with him that helped his blood flow while we listened to Howard Stern on the radio. We played this video game—*Viral Control III*—that he loved because he could beat me and my real working fingers with his puff-and-sip sensors and the switch that he pushed with his chin.

We watched political shows on TV and talked about the day's news.

I tried to tell him the truth as I saw it: "We screwed it all up. Oh, some things are better now. When I went in, Nixon was president, and now we have this very smart black guy. Smart enough to transfer *into* Columbia and actually graduate, unlike some people I know. But who cares about a minor Ivy, right?"

Derek snorted, "No shit."

"I'm sorry, kid," I said. "But my generation let you down. We let the bad guys win. The greedy exploited the gullible, and now everybody hates everybody."

When Derek's eyes got tired from the TV and game playing, I read to him, just as I read to the Doggies, a million years ago. "*Once upon a midnight dreary, while I pondered weak and weary...*" I read him the Dylan Thomas that he loved and some Emily Dickinson that blew both our minds.

I told him my prison stories, which he couldn't get enough of. I guess it's good for me to get some of this stuff out. I certainly couldn't tell Betsy. I don't want those pictures in her brain. Hell, I don't want them in *my* brain. But you know what *mon ami* Montaigne said about nothing fixing a thing so intensely in the memory as the wish to forget it. Even when you remove a nail from a wall, the hole is still there forever.

⌒

Betsy didn't want a big wedding. ("I did that once before," she said. "I don't need to do it again.") But I wanted some kind of party. Even if we got married at city hall, I thought that we should have a party. If not, it would be as if we were hiding the fact that we got married, and I was proud to be getting married to a wonderful woman like Betsy Hull. That would be the truest sign of all that I had finally achieved my impossible dream of spending what's left of my life as a normal person who lives a normal life. The ultimate Grace and Thanks.

At first it was going to be a small wedding—just a few people in the empty store, which was now a big open space: perfect for a party. But we wound up inviting a lot of people. I mean, why not?

Betsy invited the book club ladies and their husbands/boy-friends/whoever they wanted. She invited several people from Thomas Paine—"but *not* Croll"—including Larisha and her enormous husband, Tremaine, who used to play for the Jets. And of course, we invited Kelly; Jimmy; his wife, Jean; and Betsy's relatives.

I invited some people from Clemency, just to show I had no hard feelings: Javier and his wife, Jessica; and Rosemary and her husband. I had only a few people to invite, but at least I had some.

At first, we felt that we had to invite Bob Jensen, even though neither of us liked him very much. Finally, we decided we were both too old to have anyone at our wedding we didn't like, so no Bob Jensen.

We debated about inviting Jonathan Klein—after all, it was his generosity that allowed a lot of this to happen—but I decided we shouldn't. I told Betsy, and she agreed, that sending an invitation was like trolling for an expensive gift, and Klein had already given us more than enough. Of course, I knew not to invite him because of our no-further-contact understanding. Betsy still didn't know what happened in the Bahamas, and if it were in my power, she would never know.

Kelly said we should hire a wedding coordinator, and I agreed with her. But Betsy said if we needed a wedding coordinator, then the wedding was too big. She said it was going to be very casual and we could do it all ourselves, and then I had to agree with *her*. (Of course, we should have hired a wedding coordinator. Not that we didn't have a great time, but it would have been easier for Betsy. All the real work and planning fell to her; I just did as I was told.)

Fortunately, the Ellisons kept wanting more hours from me, and I was glad to oblige. Derek really seemed to respond to me. We spent a lot of time just laughing and bullshitting while we watched videos on YouTube, but that seemed to be what the Ellisons wanted from me. And I got paid for it.

I showed him the James Brown *T.A.M.I. Show* from when I was a kid, which blew his mind. We watched a lot of Bruce Springsteen shows, which blew *my* mind. Derek told me that once he saw the Boss from "the pit"—the standing room right in front of the stage—maybe twenty feet away from Springsteen.

"I won't be doing standing room anymore," Derek joked.

"Baby, you were born to roll," I answered.

Derek loved any kind of joke, the darker the better.

We also watched a lot of Frank Sinatra clips, which made me think about my Dad who loved "Frankie" so much. It was gratifying to pass that love on to Derek, who quickly understood Sinatra.

"He sings like a *man*," Derek declared. "You know, between Sinatra and Springsteen, we may have to rethink New Jersey."

We thought about it briefly and concluded, "Naahh!"

After some resistance—"What's the point?"—I got Derek to think about doing some online classes that would allow him to finish his Dartmouth degree. Catherine was especially grateful for that.

The Ellisons had bought a nice Honda Odyssey minivan that they had converted for wheelchair access so Derek could be driven around. He seemed to be willing to go out in the world with me, braving all the pitying stares—and averted eyes. I was his shield. We didn't care about anyone else.

We went to a 3-D movie, the first one I've ever seen. There are special reserved places for wheelchairs in the theatres now, a good idea. And big leather loungers, even better. Movies are so expensive these days. You wouldn't believe what they charge for popcorn, but the Ellisons paid for everything. At least I got in with a senior citizen discount, and Derek really seemed to enjoy himself. Young men like superheroes. When you're an old man, you realize that ordinary people, getting through everyday life, are the true superheroes.

Golf had been a big thing in Derek's life, something he really missed. He made us watch golf on TV, which is, shall we say, an acquired taste. So it was a real treat for him when Charles got tickets for Derek and me to a big tournament at the Westchester Country Club.

I told Charles he should've gotten three tickets so we could all go.

He sighed and said, "No, he'll have a better time if it's just the two of you."

I felt sorry for Charles. I knew how much he loved his son. Unfortunately, his son didn't want his love.

Derek and I wound up having a lot of fun at the golf tournament, yelling, "BA-BA-BOOEY!" after every other tee shot. It's a Howard Stern thing, and it pissed a lot of people off, but it amused Derek no end. I never saw him laugh so hard. By the end of the afternoon, he had some good color in his cheeks and looked, from the neck up, like a happy, healthy young American male. I felt proud that he was doing better since I had come into his life. At least that's what his mother kept telling me. Whatever else I've done in my life, I've done something good for someone.

TWENTY-NINE

The day of the wedding was like a dream I didn't deserve, the dream of a better man: Grace and Thanks beyond anything I could have ever hoped for. Betsy had insisted that I get a nice new suit. I told her what Benjamin Franklin said about "beware of all enterprises that require new clothes." But she said that was ridiculous; she wanted me to look nice.

"And besides," she added, "that was Thoreau." You see why I love her?

So she took me to a Men's Warehouse and got me a dark blue suit, fancy shirt and tie, and new shoes.

I made Derek my best man. He said he was "very honored" that I asked him (and it was my way of assuring that, despite his self-consciousness when in public, he came to the wedding). He gave us a nice winemaking kit—"so you can launch Chateau de Pruno"—as a wedding gift. The Ellisons came to the ceremony too, and gave us a ridiculously generous monetary gift.

Kelly was maid of honor, Emily—my Lego friend, Betsy's grandniece—scattered rose petals, and little Brendan was the ring bearer. Betsy planned the whole thing, and we had a rehearsal the night before. It was pretty casual, and we got pizza for everybody. I didn't make Derek come to the rehearsal; that would have been too much for him. But I coached him the day before on everything that he'd be expected to do.

"I'm going to be nervous," he said.

"What about me?" I shot back, which made him relax a little.

The caterer turned out to be a complete screw-up. She was the niece of one of the book club ladies who was just starting her company, and Betsy agreed to let her do the food. Big mistake.

At the last minute, Gassim and a couple of his workers jumped in and saved our asses.

"I don't know how to thank you, Gassim," I said. "You really saved us."

"My pleasure, my friend," he said. "Together, you and I can show the Middle East how to make peace."

I didn't really know what he meant.

He smiled. "I am a Palestinian, and you are a Jew. And yet we are friends."

"Of course, we're friends!" I said. "No matter what anybody says, this is still fucking America, and it's for everybody."

"Allahu akbar."

"Whatever."

We both laughed and drank together like brothers: me a beer, him a club soda.

⌒

The ceremony was performed by June Hackett, an older black woman who was the aunt of Shirley, one of the book clubs ladies. June was a "life minister" and had married hundreds of couples. Betsy knew her and said that I would love her, but I didn't really care: it was Betsy's choice.

I met June for coffee a couple of days before the ceremony. Apparently she didn't like to marry two "total strangers," so I agreed to meet her. The coffee turned into three hours.

June was a real trip, what they call a "big personality." She was also big physically, at over six feet tall and well over two hundred pounds. Her smile and huge tangle of silver dreadlocks were big too. We really bonded when she found out I did time in the same joint—Elmira—as her brother.

There was a party with music and food and lots of laughter. But what I remember most is what Betsy and I said to each other. Javier made a video of the ceremony and put it on both a DVD and a flash drive for us, so these are the exact words. In her beautiful dress of lavender lace, this is what Betsy said:

Me first? OK. I'll go first. I wrote something down
to say, but then I decided that I should just speak
from my heart.

[From the crowd: Louder! Sssh!]

OK, I'll try to be louder!...I just want to say how
thrilled I am today—to see all of you here—and
thrilled to be marrying this man who I love so
much. This man I thought I would never find.
Loneliness is a hard thing to deal with. You don't
want to even admit that you're lonely when you're
living that way. You can learn to live alone, but
it's much, much better to have a partner. Even
someone who takes up all your very limited closet space. [*Laughs.*] Someone to come home to.
Someone to say, 'How was your day, honey?'
He really says that: 'How was your day, honey?'
And I tell him. And he listens. He really listens to
me, or else he's a very good pretender. [*Laughs.*]
But that's all a person wants: someone to listen
to them...and love them anyway. Larry loves me
anyway. That's what he tells me, and I believe
him. He's a good man. Not a perfect man, but he's
trying. He's trying very hard. And now he's my
man. I've been waiting for him a long time, and
now that he's here—in my life—I'm not going to
let him go.

Then I said:

Well, I don't know what to say after that. Maybe
I should just keep my mouth shut and be grateful
for this day. For I am truly that: grateful. As most
of you know, I haven't had the greatest of lives...
until recently. I lived without anything approaching love for a very, very, very long time. But then
something happened, and I got a whole lotta love

at the end. Somehow, I got this wonderful woman to love me. I must have tricked her in some way. She still doesn't see the real me, or maybe she brought out a me that was there all along, the man I was supposed to be. I don't know. I only know that I love her and I'm going to try my hardest to be worthy of her, and love her as she deserves to be loved. Everybody deserves love, but especially this woman who I am very, very proud to call my wife.

Then June Hackett said the legal words, and we were married. As I said, it was like a dream come true. The party was great. I danced with Betsy (badly). I danced with June Hackett and her beautiful wife, Toni. I had too much wine, but Betsy, as always, took care of me.

We decided to postpone a honeymoon. I was seeing Derek virtually every day, and that was a good thing for him—and for our bank account. Plus I didn't want to have to ask Fusco for permission to leave the state. And Betsy seemed satisfied.

"When the time is right," she said, "we'll take a little trip somewhere."

The night of our wedding, we slept in our own bed, which only seemed right. It was where we were most comfortable; it was where we were ourselves.

⌒

Betsy and I had the bottom level of the store fixed up—the floors redone, the walls repainted white—and Roland's old apartment and office demoed so now there was a huge open space. I got three estimates for the job, just like my Dad would have advised, and picked the middle one. Then I checked the guy's references, just to be sure.

The results were great: the store looked fresh and new. But we had trouble at first renting it out. Under some peer pressure, Betsy let one of the members of her book club, Miriam Landis, who was a real estate broker, handle the listing. She wanted to do it as a favor to Betsy and agreed to take a lower fee, so what could I say? Miriam was loud and talkative and not my type at all, and I let Betsy deal with her.

The problem was that City Island's relative isolation—the source of much of its charm—made it unattractive to potential renters. You had to give people a good reason, other than salt air and Cape Cod charm, to drive there.

There was also the situation that we wanted to stay in the apartment above the store, which some renters might object to. But that was our plan, and we were going to stick to it. It's what Betsy wanted.

It was sad at first, putting a big "For Rent" banner across the old City Island Nautical Treasures and Antiques sign, but it had to be done. It was a sign of progress.

Finally, we got some interest in renting the store. I have to admit that Miriam backed up all her talk and promises with action. Two young women—Laura and Sandy—fell in love with City Island and wanted to put in a yoga studio and "natural products" store. Our space would be perfect for them if we could put up a wall with a door to cut the store into two parts: a smaller front part for the store and a larger space in back for the yoga studio.

"That wouldn't be difficult," I said.

"I've met them," said Betsy. "And they've very nice. And they'll be quiet and peaceful underneath us. I mean—a *yoga* studio!"

"Hey," I said, "as long as they pay the rent on time, I don't care if they practice *voodoo*."

And the best part was that we could afford—just barely—to keep the building and continue living upstairs, just the way Betsy wanted.

It was so easy for me. I let Betsy do the whole thing. I wasn't even there when the papers were signed. When Betsy came back from the signing, she was so excited and optimistic.

"I hope you don't mind," she said, "but I had them add one more thing to the lease."

"What was that?"

"That you and I get free yoga classes," she said. "As many as we want."

"Are you kidding?" I laughed. "Me? Yoga?"

It turns out I *love* yoga! I started doing it, and after a few weeks, I realized I should have been doing it all my life. I think—I *know*—it would have helped me get through the years in prison, both physically and mentally. They should make everybody in prison—convicts *and* guards—do yoga all the time. It would cut down on the recidivism rate plenty.

Betsy started to take classes almost every day, and now I think she wants to become a yoga teacher. Hey, whatever she wants. Laura and Sandy love Betsy—who doesn't?—and they are encouraging her. It turns out that her extra clause in the lease, that she and I should get free unlimited classes, was a "Santa" clause.

⌐

But, of course, pure happiness exists only in books or movies. I kept seeing Klein's name in the financial news. He did beat an SEC investigation headed by this Vera Kassakhian, a zaftig prosecutor with a head of wavy hair and the eyes of a sniper, who often got her picture in the news and wants to be attorney general of New York. I think one of the Doggies mentioned her at Le Bernardin. But Klein's "increasingly erratic" behavior was also being reported by sources too frightened by the threat of retribution to be named. Klein was also trying to take over some company and was fighting with some other rich guy. Still, I saw nothing about what happened in the Bahamas, nothing about Avery. Maybe he did make that particular nightmare go away, just as he said he would. But I know that Jonathan did not like all this attention in the media. And, frankly, neither did I.

⌐

We made good money from the rent we charged Laura and Sandy, and we had one more year of Betsy's salary, but the building cost money every month for utilities, insurance, taxes, etc. We had to put several thousand dollars into overdue repairs for the Jeep. And, of course, there was the cost of the wedding and all the other bills that didn't stop. The Klein money was almost all spent (not counting the reserve we kept back for taxes), so the money I made from watching Derek came in very handy. Make that "was essential."

So just when things were beginning to settle down, there came a surprise I was not ready for.

"My father's been asked to be a dean at this law school in California," Derek said, "and they're thinking it would be good for me to move to a warmer climate."

I panicked but tried not to show it. *Move to California?*

"Well, what do *you* think?" I asked him neutrally.

"I don't know," he said. "The weather's better, I guess. It would be different. But I told them I wouldn't move unless we could take you with us. I mean, we would help you and Betsy move out to California so you could keep, you know, working for us."

Instantly, I unclenched...a little.

"Well," I said. "That's...an interesting idea."

I didn't say anything to Betsy about it when I got home, since I wasn't entirely convinced it would happen. But I was worried: this job with the Ellisons was our steady extra cash flow.

⌒

Amid this new uncertainty, one very good thing happened: my parole finally ended. Really. I was actually and forever leaving the System. At my last meeting with Fusco, I got my parole discharge card, which tells the whole world—and the rest of the criminal justice system—that I am a free man.

Fusco even shook my hand.

"You made it, Ingber," he said. "I didn't think you would."

"Well," I said, "you were wrong."

I wanted to tell him off. I wanted to let everything out—all the bitterness, all the hatred, all the truth—that I had stored up inside me from all those years in the joint. I wanted to quote Dostoevsky as I have a million times: "The degree of civilization in a society can be judged by entering its prisons." I wanted to laugh in his face and say, "You never got me, Fuck-so, even though I left the country right under your nose and got involved with some bad, bad things."

But I said nothing. I just shook his hand, walked out his office forever, and didn't make things worse. Maybe I was learning something in my old age.

When I got back home, I showed Betsy my discharge card. She was sitting in her favorite reading chair in the living room.

"You should celebrate tonight," she said, handing it back to me.

"No," I countered, "*we* should celebrate!"

"Oh." She sighed. "I'm feeling kind of tired."

"There's nothing wrong?" I asked with some concern.

"No-no-no," she said, trying to calm me down. "I'm just a little—why don't you go down to Gassim's? You two talk. Go and have a drink."

"I don't like to drink alone," I said. "Gassim just drinks club soda."

"Go see Gassim," she said with a gentle smile. "We can celebrate tomorrow night...and for the rest of our lives."

"Well," I said, "when you put it that way."

I liked hanging out with Gassim. After Roland died, Gassim's was the best place for me to go for a vigorous, good-natured political argument and cultural discussion. Gassim had been an electrical engineer in his home country and knew four languages, so he had a good mind. Even though he was a Muslim, he didn't mind that I drank in front of him while he sipped his club soda. Hell, he served liquor in his restaurant, so it couldn't have mattered to him that much.

The walk down to Gassim's was a pleasant, head-clearing, lung-filling experience with my old friend the sky. By the time I got down to his place, I had even worked up a little thirst.

Gassim was always glad to see me. He put me in the corner booth, Roland's favorite, and brought me a beer.

"Here, my friend," he said. "I'll be back."

I watched Gassim strut around the restaurant, chatting with customers, telling a bus boy to clean up a spill, whispering something to a waiter, going in and out of the kitchen. He seemed so comfortable, so in charge of things, the master of this little world of fried shrimp, lobster rolls, and cold, cold beer. Just like Charlie Wagner, except he wasn't a dick.

"Stay here," he said. "We'll go for a walk, but let me talk to Amir first so he doesn't burn the place down."

Later, Gassim and I walked out in the cool dark night.

"He's a good boy," said Gassim, "but sometimes I wonder if he has his head screwed on properly."

Amir was Gassim's son, probably in his late twenties, and Gassim's assistant running the restaurant. He was as gangly and nervous as Gassim was portly and calm.

"I have to leave him in charge sometimes," he continued, "so that he learns. That's what his mother says."

"She's right. And *you* have to get out too, sometimes," I added.

"I suppose so. My doctor says I should walk, so I walk. Twenty minutes won't kill me."

"Who knows? It might even help," I said. "And it's a beautiful night."

"Yes, business is very good."

"Is that all you think about?" I razzed him.

"Is there anything else?"

"Yes," I countered. "This beautiful night!"

He laughed. "Spoken like a newly married man."

We went down the block at an easy pace, feeling the sweet breeze.

"It sounds funny when you say it like that," I said.

"It just shows that anything is still possible in this world," he said.

"*Hey!*"

A rough voice from a passing car yelled to us. We both turned and—

"*Fuckin' sand nigger!*"

Someone in a car going past us threw a can of beer out the window. It sprayed all over the both of us, and the can hit Gassim in the shoulder.

The car—a black muscle car—roared away from us with some laughter, a blast of the engine, and the smoky screech from its fat tires.

"Hey!" I yelled back at them, but it was too late. They were gone down City Island Avenue.

Gassim was both laughing and gasping, rubbing his shoulder. "Can you believe it? The dirty, rotten punks!"

I checked myself—the beer got all over my pants and some on my jacket. "Yeah, Gassim. Unfortunately, I can believe it."

⌐

When I got home, I wasn't going to tell Betsy what happened. I didn't want to upset her, but my clothes stank of beer and she smelled it soon after I walked in.

"But that's horrible!" she said. "Right on City Island Avenue? Right in the middle of town?"

"Right down the middle," I confirmed sadly.

"And there wasn't a cop to chase him down?"

"There wasn't anybody," I said. "No witnesses or anything. Just Gassim and me."

"Was he hurt?"

"His pride more than anything," I replied. "I wonder if it was those guys from that dive up the way, that bar where I got those bad vibes."

"You think it really was them?"

"I don't know," I answered. "The depressing thing is, it could have been anybody."

The next day, Betsy made a plate of chocolate clouds and brought them down to Gassim, to make him feel better after the assault. Not all people are bad. He appreciated the gesture, but I don't think it really addressed the situation. It would take more than a sweet treat to relieve the pain of racism and hatred, right on his own street, in his own neighborhood.

⌐

Unfortunately, I kept seeing Jonathan Klein's name in the news. Someone was trying to takeover one of Klein Global Partners' companies, and he was fighting them, but the board was on the other guy's side. Billionaires fighting with billionaires. Who cares except that Klein was on the losing end, and investigations of him were only going to intensify. I felt this bond with Klein, and I didn't completely like it.

Then another odd thing happened. From out of the blue, I got a call from a man named Lou Aronica, who runs a book publishing company called The Story Plant. It turns out all those pages I wrote after my first trial for Mantell when he was my lawyer— that non-confession/confession I wrote for the judge during my sentencing phase a million years ago—somehow has survived. I never knew what happened to it after Mantell had sent it to Judge Jordan, who presided over my trial. I thought it was lost, not that I cared. Once my sentence was handed down, it really didn't matter anymore. (I think Thomas X. Jordan was a basically fair man. I mean, he could have thrown out the charges against me, but that wasn't going to happen. Not with three dead bodies, and me left alive.)

In any case, this Aronica fellow wants to publish the manuscript since, apparently, it was passed around for years by psychologists and criminologists who wanted to understand the thinking of fucked-up, smart-ass young people like I was then— how crazy was I when I was nineteen, how crazy-in-love? He thinks there might be a market for it. I guess people like to read all kinds of things. Maybe someone can benefit from reading about my personal hell...though, if I recall, there were some delusions of heaven in there too.

And who knows? Maybe I'll make a couple of bucks from it someday.

⌒

Which was good because it turned out that the Ellisons were dead serious about moving to California. And Derek was now completely in favor of the idea but for another reason.

"You have to keep this totally confidential," he said, his eyes lively with excitement as I approached his bed. He had asked the nurse—he had several regulars—to leave the room. "I've been

talking to my ex-roommate from Dartmouth. He's from California, right near where my father is going to run the law school."

"So you think this is really going to happen?" I asked, trying
not to sound too concerned.

"Oh, yeah!" he said as if it were already a done deal. "But forget about that for a minute. This guy—I can't tell you his name,
but I will say that I think he's a scientific genius."

"A genius?" I said skeptically.

"Listen to what he's done," he whispered. "It's the greatest
thing you've ever heard of."

I walked closer to the bed, where he was strapped into a sitting position.

"He's invented"—Derek paused for effect—"a cool"—he
paused again—"*blanket*."

"What do you mean, a—?"

Derek burst into laughter. "I don't mean a cool blanket like
it has a cool design. I mean it's a blanket—a thin blanket—that
keeps you cool. You put it around you, and it's like air-condition-
ing. It keeps you cool, the way a warm blanket keeps you warm.
It's going to *revolutionize* life in warm climate zones!"

I admit I was intrigued by the concept. "He's really invented
this?" I asked. "He's not just blowing smoke?"

"No!" He laughed. "This is a very serious guy. Really brilliant. A physics and computer science double-major. But he's
very shy and kinda private, y'know, so when we settle in California, we can help him launch it."

I could see that this move really was going to happen.

"Come on, Larry," Derek enthused. "It'll be fun: we're talking
about California! The Beach Boys! Surfing and Big Sur and all
those girls with their suntanned bodies!"

He was more enthusiastic than I had ever seen him.

"Didn't my parents tell you they'd pick up all your moving
expenses and help you get settled?" he asked as I thought: *California? What will Betsy say? She likes City Island so much.*

"Come on, Larry!" he urged. "Where's your sense of adventure?"

"I'm too old for adventure."

"Bullshit!" he shot back. "You're still alive, aren't you?"

He stopped me with that.

"If I can do it, you can do it," he declared. "Let's just fuckin' *move* to California and launch the cool blanket. We'll find the venture capital, and you'll be in on it from the ground floor. Come on, we can change the world—*and* make some money. Tell me what's wrong with that."

⌒

I drove back to City Island confused and uncertain. I liked Derek and the Ellisons (I even had developed a decent-enough relationship with Charles), but relocate to California? Would Betsy want to? Once she was free of Croll and Thomas Paine, who knows what she might want to do. Stay here and become a yoga teacher like Laura and Sandy? I didn't know what to tell her about California and when. I'd have to talk again to Catherine Ellison about exactly what kind of financial help they'd give Betsy and me, if we decided to move with them. What kind of guarantees they'd offer. It seemed like such an out-of-left-field idea, and yet after what happened to Gassim and me in the street, maybe it was time to consider moving to a different place.

And it might not be a bad idea to put three thousand miles between me and Jonathan Klein.

⌒

I arrived back home just in time to catch a late yoga class—can you believe I actually said that?—and tried not to think about things. Unsuccessfully. Yoga is good for clearing the mind because you have to concentrate on the poses and your breathing, but it doesn't always work. Sometimes, thoughts from Real Life come sneaking in.

The way the studio was set up, there was a window in the wall between the natural products store in front and the yoga studio in back so that people in the store could see the class going on and people in the class could see when someone was in the store.

I was in a class led by Laura, doing my cobra pose—and no, I wasn't the only guy there; there was also a biker guy named

Marco, a bald ex-marine, who came all the time—when I noticed a young, well-dressed black woman in the store looking through the window.

Good, I thought. *Another client for Laura and Sandy. The place is really starting to do well.*

But when I looked over a few minutes later, doing a reverse warrior, I could see that she was still there at the window—and she was looking straight at me. I got a sudden bad feeling, and it lasted throughout the savasana. That's the relaxation period at the end of each class. For some reason, I couldn't quite relax.

When the class ended and everyone filtered out after thanking Laura, I got my keys and wallet out of my cubby and changed back into my street clothes in the bathroom. When I walked out, sure enough, the woman was still there, looking through the window, looking for me.

I figured, what the hell and went out into the store. I had to go around to the staircase in the back to get up to our apartment. When we redid the store, we closed off the door at the top of the staircase that up led to our apartment from inside. Before I got five steps into the store, the woman came up to me, cutting me off before I got to the front door.

"Mr. Ingber?" she said.

"Yes?" I answered, looking her over. She was young and pretty, maybe in her mid-twenties, and dressed in a dark gray business suit.

"Excuse me, Mr. Ingber," she repeated. "Do you have a minute?"

Before I could answer, she put out her hand. "I'm Diana Pritchard, Myles Pritchard's daughter."

I was chilled. She probably expected me to be surprised, and I was, even as I tried to conceal it. I didn't dare take her upstairs, because Betsy was there and would ask questions. All she had to do was meet Diana Pritchard, and she would know that something from the clusterfuck in the Bahamas had tracked me down.

"Why don't we get out of here?" I proposed.

We walked down the sidewalk a ways. I figured no one would overhear us if we kept moving. I could tell she had something to say—why else would she come all the way out to City Island?—and I had a feeling it wasn't good.

"I've never been out here," she said. "It's very different. Not like Manhattan at all."

She had that lovely Bahamian accent that made music out of every phrase. I always was attracted to musical voices, but I could see that she was here for a definite reason, so I spared her any more small talk.

"So, Miss Pritchard—Diana," I said crisply. "What can I do for you?"

She stopped walking and faced me straight on. "Janet Ko is dead."

That hit me like a rock.

"Janet Ko is dead, and my father is missing. No one has heard from him in more than six weeks—just around the time that Janet was found."

"Found?" I asked. "Found how?"

"They said it was an overdose of pills," she said, "but I don't believe it."

"Why?"

"Did you ever meet Janet Ko?"

"Yes, I did."

"Well, do you think she was someone who would overdose on pills in a hotel room in San Francisco?"

"No."

"Neither do I."

"You're the one studying criminology at George Washington, right?"

"How do you know that?" she asked, her eyes narrowing in on me.

I could see how uneasy she was, and it made me uneasy too.

"Diana, why don't you let me buy you a cup of coffee? Then you can tell me everything."

I kept my mouth shut while she talked. I wasn't going to give away anything, so I just sat across from her in the corner booth at Gassim's and listened. Diana Pritchard seemed to be a very smart young woman, so I had to be very careful of what I said. She recounted every step of her pursuit of information about her father's whereabouts. Fortunately, she mentioned nothing about Avery's murder or anything about that night. Still, I was cautious.

"I'm sure your father will turn up," I said. "Maybe he's on some kind of secret assignment for Klein, or something."

"That's not what Mr. Klein said," she replied, shaking her head. The concern on her face was obvious. "I spoke to him, but he said he didn't know anything about where my father is. Quite frankly, he sounded kind of evasive. Mr. Klein is a wonderful man," she insisted. "He pays for my college. He's helped my whole family, not just me. But I'm worried. He doesn't seem to want to help me now."

She didn't know it, but I wasn't going to help her either.

"Here is my phone number and my email address," she said, sliding a piece of paper across the table. "I know that you and Mr. Klein are friends, and that you were with Mr. Klein the last time he was in Nassau. If you see or hear anything, please contact me."

I felt guilty taking her information.

"Michael said that you seemed to be very close to Mr. Klein."

"Who's Michael?" I asked.

"Oh," she said, surprised that I didn't know. "He's the under-butler at Jamboree."

I didn't say anything because my mind had already gone to a bad place: *Janet Ko dead and Myles Pritchard missing? Did Myles kill her on Klein's orders, and would he now come after me? Or was Klein going about eliminating everyone who knew anything about the Avery murder? But why did he give me all that money if it wasn't hush money? Didn't he just pay everyone off? He knows that I wouldn't blackmail him; anything I could say would only incriminate myself. But, as we know, when a murder's been committed, people do strange things.*

"You don't know me, Mr. Ingber," she said, "but I'm not the kind of person who gives up on anything. Especially when it comes to my father. Something happened down there. I don't know if it was at Jamboree or not, but I'm going to find out what it was. My father didn't just disappear, so whatever it takes, I'm going to find out the truth."

She sounded dead serious, no pun intended. I said nothing. I really didn't know what happened to Myles, but I had my suspicions. I felt sorry for his daughter, but not sorry enough to give her any help.

"Please call me if you hear anything," she pleaded. "When you talk to Mr. Klein, or even if my father gets in contact with you."

"Why would he do that?" I said, betraying nothing.

"No reason." She shrugged with a forlorn look. "I'm just getting a little...desperate. So call me or email anytime, please, if you hear anything about my father, or talk to Mr. Klein and he mentions anything."

"I will," I lied.

I could see she didn't trust me, but I had to be careful now that this smart young woman was digging around. Studying criminology? Better steer clear of her. Anything she discovers is not going to do me any good.

She tried to pay for my coffee, but I insisted on paying for hers. I walked her to her car and watched her drive away. I felt bad about not telling her what I knew, and I felt truly sorry for her, trying to find her father.

But now I had an even bigger problem facing me: was I too on Klein's list for elimination? What if he didn't trust me anymore to keep his secret, thinking that I would flip on him if someone connected us to the killing of Avery? If he could get rid of Janet Ko and Myles Pritchard, he would have absolutely no problem getting rid of me. Of this, I have no doubt.

> So let me say—right here, right now, before I forget—that if for any reason I turn up dead, or don't turn up at all where I'm supposed to be, look for a trail of clues that leads directly or indirectly to **JONATHAN KLEIN**, who is having me murdered because I was an eyewitness to his killing Mr. Lester Mantell a/k/a Brandon Avery of Mineola, New York, and Nassau, Bahamas, in the Seabreeze Canal on September 27, 2014. Jonathan Klein is the guilty party.

Over the years, I've had death threats, but this one genuinely scares me. Against Jonathan Klein's money and power, I have no protection.

And on top of all this, I got another email from Lou at The Story Plant, asking me if I was done reading and correcting all those pages he sent me. Of course I hadn't. Truthfully, I tear up when I read a lot of it, that cry of pain, that confession, for that's really what it was. I can't believe how *young* I was. How stupid and innocent and obsessed and detailed I was. And how, despite all the years of punishment and confinement, blank walls and wasted decades, I'm still basically the same person I've always been, hopeful and hopeless, trying desperately not to screw up my life—with decidedly mixed results. It's a hard truth to face.

Still this Aronica fellow's after me to get them read and turned around quicker. I can't blame him; I signed a contract. Frankly, if I knew doing a book was this much work, I would never have started in the first place. Screw the money.

⌒

In the midst of all this uncertainty, we had one fun time. I don't want to call it our last fun time in New York, but I felt the sure sense of an ending about it. It was New Year's Eve. The Ellisons were going out, of course, and wanted to know if Betsy and I would spend New Year's Eve with Derek. They offered to have a dinner catered in their house for the three of us. I was never a big fan of going out on New Year's Eve—all that forced joy among strangers seems phony—and Betsy thought it was a good idea not to leave Derek alone.

She and I got dressed up. Catherine put Derek in a nice dress shirt. And we had a wonderful dinner in the Ellisons' candle-lit dining room. The food was fantastic. Catherine had found a chef—her name was Sophia Something—and she made this gourmet dinner that was all easy to eat so that Derek could get it down. Lobster polenta and pureed peas and a yam soufflé and mango sorbet.

"This is like deluxe baby food," Derek said as he ate another spoonful enthusiastically. (Did I mention that he had to be spoon-fed?)

"I'm going to have to get the recipe for these peas," Betsy said. "They don't even taste like peas."

"That's why they're so good," I said.

Betsy was so considerate. She made sure that Derek's nurse—a substitute named Jasmine—joined us for dinner.

"She shouldn't have to eat alone," Betsy reasoned correctly.

"Where's Edwina?" I asked Derek about his regular nurse.

"She's off tonight," he said.

"She deserves it," I said.

"What?" Derek cracked humorously. "Am I so hard to deal with?"

"No," I replied honestly. "I think you're doing pretty OK, kid."

And he was. He was doing a lot better, physically and mentally, in the past few months. In fact, we had signed him up to finish his Dartmouth degree online, which thrilled his parents. It wouldn't take him that long, and I could help him. A long, long time ago, I was good at schoolwork.

After dinner, we had fun watching things from YouTube on Derek's giant TV screen. I finally got to show him who Guy Lombardo was. Betsy and I danced to the Royal Canadians at the Waldorf Astoria as Derek laughed at the music.

"This is really terrible!" said Derek appreciatively.

"Didn't I tell you?" I said as I tried my best to keep up with Betsy's dancing.

"It's so *white*," exclaimed Derek.

"You are so right, Derek," Betsy concurred. "Thank goodness *some* things have changed."

Soon we got off Guy Lombardo and watched a bunch of other things, better things. All our favorites: Frank Sinatra, Bruce Springsteen, the Beatles, and the Stones. We played a lot of oldies and Motown and soul music. We played a lot of Van Morrison, Betsy's favorite. Derek had never really gotten into Van's music, so we gave him an extra reason to live. Right before we left, I made sure to play The Kingsmen doing "Louie Louie" so we could sing, "We gotta go," to Derek, which he appreciated. We even made it till midnight. Then Jasmine took over, and Betsy drove us home.

To the drumming of the road, I sat back in my seat with my eyes closed and thought about everything. I thought about Jonathan Klein and what I wasn't telling Betsy. I thought about how

I was connected to Klein from now on, no matter what. And how, no matter what I said in that cemetery, I was still, in a way, connected to Rachel Prince, even if I didn't want to be. And I was connected to those two dead people and connected to my parents. I was connected to everybody I've ever known—every cellmate, every bull. All the Doggies and the people at that camp. The people at Clemency. Roland. Gassim. The guys in the kitchen at Charlie Wagner's. Even Brian Halliwell. And poor Janet Ko. I was connected to all of them, forever. There is an infinite web of feelings and memories that connects everybody across the world like the stars in the Milky Way. And I was just a small part of it, trying to survive and not dishonor my birthright any more than I already had, being driven home drunk and mellow by the kindest woman in the world—she who found me, pitied me, and took me in. Talk about Grace and Thanks.

⌒

Finally, Betsy and I had to talk seriously about the moving-to-California situation. I never told her exactly what happened in the Bahamas, so I couldn't tell her that my life might now be in danger from Jonathan Klein. And now I wanted her to move with me away from her family and friends to California—a place neither of us had ever been—based on what? Faith in me?

The next day—New Year's Day—we took a long, slow walk after dinner, arm in arm down City Island Avenue, making our way toward Gassim's and the water. Even though it was January, for some reason, it wasn't particularly cold. I walked us on the other side of the street from where Gassim and I were ambushed and watched out for that black muscle car. Cars passed us, but nothing bad happened. Nonetheless, I kept a lookout.

I reconstructed for her my most recent discussion with Catherine, reinforcing the assurances she had given me about covering our moving expenses to California and guaranteeing me enough hours watching Derek when we were there so we'd have enough money to live on.

I repeated Catherine's exact words: "'Nothing is more important than my son's happiness.'"

"Well," said Betsy, "what a nice woman."

"She can afford to be nice," I said.

"But *still*," she countered. "Her heart is in the right place. A lot of rich people aren't so nice."

We walked on, passing from darkness to streetlight and back to darkness. I could almost *hear* Betsy thinking it over. Not telling her that we were going on the run, I felt dishonest. I loved her so much, and here I was, if not outright lying her, concealing the truth.

"You know," she remarked, "Sandy and Laura asked me again if we would sell them the building outright."

"You know," I added, "eventually we're not gonna want to climb all those stairs in the back to get up to the apartment."

"It's a lot of stairs *right now*," she said, "especially when I have groceries."

"Did Sandy and Laura mention a price?"

"No," she said, "but I'm sure it would be fair."

"Are they doing that well?"

"Evidently," she affirmed. "You see how full the classes are getting. And they *are* great teachers."

"It's true," I said.

"Yoga in the Bronx! Who'd a thunk it?"

I snickered. "Yeah, it used to be just Yog*i* in the Bronx." Which made her laugh. I loved to make her laugh: it signified approval, which I wanted more than anything. *Even more than telling her the truth?* I wondered.

We walked for a while, and then I said. "I think they do a lot of yoga in California."

"I think you're right," she replied.

We walked on a while longer, letting her think. Sometimes the best thing to do is just shut up and hope.

"I'd miss Kelly and the kids," she said pensively, "and my book club and all my family. Well, *most* of my family."

I nudged her as we walked, but I could tell she had real misgivings about the plan.

"They can come visit," I said. "There's a lot to see in California, supposedly."

"But what if *I* don't like it?" she said. "Really."

"Then we'll come back," I said. "I promise."

I let her think a little more as we walked.

"You know," I began, "we really can't keep walking up and down those stairs for many more years. I know it's good exercise, but falls are what get old people. You fall down and break a hip? You're in trouble."

"We're not really *old*-old," she scoffed.

"I'm saying in a few years. Maybe the time to move to a warmer climate is now. Before there's a problem."

"A warm climate without stairs..." Betsy thought out loud. "What about all my books and things? All my stuff, all the furniture?"

"Some we could take with us. The Ellisons say they'll pay for the move," I said. "And the rest we could put into storage. We could make it work. This might be the right thing to do, just at the right time."

"It's a pretty big step, Larry."

"You'll see. I'll take care of you."

"Oh, Larry, you can barely take care of yourself."

"Then we'll take care of each other."

She liked that, and we walked on, holding each other closer as we got nearer to the edge of the ocean at the end of Gassim's parking lot. We could see the lights of the Throgs Neck Bridge shimmering in the water with the dark velvet sky above us.

I felt guilty not telling her about Klein, but I needed her to be with me. I vowed inwardly that I would be so good to her when we got to California that I would make the move the best thing she ever did in her life. I told myself that it would be good to change things boldly and embark on a new adventure, a new life. Carpe fuckin' diem.

"You know," I said, "when we move out to California, maybe I should change my name to something that isn't so famous. I'm tired of *Laurence Allan Ingber*. Maybe I'll try something else, something completely anonymous."

Betsy laughed. "What would you change it to? Something very Hollywood?"

"I don't know," I said, "but I'll think of something."

Maybe a name change will do me good, make it harder for Klein to find me. Whatever it is, Betsy will be safer with me in California than she'd be in New York, because I'm not going to let her go, no matter what.

Is that selfish of me? Probably. If I really cared about Betsy, I would clear out so she wouldn't be in danger when Klein wants me eliminated if and when that time should come. But I'm sorry, I can't leave her now. All my life I believed in "negative learning"—learning what you *don't* want is as important as learning what you *do* want. And I've learned that I don't want to be without Betsy Hull for the rest of my life, however long I have left.

"You know," she said measuredly, "Jonathan Klein can find you in California."

I stopped.

I turned to her and asked, "What exactly do you know? How do you know everything?"

She threw her head back and laughed. "I don't know everything." She took my arm. "But I know enough."

I didn't want to tell her about Diana Pritchard snooping around, digging up dirt that could incriminate me, but she probably knew about that too. I wondered if perhaps Diana had called *her*.

Holding my arm tightly, she said, "I was just reading that there are some old religious cults that believe this whole world is really just a prison. It imprisons our individual souls, and it's only when we die that we truly escape from this human prison and rejoin the one great big soul in the sky."

"I know what prison is, and this world isn't quite that. You know, I admit I was scared when I got out," I said, leaning into her. "I felt so alone. But I knew there had to be some reason that I got out. That reason was you."

She stopped walking, and I turned her to face me.

"OK, so maybe we're never really *really* secure, any of us," I said. "Everyone is under intense everyday pressure out here, but maybe that's just the way life is. And when you add in all the violence and terrorism and hatred and racism and guns on top of that, it's almost too much to bear—whether you're in prison or out. Everything is so *precarious* and *combustible*—it could get pretty ugly if the wrong person, some demagogue, lights a match."

I felt like crying but I didn't.

"It's so crazy: with so many problems from just normal life, why do people make things worse? Why are there all these wars over religion and what other people believe and how they behave? Over who prays correctly to which imaginary friend? Didn't we have the Enlightenment? Why are people still heeding the words of ignorant shepherds from thousands of years ago—and killing any people who believe differently? And why does everyone need the Miracle of God anyway? Isn't this world miracle enough??"

I spread my arms wide, trying to show her what I meant.

"Just look: *this* is the miracle!" I shouted. "Everything around us. You, me, the sky, the ocean, the bridge, that couple over there, the music and the traffic in the distance—it's all a miracle! We don't have to look anywhere else. Everything we need is right here for us to be happy, if we just open our eyes. It's all so sad and beautiful. It's almost too much to feel. And to think I almost missed it all."

With tears in her eyes, she put her arms around me.

"I'll go to California with you," she said, "if that's what you really want to do. Whatever your name is, you'll still be the same person."

"No, I'll be better." I pulled back. "I promise."

"You know what? I'm ready for a change, another one. First it was you coming into my life. And now *this*. Maybe it's time for me to get off *my* island."

She smiled like the Mona Lisa.

"And I bet it could be fun!" she said. "We could drive across the country to get there. I've always wanted to do that. It could be our honeymoon!"

I gave her a big, thankful kiss, held her, and briefly considered telling her about the "cool blanket" idea. But that could wait. There would be time for everything.

I could almost feel our hearts beating together.

"You know the world as we know it is going to end pretty soon," I said. "In a couple hundred years, maybe less. The oceans will rise as the climate changes. A lot of the earth will become uninhabitable. There will be floods and famines and great waves of refugees. Things are going to get worse. A lot worse."

"You really think so?" she said, settling in my arms. "I hope not. Maybe people will smarten up before it's too late. There are some very smart scientists out there."

"Don't worry. We'll be long gone way before that happens. By then we'll have joined that long parade of the dead, passing through time into eternity."

"Maybe it won't be so bad," she whispered. "It will be just like we're asleep but forever."

"You know, it could actually be better than sleep. I won't have to get up in the middle of being dead to pee *four* times every night. I'll able to lie there in peace."

She laughed and shook her head.

"You know?" I crowed. "Now I really have something to look forward to when I die. There might be some real advantage there."

We laughed together, and I kissed her. And then her smile faded.

"But when we die," she said, "I'll never see you again."

"But we're together now," I countered. "We found each other. That's the main thing. Besides, everything is temporary."

"Except us," she corrected me. "Right here. Right now."

She smiled and tilted her face up to me for a really long, deep kiss. We turned to look at the bridge all lit up, with glittering, unattainable Manhattan in the distance and the infinite black sky above us.

"And right now," I said, "right at this very moment, I'm free, and I'm actually...happy."

She put her head on my shoulder and gently concurred, "I'm happy too."

PUBLISHER'S NOTE

As of the date of publication of *When I Got Out*, the writer of
these pages is still alive.

Acknowledgments

I thank my publisher Lou Aronica for all his efforts on behalf of my work: his ideas, his energy, and his good advice. I thank my agent Nancy Cushing-Jones for her guidance and her editorial eye. I thank my copyeditor Lisa Kaitz for improving this book in many ways. I thank my brother Bruce Robinson, an early reader and good idea-giver. I thank Kate Klimo and Mark Watt who also gave me important help.

I want to thank my niece Claire Shutt for helping me stay afloat in the digital age. And I thank Kim Dower for helping me get the word out.

I especially thank my family—my son Jesse, my daughter Daisy, my daughter-in-law Katrina, and my grandsons Calder and Silas—for giving me the other big reason to live.

I'd like to apologize to my father Lester Robinson for naming the bad guy in my books "Lester." If I had known at the beginning that Mantell was going to be the villain, I would have given him a different first name. My father was anything but a bad guy, and I wouldn't want anyone to think that I had anything but love for him. It was just the name, Dad.

And finally, as in most things, I want to thank the former Mary Elizabeth Shutt for making every day of my life better, sweeter, more fun. Everything. No matter what.

About the Author

Peter Seth is a writer living in Los Angeles. He has written for television shows produced by Gary David Goldberg and Glenn Gordon Caron and has written several screenplays. He wrote, produced, and directed the award-winning short film *Lunch with Louie*, which appeared in more than thirty-five film festivals around the world. He was born in Brooklyn and raised on Long Island.

What It Was Like, his first novel, was greeted by praise from readers all across the country. He writes a blog at peterseth.com.